SOBER JUSTICE

JOSEPH H. HILLEY

RiverOak®
Good News in Fiction

An Imprint of Cook Communications Ministries
COLORADO SPRINGS, COLORADO • PARIS, ONTARIO
KINGSWAY COMMUNICATIONS, LTD., EASTBOURNE, ENGLAND

River Oak® is an imprint of
Cook Communications Ministries, Colorado Springs, CO 80918
Cook Communications, Paris, Ontario
Kingsway Communications, Eastbourne, England

SOBER JUSTICE
©2004 by Joseph H. Hilley

Cover Design: Marks & Whetstone
Cover Photo: Royalty-Free/CORBIS

First Printing, 2004
Printed in United States of America
1 2 3 4 5 6 7 8 9 10 Printing/Year 08 07 06 05 04

Library of Congress Cataloging-in-Publication Data

Hilley, Joseph H.
  Sober justice / by Joseph H. Hilley.
     p. cm.
  ISBN 1-58919-015-7 (pbk.)
 1. Lawyers--Crimes against--Fiction. 2. Attorney and client--Fiction.
3. Trials (Murder)--Fiction. 4. Conspiracies--Fiction. I. Title.
  PS3608.I439 S63
  813'.6--dc22

                                        2004008212

SOBER
JUSTICE

For Joy

I know a man in Christ who fourteen years ago was caught up to the third heaven. Whether it was in the body or out of the body I do not know—God knows. And I know that this man—whether in the body or apart from the body I do not know, but God knows—was caught up to paradise. He heard inexpressible things, things that man is not permitted to tell.

Paul's Second Letter to the Corinthians

PROLOGUE

Sweat soaked through Avery Thompson's blue work shirt as he walked along the edge of Short Haul Road, a narrow ribbon of pavement that wound through the delta swamp at the northern end of Mobile Bay. The road connected the shipyards on Pinto Island to the causeway that spanned the upper reaches of the bay. Heavily traveled in the morning and afternoon, the road was deserted and quiet as evening approached.

Waves of swamp grass on both sides of the road stretched as far as he could see, a sea of brown dotted by clumps of low, shrubby ty ty bushes. Behind him were the gantry cranes and warehouses of Alabama Shipyard. To the left, the buildings in downtown Mobile seemed to recede into the creeping shadows, swallowed by the growing darkness and sprawling limbs of moss-covered oaks that shrouded the city. Night was coming on. A gentle, warm breeze blew in from the bay. It was that moment at the end of the day, just before twilight, when the sweltering heat of the day lifted, and the sultry night descended.

Thompson paused and let the breeze pass through his shirt, then continued walking.

A few minutes later, he rounded a curve in the road. A white Cadillac was parked on the shoulder of the road to his left. His spirits lifted. He glanced behind him to check for traffic, then crossed the road toward the car. As he neared it, he saw two people sitting in the front seat. His heart sank.

"White folks," he mumbled to himself. "Ain't no white folks going to be interested in helping me."

He continued toward the car, growing more apprehensive with each step. The person behind the steering wheel was not only white, but a woman. The man beside her was staring out the window on the opposite side of the car. Apparently, they hadn't noticed Thompson approaching.

A few feet away, Thompson heard the woman's voice. She seemed to be pleading with him. Her face was turned away from Thompson toward the man sitting across the seat from her.

Lovers, Thompson thought. *Just my luck. Car quits and now this.*

He hesitated, then through the window he saw a cell phone lying on the seat. He rapped on the driver's window with a bare knuckle. The woman behind the steering wheel jumped. The man with her leaned around from the far side of the front seat and stared at Thompson. They both looked apprehensive.

Well over six feet tall, and almost three hundred pounds, Thompson was an imposing figure. He took a step back from the car and folded his hands at his waist, just above his belt. A smile appeared on his face. He did his best to seem harmless.

In a moment, the woman in the car pressed a button on the door panel and lowered the window a few inches.

"Excuse me, ma'am," Thompson began. "My car broke down and ..."

The woman shook her head.

"I'm sorry," she replied. "I can't help you."

"Please ma'am," Thompson insisted, "it's a long way to anywhere. Could you maybe call somebody?"

She shook her head and raised the window.

As they talked, a blue Ford pickup truck rolled to a stop a few feet from the Cadillac's rear bumper. The driver, clean-shaven and athletic, stepped out. His faded blue jeans were dirty and frayed, and he wore a tattered white T-shirt. Even though it was June, he wore a blue denim jacket with a Harley-Davidson patch sewn onto the left sleeve.

Thompson glanced at him as he approached, but only for an instant. The cold, detached look in the man's blue eyes made him turn away. A chill ran up his spine. Thompson backed away from the car, then turned and ran across the road. Tires screeched as an approaching truck swerved to miss him. He darted to the left, avoided the truck, then disappeared into the marsh grass and bushes on the opposite side of the road.

Seconds later, the muffled sound of a gunshot sent Thompson diving headfirst into the swamp grass and the mucky black mud beneath it. He spread out flat and closed his eyes, his face only inches above the stinking black goo. The pungent aroma stung his nostrils, but he didn't dare move.

A woman's scream pierced the air, followed by two more shots, muffled as the one before. Thompson lay on the ground, straining to hear over the pounding of his heart. In a moment, he heard a door close. He listened as the pickup drove away. He waited a few minutes longer, then carefully raised up on his knees and looked around. The Cadillac sat alone by the side of the road.

He stood, his clothes muddy and wet, and walked to the edge of the marsh grass along the shoulder of the road. The woman was out of the car and leaning against the driver's door. Her hands covered her face. She was crying uncontrollably.

As Thompson watched, a black Lincoln Navigator approached from the right. He retreated to a nearby bush and watched through the branches. The SUV stopped alongside the woman. The rear door opened.

"How could you?" she screamed. Her clenched fists

pounded the air. "How could you? Look. It's all over my clothes."

Someone in the back seat pulled her inside. The door closed, and the Lincoln started forward. As it moved away in one direction, the Cadillac drove off in the opposite.

Thompson waited until they were out of sight, then slipped from his hiding place. On the other side of the road, near the edge of the marsh grass, a man's body lay in a crumpled heap. Thompson checked to make sure no one was coming, then hurried across the road.

One

*D*awn came shortly after five o'clock. The night sky turned gray as morning crept toward the horizon. Minutes later the sun burst over the treetops along the eastern shore of Mobile Bay in a blaze of light, drawing the downtown buildings from the receding shadows into the early morning glare.

A man sleeping on a park bench under the massive oak trees in Bienville Square rolled on his side and draped his arm across the side of his face, shielding his eyes. Another lying on a nearby bench pulled yesterday's newspaper over his head. By five-thirty the cool of the night was gone. In its place, stifling heat and suffocating humidity enveloped the city.

Across Bienville Square on Dauphin Street, the Warren Building looked out on the waking city. Constructed in the 1920s, it had been the marvel of the downtown business district in its day. Its central air conditioning and gleaming elevators were the first of either in the city and made it the location of choice for most of the prestigious firms. Now worn and tired, it was home to a collection of private investigators, sleazy plaintiffs' attorneys, and Mike Connolly.

That morning, Connolly was fast asleep in his third-floor office. Slumped forward in his chair, his head rested on top of the desk. Both arms dangled at his side. To the left of his head was the telephone. Next to it sat a round pencil holder filled with pencils, pens, and a letter opener. To the right, a half-empty gin bottle sat a few inches from his nose.

Shortly before eight o'clock the telephone rang. The ringing pounded in Connolly's head and beat against his ears until he was roused from sleep. Thinking it was an alarm clock, he swatted with his hand to turn it off. His hand came crashing down on the pencil holder. Two pencils turned pointed end up stabbed him in the palm of his hand.

Startled by the pain in his hand, he jerked his head up from the desk so fast he strained a muscle in the back of his neck. He grabbed the phone with his left hand and clutched his neck with the other.

"Hello," he growled.

In response he heard only a dial tone. He slammed down the phone and leaned backward. His head flopped against the back of the chair and sent a stabbing pain through the muscles of his neck. He moaned and closed his eyes.

In a few moments, the phone rang again. This time, he rocked forward without moving his head and grabbed the receiver on the first ring.

"Hello," he said.

"Connolly?"

"Yeah."

"Connolly, this is Walter in Judge Cahill's court. Judge wants to see you."

"When?"

"Now."

"Alright. I'll be right there."

Connolly hung up the phone and gently returned his head to the desktop. The muscles in his neck throbbed. A pounding headache made him dizzy. He closed his eyes.

Sometime later, the phone rang again. Once again he

jerked his head up from the desktop. The ache in his head was more intense than before. His neck muscles were in knots. He lifted the telephone to his ear.

"This is Walter in Judge Cahill's court. You coming over here this morning?"

"I just told you I'd be right there," Connolly groused.

"That was forty-five minutes ago," Walter replied. "Judge wants to see you right now."

Connolly checked his watch.

"Alright," he groaned. "I'm on my way."

He hung up the phone and pushed himself up from the chair. With one hand against the wall for support, he made his way around the desk to the doorway and shuffled out of his office.

A little way down the hall was a tiny room that served as both a break room and copier room. In the far corner was a sink with a cabinet above it and a small mirror on the wall behind the faucet. A refrigerator sat next to the sink with a microwave oven on top. A small table by the door held a fax machine. The photocopier took up the rest of the space.

He opened the cabinet above the sink and reached inside for a toothbrush. When he finished brushing his teeth, he splashed water on his face and ran his fingers through his hair. As he did, he caught a glimpse of himself in the mirror. His hair was still thick and full, though most of it was turning gray. Tiny wrinkles stretched from the corners of his eyes. Beneath them, large dark circles sagged toward his cheek-bones. He rubbed lightly across his face with his fingers and felt the stubble of his beard.

No time to shave, he thought.

He buttoned the top button of his shirt and pulled the knot of his tie up tight against his neck. At least he had avoided the thick jowls and double chin most men his age acquired. Though he was fifty-eight years old, his chin was still square and sharp, his jawline straight and lean. Drinking didn't leave much time for eating.

Back in his office, he rummaged around in the desk and found a legal pad with a few clean pages. As he looked through the drawer, the gin bottle on the desk caught his eye. He wanted a drink but Judge Cahill would smell it on his breath for sure. Instead, he put the cap on the bottle and shoved it in the bottom drawer of the desk. He took a pen from the pencil holder, grabbed his jacket, and headed out the door.

Downstairs, he slipped out the back of the building into Ferguson's Alley. He made his way down the alley, across Conti Street, and emerged at Government Street directly opposite the courthouse. He arrived in Cahill's courtroom a few minutes later.

Walter sat at a desk to the right of the judge's bench, busily working through a pile of court files. He looked up as Connolly entered the courtroom.

"He's in his office," he said, nodding toward the door behind him.

Connolly walked around Walter's desk and disappeared through the door to the judge's chambers.

Beyond the door was an outer office furnished with non-descript chairs and a small table with a lamp. On the wall to the left was a picture of Judge Cahill and the governor. To the right was a citation Cahill received while serving in the Alabama National Guard. At the far end of the left wall was the door to his office. The door was slightly ajar.

"Walter," Cahill called, "did you get in touch with Mike Connolly?"

Connolly stepped to the door and peered through the opening. Cahill was seated behind his desk across the room facing the door. His desk was covered with stacks of court files. He glanced up as Connolly appeared.

"Come in here, Connolly," he called.

Connolly pushed the door open and stepped inside.

"Good morning, Your Honor."

"It doesn't look so good for you," Cahill frowned. "You look as rough as I feel."

Connolly managed a nervous smile, suddenly aware of his rumpled appearance.

"Sorry, Judge. They said you wanted to see me. I just came right over. Didn't have time to go home and get cleaned up."

Cahill shook his head. He gave a long, heavy sigh.

"You need to lay off the gin."

"Probably so," Connolly replied. "Probably so."

His voice trailed off as he crossed the office and stood in front of Cahill's desk. Cahill picked up a file from the stack in front of him.

"I'm going to appoint you to a capital murder case. Think you can handle it?"

"I've done it before."

"This one's a little different," Cahill said. "You watch the news last night?"

"Ahhh ... saw the first part."

"Then you probably know Keyton Attaway's dead."

"Yeah," Connolly lied. He hadn't watched television in months. "I fell asleep in the middle of the report," he continued. "Where did they find him?"

"Pinto Island. Not far from the shipyard."

"How'd it happen?"

"Not sure. Police think it might have been part of a robbery."

Connolly's forehead wrinkled in a look of concern.

"I'm sorry to hear that," he said. "Keyton was a good man. Any idea who did it?"

Connolly didn't realize how ridiculous the question sounded until the words were already out of his mouth. He stared at Judge Cahill a moment, as if expecting an answer, then a broad smile broke across his face.

"Police think Avery Thompson did it," Cahill snorted with laughter. "They've charged him with capital murder." He tossed the court file toward the edge of the desk in front of Connolly. "Here. Take a look at the file. You can get somebody to help you if you like. Or, you can work it by yourself. I don't care."

Connolly picked up the file and opened it. Cahill leaned back in his chair and draped both arms over the top of his head.

"You got any problem defending him?"

"No," Connolly replied. "I guess not." He was supposed to know Keyton Attaway. The name sounded familiar, but right then it was a struggle to remember his own name much less anyone else's. Still, his momentary lapse of memory didn't stop him from continuing the conversation. "I knew Keyton," he said, "but we weren't that close."

"Alright." Cahill lowered his arms and leaned forward again. "Thompson's up in the jail. You can go see him when you get the time."

Cahill picked up another file from his desk and opened it, a signal for Connolly to leave.

"What about bail?"

"No bond," Cahill snapped.

He was already reading the next file. He didn't bother to look up as he spoke.

"You saying you didn't set an amount," Connolly asked, "or you saying you've ruled he's not entitled?"

Cahill glanced at Connolly, then back to the file in his hands.

"I've considered the question of bail. He's in on no bond. You can request a hearing if you want to," Cahill said. "But I'm not letting him out."

Connolly stepped to the door. Cahill tossed the file he was holding into a bin on the corner of his desk, then picked up another.

"Give the file to Walter when you get through with it," he mumbled as he reached for the next file.

Connolly took a seat at the counsel's table in the courtroom and opened the court file. There wasn't much inside. A cover sheet, a warrant, and a booking sheet created when Thompson was processed in at the jail. He made notes from what little information he found.

Avery Thompson was forty-eight years old. He was accused of murdering Keyton Attaway with a pistol. Because he had previously been convicted of murder, the charge against him was a capital offense for which he faced the possibility of the death penalty. Information in the file indicated forty dollars in cash and a watch valued at one thousand dollars had been taken from Attaway, but there was no indication Thompson was charged with robbery. Connolly jotted down the information and handed the file to Walter.

"We'll have a preliminary hearing sometime in the next three or four weeks," Walter said. He took the file from Connolly and tossed it on a cart behind his desk. "I'll let you know."

"I'll be waiting," Connolly replied.

From Cahill's courtroom Connolly took the elevator to the courthouse lobby and made his way to the front exit. A blanket of summer heat wrapped around him as he stepped through the door. Sweat seeped from every pore in his body. The air was thick and humid. Two steps up the sidewalk he peeled off his suit jacket, slung it over his shoulder, and trudged toward the office.

Myrtice Gordon, Connolly's secretary, was seated at her desk when he returned. At seventy-five she was long past retirement age, but she refused to quit. Always at her desk by eight-thirty in the morning, she remained there until five-thirty each evening, a routine she had followed for thirty-four years. She was the only secretary he had ever had.

"Good morning, Mrs. Gordon," Connolly said as he passed her desk.

"Have you been to the hospital this morning?" she asked, ignoring his greeting.

"No," he frowned. "Why?"

"Your daughter ..."

Halfway down the hall Connolly whirled around to face her. He looked stricken.

"Rachel?"

"She had a baby last night. Your first grandchild," Mrs. Gordon said. The tone of her voice indicated it was a matter they had already discussed. "Didn't you go over to the hospital to see them?"

"Oh," he said. He turned away. "No. I didn't make it."

He walked down the hallway to his office, hung his jacket on the coat rack, and flopped into the chair behind his desk. When he looked up, Mrs. Gordon was standing in the doorway holding a neatly wrapped gift.

"I bought this for you to take with you," she said.

She stepped toward the middle of the room.

"What is it?"

"It's a gift for the baby," she said. She set the package on his desk and glanced at her watch. "If you go now you can see her before Rachel has to feed her again."

"Her?"

"She had a little girl, Mike. You need to go see her."

He looked away.

"I haven't seen or heard from her in over a year."

"Rachel's your daughter," Mrs. Gordon replied. "Go see her."

She stepped to the door and walked up the hallway. Connolly leaned around the end of the desk and looked to make sure she was gone. Satisfied she was out of sight, he slid open the bottom drawer of the desk and took out a bottle of gin.

Two

*L*ater that morning Mrs. Gordon left the office on an errand to the post office. While she was gone, Connolly picked up the gift from the desk and took the elevator to the lobby.

On the street in front of the building he paused and tried to remember where he parked his car. A dark blue 1959 Chrysler Imperial, it should have been easy to find, but he had no recollection of the previous day. As he struggled to recall the car's location, he wandered down the sidewalk. He was almost to Conception Street when he saw it, parked at the curb in front of the Port City Diner. He slid in behind the steering wheel, placed the gift beside him on the front seat, and started the engine.

From Dauphin Street downtown, he drove to Government Street and then west toward midtown. At Carondolet Street he turned left and drove two blocks to his apartment. He parked out front under a large oak tree and trudged up the steps to the second-floor landing. Tired and aching from the night before, he struggled to unlock the door.

Once inside, he slipped off his shoes and walked quietly down the hall to the bedroom. Through the doorway he could see Marisa asleep in bed. Only the top of her blonde head was visible from beneath the cover. He slipped off his clothes and laid them on a chair, then crawled in beside her. She moaned lightly at the interruption, then squirmed her naked back against his chest.

Her real name was Linda Marie Mayhew. When they first met, she lived with her parents on Bayou Cumbis, a dank little place on the coast near Pascagoula. She worked as a barmaid at the Imperial Palace, a club on the Alabama-Mississippi line, thirty miles west of Mobile. Connolly was a regular there. Newly divorced, he was an easy mark.

She moved in with him a month after they met. Two months later, she convinced him to pay for cosmetic surgery. Overnight, she was transformed into a buxom beauty of unnatural proportions. Equally as quickly, she moved from barmaid to exotic dancer and began calling herself Marisa. She was an instant success. Attendance at the Imperial Palace doubled.

A few months into her new career, Connolly came home to find she had moved out. A note on the kitchen table said she was moving to Florida with Frank, a banker from Panama City. He put her in a condo in Destin, which was owned by his wife. As it turned out, Frank had little interest in business and even less in hard work, becoming a banker only because his wife inherited Palmetto State Bank from her father in Panama City.

Marisa took a job at The Gold Coast, a club that catered to the upscale tourist crowd that frequented the Florida beaches in and around Destin. Frank came to see her every Tuesday and Thursday. Then, his wife came over to check on the condo and found Marisa in the shower. Not long after that, Marisa showed up at Connolly's apartment.

As much as he wanted to be angry with her, Connolly was glad to see her. The Imperial Palace was glad to see her too. Business had been off in the months since she left. Soon, she was dancing again at the Palace and sleeping in Connolly's bed. She'd be gone before long with someone else who promised to take her places she'd never been, but he liked the way she made him feel.

He wrapped his arm around her waist and pulled her closer. She felt warm and soft in his arms, and he squeezed her against him. Soon, they both were sound asleep.

Connolly awoke in the middle of the afternoon. He slipped out of bed and put on his trousers. As he did, Marisa opened her eyes.

"What time is it?"

"Two," Connolly replied.

She rolled on her side to face him.

"Where you going?"

"To the office," he said.

She smiled again and closed her eyes. Connolly dressed and stepped toward the door.

Downstairs, he got behind the steering wheel of the Chrysler and drove away from the curb. At the corner, he made the block and drove back to Government Street. Instead of turning right, toward the office downtown, he turned left and drove west. He reached St. Joseph's Hospital in twenty minutes.

Located in the suburbs west of town, the hospital was a modern structure of concrete and glass situated in the midst of a lush, green campus. Sleek, efficient, new, it stood in stark contrast to the old brick and stucco buildings downtown.

He parked near the front entrance and went inside. An aide at the information desk directed him to the visitor's elevator.

At the fourth floor, he followed signs toward the maternity ward. Around the corner from the elevator, he passed through double doors to a corridor that led past the nursery. Curtains were drawn over the nursery windows, but he paused there anyway, examining his appearance in the reflection of the glass. He ran his fingers through his hair and checked his tie, then moved on down the corridor.

In a few minutes, he located Rachel's room. At the door, he hesitated. From inside he heard voices, but they were the quiet sounds of easy conversation and were unrecognizable. He took a deep breath. Gift in hand, he tapped gently on the door.

"Come in," someone called from inside the room.

He eased open the door and stepped inside.

Rachel lay in bed, her head and torso elevated. Her hair was unkempt and oily and lay flat along the outline of her head. Her skin was pale, almost without color. Her eyes looked tired. Against her chest she held a tiny newborn baby bundled in a blanket.

Across the room, on the opposite side of the bed stood a man, his hair cut neat and short, dressed in blue jeans and a freshly laundered blue work shirt starched and pressed with a sharp crease down each sleeve.

As Connolly entered the room, he made eye contact with Rachel first. When she saw him, her tired, listless eyes suddenly became alive and alert.

"What are you doing here?" she hissed through clenched teeth.

She pulled the baby closer and covered her head with the blanket.

"Just came to see my granddaughter," Connolly replied, smiling.

The man stepped forward and extended his hand.

"Good afternoon," he said. "I'm Craig Jackson. You must be Mr. Connolly."

"Yes," Connolly replied.

"Rachel has told us a lot about you," Craig said.

"Us?"

"Yes. Me and Mark."

Connolly's countenance dropped.

"Oh," he said. Inside he felt a stab deep in his soul.

Rachel left home at nineteen to attend college. Halfway through her second year she dropped out and moved in with a man twice her age who was married and had two children. They lived together for two years, then she became pregnant. He reconciled with his wife and moved back home, leaving Rachel to fend for herself. Pregnant and alone, she moved in with Craig and Mark. The trio shared a three-story house on Texas Street in a rundown section of midtown.

Connolly forced a pleasant smile. He had driven by the house a time or two, just to check on things, and he was surprised to find Craig looking neat and clean. Not what he had expected from the looks of the house.

Rachel pulled one arm free from around the baby and pointed toward Connolly.

"Get him out of here," she railed at Craig. "I don't want him anywhere near me."

Her voice was no louder than a whisper but carried the force of a shout. Her pale face was now red with anger.

"Come on, Rach," Craig replied plaintively, "she's his granddaughter."

"I just wanted to see how you're doing and bring her a gift," Connolly said.

"You don't care how I feel," Rachel snapped. Her voice was again a shout no louder than a whisper. "You've never cared how I felt."

Connolly set the gift on the end of the bed.

"Can I see the baby?"

He stepped toward her.

"No. Get away," she demanded, pulling the baby even closer with one arm and slapping at him with the other. She turned to Craig and burst into tears. "Please, get him out of here," she sobbed, her voice at once dissolving into a pleading whine.

Craig moved around the foot of the bed and placed his hand on Connolly's shoulder.

"Come on, Mr. Connolly," he said calmly. "Maybe you should come back later."

Connolly stood there, staring at the bundle in Rachel's arms. As he watched, the baby squirmed. The blanket fell from around her head revealing her smooth face, and thin red hair appeared. A lump rose in Connolly's throat. His eyes grew full and moist.

Rachel saw the look on his face and snatched the blanket over the baby's head. Connolly backed away. Craig guided him toward the door.

In the hall, Connolly turned to Craig.

"What's her name?"

"Excuse me?"

"The baby," Connolly said. "What's her name?"

"Elizabeth," Craig replied.

Connolly paused. Elizabeth. It was his mother's name, and hearing it brought back a flood of memories long buried deep in his soul. Without replying, he turned away and walked up the corridor.

Three

From St. Joseph's, Connolly drove toward town. He reached the county jail around four o'clock that afternoon.

The jail sat one block west of Water Street across from the banana wharves that lined the Mobile River. Ten stories high, it was built of dark brown brick that gave it a hulking, formidable appearance. Steel bars, rusted from the salt air that drifted in from the bay, covered the windows adding to the building's imposing character.

Inside, it was a dreary place. Built in the 1950s and never remodeled, it was dirty, worn, and cramped. Filing cabinets lined every inch of the walls filling the entrance lobby and hallways. Papers and files seemed to be stacked everywhere. A metal detector stood in the middle of what was left of the lobby. It was the building's lone, begrudging acknowledgment of modern technology. Next to it was a small metal desk. Beyond the metal detector was a large steel door that led into the booking area.

A guard sat at the desk. She looked up as Connolly approached.

"May I help you?" she asked.

"I'm here to see a prisoner. Avery Thompson," Connolly replied. "He's my client."

"Empty your pockets and step through the metal detector," the guard ordered.

Connolly laid his car keys on the desk and walked through the detector. When he was through, the guard handed him his keys and banged on the steel door with her fist.

"Visitor," she shouted.

In a few moments a rattling sound could be heard from the other side of the door as a guard inserted a large key into the lock. Then, slowly, the door swung open. Connolly stepped over the threshold and through the doorway. He made his way past the booking area to the elevator near the rear of the building. Thompson was waiting for him in an interview room on the eighth floor. A guard met Connolly in the hallway and let him into the room.

"Avery Thompson?" Connolly began.

Thompson nodded.

"I'm Mike Connolly. Judge Cahill appointed me to represent you."

Thompson sat on a stainless steel bench on one side of a stainless steel table that was bolted to the wall and floor. He extended his hand to Connolly but did not stand. Connolly reached across the table, shook his hand, then took a seat on the bench on the opposite side of the table.

"Do you understand the charge against you?"

Connolly spoke without looking at Thompson. While he waited for a response, he looked through the notes he had made from the court file earlier that morning.

"Yeah," Thompson replied. "I understand."

"They have you charged with capital murder in the death of Keyton Attaway."

Again Connolly fumbled with the pages in the legal pad.

"I understand the charge," Thompson repeated.

"Alright," Connolly said, turning to a clean sheet in the legal pad. "Suppose you tell me what happened."

As he removed a pen from his jacket, he glanced at Thompson for the first time.

"Well ..." Thompson began, "I was coming from work over at Alabama Shipyard. Got off late. When I got up on Short Haul Road, my car broke down. I started walking. Little way up the road I seen a car ... a Cadillac parked on the side of the road. Was two people in it. A man and a woman in the front seat."

"Where was the man?"

"Passenger's side. Woman was behind the wheel. I walked up to the car and tapped on the window."

"Driver's side?"

"Yeah. The lady rolled the window down a little way. I tried to tell her my car broke down, but she said she couldn't help me and rolled the window up."

"Could you tell what they were doing in the car?"

"Not really. Looked like they was talking. She was turned in the seat kind of sideways, facing him."

"Did you recognize them?"

"No. I'd know them if I saw them again, but I hadn't never seen them before."

"What happened next?"

"She rolled the window up. I was standing there thinking, 'I can't believe this,' when a pickup truck pulled up behind the car."

"What kind of truck?"

"Blue. Ford. I don't know the year, but it wasn't too old."

"What happened after that?"

"This guy gets out of the truck. Had on a ragged old T-shirt and blue jeans, but his shoes were black and shiny, like military shoes, and he had a fresh haircut. Something didn't seem right about him. Had a look in his eye like something serious was up. Gave me the creeps."

"What did you do?"

"I backed away from the car and ran fast as I could."

"Where'd you go?"

"Ran across the road."

"Isn't that a little swampy around there?"

"Yeah, but I didn't care. I ran into the bushes as fast as I could."

"Then what happened?"

"When I was running into the bushes I heard this sound like a gunshot. I dove to the ground. Then I heard two more shots."

"You still on the ground?"

"Still on the ground. Flat as I could get. In a few minutes I heard the truck drive off. I waited a little bit and then walked back toward the road. When I got to the edge of the bushes, I seen the lady standing outside the car, screaming and crying and carrying on. I thought about going over there to see about her but ... you know ... black man and white woman out like that ... I was sure the man was dead. So I hung back in the bushes and watched."

Connolly began to sweat. His hands were sticky, and it was hard to concentrate. Notes on the pages of the legal pad, never very legible, became random marks.

"Anything else happen?"

"While I was standing there, a black ... One of those big things."

"An SUV?"

"Yeah. An SUV. Looked like one of those Lincolns. I can't remember what they call 'em. It pulled up beside her. The back door opened. Looked like she knowed whoever was in it 'cause she started yelling at 'em."

"Could you hear what she said?"

Connolly wiped his forehead with the back of his hand and rubbed his palms on his pants legs.

"Sounded like, 'Why did you do that?' or something like that."

"But she knew them?"

"Looked like it to me. They pulled her inside and drove away."

"And then where did you go?"

"I ran back through the swamp. Came out over on the causeway by Johnny's Crab Shack and headed east."

"And that's when the police found you?"

"Yeah." Thompson's voice dropped, and he lowered his head. "By then they was all over the place."

"How did they know to look for you?"

Thompson shrugged.

"I don't know."

"Anything else?"

Sweat rolled down the middle of Connolly's back. His hands shook, and his mouth became as dry as cotton. He hadn't had anything to drink since he left the office that morning.

"You alright?" Thompson asked. "You don't look so good."

"I'm fine," Connolly replied. He stood and picked up the notepad. "I haven't talked to the district attorney about this case yet. I'll do that today or tomorrow, and then we can talk about this again. Anything else you need to tell me?"

"No," Thompson responded. "Think we can win?"

"I don't know," Connolly replied. He moved toward the door. "I'll be able to tell you more about it after I see the district attorney."

"You'll be back tomorrow?"

Connolly fumbled with the pen as he tried to slide it into the pocket of his jacket.

"Tomorrow or the next day," he said. "Just ... ahhh ... just depends on when they can see me."

Connolly banged on the door to get the guard's attention. Splotches of sweat soaked through his shirt, and his hands trembled. The guard opened the door. Connolly darted toward the elevator.

When he reached the car, Connolly took out his keys to unlock the door. As he struggled to put the key in the lock, the keys slipped from his hand and fell to the ground. He picked them up and tried again. Once more the keys slipped from his fingers. Finally, he laid his jacket and the legal pad on top of the car and held the keys with both hands. With great effort, he managed to open the door.

Inside, he lunged across the front seat toward the glove box. With a swat of his hand, he hit the lock button on the glove box door. The door fell open. He reached inside and grabbed a small, silver flask. In one quick motion, he twisted off the top and took a long gulp of gin, then another. After the third, he propped himself up in the seat and lowered the car windows.

He sat there in the parking lot outside the jail and continued to sip from the flask. Slowly, his hands stopped shaking. A hot breeze blew through the car. It drifted across his wet shirt sending a chill through his body. He took another sip from the flask and glanced around to see if anyone noticed.

By the time he finished off the flask, he was calm enough to function. He pulled himself to a sitting position behind the steering wheel and started the engine. He screwed the cap on the flask and laid it on the seat beside him. He put the car in gear and pulled out of the parking space. As he did, a flash of yellow in the rearview mirror caught his eye. The yellow legal pad blew off the top of the car and tumbled to the pavement behind him. His jacket tumbled from the car top onto the trunk. He stopped the car and ran to retrieve them.

Across the way a man sat alone in a dark green Taurus. Connolly flashed a nervous smile in his direction, tucked his jacket under his arm and picked up the legal pad.

Four

Connolly checked his watch as he drove away from the jail. It was almost five. If he hurried, he might be able to get to the district attorney's office before everyone left for the day. He would hear their side of the story, and that would be the end of it. They'd have the evidence. It would all fit neatly in place. No room for any lawyering. No need for any work. Then he could go back to the office and forget about Avery Thompson.

The district attorney's office was located on the fourth floor of the newly constructed courthouse building. Connolly parked behind the building in a space reserved for sheriff's deputies and took the elevator.

Juanita, the receptionist, gave Connolly the once-over as he approached her desk.

"May I help you?"

Her voice was at once both cordial and condescending.

She was as old as dirt, but her skin was as smooth as porcelain, and she had a certain air of dignity about the way she carried herself that left one wondering whether her gruff disposition was merely an act. Beyond the tone of her voice, however, there was little emotion about her. No frown. No scowl. Only that voice, and eyes that rolled up to the top of her eyelids as she looked over the top of reading glasses perched in the middle of her nose. And once in a while, if she was particularly perturbed, the corners of her mouth turned down.

Connolly approached her with caution.

"I was wondering if I could see Paige Huddleston?" he said.

"What about?"

The tone in her voice put him on the defensive.

"A case," Connolly replied.

As he spoke, he slipped a breath mint from his pocket and popped it into his mouth.

"Whose court?"

"Judge Cahill."

"She isn't in that court anymore," Juanita said. She lifted the telephone receiver and began punching a number on the telephone key pad. "She's in Judge Pearson's courtroom now. You need Henry McNamara."

Connolly vaguely remembered seeing McNamara in Cahill's courtroom once or twice.

"Alright," he replied. "Can I see Henry?"

Juanita stared at him as she waited for McNamara to answer the phone.

"It's late," she said, holding the phone against her ear. "I'll see if he has time to meet with you."

As she glared at him, the corners of her mouth turned down.

Connolly moved away and wandered to the far side of the room. He took a drink from the water fountain near the entrance, then flipped through a magazine from a nearby table.

"Henry will be out in a minute," Juanita called, her voice loud and flat. "Have a seat."

Connolly did as he was told and sat in a chair as far from

her as possible. He hid his face behind the magazine and tried to become invisible.

In a few minutes, McNamara appeared near Juanita's desk. Almost six feet tall, McNamara had broad shoulders and an athletic physique, which he carried well. But his innocent, round face and boyish manner made him seem even younger than he was.

Barely a year out of law school, he had only recently been allowed to handle preliminary hearings by himself. Having this case assigned to him struck Connolly as odd, but he pushed the notion aside, tossed the magazine on a nearby table, and started across the room.

"Come on in, Mr. Connolly," he said, holding the door open. "I assume you're here about that Avery Thompson case."

"Yeah. Judge Cahill called me this morning. I thought maybe we could talk a minute."

"Sure."

McNamara led him through a labyrinth of offices and cubicles to a small conference room on the far side of the building. Sparsely furnished, the room held only a plain folding table and four chairs. The walls were bare and windowless. A fluorescent light in the ceiling above the table made the room seem even more stark. McNamara's file lay at the far end of the table.

"Have a seat," McNamara said.

He closed the door and moved to the end of the table.

"I don't normally do this," he said, "but because this is a capital case, I'll let you see most of what's in my file."

He pulled a chair from the table and sat down. Connolly took a seat nearby.

"I made copies of the arrest and incident reports for you," McNamara continued.

He slid the copies across the table to Connolly as they talked.

"Thanks," Connolly replied. "What kind of physical evidence do you have?"

"We have the clothes the victim was wearing, along with personal effects from his pockets. They removed some bullets from him during the autopsy. I think they sent those to us too. They might still be at the lab. I'm not sure."

"He was shot more than once?"

"Yeah. Once in the head and once or twice in the mouth."

"Got a ballistics report on the bullets?"

"Not yet," McNamara replied. "It should be in any day."

"Any chance I can look at the clothes and whatever else there is?"

"Yeah. I'll have to call the detective. He has it in their property room."

"Alright," Connolly replied. "Who's the detective?"

"Anthony Hammond."

Connolly nodded. He had no trouble remembering Hammond. Their paths had crossed several times.

"What else you got?" he said.

"I have a written statement from a witness," McNamara replied. "Let me see if I can find it in here." He searched through the papers in the file while he talked. "And then there's the gun we took from your client when we arrested him."

Connolly was caught by surprise. He was sure Thompson hadn't mentioned a gun when they spoke in the jail. He would have remembered something as important as that. McNamara noticed his surprise.

"He didn't tell you about the gun?"

Connolly smiled and shrugged his shoulders.

"You tell me about the gun."

"Nothing special," McNamara said. "Five-shot, thirty-eight caliber revolver."

"Do any testing on it?"

"Sent it to the lab. They haven't issued a report yet, but I'm sure it matches the bullets from Mr. Attaway's body." McNamara slid a piece of paper out of the file. "Here's the statement," he said, handing the paper to Connolly. "Witness' name is Bill Sisson."

Connolly held the incident report in his left hand and Sisson's statement in his right. He scanned through both reports. He shook his head as he studied the two documents.

McNamara smiled.

"Something wrong?"

Connolly laid the two reports side by side on the table.

"Look at this," Connolly said, pointing to the report. "The incident report says the victim was sitting in a car, but it doesn't describe the car. Any idea where the car is?"

McNamara looked at the report.

"No," he replied, puzzled. "I don't think we recovered one. Must have been the victim's car."

"But look at Sisson's statement," Connolly continued. "It doesn't say anything about a car."

"So?"

"So, where did the officer who wrote up the incident report get the information about the victim being in a car?"

"I don't know."

"You got any other witnesses who could have given him this information?"

"Not that I know of."

Connolly scanned the report once more.

"Is this report saying Attaway was in a car when the police got to the scene?"

"I don't think so," McNamara replied. "Attaway's body was found on the side of the road. Somebody called it in to the police. Might have been Sisson. When the officers got out there, they found the body lying on the shoulder of the road."

McNamara began gathering papers from the table and stuffing them in his file. Connolly continued to press him.

"Was Sisson at the scene when the police arrived?"

"I think so. Like I say, he may have been the one who called it in. You know, drove down the road to a phone, made the call, then came back. I don't know."

Connolly laid the two documents on top of his legal pad.

"You sure you want to charge my client with capital murder?"

McNamara grinned.

"Thompson has three prior convictions," he explained. "One of them was a conviction for murder. And, since that prior conviction happened within the last twenty years, that makes this case capital murder."

Connolly chuckled.

"That's it?"

"That's it," he replied.

"Kind of thin for a capital case, don't you think?"

"I think it's a good case," McNamara said, a hint of irritation in his voice. "Plenty of people have been convicted on less evidence than this."

"I've seen them acquitted on a whole lot more too. Judge Cahill said the police thought this was a robbery."

McNamara closed his file and laid it on the table in front of him. He folded his hands on top of it.

"Mr. Connolly, I don't develop the cases. I just prosecute them. When that ballistics report comes back matching the pistol from your client to the bullets in Mr. Attaway, it'll be over. With your client's previous murder conviction, he'll be looking at the death penalty, and we won't have to worry about whether he was trying to rob anyone."

McNamara was right. Connolly picked up Sisson's statement from the table. He scanned it for a moment as he tried to think of something to say.

"You got an address for this witness ... Sisson?"

"Yes," McNamara replied. "But he was a little concerned about us giving it out. You know, this being a capital murder case and all."

Connolly lowered the report and looked at McNamara. He cocked his head to one side and raised an eyebrow.

"I need to talk to him."

"I told him that," McNamara said. "Just be careful, and if you would, make sure your client doesn't get the address."

"I'll do my best."

McNamara looked at the cover sheet on top of his file.

"He lives at 2209 Forrestwood Drive. Let me call him first and tell him you're coming."

"Alright. Got anything else?"

"I think that's about it."

"You want to talk about settling this case?"

"If he pleads to capital murder, we'll recommend life without parole," McNamara replied. The smirk on his face and the smug tone of his voice made something in Connolly recoil. "Otherwise, we're looking at the death penalty."

Connolly gave him a cold, emotionless glare.

"I was talking about settling, not caving in," he said.

"Read the statement," McNamara chided. "Sisson puts your man at the scene. Your client has three prior felony convictions. And when the jury hears we found the murder weapon on him when we caught him, they won't be out more than thirty minutes."

For the first time in a long while Connolly felt angry. McNamara's cocky, sarcastic tone set his teeth on edge.

"Well, I guess we'll see about that, won't we?" Connolly said.

"Yes, sir," McNamara smiled. "We will."

He stood and moved toward the door.

Late that evening, Connolly returned to St. Joseph's Hospital. Instead of using the front lobby he entered through the back of the building and took a service elevator to the fourth floor. There, he made his way to the maternity ward on the opposite side of the hospital. When he arrived, a nurse was drawing the curtain closed in front of the nursery. He pressed against the glass and scanned the room for his granddaughter. The nurse paused and stepped away from the window. In a moment, she appeared through a door a little way down the hall.

"Which baby were you looking for?"

"Connolly," he replied. "Elizabeth Connolly."

The nurse entered the nursery and took Elizabeth from her bassinet. She cradled her in both arms and walked to the window. Connolly pressed closer, his nose touching the glass as he did his best to soak up every detail of his granddaughter's appearance. A minute or two later the nurse lifted the baby's tiny hand and moved it up and down as if to wave goodbye, then returned her to the crib. Connolly watched a moment longer. The nurse drew the curtain closed. He turned to leave.

As he stepped from the window, he bumped into a woman standing behind him.

"Pretty, isn't she?"

The sound of her voice caught him by surprise. A flood of

emotions washed over him. He shoved them aside as best he could and struggled to smile.

"H ... hello, Barbara," he said.

His voice caught in his throat. When he finally forced the words out, they sounded thin and raspy. He felt awkward and nervous. Barbara seemed not to notice.

"Rachel know you're out here?"

"Ahh ... no," he replied. He glanced away, averting her piercing gaze.

"Bring your ... live-in with you?"

Her eyes bore down on him as she awaited his response.

"Don't start," Connolly snapped. "I don't tell you how to live your life. You don't tell me."

Barbara folded her arms across her chest.

"Rachel said you came by earlier. I hear she ran you off."

Connolly shoved both hands in his pants pockets.

"That's something, isn't it?" He looked at her with a pained, tight-lipped smile. "Have to come out here like a visitor to see my own granddaughter."

"You had a lot of nerve coming to see her at all."

She glared at him, her finger jabbing the air with each word. Connolly cowered at the sound of her voice.

"Yeah, well ... seemed like the thing to do."

Barbara pressed her point.

"That was always your problem—"

Connolly held up a hand.

"Don't start on me," he growled, interrupting her. "I took twenty-five years of that off you. I'm not interested in hearing it tonight."

As he spoke, a man stepped to Barbara's side and gently laid his hand against the small of her back. Connolly had not noticed him before.

"Who are you?"

"Lamar Edwards," the man replied.

He thrust his hand toward Connolly. Connolly ignored him, looking past him to Barbara. Now it was her turn to cringe. Her gaze dropped to the floor.

"When did this happen?"

She did not reply. Lamar pulled her to his side. Connolly turned away and walked down the hall toward the elevator.

Five

The next day Connolly returned to the county jail. Once again, he rode the elevator to the eighth floor and met Avery Thompson in an interview room. Thompson was already seated at the table.

"Why didn't you tell me about the gun?"

Thompson looked puzzled.

"The gun?"

"Yeah. The gun," Connolly said. He made no attempt to hide his anger. "The thirty-eight caliber pistol they found on you when they arrested you."

"Nah," Thompson said, waving his hands and shaking his head. "No way. They can't use that. That ain't nothing, man. That arrest was illegal. You got to get that pistol suppressed."

"Where did you get the pistol?"

"Found it."

"Where?"

"On the ground, a few feet from the dead man."

Connolly was beside himself.

"I thought you watched from across the road."

His voice was sharp and caustic.

"I did," Thompson cried, his voice rising in volume to match Connolly's. "But after they left, I walked over there to look around. When I seen him lying there, I got scared.

Thought they might come looking for me. I saw the pistol lying there. I picked it up and ran away."

A wry, sarcastic smile spread across Connolly's face.

"And you expect a jury to believe that story?"

Thompson stood and moved away from the table toward the door.

"Ain't done nothing," he mumbled, "and here I am, stuck up here in jail with a drunk for a lawyer."

Connolly stepped in front of him, blocking his way.

"Drunk? Who you calling a drunk?"

"You had the shakes so bad yesterday, I doubt you even remember being here."

Thompson pounded on the door with his fist for the guard.

"You supposed to get me off," Thompson continued. "That's your job. Why don't you lay off the booze and get to work?"

"It would help if you would tell me the truth," Connolly said, his voice even louder than before. "I looked like an idiot trying to talk about your case to the DA."

Thompson leaned toward Connolly. Their noses almost touched.

"Who you calling an idiot?"

Connolly stepped back and took a deep breath.

"Wait a minute," he said. His voice was lower, his tone less combative. "Sit down and let's talk about this."

Thompson glared at him.

Just then, the clanking of the guard's key in the door interrupted them. The door opened. The guard appeared in the doorway.

"Y'all alright in here?"

Thompson stared at Connolly.

"Yeah," Connolly said. "We're alright."

"Well, keep it down," the guard replied. "Everybody on the whole floor can hear you."

The door banged closed. Connolly took a seat at the table.

"I talked to the DA," he said. "There's a witness."

Thompson turned from the door and stepped to the table. "What witness?"

He stepped over the bench and took a seat. Connolly sat across from him.

"His last name is Sisson," Connolly said. "He gave the police a written statement. Do you remember seeing his truck?"

"The blue one?"

"No. One in the road. You dodged it as you ran away."

Thompson shrugged his shoulders.

"I don't know," he said. "I was scared." Thompson folded his arms on the table and rested his chin on top. "This case sounds like a setup."

"A setup?" Connolly felt frustrated. His tone once again became sharp. "Who knew you would be out there? Huh? Who set you up?"

Thompson sat erect.

"Man, that's your job," he said, slapping the table in disgust. He leaned against the wall and glared at Connolly. "How they going to prove this is a capital case, anyway?"

"They say you have a prior murder conviction," Connolly explained.

Thompson sighed and looked away.

"Should have been manslaughter," he muttered.

"Doesn't matter what it should have been," Connolly said. "They won't get into all that."

"Man pulled a knife on me," Thompson said. "I shot him. Didn't have no choice. It was self-defense."

"They won't get into all of that," Connolly said again. "They only have to prove you were convicted of murder within the past twenty years. They can do that with a copy of the court record. There won't be any opportunity to get into the underlying facts of that case."

Thompson's head sagged.

"What about a settlement?"

"Only way they'll settle is if you plead guilty to capital murder. They'll recommend you get life without parole. Saves you from the death penalty."

Thompson slapped the table again.

"You people are crazy," he said.

In one quick motion he flipped his legs over the bench and walked to the door. He banged on it with his fist and waited. A moment later, the door opened. Thompson stepped from the interview room and walked toward the cell block door.

Connolly grabbed his notepad and left in the opposite direction toward the elevator.

Sometime in the night Connolly became aware he was lying face down on the floor of his office. He rolled over on his back and looked around the room.

It was late, perhaps late enough to be early. The office was dark except for a single small reading lamp to one side of the desk that cast a circle of light in the center of the desktop. A file lay open near the lamp. To one side, at the edge of the arc of lamplight, sat a half-empty gin bottle.

He rolled onto his side and forced himself to his knees. A stabbing pain knifed through his head. Grasping the edge of the desk, he managed to haul himself up to his feet. Standing made his head throb all the more, and he found it difficult to focus his eyes. The room began to spin around him. Leaning against the desk to steady himself, he moved around to the far side and collapsed in the chair.

Inside the top drawer, he found a bottle of aspirin, counted out five or six, and threw them into his mouth. A swig from the gin bottle washed them down. Another made sure they dissolved. He screwed the top on the bottle and returned it to the bottom drawer, then looked at his watch. It was two o'clock in the morning.

He picked up the file from the desk. Along the top of the file he noticed the name Avery Thompson. He rubbed his eyes and tried to remember who that was and why it was important. Frustrated, he tossed it aside and leaned back in his chair. He rested his head against the wall and closed his eyes. Soon, he was fast asleep.

Six

Until his death, Keyton Attaway was a partner in the law firm of Owens, Attaway, Glover, and Polack. Although the firm was relatively young, it enjoyed a growing reputation for successfully pursuing plaintiffs' cases against large, multinational corporations. Over the past three years, Attaway had become the most successful member of the firm.

The firm's offices were located in a building on St. Francis Street, across Bienville Square from Connolly's office. The site had once been home to Parker Stevedore Company. When Parker's closed, the Longshoreman's Union took the space. When they vacated the property, the building was left empty. Vagrants used it for a number of years until Attaway convinced his partners to buy it. They renovated the inside and restored the exterior to its original luster, complete with ornate wrought-iron railings on the balconies and workable shutters on the windows.

Attaway's office was located on the corner of the third floor, overlooking St. Francis Street and the square on one side, and Royal Street on the other. The windows on the St. Francis Street side opened like doors, allowing access to a small balcony above the sidewalk.

Connolly knew Attaway, but they were not friends. Their wives, however, were much better acquainted, a fact that forced Connolly and Attaway to see each other at social gatherings before Connolly and Barbara divorced, then made it awkward after the marriage ended.

By contrast, Charlie Miffin, one of Attaway's partners, once was Connolly's neighbor. In a time that seemed an eternity ago, they entertained each other in their homes. Their children attended the same schools, played on the same teams, swam at the same country club.

With a little persistence, Miffin agreed to allow Connolly a brief look around Attaway's office.

At noon, Connolly walked across Bienville Square. Near the fountain at the center of the square he slipped off his jacket and slung it over his shoulder. Sweat appeared on his forehead. In spite of the shade from the sprawling oaks, the midday heat was stifling. He felt his shirt stick to his back.

Connolly reached the opposite side of the square and crossed St. Francis Street. He opened the door to Attaway's building and felt a rush of cold air. Miffin met him in the lobby.

"You can't take long," he said.

"I won't," Connolly replied.

"And you have to be out of here before Glover comes back from lunch."

"I will."

"And you can't look at any files."

He led Connolly across the lobby to the elevator.

"Relax, Charlie," Connolly replied. "I don't want to look at the files, and I won't take long."

Charlie smiled nervously as they waited for the elevator.

"Don't know what good it will do," he said.

"You never know," Connolly replied.

They stepped inside the elevator. The door closed. Miffin glanced at Connolly.

"Let me ask you something, Mike."

"Sure," Connolly replied.

"Off the record, just exactly why did this guy kill Attaway?"

"Charlie," Connolly said, "I'm beginning to think he didn't do it."

"That's what all you criminal lawyers say," Miffin chuckled. "Never had a client that was guilty."

"No. I mean it," Connolly insisted. "There are some big holes in the State's case. I think they may have the wrong man."

The elevator reached the third floor. The door opened. Miffin led Connolly down the hall.

"Your guy wasn't there?"

"Oh, he was there alright," Connolly replied. "But there's a lot more to it than that."

They reached Attaway's office. Miffin opened the door.

"There it is," he said.

Connolly peered in from the hallway.

Light filtered into the room through broad wooden blinds on the windows. Two green leather wing backed chairs sat across from the door, facing to the right. A small table stood between them. A Persian rug covered the floor between the chairs and Attaway's desk, which sat further to the right at the far end of the room. The floor beyond the rug was made of hardwood boards polished to a gleaming shine.

On the desk, a handful of pens were neatly arranged in a brass cup that sat to one side of the desktop. A picture of Attaway's wife sat on the other side. A blotter lay in the middle in front of the chair. A calendar book lay on the blotter, opened flat.

Behind the desk was a credenza made of the same wood as the desk with shelves on the wall above it. The telephone sat on the credenza to the right, a notepad next to it and another brass cup filled with still more pens and pencils. To the left sat another picture.

Everything was neatly arranged in its place. Too neatly.

"Who cleaned the office?"

"No one," Miffin replied. "This is just like he left it the last time he was in here."

"I've seen a lot of lawyers' offices," Connolly said. "Most of them have so many files sitting around on the floor you can barely move."

"Not Attaway. He couldn't stand the clutter."

Connolly stepped into the office and looked around, slowly making his way toward the desk.

"Nice rug," he observed.

"He was pretty proud of it," Miffin said. He followed behind Connolly, keeping a close eye on him. He glanced over his shoulder at the door every few seconds to see if anyone noticed them. "Said his wife got it in Atlanta. Supposed to be an antique."

"You sound skeptical."

Connolly reached the front of the desk. He moved around behind it as they talked.

"Ahh, you never know," Miffin said. "I got a catalog from a place the other day where you can buy reproductions that are made to look old, including the worn and faded spots."

The calendar on the desk was opened to June, the current month. Connolly lifted the page on the right to see the entries for July. Miffin stepped closer and leaned over the desk to watch. Connolly glanced quickly at the calendar. Attaway had two trials and several depositions scheduled that month but nothing that seemed out of the ordinary. Connolly could feel Miffin growing tense. He dropped that page and picked up the one on the left, revealing May.

"I don't know whether you should be looking at that," Miffin said.

He glanced back at the door.

"Relax," Connolly said. "I'm not interested in your cases."

He scanned the entries for the month of May.

"What are you looking for?"

"I don't know," Connolly said. "Just wanted to look around."

Most of the activities in May dealt with the firm's clients and seemed to be routine. He was about to lower the page when an entry caught his eye.

"What's this mean?"

Connolly pointed to an entry for Saturday, May 23. Miffin moved around the desk and looked over Connolly's shoulder.

"Alpaca," Connolly said, reading from the calendar. "Any idea what that means?"

The word was written in large letters across the twenty-third, but it had been crossed out.

"No," Miffin replied. "Might be initials. A-L-P-A-C-A instead of a name. Isn't an alpaca some kind of rare animal from ... South America?"

"I'm not too well versed on South American animals," Connolly said, shrugging his shoulders.

He turned around to the credenza and tore off a piece of notepaper from the notepad beside the phone. With a pen from one of the brass cups, he scribbled down the entry from the calendar. As he did, he noticed the picture on the credenza. He shoved the note in his pocket and picked up the picture for a closer look. Miffin took a deep breath; he was growing more tense by the minute.

"That looks like Hogan Smith," Connolly noted, pointing to a man in the photograph. Smith was seated next to Attaway.

"It is," Miffin replied. "He and Attaway were pretty good friends. That's John Agostino and Truman Albritton standing behind them."

"How did Keyton get to be friends with Senator Smith?"

"Attaway, Agostino, and Albritton all worked together on Hogan's campaigns."

Connolly continued to study the picture.

"Looks like they were on vacation together too."

"Like I said, they got to be pretty good friends," Miffin replied. "Every year they get ... got together at some little place in the Bahamas."

Connolly looked at the picture again. Attaway was holding a drink. They all were dressed in shorts and golf shirts, smiling and looking comfortable.

"Looks like fun."

"I think they had a good time together. I believe they were supposed to go down there last month, but seems like something came up at the last minute." He glanced at the door again. "You about through here?"

Connolly set the picture in its place on the credenza.

"Just about," he replied.

He moved from behind the desk and looked around the room again.

"Think Smith will run again next time?"

"I don't know. I really don't pay that much attention to politics. You'd have to ask Truman Albritton about that."

Miffin looked at his watch.

"You need anything else?"

"No," Connolly said. "I've seen enough."

They started toward the door. As Connolly neared the edge of the rug, he noticed a cross on the table between the chairs near the door.

"I didn't notice this when we came in," he said.

He stopped to admire the piece. Dark and rough, it appeared to have been chiseled from stone. He picked it up.

"Heavy."

"It's a Cross of St. Anthony, I think," Miffin said. "I skipped most of catechism class. I'm not up on religious icons too much."

"Sort of unusual for a lawyer's office," Connolly noted.

"Keyton brought that in here a few months ago," Miffin replied. He glanced through the doorway into the hall. "Part of the reason the office is so neat."

Connolly returned the cross to its place on the table.

"What do you mean?"

"He wasn't here much the last few months," Miffin said. "Spent most of his time either at home or at church."

He stepped toward the door, hoping Connolly would follow.

"Church? What church?"

"St. Pachomius," Miffin said.

"The one behind the courthouse?"

"Yeah."

"What was he doing there?"

"I don't know. We all were too busy to pay attention to the details. I just know he wasn't here much."

The strain in Miffin's voice indicated the matter had been a sore point for the firm.

"Not producing enough income?"

"I wouldn't say he wasn't pulling his weight," Miffin replied. "But his priorities had definitely changed."

Miffin held the door. Connolly stepped into the hall.

"Have the police sent anyone over to look at the office?"

"No," Miffin replied. He paused to make sure the door was closed. "They haven't. I think you and I are the only ones who've been in there since Keyton died."

Connolly nodded and pursed his lips in a thoughtful manner.

"Come on," Miffin said. "I'll walk with you to the lobby."

Connolly left Attaway's office and crossed Bienville Square to his car. From there, he drove across town to St. Joseph's Hospital. He parked near the front entrance and went inside. He crossed the lobby and made his way to the maternity ward on the fourth floor.

The curtains were open in the nursery. He stood at the window a few minutes and scanned the rows of bassinets looking for Elizabeth. A nurse recognized him and stepped into the hallway.

"They checked out already," she said.

Connolly looked puzzled.

"Rachel Connolly?"

"Yes," she said. "They went home this afternoon."

The nurse returned to the nursery. Connolly turned away and walked up the hall to the elevator.

Outside the hospital, he sat in the car and watched as the sun sank low in the sky. He opened the glove compartment and reached for the flask. He twisted the top off and took a quick sip, then another.

Seven

A check of police records indicated two Ford pickups had been reported stolen. Neither of them met the description of the blue truck given by Thompson. A third had not been reported stolen but had been found abandoned and burned in a remote community known as Mon Louis Island, located in the low country some thirty miles south of Mobile. It had been towed to Yates Wrecker Service where it was impounded by the sheriff's department.

The next morning, Connolly drove out to look at it.

Yates Wrecker Service was located on Moffat Road, a corridor of used car lots and mobile home dealers extending west from Mobile. Yates's business sat between Mobile Tractor Company and Tiny's Used Mobile Homes. Hubcap Annie's was across the road.

Connolly turned into the parking lot and maneuvered the Chrysler past two large mud holes. He parked in front of a small office trailer near the road and got out. Behind the office lay a sea of junked vehicles. Three fiberglass fishing boats were piled against a fence to the right of the dirt parking lot. A twisted mobile home lay to the left.

Connolly opened the door to the office and stepped inside. As he did, a cloud of cigarette smoke rolled over him, stinging his eyes and burning his nostrils.

Larry Yates sat behind a gray metal desk. An air conditioner hung precariously out a window a few feet to the left. It pumped out cold air but rumbled loud enough to make conversation difficult.

"Can I help you?" Yates asked. He spoke loudly to overcome the noise.

"Yes, sir," Connolly replied. "Police report says you have a pickup you towed in a few days ago. Burned out. Might have been a blue Ford." He handed Yates the report. "I was wondering if I could take a look at it."

Yates scanned over the report, then handed it back.

"Who are you?"

"Mike Connolly. I'm a lawyer. I think that truck may have been involved in a case I have."

Yates stood and pointed out the window above the air conditioner toward the rows of cars and trucks in the junkyard behind the office.

"You see that gray Mercedes with the front smashed in?"

Connolly moved closer and looked over Yates's shoulder.

"Yeah."

"Walk out to the Mercedes, turn right. The truck you're asking about is up there on the right a little ways past the Mercedes. The cab's pretty much covered in rust where it was burned, but the bed in the back is still blue."

"Thanks."

Connolly left the office and walked to the gray Mercedes. Several yards beyond it, he found the truck. Like Yates said, the cab was covered in rust from a fire that apparently started in the engine compartment. Heat from the fire destroyed the dash, but the seats were still intact, and the windshield was in place. Behind the cab, the bed of the truck was unscathed except for a long scratch that extended down the driver's side.

He walked to the rear bumper. The tag was still attached. He noted the number, then returned to the driver's door. It was hanging open. He looked inside.

"You won't find anything," Yates said.

The sound of his voice startled Connolly. He jerked around.

"Why not?"

Connolly slid his hand between the seat bottom and the back.

"Police came out here three days ago," Yates smiled. "Went all through it."

Connolly stepped around the door and moved to the opposite side. The door to the glove compartment dangled from one hinge. He took a pen from his pocket and raked through the ashes. Above the charred remains of the dash, he flipped down the sun visor. Finding nothing there, he checked the pockets in the door.

"Well, looks like they pretty much cleaned it out," Connolly said, stepping away from the truck.

"I don't think they found much either," Yates said.

"Did they lift any prints?"

"I don't think they checked."

"Not any dust around," Connolly said. "They usually leave a mess when they do that. Although it's hard to tell with all the soot from the fire." He backed farther away from the truck. "Mind if I take a picture or two?"

"Help yourself."

Connolly took a disposable camera from the pocket of his jacket and moved around in front of the truck. He put the camera to his eye and snapped a picture. As he did, he noticed a green sticker at the top of the windshield. He snapped another picture.

"Did you put that sticker on the windshield?"

Yates looked puzzled.

"Sticker? What sticker?"

"That green one," Connolly said, pointing. "Right corner, above the steering wheel."

Yates looked again.

"No," he said. "That didn't come from us. It was already on there when we got it."

He stepped to the driver's door and leaned over the windshield.

"Looks like it had some writing on it," he continued. "Can't make it out though. Pretty faded."

Connolly snapped another picture, then slipped the camera into his pocket.

"Thanks," he said.

"No problem," Yates replied.

They walked together to the office trailer. Yates stopped near the door. Connolly walked to the Chrysler and opened the car door.

"Where'd you get a car like that?" Yates asked.

"Took it for a fee in a case," Connolly replied, smiling.

"What is it? A '54 Plymouth?"

"'59 Chrysler Imperial," Connolly said, proudly.

"Interested in trading?"

Connolly shook his head and smiled.

"No way."

Connolly slipped behind the steering wheel, closed the door, and backed the car away from the building. He turned the car around and stopped at the edge of the parking lot. Across the road, a green Taurus sat facing him. The driver motioned for Connolly to go ahead of him. Connolly nodded and turned the Chrysler onto the road.

Mrs. Gordon was at the copier when Connolly returned to the office. He paused at the break room door on his way down the hall.

"Did Henry McNamara call?"

"No," she said, not bothering to turn around to face him. "Was he supposed to?"

"He's supposed to tell me when I can go see Bill Sisson."

"Bill Sisson? Who's that?"

"A witness."

Irritated that McNamara had not called, his voice was unusually gruff.

He moved away from the door and stepped into his office.

"You want me to call Henry and set it up?" Mrs. Gordon called after him.

"Yeah," Connolly replied. "Maybe you can get him to return your calls."

He closed the door to his office and dropped into the chair behind the desk.

Eight

When he awakened from his nap, Connolly walked from his office to the courthouse and made his way to the motor vehicle registration office. Using the tag number from the blue Ford pickup at Yates's Wrecker Service, he learned the truck was registered to Vern Eubanks. According to the vehicle records, Eubanks lived in Grand Bay, a small town south and west of Mobile near the coast, not far from the Alabama-Mississippi state line. Late that afternoon, Connolly rode out there. It was almost dark when he arrived.

Eubanks lived in a dilapidated wood frame house surrounded by a dozen junked automobiles and stacks of used lumber. A shrimp net hung between the trees in the yard. Trash littered the place. Laundry hung from a rope strung between posts on the porch.

As Connolly stepped from the car, he could hear a television blaring through the open front door. He approached the porch steps with caution. Suddenly, a woman appeared in the doorway.

"You looking for somebody?"

Her unexpected appearance startled Connolly. The few front teeth she had were black with decay and her mouth seemed to sag into the open areas created by the missing teeth. Her hair, white as snow, stuck out from her head in all directions. She wore a thin cotton dress and no shoes. Standing in the doorway, she was surrounded by the glow from the television inside.

"Yes, ma'am," he said, as politely as possible. "I'm looking for Vern Eubanks."

"He's around back in the shed." She wandered back into the house as she spoke. "Prob'ly find him under one of them old cars."

Connolly walked around the corner of the porch. A shack of a building stood fifty feet behind the house. Pieced together with tin and corrugated fiberglass siding, it looked ready to collapse at any moment. He picked his way around an engine block, three transmissions, and a pile of discarded water heaters.

About halfway across the back yard, a bulldog appeared from around the corner of the shed. Connolly froze. The dog ambled over to him and nuzzled around his thighs and crotch. Connolly held his breath.

Suddenly, the door to the shed burst open, and a tall, lanky man stepped out. He wore greasy coveralls and a dirty red cap. His shoes were crumpled and misshapen, held together by layers of gray duct tape.

"Skip!" the man yelled. "Get out of here!"

The dog turned and lumbered back around the corner of the building. Connolly relaxed.

"He won't really hurt you," the man said. "But he's mighty intimidating."

"He made a believer out of me," Connolly said as he stepped closer. "Are you Vern Eubanks?"

"Yes, I am," Eubanks said. "You look like the law."

His jaws worked back and forth on a wad of tobacco as he talked.

"No," Connolly replied. "Just a lawyer. My name is Mike Connolly."

"Lawyer? That's worse than the law," Eubanks growled. "Go where you're not wanted, take what's not yours, and call it justice. Can tell you fellas a mile away. Ain't no need to come no closer. You don't want to shake my hand," he said, holding up a greasy palm.

Connolly stopped a few feet away. Eubanks stared him in the eye.

"What you want with me?"

"County records show you own a blue Ford pickup truck," Connolly said. "Maybe a 1980 model."

"No, sir," Eubanks said.

"There's one out at Yates's Wrecker Service. It's registered in your name," Connolly countered.

"I took that truck in on trade from a fella that owed me quite a bit of money for some work I did." Eubanks paused. He spat a stream of brown tobacco juice on the ground near Connolly's feet. "It was registered in my name, but I sold it about two weeks ago."

"Who'd you sell it to?"

"Young fellow. Had a funny accent. Like he was a Yankee maybe. Tall, slender build, short haircut. Law enforcement type ... maybe military."

"How much did he give you for it?"

Eubanks's jaw stopped working the tobacco in his mouth. His eyes were like fire.

"I doubt that's any of your business," he said.

He began chewing again, more rapidly now than before.

"I'm not trying to be difficult," Connolly said. "I'm just trying to investigate a murder."

Eubanks crossed his arms and stared at Connolly a moment.

"Two thousand dollars," he finally said. He spit another stream of tobacco juice. "Paid cash."

"Anyone with him?"

"Somebody brought him out to get the truck. They stayed in the car. I didn't see what they looked like."

"Man or woman?"

"Couldn't really tell."

"Did you happen to get the name of the man you sold it to?"

"Said his name was Sanders ... Sanderson. Something like that. After he pulled out the cash, I didn't really care who he was."

"What did you do with the cash?"

Eubanks's jaw stopped chewing the tobacco again.

"What difference does that make?"

"I don't know," Connolly replied. "I'd just like to see it."

Eubanks rolled the wad of tobacco from side to side in his mouth. Then, he started chewing it again, his jaw moving rapidly up and down. He spit a long stream of tobacco juice on the ground, then disappeared inside the shed. He returned in a few moments with a grease-smudged envelope in his hands. He handed it to Connolly who peeked inside. The envelope contained a stack of crisp, new one-hundred-dollar bills.

"Has anybody else asked you about this?"

Eubanks snatched the envelope from his hand and stepped back to the door.

"I got this money fair and square," he snapped. "I don't know who that fella was, and I don't know who you are. For all I know you're in with him and just trying to beat me out of my money. Now unless you got a warrant and a badge, you can get off my property."

Connolly gestured for calm with both hands.

"Hold on now, Mr. Eubanks. I'm not looking for trouble."

"Well, for a man that ain't looking, you're sure about to get your fill of it."

"Calm down," Connolly repeated.

"Skip."

The bulldog appeared at the corner of the building, muscles taut and ready to spring. He crept forward, low to the ground, eyes fixed on Connolly. As he approached, he gave a low growl. Eubanks stepped inside the shed. Before Connolly could react, Eubanks returned with a double-barreled shotgun in his hands.

"Alright, Mr. Eubanks," Connolly said as he backed away. "I'm leaving."

It was well past five when Connolly returned to the office. Mrs. Gordon was gone. The office was dark. He switched on a light near her desk and made his way down the hallway to his office.

A stack of phone messages lay on his desk. He picked them up and read through them. The second message was from Henry McNamara informing him he could see Sisson the following morning. Connolly shoved the note in his pocket and tossed the others aside.

He took a seat behind the desk and propped his head against the wall. A few moments later, he opened the bottom drawer and took out a bottle of gin.

Nine

*B*ill Sisson lived in a nondescript subdivision on the western side of Mobile. His house was located on a street of modest two-story brick homes, neatly trimmed lawns, and concrete driveways. Connolly drove out there the following day. After several wrong turns, he found the address sometime in the middle of the morning.

He parked the Chrysler on the street in front of the house, crossed the lawn to the front door, and rang the doorbell. Sisson opened the door, dressed in cotton shorts and a T-shirt.

"Mr. Sisson, my name is Mike Connolly. I—"

"Yes, sir," Sisson replied, interrupting him. "The DA's office said you'd be coming. Come on in."

He held the door open for Connolly.

"Come on back to the kitchen," Sisson said, as he waddled through the house. "I work nights. I'm usually asleep by now, but they said you would come by so I waited. Come on back to the kitchen. I was just having something to eat."

Connolly followed close behind. The house was neat and orderly, but the heavy scent of bacon grease and burned toast hung in the air.

"Sorry to bother you," Connolly said.

"Don't worry about it. Have a seat," Sisson said, pointing to a chair at the kitchen table. "They said you wanted to talk. Thinking about it got me wide awake."

Sisson dropped into a chair. Connolly sat opposite him and laid his notepad on the table. He removed a pen from the inside pocket of his jacket.

"Why don't you begin at the beginning," he suggested. "What did you see?"

"Alright," Sisson said. "I was coming down Short Haul Road, over on McDuffie Island."

"McDuffie Island?"

"I'm sorry ... Pinto Island. I've been up since sometime yesterday afternoon."

"That's alright."

"Short Haul Road runs between the shipyard and the causeway. It's pretty swampy around there. Lots of marsh grass and bushes. There's a little section where the road curves one way then another. It's pretty secluded. When I came around the first curve there was a white Cadillac parked on the side of the road."

"Which side?"

"My left side. Would have been the ... north side of the road ... I guess."

"Okay."

"So, the Cadillac was sitting on the side of the road. Two people in the front seat. Looked like it might have been a woman behind the wheel, but I can't say for certain."

"A woman?"

"Yeah. Maybe. I couldn't say for certain, but it looked it."

"Did you tell the police about the Cadillac?"

"Yeah. Why?"

"The Cadillac isn't mentioned in your written statement," Connolly explained. "But there is mention of a car in the incident report."

Sisson nodded.

"I know. I told them about the car when they talked to me that day. The officer took notes. The next day a different officer brought me the typed statement to sign. I read it and told him there wasn't anything in the report about the car. He said it would be alright and to sign it anyway. So I did."

Connolly scribbled notes furiously.

"Okay. You saw the car. What happened?"

"There was a blue pickup parked behind the Cadillac."

"What kind was it?"

"Ford. Like maybe an early '80s model. Scratched and banged up some. Now, I don't know whether they mentioned that in the police reports or not. I don't think I told them about the blue pickup."

"Why didn't you tell them about it?"

"They didn't ask me very many questions, and I just didn't think about it."

"Anybody in the pickup?"

"Didn't see anyone. Only other person I saw was a black guy. When I drove up, he darted across the road in front of me. I had to swerve to keep from hitting him."

"So, when he ran out in front of you, you looked away from the Cadillac?"

"Yeah. I was trying to dodge him."

"Where was he going?"

"He ran across in front of me and off into the swamp on the other side of the road."

"How did he look? Was he scared?"

"I'd say scared. Darted right out in front of me, like something was happening. Never looked, just came right out in the road. He never stopped when he got across the road either. Just kept hightailing it into the swamp."

"You watched him?"

"Yeah. I watched him for a moment. Then looked in the mirror to make sure I wasn't about to get hit myself."

"Then what did you do?"

"I drove on to the causeway, but it bothered me, you know, that guy running across in front of me and all ... it just didn't seem right. So when I got to the causeway, I turned around and drove back. By the time I got back to where this had all happened, the car was gone. Then I saw the body lying over near the weeds."

"What did you do?"

"I stopped and waited. Thought someone would come along, and I could send them for help, but it was late. I wouldn't have been there then myself except I had to work late. Nobody came, so in a few minutes I went back to the causeway and called the police."

"Where'd you call from?"

"Hank's Fish Camp."

"See anything else?"

"No, sir."

"Get a tag number off the car or truck?"

"Nah. Never even looked. They were headed in the opposite direction from the way I was going."

"Anything about the car that you remember?"

"Nothing in particular. Just a white Cadillac. It was clean."

"What about the truck? Remember anything about it?"

"Well ... let's see ... it was scratched down the bed pretty good on the driver's side, behind the cab. Had side mirrors, like the after-market kind that sort of stick out pretty far from the doors. It was blue. And I remember it had a green sticker at the top of the windshield."

"Where?"

"Up at the top. In the corner above the steering wheel."

"Anything else you remember about the truck?"

"No. I think that's about it."

"After you called the police, what did you do?"

"Went back out there and waited."

"Anyone out there with you?"

"No."

"And you're sure you told the police there was a Cadillac?"

"Yeah." Sisson looked perplexed. "Wonder why they left it out?"

"I don't know."

Connolly reviewed a few more details with Sisson, then closed his notepad.

"Mr. Sisson," he said, standing. "I appreciate your time. I may have some more questions later, but you've been very helpful."

Sisson stepped toward the hall.

"All I can say is what I saw."

He led Connolly through the house again, retracing the path toward the front door as they talked.

"And that's exactly what I want you to do," Connolly said. "Just tell the truth."

They reached the front door. Sisson opened it and moved aside. Connolly shook his hand and stepped outside. Sisson closed the door.

Connolly walked across the lawn to the Chrysler. He opened the car door and slid in behind the wheel. He tossed the notepad on the seat beside him, started the engine, and steered the car away from the curb. As he drove down the street he opened the glove compartment and reached for the flask. He twisted off the top and turned it up to take a drink only to find the flask was empty. Frustrated, he tossed it on the seat and slammed the glove compartment closed. His hand on the steering wheel trembled.

At the corner he turned right and drove a few blocks to the intersection at Airport Boulevard. At the intersection, he swerved into the parking lot of the Jiffy Mart convenience store. He parked at the end of the building and went inside. He returned to the car a few minutes later with a six-pack of beer. The first can was empty before he left the parking lot. The second before he reached the office.

Mrs. Gordon was at her desk when he arrived.

"You had some calls," she said, as he came through the door.

Connolly smiled.

"Good morning to you, too."

He picked up the mail from the corner of her desk as he walked past.

"It's not morning," she retorted. "It's almost lunch."

He shuffled through the mail as he wandered down the hall toward his office. Mrs. Gordon called after him.

"Did Rachel like the gift?"

"What gift?"

"I gave you a gift for her three days ago. Didn't you take it to her?"

"Oh," he said. "Yeah. I gave it to her."

He was out of sight down the hall near the door to his office. Mrs. Gordon pushed her chair away from her desk and leaned around the corner.

"What did she think of it?"

"Don't know," he replied. "She wasn't in the mood to open it."

"I hope you didn't make a scene. Did you see the baby?"

"Yes," he said, turning to close his office door. "She's red-headed like her mother and just as stubborn."

He closed the door, tossed his jacket across a chair, and took a seat at his desk. From the bottom drawer he removed the gin bottle and took a gulp. Then another. A moment later, Mrs. Gordon tapped on the door. He dropped the bottle in the drawer and shoved it closed. She opened the door without waiting for him to respond and entered the room as he was closing the drawer.

"I thought you were going to quit that," she chided.

She moved past the desk to a row of filing cabinets on the far wall. Connolly looked away.

"Quit what?"

"You know what I'm talking about," she said. Her voice was as cold as the scowl on her face.

She opened a file drawer and reached inside, her back to him. He wiped his mouth and cupped the palm of his hand in front of his lips to check his breath.

"They hate me, Mrs. Gordon," he sighed.

He would have tried anything to change the subject.

"Who hates you?"

He propped his feet on the desk and leaned back, arms folded behind his head, eyes closed.

"Rachel ... Barbara. Judge Cahill. Henry McNamara."

"Rachel and Barbara, yes," she said. She shoved the file drawer closed. "I doubt Cahill or McNamara give you a second thought."

"That's just it," he said. "That's what I mean. That's why they gave me this case."

"What case?"

She stepped away from the filing cabinet.

"Avery Thompson. Judge Cahill gave it to me to get it off

his docket without much fanfare. He thinks I'll roll over. Thinks I'll waive the preliminary hearing and let Henry take it to the grand jury without a fight."

She started toward the door.

"You always do."

"And Henry thinks he has the case already won."

She reached the door and grasped the doorknob to pull it closed behind her.

"He usually does."

He opened his eyes to look at her.

"You're a big help, Mrs. Gordon."

"I try to be," she said.

She closed the door. He soon was fast asleep.

Ten

In the afternoon, Connolly drove to Mobile General, the county hospital. Unlike St. Joseph's in the suburbs, Mobile General was a stone and masonry edifice located at the edge of Mobile's downtown business district.

A huge building, it sat not on a manicured campus, but at the edge of Broad Street. A long run of steps swept up two floors from the sidewalk to a wide portico. Huge round columns supported the portico roof that soared to the top of the building five floors above.

A grand and elegant structure on the outside, inside it was a crumbling heap of decay and inefficiency.

Connolly steered the Chrysler to the back of the building. He parked near the emergency entrance and went inside. Notepad in hand, he crossed the waiting area by the door and walked past the receptionist desk to a corridor that led toward the interior of the building. A little way down the corridor, he turned right and made his way to the county morgue at the end of the hall. Large double doors separated the morgue from the remainder of the hospital. He pushed open one of the doors and stepped inside.

Directly across from the doors was the county's single autopsy suite. Inside, the white ceramic tile floor was clean and bright. To the left of the room, a stainless steel counter ran along the wall. The autopsy table stood in the middle. A lab technician sat at the counter busily labeling vials of samples from the latest corpse. She paid no attention to Connolly.

To the left of the door was the cooler where corpses were stored while awaiting final disposition. An empty gurney sat nearby. Bloodstained linens lay in a bundle on the floor beside it.

The place was kept cool throughout the year by cold air that seeped from the cooler. But it had a distinctive odor. A combination of death, blood, raw flesh, and an antiseptic hospital smell. Connolly felt his stomach rumble in response. He didn't mind seeing dead bodies, and the sight of blood had never bothered him. But he was particularly sensitive to odors. A wave of nausea washed over him.

To the right was the coroner's office. Ted Morgan sat at his desk reading the morning newspaper. A Styrofoam plate of unfinished lunch sat in front of him. The door to the office was open. Morgan smiled when he saw Connolly.

"Kind of early in the day for you, isn't it?" Morgan said. "You usually don't get started 'til the middle of the afternoon, do you?"

Connolly smiled in reply.

"You know me, never one to rush the day."

Like Connolly, Morgan came up the hard way. Worked his way through college. Struggled to pay for medical school. But Morgan was an oddity to his colleagues. In a profession focused on giving life, he found himself fascinated with death. After completing a residency he tried his hand at family practice, but when the coroner's position opened, he jumped at it. Over the years he became an expert in forensics. Connolly met him while working on his first criminal case. They had been friends ever since.

"You here to talk about Keyton Attaway?"

Connolly slid a chair across the room and sat down near the desk.

"Thought it might be good to know what you found in your autopsy before we get to the preliminary hearing."

Morgan scowled in response.

"They didn't give you the autopsy report?"

"Yeah. I got the report," Connolly replied. "But I'd like to hear about it from you."

Morgan had a penchant for finding details others either overlooked or ignored. When he first became coroner, he included many of those details in his written reports. Everyone was impressed, initially, but then his reports started casting doubt on the investigative skills of one or two detectives. Under pressure from the sheriff and the district attorney, Morgan's autopsy reports became more generic. Now, he included only those details essential to show the time and cause of death. He still found intriguing information, only now anyone interested in it had to talk to him in person to get it.

Morgan lay the newspaper aside. He pulled open one of the desk drawers, propped his feet on it, and folded his hands in his lap.

"How'd you get stuck with this case?"

Connolly shrugged his shoulders.

"I guess I was next on the list," he said. "Judge Cahill appointed me."

"Cahill. I've testified in his court a time or two. I hear he's a pretty good guy."

"Loves the cops."

"Yeah. But I've seen him give the other side a fair shake too."

"He's not too bad," Connolly said. "Helped me out a time or two."

Morgan nodded.

"What do you want to know about Mr. Attaway?"

"Did you go to the scene?"

"Nah. I don't do that much anymore. We leave most of that stuff to the police, unless they call us. Detectives are usually pretty good about handling the body, and if they aren't, I don't worry about it."

"Bag the hands?"

"I don't think so."

Morgan lowered his feet to the floor and turned to a filing cabinet behind the desk. He opened the top drawer and took out a file. He laid it on the desk and opened it.

"Let's see ..." Morgan scanned his notes. "No. The hands were not bagged when we received the body."

"Isn't that standard procedure?"

"Yeah. I guess."

"Report says there were wounds to the head. Any wounds anywhere else?"

"No. Few scratches, that sort of thing. Nothing major."

"Any question about identity?"

"Not really." He continued to review his notes as he spoke. "The face was in poor shape. Bullet from the temple blew out a large portion of the forehead. Exited the jaw on the left side. Tore that up. And then he had been shot through the mouth several times. That tore out the back of the skull. But I knew who he was."

"You still had someone come in and officially identify him?"

"Oh, yeah. We did that. Someone came in ... let me see who that was ..." He turned to another page in the file. "Yeah.

Truman Albritton came in and identified the body for the family."

Connolly frowned.

"Truman Albritton?"

"Yeah. Says so right here in my notes."

He held the file for Connolly to see.

"Does that say when he came in?"

"Came in the day we got the body. Looks like he was here around seven o'clock that evening."

"How did he know you had the body?"

"I don't know," Morgan said. "You'd have to ask him. As I recall, he showed up and said he heard we had a body down here. One of his clients had been notified it was the body of a family member. He asked to see it. We had the body on the table ready to begin the autopsy. I took him in there. He told me it was Keyton Attaway. How his client knew to send him, I don't know."

"You knew Keyton."

"Yeah. I knew Keyton. And, like I said, I knew that was him lying on my table. But we had to have someone else identify him. At least that's what the DA tells me."

"Now, your report says the bullet to the temple killed him. How do you know that?"

"By the location and the damage," Morgan replied.

"The other shots wouldn't have killed him?"

"Might have, but they came after the one to the temple."

"How do you know that?"

"One of the wounds through the mouth crossed the track of the bullet from the temple."

"You could tell which one went first?"

"Yeah."

"Could you tell where the shooter was standing?"

"Based on the angle and the trajectory of the bullet, I'd say Keyton was sitting when he took the first shot. Sitting in a car, actually. The shooter was standing to his right, slightly behind him." Morgan looked up at him and smiled. "If we had a couple months to work on it, I could probably get you a make and model on the car."

"I thought they found the body on the side of the road?"

"Yeah." Morgan's smile broadened. "They did."

"So, how do you know he was in a car?"

Morgan's smile became a grin.

"Found tiny slivers of glass in the wound to the temple. And I found larger chunks of glass in his shirt pocket. I'm sure it was shatter-resistant automobile window glass."

Morgan propped his feet again on the open desk drawer.

"The pocket wasn't starched closed?"

"No."

"Anything else in his pockets?"

"No. Not in the shirt pocket. Usual stuff in his pants pockets. Change, car keys. I gave all that to the detective." He glanced at the file. "Anthony Hammond."

"What about the other shots? Through the mouth."

"Opened the door, stuck the gun in his mouth, and pulled the trigger."

Connolly winced and looked away.

"Powder burns look like the muzzle was inside his mouth."

Connolly sighed and shook his head. After a moment, he turned back to Morgan.

"Anything else interesting?"

"No. Not with the autopsy."

Morgan closed the file. The tone of his voice indicated he had more to say.

"Something else catch your attention?"

"Well, just that they seemed rather anxious to get the body to the funeral home. At least Albritton was. Had it cremated, I believe."

Connolly looked puzzled.

"I thought I saw a picture of them carrying his casket out of the church after the funeral?"

"Oh, they had a casket alright." Morgan nodded his head for emphasis. "But there wasn't anything inside it. Hagan Brothers did the funeral. I know a guy over there, Bob Hunt. He said they cremated the body the same day I released it. I think Attaway's wife scattered his ashes in the bay down there near where they live."

Connolly rubbed his chin.

"Interesting."

"Yeah. A little odd. But, I've seen stranger things."

Connolly stood. They shook hands.

"I appreciate your help."

Morgan acknowledged him with a nod.

"Always glad to help, Mike."

Morgan slid the Styrofoam plate into the trash and picked up the newspaper. Connolly walked through the double doors and made his way to the car.

Eleven

*L*ater that afternoon, Connolly drove to the county jail to see Avery Thompson. The guard at the desk out front scanned a long list of inmates. She looked at several of the pages twice, then shook her head.

"We don't have an Avery Thompson," she replied.

"Sure you do," Connolly said. "Eighth floor."

She checked the list for eighth floor.

"No. Sorry." She shook her head again. "He's not here." She held up several pages for him to see. "This census was run this morning," she explained. "If he's not on this list, he's not here."

Connolly gave a heavy sigh of frustration.

"Well, I need to find out where he is. Who can I talk to?"

"Wait here," she said.

She disappeared around the corner. Connolly leaned against the desk and waited. In a few minutes she returned.

"Thompson was transferred last night," she said. "He went to Aikers Hospital in Jackson."

Connolly was perplexed.

"Aikers? That's a mental hospital."

"Yes, sir."

"Why was he sent there?"

"I have no idea. We got an order to send him up there. A van took him up around eight o'clock."

"When is he coming back?"

She shrugged her shoulders and shook her head.

"Sir, I've told you all I know."

Connolly left the jail and hurried to the courthouse. Judge Cahill was conducting a preliminary hearing when he arrived. He took a seat in the back of the courtroom and waited. When the lawyers finished with the witness on the stand, Cahill called a recess.

"Let's take ten minutes," he said.

He looked to Connolly.

"Mike, you need to see me?"

"Yes, Your Honor."

Connolly strode to the bench.

"Judge, I went over to the jail a few minutes ago to see Avery Thompson on that capital case you gave me. They moved him to Aikers Hospital last night. Said they had an order to transfer him."

Cahill glanced at Walter, who was seated at his desk below the judge's bench.

"Signed the order yesterday morning, Judge," Walter said. He gave Connolly a sarcastic smile. "You filed the motion asking for it. Probably don't remember it."

"I didn't file any motion," Connolly retorted.

Cahill pushed his chair away from the bench and stood.

"Walter," Cahill said, "get Henry McNamara up here, and call down to the clerk's office for the file."

"Yes, sir, Judge."

Walter picked up the phone and placed the calls.

"Just have a seat," Cahill said to Connolly. "We'll get everybody up here."

Cahill disappeared through the door behind the bench.

Connolly took a seat on a bench behind the counsel tables near the front of the courtroom.

In a few minutes, Cahill returned. The preliminary hearing resumed. Before long, Henry McNamara arrived. Cahill motioned for him to take a seat next to Connolly.

"What happened to Avery Thompson?" Connolly whispered.

McNamara opened his file and took out a single sheet of paper. It was a motion for psychiatric examination. Connolly's name was scribbled across the signature line. He handed the paper to Connolly.

"Where'd this come from?"

"Got it day before yesterday," McNamara whispered.

"Who sent it to you?"

"Has your name on it," McNamara smirked.

"That's not my signature," Connolly said. "I didn't send this to you."

Walter slid into a seat next to Connolly and leaned around him to face both men.

"Judge said if y'all want to talk to take it out to the hall."

Both men nodded in response and fell silent. Walter returned to his desk. McNamara scribbled a note to Connolly on his legal pad.

"We got a copy. The jail got a copy. I guess Judge Cahill signed an order for it."

Connolly shook his head in disbelief.

In a few minutes, Judge Cahill concluded the preliminary hearing. Walter handed him the file on Avery Thompson.

"Y'all come on up here," Cahill said.

Connolly and McNamara stood in front of the judge's bench. Cahill looked through the file as he talked.

"Mike, looks like I signed an order yesterday sending

Thompson up to Aikers Hospital. Here's your motion asking me to do it."

Cahill lifted the paper from the file so Connolly could see it. Cahill was not in good humor.

"Your Honor," Connolly replied, "Henry showed me a copy of the motion. It has my name on it, but that's not my signature, and I didn't file it."

Cahill stole a glance in Walter's direction. Walter was listening to every word, but his head was bent low over a stack of files on the desk in front of him.

"Let's see," Cahill said, shuffling through documents in the file. His voice dripped of skepticism. "Here's the motion. Filed day before yesterday." Cahill looked askance. "Mike, you sure you didn't file this and just forget about it?"

The implication was obvious. Connolly was incensed, but he held his emotions in check.

"Judge," he said, his voice low, even, and tense. "That's not my motion, and that's not my signature. There are plenty of documents in that file with my signature on them. I think if you compared the signature on that motion to my signature on the other things in the file, the difference would be obvious."

Cahill lifted several pages in the file and compared the signatures.

"You know," he said, slowly, "I'd say you're right. Actually, this signature doesn't even come close to these others."

Cahill looked to McNamara. Still skeptical of Connolly, he was a little more interested than before.

"Henry, any idea who sent you this motion?"

"No, Your Honor," McNamara replied. "It showed up in my box at the office."

"Judge," Connolly said, "If you don't believe me, I can get

my secretary over here to testify she never prepared a motion like this for me."

Cahill dismissed the suggestion with a wave of his hand.

"You want him returned?"

"Yes, Your Honor."

"Alright. I'll order him back. Walter."

Walter rose from his chair and leaned over the judge's bench. Cahill handed him the file.

"Prepare an order returning Thompson to the jail. See if they can get him back today."

Walter took the file and returned to his seat. Cahill turned to Connolly.

"Anything else?"

"I'd like to know who did this."

"I would too," Cahill replied. He glared at Connolly, one eyebrow raised, still doubting Connolly's story. "But if Henry doesn't know, and you don't know, I don't think there's any way to find out. Important thing is to get him back. We'll get the order to the jail today."

Twelve

---

*T*he following morning, Connolly telephoned the jail. Avery Thompson had not been returned.

"Our records show he's still assigned to Aikers Hospital," the clerk said.

Connolly felt angry.

"Did you receive Judge Cahill's order returning him to the jail?"

"Ahh ... let me see ... Yes," the clerk replied. "Looks like it came in late yesterday. We don't make a run up there every day," the clerk explained. "It'll take two or three days to get him back."

Already suspicious of foul play, Connolly was not satisfied with the answer. He slammed down the telephone and leaped from his chair. He snatched his jacket from the coat rack and charged up the hallway.

"I'm going to Jackson," he growled.

"Tell Mr. Thompson hello," Mrs. Gordon said.

The door banged closed behind him.

Aikers Hospital was located on the outskirts of Jackson, a small community twenty miles north of Mobile. An odd assortment of modern and decrepit buildings, the site originally was built as an army training station. The grounds were well maintained with a lush, green lawn and neatly trimmed bushes. A modern administration building sat near the front entrance. However, most of the patient facilities were in former barracks constructed before World War I. A high fence surrounded the complex. Guards were posted at each entrance.

As Connolly approached the main entrance, one of the guards stepped from the guard shack and motioned for him to stop. Connolly rolled down the window.

"Just going to the administration building," he said.

The guard reached through the window and placed a visitor's card on top of the dash, then waved him forward. Connolly steered the Chrysler past the guard and parked in front of the administration building. Inside, he crossed the small lobby and stopped at the receptionist's desk.

"I'm here to see Avery Thompson," Connolly said. His voice was curt and stern. "He's one of your patients. I'm Mike Connolly, Mr. Thompson's attorney."

The receptionist opened a large black notebook and scanned through pages of names.

"What was that name?"

"Thompson," Connolly repeated. "Avery Thompson."

"I don't see any Avery Thompson on our list," the receptionist said.

"He was sent up here from the jail in Mobile."

"Let me look again." She ran her finger down the list. "Got a George Thompson ... and a Bill Thomason ... Avery Thompson. Here he is." She closed the book and smiled. "You'll have to see Mrs. Holsombach about him."

Connolly did his best to control his frustration.

"I'm his attorney," he said. "I just want to—"

"I don't know about that," she said, holding up her hand to stop him. "You'll have to see Mrs. Holsombach about that."

"Where is she?"

"Down the hall. Third door on the right."

Connolly walked down the hall and knocked on Mrs. Holsombach's door.

"Come in," a voice said from inside.

Connolly pushed the door open and stepped inside. A middle-aged woman sat behind a large metal desk directly opposite the door. Slender, with hair dyed black, she wore a black dress. A gold necklace hung from her neck, and she wore rings on each finger of both hands. She was smoking a cigarette when Connolly entered.

"May I help you?"

"I'm looking for Mrs. Holsombach," Connolly said.

She took a long draw on the cigarette, then slowly exhaled blowing the smoke out the corner of her mouth.

"What may I do for you?"

"My name is Mike Connolly. I'm an attorney. I represent a man named Avery Thompson. He was sent up here from the county jail in Mobile a few days ago. I'd like to see him."

"Can't," she said. "At least not today."

She stubbed out the cigarette in an ashtray on her desk.

"Why not?"

"He's being tested. Have to wait until the tests are complete."

Mrs. Holsombach folded her hands in her lap. Connolly's eyebrows narrowed in an angry scowl.

"Judge Cahill ordered him returned to the county jail," he said. "He's not supposed to be tested. Didn't you receive his order?"

"He was sent up here on an order from Judge Cahill to have him tested to see if he was mentally competent to stand trail," she replied. "We haven't received anything to the contrary. He's being tested. You can't see him until we're through.

If you do, you'll negate the validity of our tests. We'd have to start over."

Connolly glared at her. Mrs. Holsombach took a cigarette from a pack on her desk and lit it. She took a long draw from it and once again let the smoke escape from the corner of her mouth.

"Rules," she said. "We have rules we have to go by."

Connolly sighed and looked away. There was no point in venting his anger on her. He ran his fingers through his hair and forced his body to relax. A pleasant expression returned to his face.

"When can I see him?"

"Be finished with him in about two days."

"Alright." Connolly stepped toward the door. "I'll be back in two days."

Connolly left Mrs. Holsombach's office and walked outside to the Chrysler. He opened the door and dropped into the front seat. The sense of frustration he felt inside now seemed overwhelming, only now it was frustration with himself. That bogus motion with his forged signature should have alerted him to trouble. He should have come to find Thompson immediately, instead of relying on Judge Cahill and the staff at the jail to get him back. He struck the steering wheel with his fist. All he could do now was wait.

He placed the key in the ignition and started the engine.

Thirteen

The following morning, Connolly left his apartment and drove downtown. Instead of going to the office, he turned off Government Street near the courthouse and drove one block to Church Street. There he turned left. The Chrysler idled along in the morning sun as Connolly stared ahead at St. Pachomius Church in the middle of the block behind the courthouse.

St. Pachomius was a massive building that sat in regal splendor beneath a canopy of huge oak trees. The oldest church in the state, it was constructed of stone. Steps led up from the sidewalk to a front portico supported by stately round columns. Behind those columns, huge doors, fifteen feet tall, stood like sentries guarding access to the sanctuary beyond.

Connolly parked the car in front and gazed at the building. After a moment, he closed the car door and slowly walked up the steps. At the top, he moved past the columns and pushed against one of the doors. The door swung open. Inside, the sanctuary was cool and dark. He closed the door behind him and looked around.

The walls on either side were lined with stained-glass windows depicting scenes from the life of Christ. At the far end of the nave, a railing separated the congregation from the chancel that sat three feet above the sanctuary floor. An opening in the railing allowed access to marble steps that rose from the sanctuary floor to the chancel.

The floor of the chancel was made of marble as well. Near the front, lecterns stood on either side facing the nave. Toward the back, pews were arranged on either side for a split chancel choir. Beyond the choir, the altar stood behind still another railing near the rear wall of the church.

Connolly studied each of the windows as he moved down the aisle. At the railing he knelt, touching one knee to the floor, and made the sign of the cross on his chest. As he stood, a door to the right opened. A man dressed in a dark suit and clerical collar entered the sanctuary.

"Sorry," he said. "Didn't know anyone was in here."

His presence startled and unnerved Connolly. Suddenly, he felt out of place.

"I didn't mean to intrude," Connolly replied.

"No intrusion. I'm Scott Nolan," the man said, extending his hand toward Connolly. "I'm the rector here. Most people call me Father Scott."

Connolly shook his hand.

"Mike Connolly," he replied.

"Anything I can do to help you?"

"Well, actually ... I ... I'm a lawyer," Connolly explained. "I represent a man who's accused of killing Keyton Attaway. I understand Keyton was one of your members."

Father Scott folded his arms across his chest as he listened. He nodded for Connolly to continue.

"I was wondering if there was someone here who could talk to me about him. Did you know Keyton?"

"Yes," Father Scott nodded. "We all knew him. We were horrified by what happened to him ... as I'm ... as I'm sure you were too."

"Yes. It was a terrible thing." Connolly paused a moment, then continued. "I know it's somewhat awkward, but can you tell me anything about Keyton?"

"Let's sit over here," Father Scott said, directing him toward a nearby pew.

Connolly followed him to a pew in the front of the nave. Father Scott turned to face Connolly.

"I don't know how well you knew Keyton," Father Scott began, "but the Keyton Attaway who was killed the other day was not the same person he was a year ago. He became a different man over the last year."

"I think his partners noticed a change in him too," Connolly said. "He had a cross sitting in his office. Not what you normally find in a lawyer's office."

Father Scott smiled.

"I gave him that cross."

"It's a beautiful piece. Kind of rugged but burnished and ... nice."

"Exactly," Father Scott replied. "Sort of like Keyton. Rugged, but in a beautiful way."

Connolly wasn't getting much out of Father Scott.

"Listen, if this is a bad time I can come back later."

"No, no," Father Scott replied. "You go ahead and ask me whatever you want to know. I was a lawyer once." He smiled. "Practiced law for fifteen years. You ask whatever you want, and if I can tell you, I will."

"What happened to him? I mean, if he was different, what happened to him?"

"Keyton was always a good member of this church, at least while I've been here. But about a year ago, he and Karen went on a retreat with a group to North Carolina. He found out God wasn't too much like he had always thought."

Connolly nodded. Both men were silent a moment, then Connolly spoke.

"They found his body by the side of a road not too far from the shipyard on Pinto Island. It strikes me as an odd place for him to be. Any idea why he would be out there in a place like that?"

"No," Father Scott replied. "I assumed that was just where the body was dumped. Isn't that what the news reports said?"

"Suppose it wasn't like that." Connolly paused a moment, then continued. "Suppose Keyton was out there with someone, maybe in a car, parked on the side of the road. And suppose an unidentified assailant driving a pickup truck walked up to that car and shot him, execution style ... Is there anything you can tell me about him that might explain why something like that would happen?"

A puzzled frown creased Father Scott's forehead. He stroked the side of his face and stared at the floor.

"You and I have the same problem," he said. "There is much we could tell each other, but we're both limited by privileges and confidences we can't violate."

Connolly nodded.

"I'll tell you this," Father Scott offered. "Keyton was tormented by something the last few months of his life. I had the sense it was something that had been going on for a while. I don't know what it was, but whatever it was, it conflicted with the changes he had been through and the way he now wanted to live his life. He didn't tell me much. But it was serious, and he wrestled with what to do about it."

"Any idea what he was involved in?"

"No." Father Scott shook his head.

"Did he mention any names?"

"He wouldn't name names."

"Anyone else in the church who might know what it was? A close friend, maybe?"

"I doubt it," Father Scott replied. "Karen, his wife, perhaps. But if he was going to tell anyone besides her, I think it would have been me. We were pretty close the last few months."

Connolly looked around the sanctuary once more.

"This is a neat old church."

"Yes it is. You should join us Sunday."

"I used to come to church here."

"Oh? When was that?"

"Years ago. Father Tagliano was the rector then."

Father Scott smiled.

"Things are a little different here now from what they were back then. You should come see."

A skeptical look turned up the corners of Connolly's mouth.

"I can't imagine God being interested in hearing from me," he said. His voice was quiet, and there was a hint of resignation in his tone. "Not now."

Father Scott gently slapped Connolly on the knee.

"God would love to hear from you," he said. "Come worship with us this Sunday."

Connolly held out his hand. Father Scott grasped it.

"Thanks for your help, Father."

Father Scott smiled.

"Come see me anytime."

Connolly stepped into the aisle and started toward the door.

"Maybe one day you'll get tired of the law and try dealing in grace," Father Scott called.

"We'll see," Connolly called in reply.

Moments later he reached the door. Without looking back he pushed it open and stepped outside.

Fourteen

*T*hat afternoon Connolly returned to Vern Eubanks's house in Grand Bay. As before, it was almost sunset when he arrived.

He guided the Chrysler past the junked automobiles out front and around a stack of used lumber. The shrimp net still hung between the trees near the house, and laundry still hung on a rope strung between posts on the front porch.

Connolly brought the car to a stop near a rotting wooden boat a few yards from the house. He hesitated a moment, looking for the dog. When he didn't appear, he got out.

As before, a woman appeared in the doorway. She wore the same thin cotton dress, and her snow-white hair stuck out from her head in all directions.

"You looking for ..." She recognized Connolly and stopped in mid-sentence. "He's around back," she grumbled.

"Yes, ma'am," he said, as politely as possible.

The woman disappeared inside the house. Connolly walked around the corner of the porch. About halfway across the back yard, Skip, the bulldog, appeared from the far corner of the shed. Connolly froze in his tracks. Before, the dog had ambled over to him and nuzzled around his thighs and crotch. This time the dog crouched and came at him in a slow, deliberate manner. As he drew closer, he bared his teeth in a snarl and gave a low, menacing growl. Connolly slowly moved one foot back, then the other.

Suddenly, the back door of the house banged open, flopping against the wall. A cast-iron pan shot from the doorway. It sailed past Connolly and struck the dog squarely on the head. Connolly glanced to his left and saw the woman standing in the doorway.

"Get out of here!" she yelled.

The force of the pot against the dog's head sent him to the ground with a yelp. He quickly righted himself and slunk away toward the shed.

"Vern!" the woman shouted. "Somebody here to see you!"

The back door banged closed as she stepped inside.

In a moment, the door to the shed opened, and Vern appeared. Sullen and irritable when he stepped through the door, his face turned angry and hard when he saw Connolly.

"I thought I told you to stay off my property," he said. He reached inside the door and pulled out the double-barreled shotgun.

"Wait," Connolly said. "I just want to ask you a question."

"That's what you said last time," Eubanks replied. "Right before you started trying to take my money."

He pulled the stock of the shotgun under his armpit and slipped his finger around the trigger.

"I'm not here about the money," Connolly said.

Eubanks relaxed and let his finger slip off the trigger.

"What you want then?"

"I want to know if you'd go down to the jail ..."

Eubanks raised the shotgun again.

"Wait," Connolly said quickly. "Hear me out."

Eubanks paused.

"I want to know if you'd go down to the jail and look at some photographs."

"Photographs?" The anger on Eubanks's face melted into a puzzled look. "Photographs of what?"

"I want to see if you can identify the man you sold the truck to," Connolly explained.

Eubanks thought a minute, then shook his head.

"That jail's in Mobile, ain't it?"

"Yes, sir."

"Downtown?"

"Yes, sir."

"I ain't been to downtown Mobile since I was a little boy. I reckon I ain't got no need to go now."

"I really need your help," Connolly said.

Eubanks lowered the shotgun and rested it in the crook of his arm.

"If they want me to look at some pictures, tell them to bring them out here to me."

Connolly smiled.

"They have thousands, Mr. Eubanks. And besides, it's not them who wants you to look at the pictures. It's me."

Eubanks turned aside and opened the door to the shed.

"Well, they know where to find me if they want me. I ain't going nowhere."

The door closed behind him. Connolly stepped forward to follow after him.

"Mr. Eubanks ..."

A low growl from the corner of the shed brought him to a halt. To his right stood Skip. Connolly backed carefully toward the house. As he neared the corner, the back door banged opened, and the woman appeared again. The dog disappeared behind the shed as she plopped down the steps. Halfway across the yard she picked up the pot she had thrown at the dog earlier. She smiled at Connolly as she turned to go inside.

"That dog don't mess with me," she said. Her smile turned into a grin, revealing her broken and decayed teeth. She burst into laughter. "He knows I'll bust his head if he comes near me."

She struggled up the steps and went inside. Connolly walked quickly to the Chrysler.

From Eubanks's house in Grand Bay, Connolly drove to Ogden Avenue in Crichton, a neighborhood in the fringes between city and suburb on the western edge of Mobile. Once a suburban community itself, it had now been swallowed up by urban expansion. Most of the houses there were built before 1950.

He turned left on Ogden and stopped at a single-story house with white clapboard siding in the middle of the block. As he stepped from the car Toby LeMoyne came from the house to meet him. Toby was a deputy sheriff. A tall, athletic black man, he looked both friendly and intimidating.

"What you doing out here, Mr. Connolly?" he said with a smile.

"Looking for you," Connolly replied.

"Well come on in ..." His voice trailed off, and his eyes focused on something behind Connolly. "We're about to eat supper," he said, slowly. His voice sounded distracted. He pointed over Connolly's shoulder to the street. "Is he with you?"

Connolly turned around to see a dark green Taurus parked near the corner.

"No," Connolly said. "Why?"

"He pulled in there right behind you. Looks like he's watching us."

Toby started across the yard to the sidewalk and headed toward the car. As he did, the car started forward, then made a U-turn from the curb. Before Toby could reach it, the car turned the corner onto Spring Hill Avenue. Toby watched as the car sped away.

He walked back to the house.

"I don't know who that was," he said. "I think he was following you. Did you see him when you were driving over?"

"No," Connolly said, shaking his head. "I've never seen that car before."

Toby smiled.

"If I see him around here again, he'll be spending the night at the jail." He was across the yard by then, standing a few feet in front of Connolly. "Sure you don't want to come inside?" He looked to the street as he waited for Connolly to respond.

"Nah," Connolly said, shaking his head. "This won't take long."

"What's up?"

"Judge Cahill appointed me to represent a man named Avery Thompson. He's charged with killing Keyton Attaway."

"So I heard."

"I have a witness who might be able to identify the man who actually did the shooting."

Toby nodded thoughtfully. Connolly continued.

"I was wondering if you could help."

"What do you need?"

"I need you to let him look at the booking photographs at the jail."

"Thompson?"

"No. My witness."

Toby stroked his chin in thought.

"Have to be at night," he said.

"Alright," Connolly replied. "There's one other thing."

"What's that?"

"He won't come unless you go get him."

Toby dropped his hand from his chin and chuckled.

"You want me to go get him?"

Connolly nodded.

"Where does he live?"

"Grand Bay."

"Grand Bay? He's a white guy?"

"Yeah," Connolly smiled. "He's a white guy."

Toby laughed.

"White guys out there barbecue guys like me, alive."

Connolly smiled and waited. Toby straightened himself.

"Alright," he said. "When do you want to do it?"

"When can you go get him?"

Toby glanced at his watch.

"I go on in two hours," he replied.

"Good," Connolly said. "I'll meet you at the jail."

He turned away and opened the car door. Toby grabbed him by the shoulder.

"But first, you got to eat supper," he said.

Connolly closed the car door as Toby guided him toward the house.

Fifteen

*L*ater that evening, Connolly met Toby at the rear entrance to the county jail.

"Did you get him?"

"I got him," Toby replied, grinning. "You forgot to tell me about the bulldog."

Toby held the door open for him. Connolly smiled as he stepped inside.

"If the old woman hadn't been there," Toby continued, "he'd have taken off my arm."

"She ran him off?"

"Shoved a broom handle down his throat."

"She saved me too," Connolly said, laughing.

Connolly followed Toby through the building.

"I appreciate this," he said.

"No problem," Toby replied. "Only now, you owe me."

They walked down the hall toward a cluster of offices near the front of the jail.

"He's in here," Toby said, pointing. "I got him looking at some pictures."

Toby opened a door to an office on the left. Connolly stepped inside. Vern Eubanks was seated at a table. In front of him lay a box of photographs. He was busy looking through them when Connolly entered the room.

"Might have knowed you had something to do with this," Eubanks said.

He glanced in Connolly's direction as he spoke.

"Sorry for the inconvenience," Connolly said. "It was unavoidable."

"Yeah," Eubanks replied.

His voice was flat and emotionless.

"We have thousands of photographs," Toby interrupted. "You think you could narrow it down any?"

"He gave me a description," Connolly replied. "Tall, slender, middle-aged man. Said he had an accent. Perhaps from up north."

"Yankee," Eubanks growled.

"Think he could have been from New Orleans?" Toby asked.

Eubanks shrugged his shoulders.

"Same difference."

Toby took a seat at a nearby computer terminal and entered the description.

"Let's see if any New Orleans residents fit this description first."

In a few minutes a printer in the corner made a racket as it powered up. Connolly glanced in that direction. Plastic on the front of the machine was cracked and the back was worn and dirty from the countless reams that had passed through it. As he watched, the printer began spitting out a list. Pages of track-fed paper piled on the floor as the printer whirred.

"Must be quite a list."

"Not as long as it seems," Toby said. "It's an old system and the program we have prints out a lot of information. Takes several lines for each person. This will give us everyone who has been booked here at the jail who gave a New Orleans address as their place of residence. If this doesn't work, we'll try something else."

When the printer finished producing the list, Toby folded it neatly to a manageable size.

"We need to locate the pictures for these numbers," he said, pointing to a number along the left side of each entry. "They're arranged numerically in the filing cabinets over here."

Connolly followed him across the room to a row of large gray cabinets. Toby pulled open a drawer and took out a photo.

"That's the first one," he said, handing it to Connolly.

They continued on through the evening. Eubanks sat at the table looking at photos from the box. Connolly and Toby worked through the gray cabinet gathering photos from the printout.

Sometime around ten o'clock, Eubanks shoved the box aside and laid his head on the table.

"Not yet, Mr. Eubanks," Connolly called. "There's still more for you to look at."

"Can't help it," Eubanks moaned. "Way past my bedtime."

Toby closed the file cabinet and laid a stack of photographs in front of Eubanks.

"Here, look at these," he said. "I'll go get us some coffee."

Eubanks lifted his head from his arms and rubbed his eyes.

"Make mine black," he said.

Toby laid the printout on the table and left the room. Eubanks turned his attention to the fresh stack of photographs.

Connolly paced the floor and tried to keep himself occupied. He dug out a newspaper from the trash can and scanned the front page, then looked through the daily prisoner census sheet lying on a desk near the table. The clock on the wall hummed. Toby had been gone ten minutes.

"That's him," Eubanks said.

"What?"

Connolly did not immediately realize what he had said.

"That's the man," Eubanks said, pointing to a picture in his hand. "He's the man I sold that pickup to."

Connolly stepped quickly behind Eubanks and looked over his shoulder.

"Are you sure?"

"Yes, I'm sure," Eubanks insisted. "He's the man."

As they studied the picture, Toby returned.

"Found something?"

"Yeah," Connolly replied.

"That's him," Eubanks said, tossing the photograph on the table.

Toby picked it up and looked on the back for the booking number. Using that number, he located the man's identity on the list from the computer.

"According to this, his name is Ralph Martin. Also goes by Randy Mason, Jack Moran, and Ronnie Moses. Arrested here two years ago for soliciting an undercover officer. Prostitution charge. Nothing else on him in our records. I can get a full report for you, but it'll take a day or two."

"Great," Connolly said. He slapped Eubanks on the shoulder. "Good work, Mr. Eubanks. You need a ride home?"

"Yeah," Eubanks replied. "But can I have that coffee first?"

"Sure," Toby said. He handed Eubanks a Styrofoam cup filled with steaming coffee. "Black, just like you said."

Sixteen

*C*onnolly spent the next day trying to convince Toby to obtain a warrant for Ralph Martin. Toby insisted there wasn't enough evidence.

"Besides," he said. "This is a city case. City police are handling it. If I go barging in, I'll have the sheriff and half the city police force mad at me."

Reluctantly, Connolly gave up.

The following morning, he left his apartment early and drove to Jackson. He arrived at Aikers Hospital a little after nine. He parked the Chrysler in front of the administration building and went inside.

He crossed the lobby and stopped at the information desk.

"I'm here to see Avery Thompson," he said.

The receptionist smiled as she opened the black notebook on her desk.

"I remember you," she said. "You were just up here a few days ago."

Connolly nodded and forced a smile in reply.

"Let's see," she said. She ran her finger down a list of names on one of the pages of the book. "Got a Thompson. George Thompson." She glanced at Connolly. "He was here last time."

Connolly nodded, his frustration level rising with each passing minute.

"Still here," she said. She continued down the list. "But not Avery Thompson." She closed the book. "Sorry," she said.

"What do you mean?"

"He's not here," she said.

"I'm supposed to see him. Is Mrs. Holsombach available?"

"She's not here either," she said.

"Well, who can I see?"

"You'll have to see Mr. Crawford."

"Who's he?"

"The hospital director. Take the stairs. Second floor. Down the hall, in the corner. Can't miss it."

The telephone rang. She turned away to answer it.

Connolly found the stairs and made his way to Crawford's office on the second floor.

He was greeted by a secretary.

"May I help you?" she asked.

"I'd like to see Mr. Crawford."

"And what is this about?"

"I'm an attorney. One of my clients was sent up here by mistake from the county jail in Mobile. Mrs. Holsombach told me I could see him today."

The secretary looked stricken at the mention of Mrs. Holsombach's name.

"I ... ahhh ... I'll have to ..."

A man appeared in the doorway behind her desk.

"I'll handle this," he said. He stepped toward Connolly and extended his hand. "I'm Robbie Crawford," he said. "I'm the hospital director. Come on in my office."

Connolly followed him into the office. Crawford closed the door.

"Have a seat," he said, pointing to a chair near the desk.

Connolly took a seat. Crawford slid a second chair in front of the desk and sat as well.

"I assume you're Mike Connolly?"

"Yes."

"I'm afraid Mr. Thompson isn't here."

"Why not? Mrs. Holsombach said I could see him today."

"Yes. Well, we had to send him on to Harwell Psychiatric Facility in Tuscaloosa," Crawford said. "He wasn't in good enough shape for us to handle him here. Not with criminal charges pending. We really aren't equipped to house prisoners on anything more than a temporary basis."

"Good enough shape? What was wrong with him?"

"I'm not really sure. He was on quite a bit of medication ..."

"Medication? He was fine the last time I saw him in Mobile."

"I wouldn't know anything about that. Our staff physician thinks he must have had some kind of drug reaction that really set off a chain of problems. By the time they discovered his condition, he was in bad shape. Not really sure he was going to make it there for a while."

Connolly was astounded.

"I need to talk to Mrs. Holsombach," he said. "She didn't say anything about this."

"I'm afraid that won't be possible. At least not here."

"Why not?"

"Mrs. Holsombach has left us. I think she has decided to retire."

"Retire. She was just here two days ago."

"I know. It was a rather sudden decision. Caught us by surprise."

Connolly shook his head.

"Were Mr. Thompson's tests completed?"

"Tests?"

"Yes. Tests. He was sent up here on an order signed by Judge Cahill to have him evaluated to see whether he was competent to stand trial."

Crawford frowned.

"I wasn't aware he was sent here for that. I was under the impression he was sent here because the jail was unable to manage him."

"Manage him? What are you talking about?"

"Schizophrenia."

"Schizophrenia? Who said he was schizophrenic? He was perfectly normal at the jail."

"That's not what the records indicate."

"Mrs. Holsombach told me herself he was here to be evaluated to see if he could stand trial. She said I couldn't see him because if I did it would invalidate the tests. She didn't say anything about treatment for anything."

"Invalidate the tests?" Crawford scoffed. "I've never heard of such a thing. We don't do any tests for competency. We have a certified psychologist interview them and render an opinion. Takes about a day and a half. Only thing that would invalidate that is if you were to sit in on the sessions."

Crawford called his secretary on the intercom and asked her to bring Thompson's file. In a few minutes she opened the office door and handed him the file.

"Let's look at this," Crawford said. He opened the file and laid it on the desk. "See," he said, pointing. "This note says he was sent here because the jail was unable to manage his condition. There's an order in here too." He turned several pages. "There it is," he said. He held the file open while Connolly read the order.

The order indicated the jail had found Thompson difficult to manage and that he had refused to take required medication. It purported to order the sheriff to deliver him to Aikers for evaluation and management. The signature was illegible.

"That's not Judge Cahill's signature," Connolly said. "Can you make a copy of this?"

"Sure."

Crawford called his secretary. When she appeared, he handed her the file.

"Make a copy of this file for Mr. Connolly," he said.

She took the file and disappeared. When she was gone, Crawford moved behind the desk.

"I'm afraid that's all I know about Mr. Thompson," he said. "He's in Tuscaloosa. We sent him up there yesterday." Crawford took a seat behind the desk. "She'll have that file for you in a few minutes," he said. "You can wait out front."

Seventeen

*T*he drive from Jackson to Tuscaloosa took three hours. Connolly found Harwell Psychiatric Facility without difficulty. Unlike Aikers, the administration building was outside the secure area. He parked in the visitor's lot and walked inside. In his hand he carried a yellow legal pad and a copy of the afternoon edition of the *Mobile Register.*

At the receptionist's desk he confirmed that Thompson was there. A clerk took his driver's license in exchange for a visitor's pass and directed him to a waiting area. He took a seat and began leafing through the newspaper.

In a few minutes, a guard entered. He patted down Connolly and ushered him through a metal detector. Connolly tucked the legal pad and newspaper under his arm and stepped through the detector. Another guard escorted him down a long, wide tunnel that ran underground from the administration building to the guard station at the entrance to the patient area. When they emerged from the tunnel, Connolly had a clear view of the facility.

Beyond the administration building, Harwell was nothing like a hospital at all. Surrounded by double rows of fence twenty feet high and topped with six strands of concertina wire, it was designed to house criminals. Specially trained dogs patrolled the area between the two fences, and armed guards watched from towers well above the top of the fence.

A guard at the guard station searched him again with a hand-held metal detector.

"Come with me," the guard said.

Connolly followed him down a long corridor into the heart of the facility. A hundred yards down the corridor they came to a sector partition made of steel bars. A guard sat at a table on the opposite side. He pressed a button as they approached. The bars slid to one side.

"Lawyer," Connolly's escort said. "Here to see a prisoner in D Ward."

The guard at the desk nodded. He looked Connolly over as he passed by. The steel door clanked closed behind them.

A little farther down the corridor they turned right and passed through another checkpoint. Beyond it, narrower hall-ways intersected the main corridor to the left and right. Connolly glanced down the halls as they passed.

Down each hall, rows of solid steel doors lined the walls. Halfway down each door, he could see a slot with a small ledge beneath it. Trays of half-eaten food rested on the ledges.

They passed several more intersecting hallways and came to a central nurses' station. Male orderlies dressed in green hospital togs scurried about. A male nurse sat at a desk in the center of the station. He looked up as they approached.

"Got a lawyer here," the guard said. "Wants to see a man named Avery Thompson." Everyone seemed to glance at Connolly, then turn away. The guard turned to Connolly. "When you're done, come back here and tell them. They'll call me, and I'll come get you. Wait for me. You won't be able to get out without me."

Connolly nodded. The nurse said something to an orderly standing nearby. The orderly came from behind the desk.

"Follow me," he said.

They walked down the main corridor to the first hall on the left.

"He's down here in twenty-one," the orderly said.

Connolly followed him to a steel door with the number painted in black across the top. The orderly took a key from his pocket and unlocked the door.

"I'll have to lock you in," he said. "There's an intercom near the bed. Buzz us when you're ready to leave." He pulled the door open and held it for Connolly to enter. "Don't untie him from the bed," he said.

Connolly stepped inside. The door banged closed. Connolly glanced around the room.

A toilet sat in the corner to the left. Next to it was a sink. On the far wall across from the door was the bed. Thompson lay on it, a thin sheet draped over his torso. His feet protruded at the foot of the bed where his ankles were tied to the metal bed frame. His arms lay on top of the sheet and were held tightly against his body by straps that bound his wrists. He turned his head to see who entered the room.

"Tha uu misser kernly?"

Connolly moved to the bedside. What he saw made him sick to his stomach. He swallowed hard to keep from vomiting.

Thompson's right eye sagged toward his cheek, and the right corner of his mouth drooped. Saliva drooled from the corner of his mouth onto his chin. His right hand twitched and made his right elbow flop from side to side. The smell of sweat and urine stung Connolly's nostrils.

"What happened to you?"

"Bad r'action to some drugs," Thompson said, the words slurred together.

Connolly frowned.

"What are they giving you drugs for?"

"They ain't here," Thompson said. "People at Aikers said I'm schiz'phrenic."

"When did they do this to you?"

"Soon as they got me up there."

"Is it permanent?"

"Don't know. Doctor said they gave me the wrong medicine. Polyclrhricdride, or something like that." The name of the drug was unintelligible. "Lucky it didn't kill me." He made a loud sucking sound as he tried to stop the saliva that was oozing from the corner of his mouth. Connolly leaned forward and wiped Thompson's mouth and chin with the corner of the sheet.

"Mr. Connolly ... can I ask you somethin'?"

"Certainly."

"Why am I up here?"

Connolly sighed and shook his head.

"I don't know," he said. "Someone filed a request to have you evaluated. Aikers says you were sent there for treatment because you're schizophrenic, and the jail couldn't handle you. It's all a big mess."

"Huh," Thompson grunted. "I was fine b'fore they started messing with me. Think they'll come get me?"

"I hope so, Avery," Connolly replied. "I hope so."

They looked at each other for a moment. Then Thompson smiled.

"Case kind of got serious, ain't it?"

"Yeah," Connolly said. "It's gotten serious."

They were quiet a moment. Connolly was unsure what to say, then he remembered Vern Eubanks.

"I found the man who owned the blue pickup," Connolly said.

"Yeah?" Thompson smiled. "That's good. Ain't it?"

Connolly nodded.

"He sold it a few weeks ago to a man who fits the description you gave of the driver. I had him go through some mug shots at the jail. He picked a man out he says bought it."

"Picked him out?" Thompson sounded excited.

"Yeah."

"That's real good."

"Yeah," Connolly sighed. "If they give us a trial."

Thompson looked puzzled.

"What you mean?"

"The way you are," Connolly said, pointing to Thompson, "judge might say you aren't fit to stand trial."

Thompson looked worried.

"What'll they do with me then?"

Connolly turned his head away.

"Leave you in here," he said, softly.

Tears appeared at the corner of Thompson's eyes.

"Don't let them do that to me, Mr. Connolly," he pleaded. "Please don't let them do that."

A lump rose in Connolly's throat.

"I'm doing my best," he whispered. "I'm doing my best."

The orderly rapped on the door.

"Time to go," he called.

"We're not through," Connolly replied, irritated.

"Can't help it," the orderly said. "Time's up. Got to serve supper."

Connolly stepped closer to the bed and squeezed Thompson's shoulder. He shifted the newspaper and legal pad to his other arm. With the corner of the sheet he wiped Thompson's eyes and dabbed the saliva from his chin.

"I'll be back," he said. "Don't worry."

Thompson turned as far toward Connolly as the straps on his wrists would allow. He clutched Connolly's arm with his hand. Connolly grasped his hand for a moment, then turned toward the door.

As Connolly turned to leave, Thompson's eyes fell on the newspaper for the first time. He pounded the mattress with his fist.

"Auts harr," Thompson shouted. "Auts harr!" He continued to pound the mattress with his fist.

Startled, Connolly turned toward the bed. Thompson lifted his chest from the bed. His neck and head strained forward against the restraints as far as possible.

"Auts harr!" he shouted.

Connolly listened intently and struggled to understand what Thompson was saying. Before he could respond, the door burst open. Two orderlies rushed past him. One grabbed Thompson's feet. The other grabbed his shoulders. Together, they leaned all their weight against Thompson and pressed him against the mattress. The male nurse came in behind them with a hypodermic needle filled with medication.

"Wait," Connolly shouted. "Wait."

He pushed the nurse aside and rushed to the bed.

"What are you saying?"

Thompson struggled to raise his left arm. Connolly pushed the orderly's hand free from Thompson's shoulder. Thompson slapped at Connolly's arm, his hand struck the newspaper.

"Auts harr," he shouted.

"Calm down," Connolly said. He lowered his own voice. "Calm down. It's alright. Tell me again."

"Auts harr," Thompson repeated. He slapped the newspaper again and again. "Auts harr."

Connolly took the newspaper from the crook of his arm and unfolded it. He held it open in front of Thompson.

"What about the paper?"

Thompson laid his hand on a picture in the top half of the paper.

"Auts harr," he sighed.

"Auts harr," Connolly whispered, still trying to understand.

"En d ker," Thompson said.

Connolly wracked his brain trying to make sense of what Thompson was saying.

"Eeen da kerrr," Thompson said again, exasperated.

Connolly's face brightened.

"In the car?"

Thompson nodded his head.

"That's the woman in the Cadillac?" Connolly asked.

Thompson nodded his head vigorously.

"You sure about that?"

Thompson nodded his head again.

The orderly at Thompson's shoulders studied the picture. Connolly quickly folded the paper and tucked it under the legal pad.

"It's alright," he said, turning to the nurse. "He was just trying to point someone out in the newspaper." He patted the paper with his free hand. "I understand what he wants."

The orderlies looked at the nurse for instructions.

"It's alright," Connolly insisted. "He won't give you any trouble."

The nurse nodded to the orderlies. They released their grip and left the room. The nurse turned to Connolly.

"I think it's time for you to go," he said. "Mr. Thompson's had enough excitement for one day."

Connolly looked at Thompson and smiled.

"It's alright, Avery," Connolly said with a nod. "I'll take care of it."

Thompson took a deep breath and closed his eyes. Connolly followed the nurse into the hallway. The door banged closed.

Eighteen

A guard escorted Connolly back to the administration building. The clerk there returned his driver's license and signed him out. Connolly left the building and walked slowly to the parking lot. He opened the door of the Chrysler and sat in the front seat. He felt a deep sinking feeling in his chest.

"Thompson was right," he thought, "this case is getting serious."

The woman in the picture Thompson pointed to was Leigh Ann Agostino. That she was in the car with Attaway when he died was troubling enough, but it was not the thing that worried Connolly the most. What troubled him the most was her husband, John, who happened to be one of two federal judges in Mobile and a man with whom Connolly had been acquainted for a long time.

John Agostino came from a prominent Mobile family. His grandfather earned a small fortune in the timber business, which he passed to John's father who then spent it. By the time John graduated from law school, only the memory of his grandfather's accomplishments remained. But money, even the memory of it, has a way of changing people, and it gave John a not-so-subtle arrogance that had the odd effect of leaving him friendly and at the same time pompous. That

Connolly and he ever became friends was rather remarkable.

Connolly had not even the memory of money. When he was ten years old his father died. His mother turned to alcohol to escape the worries of raising two children alone. Often in a drunken daze, she was frequently gone for days at a time leaving Connolly and his younger brother to fend for themselves. Then, she met a man at a truck stop in Loxley and left altogether.

On their own for good, Connolly and his brother crammed what they could in a pillowcase and hitchhiked to Bayou La Batre, a rough and tumble fishing village on the coast deep in the heart of bayou country south of Mobile. They arrived there unannounced at the home of their uncle, Guy Poiroux. He did the best he could for them, but it was a life of grueling work on shrimp boats and oyster skiffs.

Though they came from very different backgrounds, Connolly and Agostino had once contemplated practicing law together. But Agostino's personality made Connolly leery of his motives. In addition to being arrogant, Agostino had a tendency toward laziness. If there was an easy way to do anything, he found it. Connolly was a law review member, brilliant, and a workaholic. He soon realized if he and Agostino practiced together, he would end up doing all the work and giving Agostino half the income.

Yet, to Connolly's utter dismay, Agostino was the one who seemed to enjoy all the success. While Connolly struggled to earn a living, Agostino's family reputation gained him a partnership in a highly successful plaintiff's firm two years after graduation. When Connolly purchased a modest home in midtown, Agostino bought a luxurious house in Spring Hill, and not long after that, a second home on the bay at Point Clear. Then, just as the firm was beginning to understand Agostino had his grandfather's name and none of his ability, he was appointed to the bench as a federal judge, a position he could hold for the remainder of his life.

Connolly hated the way he had always compared himself to Agostino. More than that, he hated not being able to measure up. And he hated not being strong enough to put it aside.

He glanced around the parking lot to make sure no one was watching, then opened the glove box. He took out the flask, twisted off the top, and downed a quick gulp. As the gin slid across his tongue, the tension slipped away. His body relaxed.

"I should have known there was more to this case than Avery Thompson," Connolly whispered to himself. "I'm getting Agostino'd once again."

After a few more sips from the flask, he started the engine and drove the Chrysler toward Mobile.

Connolly opened his eyes the following morning and found himself staring through the spokes of the steering wheel in the Chrysler. Below him lay a black floor mat. Sweat dripped from his nose and spattered on the mat. His shirt was soaked and stuck to his body. The sour smell of body odor and liquor filled the car.

He lifted his head from the steering wheel and squinted his eyes against the morning sun that bore down on him through the windshield. He rubbed his hands over his face and shook his head, trying to remember where he was and how he got there. A bottle lay in the floor on the passenger's side. Less than a tablespoon of gin rolled around the bottom. Holding the steering wheel with one hand, he leaned over and retrieved the bottle from the floor, then tipped it up and sucked out the remaining drops.

Finally, he opened the car door and stepped outside. Suffocating heat radiated from the pavement, but it was cooler than the car's interior. He wiped the sweat from his eyes. A breeze blew across his back, sending a chill through his body. His shoulders shuddered.

The car was parked outside his apartment on Carondolet Street, that much was familiar, and he remembered seeing Thompson the day before. But he had no memory of the drive from Tuscaloosa and no memory of where the gin came from.

He placed one hand on the fender of the car for support and moved around the rear bumper to the sidewalk. He staggered to the steps and slowly worked his way up to the door of his second-floor apartment.

On the third try, he inserted the key in the lock and opened the door. Inside, he tottered down the hall and eased open the bathroom door. He glanced through the bedroom door. Marisa lay there sound asleep, the cover over all but the top of her head. He thought of crawling in bed beside her, but the stench of sweat and gin was overpowering. He dropped his clothes in a pile on the bathroom floor and stepped into the shower.

Later that morning, Connolly left the apartment and drove toward the office. Refreshed and somewhat alert, his thoughts drifted back to his conversation with Thompson the previous day.

"Why," he mumbled, "would the wife of a federal judge be sitting with a man in a place like that? And why would someone shoot Attaway and not shoot her?"

He recalled the scene Thompson described. The

Cadillac on the side of the road. The blue pickup. Gunshots. Leigh Ann standing by the car as the SUV drove up.

A chill ran up his spine.

"The guy in the blue pickup knew she wouldn't talk," he said aloud.

More questions bombarded his mind. Was she having an affair? Did she know Attaway was going to be murdered? Did she set him up? He needed to find answers, but how?

"I could just show up and say, 'Tell me how Keyton Attaway died,'" he mumbled aloud. He laughed at the thought. "Then they'd give me a bed next to Thompson's."

Halfway to the office he turned the Chrysler around and drove to the Spring Hill section of town. He had no idea what to do next, but he felt drawn to the Agostinos's home.

The drive took all of ten minutes. He slowed the Chrysler as he passed in front.

A low brick wall ran along the edge of the sidewalk by the street. Beyond it, a lush green lawn stretched to the house. A narrow walkway wound around the edge of the lawn, disappearing behind beds of large azaleas as it approached the house. The house, a rambling three-story brick structure of no particular period, was tucked beneath the canopy of two massive oak trees and hidden behind still more azaleas.

A pickup truck was parked on the street in front of the house. Behind the truck was a long utility trailer filled with lawnmowers and other lawn care equipment. Connolly maneuvered the car around the truck and trailer. In the yard, workmen mowed the lawn and trimmed the bushes.

At the corner he turned right and drove along the end of the house. A few houses down the street, he turned the

Chrysler around and drove back to the corner. He turned left and once again passed slowly in front of the house.

A sign on the side of the pickup truck read Goleman's Lawn Care. Connolly glanced at it as he rode past.

Nineteen

*C*onnolly left Agostino's house and drove downtown. As he drove, he thought about Avery Thompson. When he left Tuscaloosa the night before, he had intended to see Judge Cahill first thing that morning to tell him what had happened. Now, he wasn't sure that was the wisest thing to do. As bad as it was, Harwell Psychiatric Facility might be the safest place for Thompson right now. By the time he reached midtown, he had decided not to see Judge Cahill just yet.

Resolved to wait, he turned his mind to the matter that troubled him even more, Leigh Ann Agostino. If Thompson was right, and she was present when Attaway was shot, he needed to know what she was up to.

He bumped his fist in frustration against the steering wheel as he thought. No investigator in town would touch a case like this, he was certain of that. Spying on the wife of a sitting federal judge was much too risky, especially in a town like this where everybody knew everyone. Besides, he didn't have the money to hire an investigator.

Lost in thought, he passed the large Victorian houses on Government Street without noticing. But as he passed in front of the courthouse, a smile spread across his face.

A block further he stopped for the traffic light at Royal Street. When the light turned green, he made a U-turn and

headed in the opposite direction driving back down
Government Street in a westerly direction.

Twenty miles outside of town he reached Irvington, a rural
community on the cusp of the low country that lay along the
coast south of Mobile. There, he turned south onto a narrow
secondary road and descended into a world few knew existed
and even fewer understood.

As the road descended toward the savannah swamps and
tidal marshes, rolling coastal farmland gave way to towering
pines. A few miles further the pines became entangled in a
mass of vines and brambles and then disappeared from sight,
obscured by giant cypress trees draped in moss.

Twenty minutes south of Irvington the road emerged from
beneath the cypress trees into a broad, open marsh dotted by
a few spindly pines. A sandhill crane rose from the marsh
grass as the Chrysler sailed by. Seagulls circled overhead. In
the distance above the grass, little patches of the blue water of
the Gulf of Mexico were visible.

A few minutes more and the road entered the village of
Bayou La Batre, Connolly's childhood home.

In the middle of town he crossed over a rusting draw-
bridge and followed a winding road that led south along the
edge of the bayou that formed the town's central corridor. To
the left, rows of shrimp boats lined the docks at the fish
houses. Lashed together three and four deep, they left only a
narrow passage near the center of the bayou for boat traffic.

Two miles south of town, he came to a large mailbox that
dangled from a rotting wooden post at the side of the road. A
driveway paved with oyster shells ran from the road at the
mailbox to a house surrounded by a grove of pecan trees.

Made of concrete blocks and painted white, the house had
jalousie windows. Below the windows, large azalea bushes

sprawled in every direction, their branches rubbing against the windows. Above the windows were large aluminum awnings. Once painted green and white, they now were a patchwork of faded green, dirty white, and dull gray metal.

Connolly turned the Chrysler onto the driveway. The oyster shells crunched beneath the tires as the car rolled slowly toward the house. He brought it to a stop near a picnic table ten yards to the right of the side door. He slid out of the Chrysler and made his way to the house.

Steps at the side of the house led to the kitchen. Through the screen door he could see inside. An aluminum table with a red Naugahyde top and four matching chairs sat to the right. Against the wall beyond the table was a gas stove. Further to the right was a refrigerator. Next to it was the sink. Connolly opened the screen door and stepped inside. Guy Poiroux stood at the sink washing dishes.

At eighty-five Uncle Guy spent most afternoons napping, but there was a time when he worked for days without any sleep at all. He dropped out of school in the sixth grade to work an oyster skiff, laboring from sunrise to well after dark. It was backbreaking work, lowering the tongs, raking them full, hauling them aboard, then shucking through bushels of shells for the meats while he rested, and all for mere pennies.

At the age of fifteen he left the skiff and took a job as a deck hand on a shrimp boat. By the ripe old age of twenty-one he became a boat captain. He spent the next sixty years piloting shrimp boats, first on week-long runs south of town, then later on trips far out into the Gulf. It was a hard life, but one that favored him.

Guy turned toward Connolly as he came through the door. "Hey," he exclaimed.

He dropped the plate he was holding into the sink, wiped

his hands on his pants, and locked his arms around Connolly in a tight hug.

"Where have you been? You haven't been down here in a long time."

"I know," Connolly said. "I should have come sooner."

"Been busy?"

"Yeah," Connolly lied. "Busy."

The truth was he'd been in a drunken haze, one that made it increasingly difficult for him to function.

Guy released his hold on Connolly's shoulders.

"Have a seat," he said, pointing toward the kitchen table. "You want some coffee?"

He was already taking a cup from the cupboard before Connolly could respond.

"Yeah," Connolly replied. "Sure."

Connolly took a seat at the table.

Across the room Guy set two cups on the counter and lifted the coffeepot from the stove. Connolly watched as the thick, black liquid filled the cups. Guy loved coffee, and he loved it hot, which meant the pot boiled all day. By afternoon his coffee was strong and bitter.

Guy brought the filled cups to the table. He set one in front of Connolly and took a seat across from him.

"So, how's Rachel? Had her baby yet?"

"Yeah," Connolly replied. His voice was flat and lifeless. He took a sip of coffee.

"You don't sound too excited about being a grandfather," Guy said.

"Not a lot to get excited about," Connolly grumbled.

"I wouldn't be too hard on her," Guy cautioned. "At least not right now. That baby needs all the help ... What is it? Boy or girl?"

"Girl."

"What's her name?"

"Elizabeth."

"Elizabeth. Nice name." Guy paused and sipped from his coffee cup. "Well, Elizabeth is going to need all the help she can get. You don't want to say too much now. Might never have a chance to get to know her."

Connolly glanced out the window. A memory of his own mother swept through his mind. For an instant, he was sitting in her lap at the table. He heard his mother's laughter as she watched him sip coffee from a cup. It wasn't really coffee but milk and sugar with just enough coffee to give it a tan color. It was a memory that made him both happy and sad in the same instant. Guy's voice brought him back.

"See Barbara any?"

"Saw her at the hospital the other night."

"How's she doing?"

"Alright, I guess," Connolly said. "Still the same old Barbara."

"Seeing anybody?"

"Had somebody with her named Lamar Edwards."

"Never heard of him."

"Doesn't really matter anymore," Connolly shrugged.

A broad grin spread across Guy's face.

"Who are you kidding?"

Connolly chuckled.

Guy took another sip of coffee. The grin disappeared from his face.

"Still got that girl living with you?"

The tone of his voice let Connolly know he did not approve of the relationship.

"Yeah," Connolly sighed. "She's still there."

Guy looked away.

"I'm sorry," he said. "It's not any of my business."

"That's alright," Connolly replied.

They sat in silence a moment.

"I see they appointed you to represent that man that killed Keyton Attaway."

"Yeah."

"Think he did it?"

"I'm beginning to have my doubts."

"Maybe the better question is, can you win the trial?"

Connolly nodded. "That's the question alright."

"Want some more coffee?"

"No," Connolly said. "I've got to go." He stood. "I need to find Hollis Toombs. Seen him around lately?"

Guy stood.

"Saw him day before yesterday at Schambeau's," Guy replied. "I imagine he's over at that shack he calls home. What you need him for?"

Connolly smiled.

"Alright," Guy said. "None of my business."

Connolly took Guy by the shoulders and drew him into a hug. Guy wrapped his arms around Connolly. Tears filled his eyes. They stood there in the kitchen, arms wrapped tightly around each other, then Connolly relaxed.

"Got to go," he said.

Guy followed him to the door and stood at the top of the steps. Connolly walked quickly to the Chrysler. He backed the car away from the house and turned it around. He glanced out the window toward the house. The old man smiled. Connolly gave a quick wave as he drove away.

Hollis lived alone in a tar paper shack along Bayou Garon

near East Fowl River, fifteen miles from Bayou La Batre in an area near the mouth of Mobile Bay known as Mon Louis Island. Located in the midst of Delchamps Swamp, Mon Louis Island was isolated by both geography and custom. A mixture of Native American, French, Spanish, and African, it was a place defined not by location but by state of mind. Centuries of marriage and intermarriage formed a tangle of relationships, language, and custom as indecipherable and unpredictable as the swamp itself, a low country stockpot that was constantly simmering.

Hollis's shack sat in a thick grove of scrubby oaks and tall pines along Bayou Garon, a hundred yards from the main channel of East Fowl River. Hollis and the shack blended well with the terrain and culture.

The land on which the shack was built once had been part of a vast tract owned by Hollis's uncle, Otis Toombs, a descendant of an unspecified band of Native Americans and a French outlaw. Uncle Otis never married, and when he died he left all his property to Hollis, much to the disdain of his twelve other nieces and nephews. When Hollis returned from three tours of duty in Vietnam, he found five cousins living on the property. He evicted them by force and spent the next fifteen years in court, which is how he and Connolly became acquainted.

He still owed Connolly a job or two.

Hollis must have heard him coming. He was standing out front when Connolly brought the car to a stop. As Connolly got out of the car, Hollis disappeared around the corner. Connolly closed the car door and followed.

He found Hollis sitting on the end of the pier that stretched out behind the shack into the bayou. A gill net hung from low pine branches, draped from tree to tree, then piled on the pier. The end of it lay in Hollis's lap where he sat mending it. His bare feet dabbled in the water.

"You got a license for that thing?" Connolly asked as he made his way down the pier.

Hollis glanced over his shoulder, then turned back to the net in his lap.

"Too long," he said. His gravelly voice rattled in his throat.

"Yeah. You're right," Connolly chuckled. "This thing wouldn't be legal even if you had a license."

Hollis continued to work on the net.

"What can I do for you? I know you didn't come down here to talk about my net."

Connolly didn't reply immediately. Instead, he watched in silence as Hollis's fingers made quick work of tying the strings that formed the net.

"Well ... ?"

Hollis's voice rose above a rattle as he raised the question once again.

"I need some help," Connolly responded.

"What is it this time?"

There was a dry sense of humor in the tone of Hollis's voice.

"I need you to get a job," Connolly said.

Hollis's hands dropped to his lap as he jerked his head around.

"A job?" Puzzled, he stared at Connolly. There was an odd smile on his face. "What kind of a job?"

"Lawn care."

"Lawn care?" Astounded by the suggestion, Hollis broke into laughter. "Look around you." He made a broad, sweeping motion with one arm. "Is there anything about this place that tells you I'm the least bit interested in lawn care?"

Connolly smiled.

"I need you to get a job with Goleman's Lawn Care."

"And just why do I need a job with Goleman's Lawn Care?"

"Because they take care of Judge Agostino's yard."

"No, no, no," Hollis said. He turned back to the net in his lap. "I ain't doing nothing with no federal judge."

"I'll match whatever they pay you," Connolly offered.

Hollis's fingers paused, still holding the net. He turned his head slightly to one side.

"In cash?" he asked, over his shoulder.

"Yeah," Connolly said. "In cash."

Twenty

The following morning Connolly walked to the courthouse for a hearing on another case. As he left the courthouse to return to the office, he stopped by the newsstand in the lobby for a copy of the *Mobile Register*. While he waited in line to pay, Harry Greenberg, a prominent defense attorney, stepped in line behind him.

"I hear you're defending the man who killed Keyton Attaway," Greenberg said, without introduction.

"Hello, Harry," Connolly replied.

"Think you can get him off?"

"All I need is one juror with a conscience."

Greenberg chuckled.

"Any idea what Attaway was doing that got him killed?"

"Not yet," Connolly replied.

"I don't know why he was killed, but he's been committing highway robbery in court." Greenberg lifted an eyebrow and cocked his head to one side for emphasis. "Especially over in federal court."

"I hear he was pretty good."

"Good? The man was born to be a plaintiff's lawyer. But no one's that good."

"Why do you say that?"

"Man never lost a case in Agostino's court."

"Never?"

"Never. Had a streak of twelve cases he'd either won out-right or got Agostino to gut the defense and they had to settle."

Connolly stepped to the counter.

"Fifty cents," the cashier said.

Connolly dug in his pocket for change and paid the clerk, then turned to walk away.

"See you, Mike," Greenberg called.

Connolly tossed Greenberg a wave without turning around. He read the paper as he walked toward the lobby door.

By the time he reached his office, Connolly had read the front page of each section in the paper. He tossed it on Mrs. Gordon's desk as he came through the door.

"Don't throw it there," she complained, grabbing it as soon as it hit the desktop. "I've already read it."

She tossed the paper in the trash can.

"How long you been working for me, Mrs. Gordon?"

"Since you became a lawyer," she replied. "How long is that?"

"I don't know," Connolly said, shrugging his shoulders. "Thirty years, maybe."

"Well, that's how long I've been here."

He took a seat in a chair near her desk.

"Where'd you work before that?"

"Judge Mashburn," she said, a frown furrowing her brow. "You knew that."

"You see secretaries for other lawyers, don't you?"

"Sure," she replied.

She had a puzzled look on her face.

"Hear gossip, don't you?"

"Yes."

Connolly slouched low in the chair, stretching his legs out in front of him. He crossed one foot over the other.

"You're pretty much up on what happens in the legal community around here?"

"Yes. I guess," she replied. The puzzled look on her face deepened. "Is there a point to all this?"

"You think a lawyer and a judge could ever get things arranged so the lawyer always won his cases?"

The frown on Mrs. Gordon's face changed to a stern, matronly glare. She liked Connolly but cared little for lawyers as a group.

"Civil or criminal?"

"Civil."

"Possible. Too hard to do in criminal cases. Those little assistant DAs see the judges every day. They'd catch on pretty fast to something like that. But in civil cases, it might be possible. And you know there are plenty of lawyers out there who'd be more than stupid enough to try."

Connolly smiled.

"You think Keyton Attaway would try something like that?"

"I doubt that," she replied. "He was good enough he didn't need something like that."

Connolly played with his tie.

"Harry Greenberg says Keyton won a string of twelve cases, all of them before Judge Agostino."

Mrs. Gordon crossed her arms as she listened.

"That sounds like sour grapes from Harry Greenberg. Probably lost all twelve of them himself."

"Hear any rumors about Agostino?"

"I ... ahh ..." She glanced away.

"Come on, tell me," Connolly interrupted. "What have you heard?"

"Not really rumors," she said. She was now embarrassed. "Some people were wondering how he ever agreed to move from a first-rate firm to a federal judgeship. That's all."

"That's a good question," Connolly replied.

He slid his body into an upright position in the chair and started toward the door.

"Where are you going?"

"Federal court. Need to do a little research."

It didn't take Connolly long at the federal courthouse to find the information he needed. Not only was Attaway on a roll, so was Truman Albritton. Neither of them had lost a case handled by Judge Agostino. All of their cases before him ended in either a settlement for their client or a verdict in their client's favor. It didn't take a genius to figure out what was going on. Proving it, however, was another matter.

Connolly left the courthouse and wandered down St. Joseph Street. He grappled with how this might have some bearing on Attaway's death and on his defense of Avery Thompson. If the two were connected, the man in the blue Ford pickup truck had not acted alone. Connolly felt a chill run up his back. He had a feeling someone was watching. He nervously glanced over his shoulder.

Lost in thought, he passed Bienville Square and the corner at Dauphin Street near his office. When he finally came to a stop, he found himself standing at the steps in front of St. Pachomius Church. The afternoon was almost gone. Shadows from the sprawling oaks seemed to cloak the building in a darkening shroud.

He took a seat a few steps up from the sidewalk and leaned against the step behind him, propping himself on his elbows. He watched as the day melted in the twilight glow.

In a little while, a car pulled to a stop at the curb. Father Scott got out.

"Looks like you're deep in thought," he said.

He moved up the steps toward Connolly.

"Peaceful place for thinking," Connolly replied.

"Yes, it is."

Father Scott took a seat next to Connolly.

"I used to come over here sometimes at noon," Connolly said. "Father Tagliano met with a couple of us, usually on Wednesdays."

"Father Tagliano was a good man," Father Scott said.

Connolly closed his eyes.

"That was a long time ago," he said.

His voice was quiet and soft, and it had a faraway tone.

"What happened?"

Connolly's eyes opened. He raised himself from his elbows to a sitting position.

"He had a stroke," Connolly said.

"No. I mean to the group he met with."

"Ahh ... you know. One or two moved away. Father Tagliano died. Things just kind of slipped away."

"They tell me you were rather successful with some big cases back then."

Connolly did not respond immediately. He picked up an acorn from the step and rolled it between his fingers.

"I had some success," he said finally.

"And then the bottom fell out."

"Yeah." Connolly admitted, letting the word roll out slowly. "And then the bottom fell out."

"What caused it?"

"I don't know." He flipped the acorn toward the sidewalk. "That was a long time ago, Father."

"I don't think so," Father Scott replied.

"What do you mean?"

"I mean the things in our past we refuse to acknowledge and deal with are always causing problems for us in the present."

"Yeah. Well, right now I've got plenty enough to worry about without having to dredge up something from that long ago."

Father Scott smiled. They sat in silence a few minutes.

"It's getting late," Connolly said. He stood. "I better get going."

"Want a ride?"

"Nah," Connolly replied. "Thanks, but I'd rather walk."

He moved down the steps to the sidewalk and walked away.

It was after seven when Connolly reached the office. His hands shook as he fumbled with the key and the lock. Sweat trickled from his forehead to the corners of his eyes. Finally, he managed to open the door. Inside, the room was dark. Mrs. Gordon had long since gone home.

He hurried down the hall and flung open the door to his office. He tossed his coat toward a chair near the coat rack as he stumbled toward the desk. With one hand, he jerked open the bottom drawer. With the other he took out the gin bottle. His hands, wet with sweat, slipped as he tried to open it. The bottle fell to the floor. He wiped his hands on his pants legs and grabbed the bottle again. Finally, he succeeded in twisting off the cap.

He put the bottle to his lips and turned it up, taking a long gulp, then another. He collapsed in the chair behind the desk and took another drink, this time a little slower. In a few minutes, his hands were steady. He relaxed.

A stack of phone messages lay in the middle of the desk. He picked up the first. It was a note from Henry McNamara telling him the physical evidence taken from Attaway would be available at ten o'clock the following morning. The note instructed him to meet McNamara at the police department.

Connolly took another drink, then picked up the telephone and dialed Rachel's number. After two rings, she answered the phone.

"Hello."

Connolly did not speak.

"Hello," she repeated. "Who is this?"

She waited a moment for a reply, then hung up.

Connolly sat at his desk, the phone still in his hand, and stared into the night.

Twenty-One

Shortly before ten the following day, Connolly entered the police headquarters. He stopped at the information desk near the main entrance.

"I'm supposed to meet Henry McNamara here," he said. "Have you seen him?"

"He's upstairs in Detective Hammond's office," the receptionist said. "Third floor."

Connolly walked across the lobby to the elevator and rode to the third floor. McNamara and Hammond were waiting when Connolly entered the room.

"Mr. Connolly," McNamara said. "I wasn't sure you'd get my message." The two shook hands. "You know Anthony Hammond?"

"We've had a few cases together," Connolly said.

Hammond acknowledged Connolly with a nod. They shook hands.

"If y'all will follow me," Hammond said, "we'll walk down to the evidence room."

They followed him to the end of the hall where a steel door guarded the entrance to the evidence room. Hammond unlocked the door and led them inside.

Beyond the door a small table with three metal folding chairs sat to the right. The table was shoved against a wall made of wire screen. On the other side of the screen were rows of shelves stuffed with boxes and bags of items collected as evidence in countless pending cases. To the left was a wall with a window that had been painted over. Ahead, opposite the door, was a second wall. Like the one to the right, it was made of wire screen. A door at the far-left side led past the wire screen into the evidence room.

Hammond pointed to the table.

"Wait here," he said. "I'll get the stuff."

He unlocked the door and stepped beyond the wire screen to the first row of shelves. There, he took out a large notebook, turned to the correct page, and noted the date, time, and evidence he was removing. Then he disappeared among the rows of shelves. In a few minutes he returned with a single large cardboard box.

"This is all there is," he said. He set the box on the table.

The box was sealed at the seams with tape. Each seam bore Hammond's signature. Using a small pocketknife, he sliced through the tape on top and opened the box.

Inside, each individual item was held in a clear plastic bag. White freezer tape, wrapped in a single continuous strand from top to bottom, sealed the bags closed. Each strand of tape bore Hammond's signature.

"If you want to open any of the bags, let me know," he said.

Connolly looked at McNamara.

"Go ahead," McNamara said. "You're the one who wanted to see it."

Connolly lifted the first item from the box, a large Ziploc bag with clothing inside.

"That's Attaway's pants," Hammond said. "His shirt should be in the package below it. Items from his pockets are in the bottom, I think."

Connolly turned over the package to see the other side, then laid it on the table. He took out the package containing the shirt, set it aside, and pulled out another package.

"That's his tie, belt, and a class ring we took from his right hand," Hammond said. "He was also wearing a wedding band, but we gave that to his wife. Thought she might want to put it on him when he was buried."

Connolly looked up at Hammond.

"Did you open this box to get it out?"

"No," Hammond said, shaking his head. "We kept it out. Figured she'd want it, so we didn't put it in here. This box hasn't been opened since I picked this stuff up from the coroner's office."

Connolly lifted another package from the box.

"That's his wallet," Hammond said.

"I'd like to look inside it," Connolly said.

"Sure," Hammond replied.

He took the package from Connolly and slit the tape seal. Carefully, he removed the wallet from the bag and handed it to Connolly.

Connolly slid a chair back from the table and took a seat. He unfolded the wallet and looked inside.

"Have you been through this?"

"Yes," Hammond said. "I looked inside it. I don't think we did a complete inventory on it, but nothing was removed, at least not since it came into my possession. The patrol officer who responded to the original call might have gone through it looking for some identification."

"This wallet is exactly like it was when you picked it up from the coroner's office?"

"Yes," Hammond said, puzzled. "Why?"

"I just want to make sure what we're dealing with,"

Connolly said. "Henry, you agree it's exactly like it was when Detective Hammond picked it up from Doc Morgan?"

"Yeah. Sure. If he says it is, I guess."

Connolly opened the wallet. In one end of the billfold portion he found several small pieces of paper. He gingerly lifted them out and laid them on the table. The first one was folded. He picked it up and unfolded it. Henry watched over his shoulder.

"What's that?"

"Tag receipt from 1999," Connolly said. "Looks like it went to a 1965 Chevrolet."

Connolly folded it and laid it aside, then picked up the next paper.

"Court reporter's business card," he said.

Next there was a small photograph of Attaway's daughter. Underneath the picture was a scrap of paper. On it was the word "Alpaca" and the numbers 41556943. Connolly felt the hair on the back of his neck stand up.

"Ever heard of Alpaca?" he asked, trying not to let his excitement show.

"No," McNamara replied. "You?"

"Some kind of exotic animal," he said, avoiding the question. "Lives in South America, I think."

"Wonder what those numbers are."

"Don't know," Connolly said.

He took out a pen and looked around for something to write on.

"I left my legal pad in the car," he said.

"I'll get you something to write on," Hammond offered.

"Don't worry about it," Connolly said. He took one of his own business cards from his pocket. "I'll write on this." He turned the card over and scribbled the name and numbers on the back.

He looked through the rest of the wallet, then peered inside the cardboard box.

"Should only be a pair of shoes left in the bottom," Hammond said.

Connolly handed him the wallet.

"I think I've seen all I need to see," he said.

"Okay," Hammond said. "I need you two to stand here with me while I seal this stuff up again. I don't want any questions about this when we get to court."

Late that afternoon, Connolly drove to Texas Street, a tough neighborhood off Broad Street south of downtown. He slowed the Chrysler to an idle. The car rolled quietly down the street. He leaned over the top of the steering wheel, looking intently through the windshield as he searched for the house. To his left a row of one-story houses faced the street, each one with a small patch of grass in front for a yard. A little further, he passed a junked car parked at the curb, its doors and hood missing. Children played inside it.

At the end of the block he crossed Galen Street. The houses there were larger, two- and three-story homes, and the yards were larger. But the houses were in no better shape. The larger ones had been turned into apartments. Trash littered the yards. In the middle of the block he found what he was looking for, 1833 Texas Street.

The Chrysler coasted to a stop at the curb in front. Connolly switched off the engine and got out. He walked to the front steps and reached for the doorbell. As he did, the door opened, and Craig stepped outside.

"I don't think this is a good time for you to be here," he said, his voice a coarse, raspy whisper.

"I just want to see my granddaughter," Connolly said.

Connolly moved to one side to step around him. Craig moved to block his way.

"But believe me," Craig insisted. "This isn't a good time."

Suddenly, Rachel appeared behind him at the door.

"Craig, who's out there?"

She craned her neck to see around him. Her eyes narrowed in anger when she saw Connolly.

"What are you doing here?" she hissed.

"Just want to see my granddaughter," Connolly replied.

Rachel stepped outside and pushed her way past Craig to face Connolly.

"Wait a minute," Craig said. He took her by the arm and pulled her back. "We aren't going to have a fight right here in the front yard."

"I told you before," she yelled at Connolly. "I don't want to see you again. I don't want you coming around here. You ruined my life. You're not going to ruin my daughter's."

Just then, the door opened again. A tall, broad-shouldered man stepped from the house. He wore a loosely fitting sleeveless T-shirt that gapped open around his arms, exposing his chest when he moved. He had the body of a weight lifter and the swagger of someone accustomed to using his size to his advantage. He strutted down the steps and elbowed his way between Rachel and Craig.

"Who are you?" Connolly said.

"This is Mark," Craig said.

Mark stopped in front of Connolly, his nose a few inches above Connolly's forehead. He glowered over Connolly.

"I didn't come here looking for any trouble," Connolly said. "I just want to see my granddaughter."

Suddenly, Barbara appeared in the open doorway behind them, holding Elizabeth in her arms. Dressed in a pink cotton dress, her hair perfectly in place, she was a stark contrast to the neighborhood that surrounded her.

"What's going on out here?" she demanded.

She glided down the steps and slipped between Rachel and Craig. Mark stepped aside to let her pass.

"Mother," Rachel snapped.

"I just wanted to see my granddaughter," Connolly repeated, his voice now quiet and calm.

Barbara stepped forward and handed her to him. Connolly slid both arms underneath the baby. Barbara gently deposited her in his arms.

Rachel was livid.

"No!" she yelled.

She pushed past Mark and Craig and stretched out her arms, groping for her daughter. Barbara moved in front of her to cut her off.

"Rachel, he's her grandfather," she said. "It won't do either of you any good to ignore it."

Connolly took the baby in his arms. Rachel burst into tears and rushed inside the house. Mark followed her. Craig waited behind Barbara near the steps.

Elizabeth was wrapped in a pink blanket. Connolly pulled it from around her face and held her close. She looked up at him and seemed to smile. A grin broke across his face. She smiled again, squirmed once, then lay still. In a moment, she drifted off to sleep. As he watched her sleeping in his arms, his eyes grew full and moist.

In a few minutes, Barbara stepped toward him and held out her hands.

"We need to get her inside," she said quietly.

Connolly bent low, as if hugging the baby, and turned his face toward Barbara.

"Is it safe for her in there?" he whispered.

"I think so," Barbara replied.

Connolly lifted Elizabeth to his face, whispered in her ear, then handed her to Barbara.

Tears streamed down his face as he turned away. He watched from the car as they went inside. When the door closed, he turned the car around and drove away.

At the corner beyond the house, he slowed for the stop sign. He reached across the front seat to the glove box and took out the flask. As he drove through the intersection, he took a sip. His body shook with uncontrollable emotion. He pounded the steering wheel in frustration. Finally, he stopped the car, threw open the door, and jumped out.

"Why?" he screamed. "Why did things turn out this way?"

He hurled the flask into a vacant lot across the street. As he did, a car horn blared. He jumped aside, narrowly missing the front fender of an oncoming station wagon.

"Are you crazy?" the driver shouted.

Connolly staggered several steps backward as the car continued past.

Behind him, a young boy stood straddling his bicycle at the edge of the street. Suddenly ashamed, Connolly turned aside and tumbled into the Chrysler. He put the car in gear and drove away.

Twenty-Two

From Texas Street, Connolly drove toward midtown. At Florida Street, he turned left and steered the Chrysler into the parking lot in front of Midtown Liquor. Not long after that, his memory began to fade.

Two days later, maybe three, Connolly opened his eyes and found himself in bed. In the pale light of dawn his eyes darted around the room as he struggled to remember where he was and how he got there. Curtains over the windows seemed familiar. Pictures on the dresser seemed to be of someone he knew. He rubbed his hands over his eyes as if to somehow wipe away the fog inside his head.

Outside, the sun was already up. It shone through a gap in the curtains, creating a line across the darkness of the room. He lay in bed and watched as the line of sunlight moved toward him. Slowly, his mind began to clear. The room, he realized, was his bedroom, but no matter how he tried he could not remember where he had been, or how he came to be in the bed.

He dropped his hands from his face and felt his arm strike something beside him. Startled, he rolled on his side and found Marisa lying next to him. She groaned and rolled on her side to face him.

"You finally waking up?" she smiled.

"Yeah," he replied, trying to remember her name. "What day is it?"

"Sunday," she said. "You okay?"

"Yeah. Why?"

"You were really out of it there for a while," she said.

"Yeah? Pretty bad?"

"You don't remember?"

"No," he said, shaking his head.

He raised his head off the pillow and looked around.

"What time is it?"

"About seven, I think."

A searing pain shot through his left temple. He dropped his head to the pillow and closed his eyes. He pressed the palms of his hands against his forehead in a futile effort to rub away the ache in his head. As he lay there, random thoughts bounced through his mind. He thought of the office, Keyton Attaway, the steps outside St. Pachomius Church.

Connolly's eyes popped open.

"Did you say it's Sunday?"

"Yes," Marisa said softly. "Sunday. We have the whole day to ourselves."

She slid her leg over his and draped her arm across his chest. Her head rested against his shoulder.

"Sunday," he muttered.

He pushed her leg away and rolled back the covers. Marisa's head flopped against the bed as he pulled himself to a sitting position.

"What are you doing?" she exclaimed.

He checked his wrist for his watch. It was gone.

"Where's my watch?"

"I found it on the floor," Marisa replied. "I put it in your pants."

She rolled away and pulled the covers under her chin.

Connolly found his pants on a chair next to the bed. He dug the watch from the pocket and checked the time.

"Seven-thirty," he grumbled.

He slid his feet to the floor and pushed himself out of bed.

"Where are you going?" Marisa sighed.

"Shower," he replied.

She threw back the covers and raised herself on one arm.

"I'll come with you," she said, smiling.

Connolly glanced at her with a sly grin, then shook his head as he shuffled out of the room.

"No time for that now," he said.

Frustrated, Marisa fell back on her pillow and pulled the covers over her head.

Sometime later, Connolly emerged from the bathroom and padded to the closet in search of a clean shirt. He opened the closet door and stared in disbelief. Inside, he found a row of neatly laundered shirts hanging next to four freshly cleaned suits.

Still in bed, Marisa glanced from beneath the cover as he entered the room.

"That lady brought those by," she said.

"That lady?"

"You know, that old lady. The one at your office."

"Mrs. Gordon?" he whispered.

"Yeah," she said. "Gordon. That's her name. Said you'd need them."

He took a shirt from the closet and slipped it on.

"You want to go with me?" he asked.

Marisa looked puzzled.

"Go with you? Where?"

"Church," he said.

"Church?" She had a sour look on her face. "Why are you going to church?"

Connolly paused, his fingers holding the top button of his shirt.

"I don't know," he said. He paused, wondering why, indeed, he was going. Finally, he shrugged his shoulders. "Seems like the thing to do. Thought I might find something there that would help."

"Help? With what?"

"With the case," he replied. "Seemed to be a pretty important place for Attaway."

Marisa looked even more puzzled than before.

"What case? Who's Attaway?"

"Keyton Attaway. You know. Avery Thompson's case."

"I have no idea what you're talking about," she said. She rolled away and pulled the sheet under her chin once again.

Connolly slipped a tie around his neck. With a few quick twists of his wrists, he tied it in a knot and pulled it snug against his collar. He stepped to the bed and slipped the cover back from Marisa's face.

"I'll be back for lunch," he said.

He pressed his lips against hers, but she did not respond. He threw the cover over her head and walked up the hall. In the kitchen, he opened a cabinet near the sink and took down a bottle of gin. He twisted off the cap and took a gulp, then another, then stepped toward the door.

From the apartment, he drove downtown and parked near the courthouse. It was only a short walk from there to St. Pachomius Church. He slipped through a side door and took a seat in the sanctuary to the left of the chancel, near the front.

From there, the door was only a few feet away, just in case he needed to slip out after the service started.

The sanctuary was quiet. He checked his watch. It was nine-thirty. He had arrived an hour before the service started.

The rack on the back of the pew in front of him held several books. He took one out and looked at the front cover. It was the *Book of Common Prayer.* As he leafed through the pages, his eyes fell on the Psalms of David, located near the back of the book. It had been a long time since he had seen a prayer book, and longer still since he had read any of the psalms. With nothing else to do, he began to read.

In what seemed like only minutes, a piano began to play in the far-right corner of the sanctuary. Not the hymns he had known as a child, songs he had never heard before. Connolly looked around. The sanctuary was full. He glanced at his watch. He had been reading for almost an hour.

The piano continued to play. Soon, the congregation was standing and singing, arms lifted over their heads, eyes closed, bodies swaying with the music. Connolly laid aside the prayer book and stood too, to avoid drawing attention to himself. This was nothing like the Episcopal Church he had known before.

He looked slowly around expecting to see the sanctuary filled with men in business suits and women in expensive dresses. What he saw left him unnerved.

Next to him was a man dressed in a white T-shirt and blue jeans. His long, oily hair was pulled into a ponytail that flopped near the middle of his back. Beside him stood a woman wearing a long, flowing dress that was tie-dyed with strange multicolored swirls like something from the sixties. Behind him was a man with a gold earring in the lobe of his right ear. Next to him was a young girl with a silver stud through the side of her nose. She noticed Connolly looking at her and smiled. As she opened her mouth to sing he saw she had a gold stud through her tongue.

Connolly wasn't sure he was in the right place.

After a while the music softened into a gentle melody. The sanctuary grew quiet but for the rustling of the congregation still swaying, eyes closed, hands lifted in the air. Then in a loud voice he heard Father Scott calling from the back of the church.

"This is St. Pachomius Church, bringing Christ to the world, and the world to Christ."

As the words rang through the sanctuary, a pipe organ began to play a traditional hymn. At the organ console situated on the left side of the chancel, near the choir, a young man dressed in a traditional choir robe attacked the keys. The organ pipes, arranged across the back wall of the balcony, made the building rumble. Connolly felt the floor vibrate beneath his feet. Around him, the congregation began to sing.

An acolyte processed down the center aisle. In his hands he carried a long, brass pole. Atop the pole was an ornate cross. Behind the cross, a second acolyte carried another brass pole. From it hung a purple banner. Next came the choir, followed by Father Scott. The congregation continued to sing as the procession made its way down the center aisle to the front of the sanctuary and then up the marble steps to the chancel. This part of the service was familiar to Connolly. He relaxed for a moment thinking the service would follow a more traditional pattern.

In a few minutes, however, someone started playing the piano again. The congregation, still standing, began singing more songs he had never heard. From somewhere near the piano a flute lifted high, shrill notes in the air. Connolly craned his neck to see who was playing. While he struggled to find the flute, he heard the sound of a violin and cello joining the music. Then someone appeared with an electric guitar, and a moment later the drums began.

Soon everyone was clapping and swaying to the music as they had before the service began. A man in the pew in front of Connolly stepped into the aisle and began to dance. Several more joined him. Connolly glanced to his left for a clear path to the exit and saw someone unrolling white butcher paper in the aisle. He watched in horror as they taped the paper along the wall, covering the bottoms of the stained-glass windows.

While several danced in front, between the pews and the chancel railing, others moved from the pews to the wall near Connolly and began to draw. The music continued to play. Everyone was singing. Those still in the pews were swaying and jumping with the rhythm.

Connolly was ready to leave.

Then he noticed his finger tapping the back of the pew in front of him. His leg moved in time with the music. He chuckled at himself and decided to stay.

He had come expecting the condescending glare of former friends who knew all too well how he lived and what had happened to his life. He was sure he would encounter an overwhelming sense of condemnation. Instead, those seated around him seemed warm and welcoming.

Twenty-Three

Monday morning, Connolly roamed around the office like a nervous cat, fidgeting with the copier, plundering through the file cabinets, and rearranging things on his desk. Finally, Mrs. Gordon appeared at the door.

"Why don't you go out for a walk?" she said. "Go down to Port City Diner for some coffee or something."

Connolly glanced up from behind his desk.

"What for?"

"You're driving me crazy," she said. "All this moving around in here. You're worse than a hyperactive kid."

Connolly slumped in his chair. Mrs. Gordon leaned against the doorframe.

"What's got you so worked up?"

"Nothing," he replied. He checked his watch. "I think you're right." He stood. "I'm going down to the diner. Want anything?"

"No," she said. "Just a little peace and quiet around here."

She turned away and walked up the hallway to her desk. Connolly took his jacket from the coat rack and followed her. Out front, he slipped past her desk and into the corridor outside.

On the street, he turned to walk to the diner, then hesitated. Instead, he walked to the Chrysler and slipped in behind the steering wheel. He placed the key in the ignition switch and turned it, the engine came to life.

He steered the car away from the curb and drove to the corner at St. Joseph Street. There, he turned right and two blocks later turned right again onto Government Street. Several blocks later, he turned onto Broad Street and then left onto Old Shell Road and continued west through midtown.

A few miles beyond Florida Street, he entered the community of Spring Hill. Houses on either side of the road suddenly became larger, the lawns more expansive. Wrought-iron fences with automatic gates kept intruders and curious sightseers at bay.

Past Spring Hill College, the road passed through a section of shops and businesses. Beyond McGregor Avenue, Connolly slowed the car and turned into a gravel parking lot in front of The Pink Flamingo, a flower and gift shop that catered to the exclusive neighborhood around it. Connolly parked the car and went inside.

The shop was owned by Tootsie Trehern, a large woman with bleached white hair and a stern, matronly disposition. She wore tiny reading glasses that she kept perched on her nose, and she peered out over them in a way that stretched her eyelids upward and arched her eyebrows in a suspicious scowl.

She was behind the counter when Connolly entered. He slipped past a shelf of glass giftware and tried to disappear behind a row of ferns in the next aisle. Even so, he could feel Tootsie's eyes bearing down on him.

He moved quickly to the back of the shop and found Barbara carefully arranging plants in a large clay pot. She lifted her head only long enough to glare at him.

"What are you doing here?"

Her voice was low, but intense. Her head was bent over the flowers in the pot.

"I wanted to see you a minute."

Tootsie appeared to Connolly's left, emerging from a cluster of tall green corn plants.

"Get that finished as soon as you can," she said to Barbara, her voice barely concealing a note of irritation. Her head was cocked forward so she could see over the reading glasses on her nose. She looked down at Barbara, ignoring Connolly. "You need to get started on those plants for Billie Crosby."

"I'll be done in a minute," Barbara smiled.

Tootsie moved away. Connolly grinned.

"Glad to see she still doesn't like me," he snickered.

Barbara shoved a handful of dirt into the pot and packed it around the plants.

"Don't start anything," she replied. "I need this job."

Two ladies dressed in white tennis skirts with pink trim passed by. Their eyes ran quickly over Connolly's rumpled suit as they glanced down at Barbara. The condescending look they gave showed in an instant what they thought of them both. They turned away and moved toward the front. Connolly noticed the imperious way they lifted their chins when they looked at Barbara. He felt a knife stab his soul. He took a breath and pushed it aside.

"I didn't come here to start any trouble," he said. "I just wanted to thank you for what you did the other day at Rachel's."

Barbara continued to work while he talked.

"I didn't do it for you," she replied.

Connolly sighed.

"Well, I appreciate it anyway," he said.

"You better go," Barbara insisted. "Tootsie will be mad the rest of the morning."

A broad grin broke across Connolly's face.

"I count it an honor to have that woman mad at me," he said.

"Yeah, well, she'll take it out on me," Barbara replied. "So, go."

Connolly chuckled as he turned to leave.

"Barbara," he said.

She glanced up at him.

"I really appreciate it."

A brief, faint smile flickered across her face, then disappeared in a frown.

"Go," she said.

She gestured with a wave of her hand.

Twenty-Four

*C*onnolly left the flower shop and stopped at the office.

"Feeling any better?" Mrs. Gordon said as he closed the door.

He crossed the reception area and took a seat in a chair near her desk.

"I'm thinking about going over to Keyton Attaway's house."

She frowned at him in disbelief.

"What for?"

"Thought I might talk to Karen."

Mrs. Gordon shook her head.

"You've been drinking something besides gin this morning."

Connolly acknowledged her with a smile.

"Think it would upset her?"

Mrs. Gordon looked askance.

"What do you think?"

"Their priest told me Keyton had been worried about something the past few weeks. I was hoping she would tell me what it was."

Mrs. Gordon turned to the work on her desk.

"I doubt she'd be interested in helping acquit the man who killed her husband."

Connolly stood and rapped his knuckles on Mrs. Gordon's desk. She jumped at the sound.

"He's not guilty until the jury says so."

Mrs. Gordon rolled her eyes.

"Right," she replied. "You'll have a hard time convincing her of that. Maybe you ought to try something else."

"Got nowhere else to go," he said. "I'm fresh out of new ideas." He started toward the door. "If I'm not back by lunch, send out a search party."

Mrs. Gordon heaved a deep sigh. Connolly opened the door.

"Don't worry," he smiled. "I'll behave."

Keyton Attaway had lived in a house on Dog River about twenty-five miles south of Mobile. The house, a large white Creole cottage, sat under moss-draped oaks on a little knoll that was just high enough to keep the house and lawn dry when the rising tide backed the river into the surrounding swamp.

Connolly eased the car up to the house and parked next to a dark green Chevrolet Suburban. As he stepped from the car door, he heard voices from the back yard. He closed the car door and walked around to the corner of the house.

Karen Attaway sat in a wicker chase lounge chair. A man sat in a chair beside her. A woman sat in a beach chair directly in front of her. They were enjoying a lively conversation until Connolly appeared. Karen fell silent. Her face became somber and serious.

"Hello, Mike," she said, as he strode forward.

"Karen," he said, nodding. "You look well."

"Thank you." She remained seated on the lounge chair. "I've had some rough days, but I'll be alright." The words caught in her throat. Her eyes grew moist. She picked up a glass of tea from the ground beside her chair and sipped from it. "Mike," she said, regaining her composure. "This is Connie Patronas and her husband, Jake."

"Good to meet you," they replied.

"You want something to drink, Mike? All I have is iced tea."

"No, thanks."

He felt awkward, standing while they were seated, but there wasn't a chair nearby.

"Well," she said, "I see they appointed you to defend Keyton's murderer." Her genteel tone of voice had a distinct edge. "That why you came out here?"

"I wanted to see you anyway," he replied. "But, yes, there are a few things I need to ask you."

Her face slipped from serious to cold.

"You haven't seen me in over a year. I doubt you care about me one way or the other. Why don't you just ask me whatever it is you want to know and get it over with? Then you can get out of here and leave me alone."

Connolly slipped his hands in his pockets. He glanced away, then back.

"Maybe this isn't ... the ... ahh."

"Well, ask them," she snapped.

Jake stood and moved away from his chair. He motioned for Connie to follow. When they were gone, Connolly moved to the chair in front of Karen and sat down.

"I've talked to several people about Keyton," Connolly said. "They seem to think he was bothered by something the last few weeks before he was killed. Did he talk to you about anything like that?"

Karen looked away.

"Not really," she said. She turned back to Connolly. "I

mean, he always had something on his mind. Nothing more than usual."

"Have you ever heard him talk about something called Alpaca?"

Karen took a sip of iced tea from the glass in her hand.

"No."

"Ever hear him mention that name?"

"No, I said." She answered before the last word was out of his mouth. Her voice grew louder. "What's all this got to do with Keyton's murder?"

"I'm not sure," Connolly said. In contrast, his voice was even and low. "The word Alpaca was written on his calendar on a Saturday in May. There was also a scrap of paper in his wallet with that name on it and a number, like maybe a telephone number or an account number."

She looked away again, avoiding his gaze.

"I ... I don't know anything about that," she said.

Connolly pressed the question.

"You sure?"

Her head jerked around as her eyes focused on him once again.

"Yes, I'm sure," she snapped.

"What about Truman Albritton?"

"What about him?"

"Were he and Keyton in some kind of business?"

She shifted in the lounge chair.

"I don't know. They were friends. I think they had some cases they worked on together."

"Did they spend a lot of time together?"

"I don't know about 'a lot.' They saw each other." She had a puzzled look on her face. "Where are you going with this? Why are you asking about Albritton?"

"Ted Morgan says Truman identified the body at the morgue."

"So?"

"Did you ask him to do that?"

"He offered to help. I didn't really care to look for myself. I made it as far as the door. Saw his feet hanging off the cart. I knew it was him. I don't see how any of that is any of your business anyway."

"So, you actually went to the morgue?"

"Yeah," Karen replied. "I went down there."

She was growing more frustrated with each question.

"Did Truman take you?"

"If you want to know the truth, Truman came down here with the police when they told me Keyton was dead."

"He rode with the police?"

"No," she exclaimed, exasperated. "He drove his own car but came at the same time. He met them down here. They told me what happened. Connie and Jake came over. They drove me to the hospital. Truman met us there." She sipped from the glass of iced tea in her hand. "You got any more stupid questions?"

"Just a few," he said. "I understand Keyton was cremated."

"Yes," she sighed. "Spread his ashes out there in the river." She pointed across the yard. "They came in a plastic bag inside a cardboard box. We buried the box and bag over there in that flower bed." She pointed to a spot near the house. "Seemed like the thing to do. Most of him's in the river. What's left is in the flower garden. How much longer is this going to take?"

"How well did Keyton know Leigh Ann Agostino?"

"What are you talking about?"

Karen glared at him. Connolly took a deep breath.

"There's some indication they might have been together in Leigh Ann's car over there on Pinto Island when Keyton was shot."

"And?"

Connolly gave a nervous smile.

"Were they seeing each other?"

"Are you out of your mind?" Her eyes were on fire. "You have no idea what you're talking about," she snapped.

Her arm flew forward hurling the glass of iced tea toward him. He ducked. The glass sailed over his head and landed on the grass. Ice and tea flew through the air.

"Listen to me," he said. "I'm only trying to—"

"I've heard enough of this," she shouted.

"I'm not—"

Connolly tried to explain, but she cut him off.

"Get off my property," she screamed.

"Karen," he implored.

"Get out of here," she screamed again. "Go soak your head in a gin bottle somewhere. Do whatever it is you do with that … that girl you have living with you. Just leave me alone."

Jake hurried across the lawn toward them. Connolly stood to leave. Jake reached Karen's chair.

"You need some help here, Karen?"

He stepped around the chair toward Mike.

"You don't want any of me," Connolly growled.

Jake stopped a few feet away and glared at him.

"Time for you to go, pal," he said.

Connolly pushed past him and walked away.

Connolly backed the Chrysler away from Attaway's house and turned it around. At the end of the driveway he glanced in the rearview mirror. Behind him he could see Jake standing beside the house, arms folded across his chest. The scowl on his face made Connolly chuckle.

Twenty-Five

*C*onnolly reached the office shortly after noon. Mrs. Gordon was seated at her desk when he arrived.

"I was about to send out that search party," she said.

Her head was bent over the files on her desk. She spoke without looking up. Connolly pushed the door closed behind him and passed her desk without replying. When he reached the hallway, Mrs. Gordon looked up. A puzzled frown wrinkled her eyebrows.

"How was Karen?"

"She's alright," he called as he moved down the hall.

Mrs. Gordon pushed her chair away from the desk and leaned her head back to see him.

"You two get into a fight?"

He reached the door to his office and turned toward her.

"I wouldn't call it a fight," he replied.

Mrs. Gordon rose from her chair and came to his office. She stopped at the doorway and leaned against the doorframe, her arms folded across her chest.

"What happened?"

Connolly flopped into the chair behind his desk.

"I asked her a few questions. She didn't like them. Threw a glass of iced tea at me. Told me to leave."

Her eyes brightened. Connolly propped his feet on the desk and leaned his head against the wall.

"Did it hit you?"

His eyes were closed. His hands rested in his lap.

"Nah," he replied. "She missed."

Mrs. Gordon's countenance dropped.

"Too bad."

She turned to leave.

"Close the door on your way out," he reminded her.

She pulled the door closed and walked up the hallway to her desk.

Later that afternoon, Connolly left the office and went downstairs to the street. Dark clouds were building to the south. Thunder rumbled in the distance. He checked the sky, looked at his watch, and started toward the corner. As he turned left toward Government Street a cool breeze blew in his face. Rain wasn't far off. He quickened his pace.

He crossed the street in front of the courthouse at a trot and hurried on to Church Street. From there, he moved quickly down the block to St. Pachomius Church. Large drops of rain fell as he rushed up the steps. He darted past the columns at the top of the steps and moved under the portico.

Rain poured from the sky in sheets driven by the southern wind. Huge drops spattered about his feet as he reached the door. In a hurry, he charged into the door, pushing against it with his shoulder and forearm. The door flew open. He stumbled forward across the threshold. He caught himself, then shoved the door closed. As he did, a bolt of lightning lit up the front of the church. Thunder tumbled through the dark clouds above the giant oaks outside and rattled the walls inside.

In the narthex, he brushed the rainwater from his shoulders and ran his fingers through his hair. He straightened his jacket, then made his way down the aisle to the right. His shoes made a clicking noise on the stone floor. The sanctuary, dim even on a sunny day, was dark except for three small lights above the altar at the far end of the chancel in the front of the church.

At the front, he made his way to the middle aisle and took a seat on a pew in the second row. The room was quiet. The sound of the rain and thunder faded away. He crossed his legs, folded his hands in his lap, and sat in silence.

"If you've come with more questions about Keyton Attaway, I'm afraid I've told you all I know."

Startled at the sound of a voice, he turned to see Father Scott coming from behind him down the center aisle.

"No," Connolly replied. "No questions about Keyton today. At least none you could answer."

Father Scott was at the end of the pew now. He nudged Connolly on the shoulder and motioned for him to move over. Connolly slid down the pew and Father Scott took a seat beside him.

"Saw you in church yesterday," Father Scott said. "For a while there I thought you were going to leave."

Connolly smiled.

"I thought about it," he said. "Not much like the St. Pachomius I knew before."

"People have changed a lot since then. Did you enjoy the service?"

"Yeah," Connolly said. He glanced around the sanctuary as he spoke. "I always liked this old church. But I was a little afraid to come back."

"Oh?" Father Scott replied. "Why's that?"

"I figured God would be mad at me."

"Was he?"

"No," Connolly said, shaking his head. "Didn't feel like it."

Father Scott nodded.

"You didn't take Communion."

"No," Connolly said, lowering his head. "Didn't seem right." His voice dropped to a whisper. "Too much has happened just to ... show up and ... partake."

They sat in silence a moment. Connolly grew uncomfortable. He glanced around the sanctuary again. His eyes fell on the stained-glass windows.

"I like the windows in here."

Father Scott followed Connolly's eyes to the windows on the left side of the sanctuary. He stood and stepped from the pew to the aisle.

"You ever look closely at them?"

Connolly shrugged his shoulders in response.

"Come on," Father Scott said.

He moved slowly up the aisle. Connolly slipped out of the pew and followed him. They stopped in front of the last window.

"All of these pictures capture a moment in the life of Christ," Father Scott said, with a broad, sweeping gesture. He paused, then pointed to the window in front of them. "This one is the one where the rich young ruler asks about the cost of discipleship."

They gazed at it a moment. Even in the dim light the images in the window seemed to glow.

"Beautiful window," Connolly said.

"Tiffany window," Father Scott replied. "Been here a long time."

"Must have been expensive, even years ago."

"Very."

Father Scott turned to move down the aisle. Connolly dropped his gaze to the bottom of the window.

"What's that?" he asked, pointing.

Father Scott turned to look. Near the bottom of the window was the image of a cat.

Father Scott chuckled.

"The lady who gave that window loved her cat," he explained. "She was certain her cat would go to heaven with her. When she gave the window, she insisted on putting that in there."

"Think she made it?"

"The woman? I never knew her. That window's been in here about a hundred years, I think."

"No," Connolly replied. "The cat. Think the cat made it to heaven?"

"I don't know." Father Scott moved a few steps down the aisle. "All of creation groans in travail, awaiting redemption."

A quizzical frown creased Connolly's brow.

"Is that Proverbs?"

"No," Father Scott replied. "Paul." He pointed to the second window. "You know what that one is, don't you?"

Connolly glanced at the next window.

"Looks like that guy in the tree. Nicodemus."

Father Scott nodded. "Zacchaeus."

"Yeah," Connolly said. "Zacchaeus."

Father Scott took a few steps farther down the aisle.

"The next one is Nicodemus," he said, pointing. "And the one after that is the woman at the well."

Connolly glanced at the third window. They stood there a moment, then Father Scott turned to him.

"Come on," he said.

Father Scott moved down the aisle and up the marble steps to the chancel. Connolly hesitated. Father Scott gestured to him with his hand and urged him forward. Connolly slowly made his way up to the chancel and past the rows of choir pews.

At the far end of the chancel was the altar railing. Beyond it was the altar table. On the table was a cross, flanked by silver candlesticks sat at either end holding tall white candles.

Behind the table, a stained-glass window rose from the floor all the way to the top of the wall. The scene on the window depicted Christ, his arms outstretched, his hands nailed to a cross.

"All of those windows out there," Father Scott said, nodding over his shoulder, "depict a moment in the life of Christ and in the lives of those he came in contact with." He paused and pointed to the window behind the altar. "This one depicts a moment in your life. A moment you can enter, or avoid."

Connolly glanced at the window, then turned away. Nervous and uncomfortable, he took a step to one side. Father Scott took him by the shoulder. Connolly jumped, startled by his touch. Father Scott didn't seem to notice.

"Let me pray for you before you go," he said.

He guided Connolly to a kneeling position at the altar rail. The building was so quiet it seemed to cause a roaring noise in Connolly's ears. He leaned forward against the rail and bowed his head. Father Scott stood behind him.

"O Lord, pour out Your Spirit on Mike as he kneels here in Your presence." Father Scott moved his hand from Connolly's shoulder to his head as he prayed, his voice echoing through the sanctuary. "Drive out all evil spirits from his life. Fill him with Your presence, with the power of Your Holy Spirit. Restore his life. Renew his life. Fill him with Your peace. In the name of the Father, and of the Son, and of the Holy Spirit. Amen."

They remained there a moment, Father Scott's hand on Connolly's head. Everything but that moment washed away from Connolly's mind. To his surprise, he found the moment peaceful and reassuring.

Connolly opened his eyes. As he glanced about, he noticed the candles on the altar table were lit. He was sure they had not been lit before. Then he felt his hands slip from the railing as he tumbled backward.

When he opened his eyes, he was lying on his back on the floor. He lay there a moment, staring at the stained glass of a skylight in the ceiling high above the chancel floor.

He raised himself to a sitting position and glanced toward the altar. His eyes moved quickly to the candles standing tall and straight in the silver candleholders. The wick at the top was fresh, clean, and unburned.

Father Scott was kneeling at the altar rail. He turned his head and smiled over his shoulder at the bewildered look on Connolly's face. They remained there in silence for what seemed like a long time: Connolly on the floor, Father Scott at the altar rail. Finally, Connolly spoke.

"What happened to me?"

Father Scott slid from the kneeler at the altar rail to a sitting position on the floor.

"The Spirit of the Living God passed over the altar."

Connolly had no idea what he was talking about.

"The Spirit ... The candles were lit."

An irrepressible grin stretched across Connolly's face. Father Scott smiled.

"The candles were lit," Connolly repeated, his almost a laugh. "Before I passed out. I saw the flames." They both glanced toward the candles. "But now they're fresh, new, unused. Like they've never been lit before." Connolly looked at Father Scott. The grin faded. The bewildered look returned. "How?"

"How?" Father Scott stood. "You know the 'how' of it. The

question you need to ask is 'why?'" He gestured with his hand for Connolly to stand. "Come on," he said. "I'll walk with you to the door."

Connolly sat on the floor, watching as Father Scott moved away. Father Scott stopped a few feet away and glanced back at him, waiting. Finally, Connolly stood. They made their way out of the chancel to the sanctuary and walked side by side up the center aisle.

"So, what was that all about?" Connolly said.

"'What' is something I can't tell you," Father Scott said. "I don't know the 'what' of it." He smiled a gentle, indulgent smile. "'Who?' Now that's a question I can answer."

Connolly felt more confused than ever.

"Who?"

"Yes. Who," Father Scott repeated. "Who passed over the altar to meet us here today? That I can answer."

They reached the doors at the back of the sanctuary. Father Scott paused as he grasped the handle to open the door. Connolly caught his eye and gave him a frustrated smile.

"You mean God?"

Father Scott winced.

"You say his name like he's just a religious concept. Religious concepts don't do what we saw and felt here today."

Connolly shrugged. He hadn't thought this much in years. The only words he thought about were the ones written on a gin bottle.

"The One who appeared today is much more personal," Father Scott continued. "The One whom we encountered today is the Ancient of Days. The Spirit who 'brooded upon the face of the deep.' Exceedingly personal. That is the One who met you here today. What he wants of you, only you can answer."

Connolly looked dismayed, his face consumed by the questions in his mind. Father Scott smiled.

"Think of it as a journey," he said. "One that has just begun. Questions are a good thing."

Connolly turned away, letting his eyes scan across the sanctuary one last time. A journey. Without forming the thoughts in his mind, he knew deep inside there were people in his life who would never make this trip. He wasn't sure he could either. A sense of sadness flittered across his soul.

"What if I don't want to go?"

He turned toward the door, the words barely audible, slipping quietly from between his lips. Father Scott's eyes bore in on him.

"Why would you ever refuse?"

He opened the door to the portico outside. The rain had stopped. Water dripped from the limbs of the oak trees hanging over the church and trickled off the eaves of the building. The air was clean but heavy and damp.

Connolly moved past him and made his way down the steps.

Twenty-Six

*I*t was late when Connolly returned to the office. Mrs. Gordon was gathering her things to leave when he walked through the door.

"Didn't expect you'd still be here," he said.

"Had to wait for the rain to let up," she replied. "Left my umbrella in the car. Karen Attaway called this afternoon."

"Yeah? What did she want?"

"Wanted to talk to you. She wants you to call her back." Mrs. Gordon handed him a note with the telephone number. "Said she was afraid she had been a little rude to you when you came to see her. I think she's feeling bad about it."

He took the note and started toward his office. Halfway down the hall he paused.

"Mrs. Gordon?"

He spoke without turning around.

"Yes?"

"Have you ever … ahh …" He tried again. "Could you …" His shoulders slumped. He threw his hands up in a gesture of frustration. "Never mind."

He continued down the hall toward his office. Mrs. Gordon watched with concern as he slipped off his jacket and hung it neatly on the coat rack near the door.

"Good night," he called, and closed the door.

In his office, he moved to the desk and opened the bottom drawer. Two gin bottles clanked together, one full, the other half empty. He lifted both from the drawer and set them on the desktop, then listened for Mrs. Gordon. The office was quiet. He slipped to the door and eased it open to look down the hall.

Satisfied she was gone, he returned to his chair behind the desk, twisted the top off the half-empty bottle, and took a sip. He felt the hint of a bite as it slid over his tongue and down his throat. He tipped the bottle up for a second drink, then paused. Slowly, he lowered it to his lap. Holding it by the neck, he rested it against his stomach and leaned back in the chair.

His mind wandered briefly back to St. Pachomius. Then, as if transported in time, he saw himself sitting on the steps outside the house on Ann Street. Barbara stood behind him. Together they watched as Rachel rode her bicycle in the front yard. It was a picturesque moment filled with laughter.

From up the street a car approached and came to a stop in front of the house. He rose from the steps and walked toward it. With each step, the expression on Barbara's face melted from bright and cheerful, to disappointment and anguish. Across the lawn, Rachel called to him. He continued forward, ignoring her.

At the car, he opened the door and leaned inside to speak with the driver. In a moment, he turned and waved to Barbara, then got inside. As the car drove away he could see the man behind the wheel was John Agostino.

The memory vanished as quickly as it came. Connolly stared ahead at the gin bottle sitting on the desk. Tears rolled down his cheeks. He had all but forgotten that day. Agostino had made partner. A group of their law school classmates hastily threw together a party to celebrate. Barbara begged him not to go. He went anyway. He made it home the next morning as Rachel left for school. In a drunken stupor, he barely noticed her.

At the time, it had been just another day. He hadn't given it much thought then, but things changed after that. Before long, he was spending longer days at the office. Some nights he didn't come home at all, and when he did, he sat in the den and drank. He had walked away from more than the steps that day, and the night he spent in inebriated celebration had been more than a benign moment in life. It was for him the beginning of a long, dark odyssey that cost him everything he ever held dear.

As he stared at the bottle on the desk, he heard the door open out front. Footsteps approached in the hallway. He wiped his eyes with the back of his hand.

In a moment, Mrs. Gordon appeared at the door, clutching her purse in one hand and a rain-soaked newspaper in the other. Her face was its usual blank slate, but her eyes were alive with excitement as if she, too, knew what lay ahead.

"Want me to take you home?"

He shook his head in response.

"You can stay with me," she said.

"I'll be alright," he said. "Marisa will be home later."

Mrs. Gordon scowled.

"Could be a long night," she suggested.

"I'll be alright," he repeated.

His voice was sharp, his tone irritable. Mrs. Gordon stared at him a moment, then turned aside and disappeared up the hallway. He heard the door to the corridor close. When she was gone, he slipped his feet from the desktop and grabbed both bottles.

In the break room, he set the full bottle on the ledge above the sink. Holding the other bottle by the neck, he turned it up to pour the contents down the drain. His hand trembled. Every cell in his body cried out for a drink. He put the bottle to his lips, but his lips refused to open. He held it there a moment without taking a drink.

"Just a little sip," his body urged. "Just enough to get home."

In the mirror behind the sink he saw himself standing there, the bottle pressed to his mouth. It struck him as humorous. A grown man, sucking a bottle. He burst into laughter.

In an instant, he snatched the bottle away and poured the gin down the drain. Without hesitating, he broke the seal on the full bottle and poured it out also. The smell of liquor wafted up from the sink and tickled his nose.

"No," he shouted. "I am not taking a drink."

Hearing himself say those words seemed to break the tension of the moment. His body relaxed somewhat, and the voices in his mind grew quiet. He turned on the water to dilute the gin. When that didn't eliminate the odor, he poured dish detergent in the sink.

With the water running, he ran back to his office and opened a filing cabinet along the wall beyond his desk. From the back of the drawer he took out another bottle of gin. He held it by the neck and walked back to the break room.

This time, he turned his head to avoid seeing the label and breathing the scent as he poured the gin into the sink.

When all three bottles were empty, he turned off the water and tossed them into the trashcan. He took a deep breath and tried to relax. The trembling in his hands grew more pronounced. His skin felt damp and clammy. He leaned against the sink for support.

As he stood there, trying to decide whether to drive home

or spend another night at the office, he glanced to one side. His eyes fell on the trash can and the three empty bottles. Less than a teaspoon of gin had collected in the bottom of each bottle. He wet his lips with his tongue and thought about the taste of just those few drops and the relief they would bring.

In a fit of rage, he snatched one of the bottles from the trash can. Raising it high over his head, he slammed it into the can with all his might. All three bottles exploded in a spray of glass sending splinters and slivers across the room.

"I am not taking a drink!" he screamed. "Don't you understand?" His face was red. The veins along his temples bulged. "I don't want you anymore."

Connolly took his jacket from the coat rack by the door in his office and drove to his apartment. By the time he got inside he was shaking so violently he could barely undress. He stripped off his clothes as best he could, pulling his shirt off over his head and leaving it with his trousers in a pile near the bedroom door. He jumped into bed and pulled the covers up around his chin.

With Marisa at the club, the apartment was quiet. He lay in bed and stared at the ceiling. In the silence he heard the clock ticking on the dresser and cars going by on the street outside. In his rush to undress, he had forgotten to throw the bottle out. Now, visions of the label from the bottle tormented his mind. The urge to take a drink was overwhelming.

He thought of little Elizabeth, his granddaughter, and imagined holding her in his arms. As he lay there he closed his eyes and concentrated, forcing himself to visualize every detail. He saw her snuggled in the crook of his arm, her mouth, her ears, her eyes. The shaking grew worse. The urge to drink raged. Sweat trickled down his face.

Images flashed through his mind. One moment he was

holding Elizabeth. The next, he was reaching for Barbara. Suddenly Elizabeth melted away, replaced by a gin bottle. He saw his hand wrapped around the bottleneck. His other hand twisted off the cap. As he did, he heard the baby give a loud scream.

"No," he shouted. "I don't want a drink!"

Convinced that what he saw was no longer just in his mind, he jerked the covers over his head and squeezed his eyes tightly shut. His body shook violently. It was a struggle just to breathe.

In a little while he drifted off to a fitful sleep. He thrashed about in the bed, jerking the sheets loose and wadding them around his neck.

Sometime later he awoke shaking more violently than ever. Night had come. The room was dark. Still bundled under his chin, the bed sheets and bedspread were soaked with sweat. It was difficult to remember where he was or why he was shaking and sweating so. He kicked the sheet and spread with his feet and covered himself again. He lay in the dark and tried to relax. And then they came.

At the foot of the bed, an angry wild dog raised its head. Black, with gray streaks across the top of its head, it bared its teeth and gave a low, tense growl. Connolly raised himself from the pillow and stared in disbelief. Another reared its head. Then another. Fear gripped him as the pack of dogs stood at the foot of his bed, barking and snarling, their long teeth glistening in the night like great white fangs. Louder and louder they barked. Two jumped onto the bed and moved toward his face. He rolled over and covered his head.

"Go away," he shouted. "Go away!"

There was a knock at the bedroom door. He jerked the covers from his head.

"Who is it?" he called.

There was no reply, only another knock.

"Who is it?" he called. His voice louder and more frightened than before.

Slowly, the door opened, and his mother, long since dead, appeared beside his bed.

"I told you not to do it," she said, her face stern and demanding. "I told you not to go to bed without feeding those dogs. They'll eat you alive."

"Mama?"

Her face melted like wax and ran down the front of her dress. Connolly screamed and jerked the covers over his head again. Rocking from side to side he moaned and howled in agony.

Being under the covers with his eyes closed sent the faces away, but the voices grew louder.

"Daddy, Daddy," Rachel cried. "Watch me. I can ride my bike."

He threw back the bedspread and looked around the room. Rachel stood near the end of the bed, smiling. As he watched, her face melded into that of one of the barking dogs. He dove back under the covers.

The night wore on in a seemingly endless cycle of voices, faces, and a cacophony of noise. Finally, he dragged himself out of bed and staggered down the hall. In the kitchen he tore open the cabinet and grasped the gin bottle by the neck. Wild-eyed and harried, he looked at it with lust. Only one quick gulp and everything would be quiet. The faces would go away. The voices would be silenced.

Instead, he wheeled around and sent the bottle sailing toward the living room. It crashed into the television shattering both the bottle and the picture tube in a cloud of dust and a shower of glass.

"I don't want another drink," he said. This time, his voice was measured and stern.

He stumbled back to bed and collapsed, his face buried in the pillow. Drained and limp, he didn't bother covering himself.

Connolly faded in and out of consciousness, losing all track of time in an endless cycle of panic and bliss, anger and peace, nightmare and rest. Finally, the terror began to pass, and he slipped into restful sleep.

It was morning when he first became aware he was awake. The rustling sound of someone folding a newspaper roused him from sleep. From the far corner of the room someone shifted positions in a chair and coughed. His heart raced as he anticipated the appearance of yet another ghoulish face. Still with his face in the pillow, he slid his knees forward until they were underneath his thighs. He pressed his hands flat against the mattress. When he could wait no longer, he flipped onto his back.

Mrs. Gordon sat in a kitchen chair in the corner of the room a few feet beyond the end of the bed. They stared at each other a moment.

"Remember me?" she said.

"I don't want another drink," he shouted.

He dove for the pillow and pulled the covers over his head.

"Good," she replied. "How much did you drink before you smashed the television set?"

He lay there a moment, unsure what to do. The fresh scent of newly laundered bed linens tickled his nose. He looked at the sheet covering his head. It had been washed and ironed. He pushed the sheet away and cocked his head to one side.

"Is that you, Mrs. Gordon?"

"Yes," she replied.

"Are you really there?"

"Oh, yes," she said. "I'm here."

Connolly rolled onto his back and looked at her.

"How'd you get in here?"

Mrs. Gordon laid aside the newspaper she had been holding.

"The landlord called your brother in Birmingham night before last. He called me. Said you wouldn't answer the door. All the neighbors were complaining about the shouting, and then they heard the television explode."

Connolly looked puzzled.

"Night before last? What day is it?"

"Thursday."

"What happened to Tuesday and Wednesday?"

Mrs. Gordon frowned.

"If you don't remember," she said, "you don't want me to tell you."

"Where's Marisa?"

"She left Tuesday morning."

"Left?"

"Yeah. She saw what was happening and packed up."

Connolly closed his eyes and heaved a sigh.

"How'd you ever get with her anyway?"

"Just one of those things," he said. "Did she say where she was going?"

"Not really. Like I say, she came home late Monday night, early Tuesday morning. Saw you. Left, in a hurry. Came back sometime Tuesday afternoon and got her stuff."

"Anybody with her when she came back?"

Mrs. Gordon sighed.

"Yes." She was hesitant to answer. "Some man she called Earl. Big guy."

"Earl," Connolly said. "He's a bouncer at the Imperial Palace."

Mrs. Gordon crossed the room to the door and disappeared up the hallway. In a few minutes she returned carrying a tray with a bowl of soup and a few crackers.

"Sit up," she said.

He did as he was told and propped his shoulders against the headboard. She set the tray across his legs.

"Better eat slowly," she said. "Craig isn't back with the towels yet."

"Craig? Craig who?"

"One of those men Rachel lives with."

Connolly looked angry.

"I had to have some help," Mrs. Gordon protested. "You were a mess. We showered you three times Tuesday night. He's down at the laundry."

"Showered me?"

"Relax," she said. A smile flickered across her face. "I didn't see anything I haven't seen before."

He sipped the soup and nibbled on a cracker.

"How'd you get Craig over here?"

"Called Barbara. She told Rachel to send him."

"Bet that went over well."

She ignored the comment.

"Eat some more of that soup if you can," she said.

Connolly took a few more sips, then closed his eyes. When he opened them again, it was late in the afternoon. The covers were neatly tucked under his chin. The room was clean and orderly. Sunlight filtered through the curtains on the windows beyond the end of the bed. He threw back the covers and sat up. He put his feet on the floor and stood. The room started to spin. He fell onto the bed.

In a few minutes, he tried again. This time he made it from the bed to the doorway. He leaned against the doorframe and called down the hall.

"Mrs. Gordon."

There was no reply.

He moved slowly up the hallway to the living room. The television was gone, and the table on which it once sat had been moved beside the sofa. In the kitchen he found a note on the counter.

"More soup in the refrigerator, and some rice. Eat slowly. Myrtice."

Twenty-Seven

Monday, Connolly appeared at the office in the middle of the morning. Dressed in a gray suit with a crisp white shirt and a silk tie, he looked alert and fit, though somewhat mellow.

"Well," Mrs. Gordon said, "you finally decided to come in."

"Yes," he replied. "But I'm not sure why."

"Think you're going to make it?"

"Absolutely."

As he moved past her desk, he reached down and grasped her hand. Bending over, he lifted her hand gently to his lips and kissed it. Without a word, he returned her hand to the desktop and stepped down the hall to his office.

In a few moments Mrs. Gordon appeared at the door. Her eyes were red, and her makeup was smeared as though she had been crying. She wiped her cheek and held her head erect.

"Truman Albritton is here to see you," she said.

She turned quickly away, hoping he would not notice her eyes.

"Alright ..." Connolly replied. He glanced away as though straightening the papers on his desk and tried not to notice. "Show him in," he said.

Mrs. Gordon returned to the front and escorted Albritton down the hall. Connolly stood as he entered.

Truman Albritton was seventy-six years old. He had been a lawyer almost as long as Connolly had been alive. Over the years, he had been known for many things. First, as a criminal defense lawyer of national renown. Then as a plaintiff's attorney who struck fear in the boardrooms of corporate empires. Throughout his career he made the most of every opportunity and exploited every moment to his own advantage. By the age of forty he was an icon in state politics. For the past thirty years not much had happened in Alabama that he had not orchestrated. Now, with Hogan Smith in the Senate, his reach extended beyond the state's borders to affairs of national interest. He was a classic Southern political boss, a power broker of the first order, the last of a dying breed.

He entered Connolly's office dressed in a navy blue suit, hand tailored and perfectly fit. His light blue shirt was made of the finest imported cotton, neatly pressed. The silk tie he wore was tied in a symmetrical knot snuggled beneath the edges of his shirt collar. Plain gold cuff links held the sleeves in place. A dark red rose in his lapel finished the ensemble. He made an impeccable appearance.

Behind his back Mrs. Gordon rolled her eyes and closed the door.

"Mike," Albritton said, stepping toward the desk. "Good to see you. Sorry to drop in on you like this."

They shook hands.

"No problem," Connolly replied. "Have a seat."

Albritton took a seat in front of the desk. Connolly pulled his chair to the desk and propped his elbows on the desktop.

"What can I do for you?"

Albritton crossed his legs and folded his hands in his lap. The cuff of his shirt slid back slightly, revealing a gold Brietling watch with a black leather band.

"I heard you've been appointed to represent that ... black man who killed Keyton Attaway. I thought we—"

"Avery Thompson," Connolly said, interrupting him.

"What? Avery—"

"The man's name is Avery Thompson," Connolly repeated.

Albritton blushed.

"Well ... I think he is black," he said. He shifted positions in the chair.

"He is," Connolly said, nodding. "But he has a name. And his name is Avery Thompson."

"Whatever," Albritton replied. He dismissed Connolly with a frown and a shrug. "I thought we ought to talk and ... get a few things straight between us."

"He's been accused, Truman," Connolly scowled, wagging his finger for emphasis. "He hasn't been convicted yet."

"Right. Well, the thing is, you've been asking a lot of questions and—"

"I've been getting a lot of interesting answers too," Connolly interrupted again.

Albritton shifted positions once more. He re-crossed his legs and propped one elbow on the arm of the chair.

"That's what bothers me. See ... I don't think you need to harass Karen Attaway anymore."

Connolly was taken aback.

"Harass? Who said I harassed her?"

"I understand there was a little ... trouble down at her house."

"She's the one who got angry. Not me."

"Surely you can understand she would be emotional about this, especially talking to someone who's defending the man who killed her husband."

Connolly leaned back in his chair.

"There you go again," he said. "The man hasn't even had a preliminary hearing, and you've got him convicted and strapped to the electric chair."

A sarcastic grin spread across Albritton's face.

"You don't think you can win, do you?"

"I think there are plenty of unanswered questions about this case."

"Oh, really? Like what?"

"Like, why are you so interested in how I defend my client?"

"I don't care what you do with your client," Albritton replied. "But I would appreciate it if you wouldn't bother Karen. I assure you, she has nothing to do with this case."

"How can you assure me of that, Truman? Do you know what this case is about?"

Albritton glared at Connolly.

"Just leave her alone," he said.

"I have a right to question anyone I want."

"I'd appreciate it if you'd see me first."

"I don't have to see you for anything, Truman. You ready to testify for her too?"

"What are you talking about?"

"You identified Keyton's body at the morgue for Karen. I thought maybe you'd like to come to court and testify at the preliminary hearing. Maybe tell us what Attaway was so worried about the last few weeks of his life. You want to do that too?"

Albritton's face grew red. His jaw jutted forward, and his eyes became intense.

"You don't have to get ugly about it," he snipped. "I was only trying to help the wife of a friend at a tragic time."

"Right."

"Listen to me," Albritton demanded. He leaned forward in his seat and tapped the desktop with his index finger for emphasis. "You have no idea what or who you're dealing with. Your client is accused of capital murder. I think it would be a good idea for you to stop asking all these questions and stirring up unnecessary trouble and find a way to save his life."

Connolly resented Albritton's tone.

"What are you saying?"

"I'm sure the district attorney would agree to life without parole," Albritton said. "Probably already offered it to you. You ought to take it."

"No," Connolly said. "I mean the part about I don't know who or what I'm dealing with. Tell me who I'm dealing with."

Albritton's eyes bore down on Connolly as if to pierce right through him.

"You've been to Keyton's office. You've been out to the junkyard to look at that pickup truck. You hunted up some uneducated buffoon in Grand Bay and nearly got yourself eaten alive by his dog. You've been to mass at St. Pachomius, and you had supper with Toby LeMoyne. Your girlfriend left you, your wife can't stand you, and your daughter won't let you see your new and only grandchild. And for all of that you've found nothing that helps your client. You need to settle this case. You can't stay sober long enough to try it."

Connolly jumped to his feet.

"Get out of my office," he shouted.

Albritton put up his hands.

"Okay. Okay," he chuckled. "I'm leaving."

He stood to leave, then paused at the door and turned toward Connolly. His face became hard as stone. His eyes grew cold.

"Just be careful you don't wind up in the bed next to your client," he warned.

Connolly was livid. He leaped from behind the desk and charged up the hall after him. Albritton was almost to Mrs. Gordon's desk when Connolly grabbed the back of his collar. Mrs. Gordon jumped to her feet.

Connolly hauled Albritton backward and shoved him against the wall. He grabbed the knot of Albritton's beautiful silk tie and pinned him in place with his elbow and forearm. He grasped the small end of the tie with the other hand and pulled it tight.

"What r oo du in?" Albritton exclaimed. His voice was garbled from the sudden lack of oxygen and the pressure on his vocal cords. He thrashed about with his arms and legs, trying to escape. Connolly pressed in close, his nose almost touching Albritton's.

"You're the one who filed that motion," he growled.

"What motion?"

"The one that got my client sent off to some psychiatric hospital. The one that just almost cost him his life."

Albritton grinned. "Settle this case," he gasped.

Albritton glared at him, still struggling to breathe. Connolly jerked the knot tighter. Albritton let out a desperate groan. Connolly let go of Albritton's tie and stepped away. Albritton collapsed to the floor and tugged the knot loose.

"You'll regret this," he growled.

Connolly grabbed Albritton's lapels and lifted him to a standing position. With both hands he shoved him toward the door. As Albritton staggered across the room, the door opened. Father Scott stepped inside. Albritton fell against the doorfacing. Father Scott was startled.

"Did I pick a bad time?"

"No," Connolly replied. "He was just leaving."

Albritton slipped past Father Scott and disappeared out-side down the corridor toward the elevator. Father Scott closed the door.

"Come on back," Connolly said, between breaths.

He started down the hallway. Father Scott followed.

In the office, Connolly flopped into the chair behind the desk. Still out of breath, he leaned back in the chair and propped his head against the wall. Father Scott sat in the chair vacated by Albritton.

"If you don't mind me asking," he began, "what was that all about?"

"He's upset because every time I talk to someone about Keyton Attaway, his name keeps coming up."

"I don't know him."

"Believe me," Connolly said. "Be glad you don't."

Father Scott smiled and changed the subject.

"Karen Attaway came to see me the other day," he said.

Connolly managed a smile.

"She tell you I came to see her?"

"Yeah. She mentioned it."

"Tell you she threw a glass of tea at me?"

Father Scott smiled and nodded.

"She and Keyton were really close," he said. "Especially the last year or so. This has been particularly hard on her."

"I understand how she feels. Look, if this guy is guilty, he deserves to die," Connolly replied. "But he's not guilty until a jury says so. Until then, I have to do everything I can to find a defense for him."

"I think she understands that," Father Scott said. "You want me to see if she'll meet with you again?"

"That'd be fine with me," Connolly said.

Father Scott nodded.

"I'll see what I can do." He paused and shifted positions in the chair. "So, how are you? I understand you had a rough week last week."

Connolly smiled.

"It was rough," he said. "But things are better now."

"Tell me about it."

Connolly rocked the chair gently. His eyes grew full as he struggled to reply.

Twenty-Eight

*L*ate that evening, Connolly drove west down Highway 90 to the Alabama-Mississippi state line. The area around the state line was cluttered with cafes, gasoline stations, and nightclubs. Originally established to provide illegal gambling, the clubs were now little more than beer joints, crumbling rotten buildings that reeked of beer, stale cigarette smoke, and sweat. The single exception was the Imperial Palace.

The Imperial Palace was a showplace. A massive building covered in neon lights, it rose from the low country marsh with a glow that lit the sky for miles. In front, a portico supported by large white columns extended out from the building far enough to allow cars to stop three abreast at the front door. Valet attendants dressed in white jackets greeted arriving customers. A paved parking lot surrounded the building.

Most afternoons it did a steady business from a motley crowd of businessmen and assorted rednecks. In the evening, a younger, more affluent crowd arrived. Cars filled the parking lot by six. By show time they lined the highway for miles in either direction. It was an odd place, a Las Vegas showroom in the heart of the low country. Garish, out of place, and immensely popular.

Connolly turned off the highway and drove under the portico. When the car came to a stop, an attendant opened his door.

"Mr. Connolly," he exclaimed. "Haven't seen you around here in a while."

He stepped from the car and slipped a ten-dollar bill in the attendant's hand.

"Treat her gently," he said.

The attendant glanced at the bill in his hand and grinned. "Yes, sir."

As Connolly approached the front entrance, a doorman stepped forward. He wore gray trousers with gold piping down the seams. His white shirt was starched stiff. A narrow black tie was barely visible at the collar. Over the shirt was a long gold jacket with shiny brass buttons. A gold bellman's hat sat atop his head.

"Welcome to the Imperial Palace," he said. As he spoke, he tipped his hat and opened the door.

Connolly nodded in response and extended his hand. The doorman grasped it. Connolly pressed a five-dollar bill into the doorman's palm.

"Enjoy yourself," the doorman said.

The front doors opened into a lobby that ran the width of the building. Brass chandeliers hung from the ceiling twenty feet above, suspended on thick brass chains. The floor was covered with dark red carpet. There were no windows, but the walls on both sides were lined with mirrors.

On the wall opposite the main entrance, huge doors, ten feet tall and almost as wide, led from the lobby into the showroom. Several stood open, guarded by doormen in uniform and large, muscular bouncers dressed in blue jeans and red T-shirts emblazoned with the gold Imperial Palace logo.

Connolly crossed the lobby to an open door. The doorman smiled and nodded. The bouncer glanced at him, then turned away. Inside, Connolly paused and looked around, waiting for his eyes to adjust to the dim lighting.

In front, opposite the door, was a low wall about waist high that separated the entrance from the main floor. A stage extended across the far end of the room with a long runway that stretched down the center toward the entrance. A bar occupied the wall to the far left. Tables, arranged in no apparent order, covered the floor between the low wall near the doors and the stage in the back. Most of the early crowd was clustered around the runway. Loud music filled the room.

"There's a five-dollar cover," the doorman said.

"I won't be staying long," Connolly replied.

"Doesn't matter," the attendant replied. "Still have to pay the cover."

The bouncer turned to face him. Connolly took out a five-dollar bill and handed it to the doorman. The doorman shoved the bill into a small box on a stand beside him and tipped his hat.

"Enjoy yourself," he said.

Connolly moved from the door around the low wall and crossed the showroom to the bar. "What can I get you?" the bartender asked.

"Ginger ale," Connolly replied.

"That all?"

"That's it."

"One ginger ale," the bartender said. "Coming right up."

He filled a glass with ice and ginger ale and set it on the bar.

"How much?" Connolly asked.

"Ahh, forget it, Mr. Connolly," the bartender said, with the wave of a hand. "On the house."

"Thanks," Connolly said. "Is Marisa here tonight?"

"Yeah," the bartender said. "Want me to tell her you're here?"

"I'll just go in the back," Connolly said.

"Can't do that," the bartender replied. "They don't let anyone but the dancers back there anymore."

Connolly took a sip of ginger ale.

"Alright," he said. "Tell her I'm here."

The bartender gestured to a barmaid standing a few feet away. She stepped to the bar. The bartender whispered something in her ear. She glanced at Connolly, then laid her tray on the bar and walked to a door in the corner to the left of the stage.

As Connolly waited, the music grew louder. Behind him, a chorus of catcalls and whistles rose from around the runway. Connolly glanced over his shoulder in that direction. A dancer moved down the runway, bumping and grinding to the music. Connolly turned away and gazed at the bottles of liquor on the shelves behind the bar.

Suddenly, the taste of gin exploded in his mouth. He could feel it sliding over his tongue. His body seemed to cry out for it. He closed his eyes and wrapped his fingers tightly around the glass of ginger ale.

In a few minutes Marisa appeared beside him. She took his elbow and nudged him off the stool. He followed her into an office near the end of the bar. With the door closed, it was almost quiet enough to talk.

She gave him a kind smile, as if she was genuinely interested in him.

"How are you feeling?"

"Fine," he said.

"I suppose Mrs. Gordon told you I left."

"Yes. She did," he replied.

"I couldn't stand the sight of you shaking and ... you know, sick and all."

Connolly nodded.

"When are you coming back?"

"I've ... ahhh ..." She looked away. "I'm not."

She turned to face him. A tense smile pulled her lips tight against her teeth. Connolly frowned.

"Who is it this time?"

Her mouth relaxed in a genuine smile.

"I guess that's the way it's been with us, isn't it?"

"Yeah," Connolly sighed. "That's the way it's been."

A knock on the door interrupted them. The bartender opened the door.

"Marisa, you're on in ten minutes," he said.

"Okay," she replied.

She turned to Connolly again.

"Well, I need to go."

"Yeah," Connolly said. "I guess you do."

She kissed him on the cheek and stepped to the door.

"Take care of yourself," she said.

Connolly smiled. She opened the door and was gone.

Twenty-Nine

*E*arly the next afternoon Connolly left the office and drove across town to Hammel's Department Store. He parked out front and went inside. Near the back of the store, he browsed through the men's suits. After a few minutes, he took a suit from the rack and walked through the door to the hall that led to the men's dressing rooms. He hung the suit in one of the rooms and continued down the hall. At the end of the hall was a door that opened into a large warehouse area in the rear of the store. He glanced over his shoulder to make sure no one was behind him, then opened the door.

He walked calmly across the warehouse floor and made his way to the loading dock. Three trucks were backed up to the dock, and workmen busily unloaded them. No one paid him any attention as he threaded his way between pallets stacked with boxes of merchandise. He walked unnoticed to the end of the loading dock and down a flight of steps to the ground.

A yellow 1979 Buick LeSabre was parked to the right behind the building. Guy Poiroux sat in the front seat behind the steering wheel reading a newspaper. Connolly opened the back door and got inside. Guy handed the newspaper over the seat to Connolly and backed the car away from the building. Connolly slid low in the seat and opened the newspaper, making sure it obscured his face.

Guy drove slowly out of the parking lot to the service road and onto Beltline Highway. A few miles north of the store, Connolly folded the newspaper and laid it on the seat.

"Anybody follow us?"

"No," Guy replied.

Connolly glanced out the back window.

"Good."

"You know the way?"

"Yeah."

Connolly slid low in the seat and closed his eyes.

They continued north on the Beltline several miles, then exited onto Wallace Highway. Twenty miles north of Mobile, Guy eased the Buick off the pavement and into the parking lot at White's Truck Stop. Connolly awoke as the car came to a halt.

"We're here," Guy said. He steered the car past the gas pumps out front and brought it to a stop at the edge of the lot. "The car is parked over there at the end of the building," he said, pointing.

Connolly opened the back door.

"Thanks for the ride."

"Don't mention it. You want me to go with you?"

"No. Just watch to see if I'm followed."

Guy nodded.

Connolly stepped from the car and walked to a gray Crown Victoria parked next to the building. He opened the door and felt under the floor mat for the key.

From White's Truck Stop Connolly drove to Tuscaloosa. He reached Harwell Psychiatric Facility shortly after four. He was met in the administration building by Fitzhugh Brundige, the physician treating Avery Thompson.

"How is he?"

"He's doing much better," Brundige said. "Paralysis has

dissipated significantly. His speech has improved. Considering how close he was to dying, I'd say he's had a remarkable recovery."

"Still tied to the bed?"

"No," Brundige said, shaking his head. "That was just temporary. PCP does strange things to people, especially in high doses. He was a little violent when we brought him in. We took the restraints off not long after you left the last time."

"Good. Now, what about trial? Is he able to do that?"

Brundige hesitated a moment.

"Yes," he said, slowly. "He is quite competent."

"What's the matter?"

"Nothing, it's just that, I ... ahhh ... I would like to keep him here as long as possible."

Brundige gave him a knowing smile. Connolly realized what he meant.

"Think he'd be ... more likely to make it to the trial that way?"

"I know that sounds strange, keeping a sound man in a psychiatric hospital. But what happened to Mr. Thompson was no accident."

"You can do that? Keep him here?"

"He can't leave until I say he's ready and issue a report to that effect."

Connolly smiled.

"I like that idea. Can I see him today?"

"Sure. Come on. I'll walk with you. I need to go that way."

Brundige waited while Connolly was cleared through security at the administration building. They walked through the tunnel from the administration building to the main guard station at the entrance to the treatment area.

Connolly was searched again, then followed Brundige

from the main guard station down the corridor to the first checkpoint. The door rolled open as they approached. Beyond the checkpoint they turned left down another wide corridor. A little way down the corridor they came to a set of gleaming metal double doors. Brundige pushed them open.

Beyond the doors was what appeared to be a typical hospital. Connolly glanced in the patient rooms as they walked by. Gone were the locked, steel doors he had seen on the other ward. By contrast, these rooms had standard hospital beds, chairs, and tray tables.

At the end of the corridor was a nurse's station. Hallways branched out from the station like spokes of a wheel. Brundige led Connolly past the station and ahead down one of the hallways. At the end, the hall opened into a large day room. Tables and chairs were arranged around the room. To the left was a television. Patients sat at the tables reading or watching television. To the right, a group was clustered around a table watching intently as other patients played dominoes.

Connolly scanned the room searching for Thompson. Brundige tapped him on the arm and pointed to the left. Thompson approached, smiling.

"Hello, Mr. Connolly," he said.

He walked with a noticeable limp, and his right arm dangled at his side, but his speech was no longer slurred, and his chin was dry.

Thompson held out his left hand as he approached. Connolly grabbed it and slipped his arm across Thompson's shoulder.

"You look much better," he said.

"I feel much better," Thompson replied.

Brundige pointed them to a table in the far corner to the right, then excused himself.

"What they going to do with me now?"

Connolly leaned over the table.

"You're going to stay here a while longer," he said.

Thompson looked concerned.

"I feel fine," he said.

"It's okay," Connolly assured him. "Dr. Brundige will issue a report saying you're competent to stand trial. But he's not going to do that until closer to the preliminary hearing."

"I can still have a trial?"

"Yes."

"Why they don't want to send me back now?"

"You want to go back to the jail?"

Thompson smiled. "Not really. The food here is pretty good."

"It's safer being here," Connolly said. "I'd rather have you here than at the county jail."

Thompson nodded. "So, we ready for 'em?"

"We're getting close," Connolly said.

They spent the next hour discussing strategy and options for the preliminary hearing. Finally, an orderly appeared and began directing patients out of the room.

"Time to eat," Thompson said.

Connolly stood. "You better go. I don't want you to miss supper."

Thompson smiled. "Thanks for coming to see me," he said.

Connolly waited while Thompson stood, then walked with him into the hall. Brundige was waiting at the nurse's station.

"Come on," he said. "I'll walk with you back to the administration building."

Thirty

When Connolly arrived at the office the following morning he noticed Hollis Toombs's truck parked on the street near the Port City Diner. He took the elevator upstairs and opened the office door. Mrs. Gordon was seated at her desk.

"He's in there," she said, nodding over her shoulder toward the hallway.

Connolly walked past her desk. From the hallway he could see Hollis sitting in his office. He moved down the hall.

"You been waiting long?"

He stepped to the coat rack and took off his jacket, then closed the office door.

"About thirty minutes," Hollis said.

"Not working today?"

"Told them I needed the morning off," he said. "They didn't seem to mind. Ain't been much rain lately. Grass kinda slowed down."

Connolly moved behind the desk and took a seat in his chair.

"Find anything interesting at the Agostino residence?"

"Yeah," Hollis said. "You got my money?"

"Money?"

"Yeah. You said you'd match what they paid me. I made two hundred dollars last week."

"Oh. Yeah," Connolly said.

He opened the top drawer of his desk and took out an envelope of cash. He counted out ten twenties and handed them to Hollis.

"Two things." Hollis said. He paused while he counted the money, then continued. "A young guy, hard, tough-looking fellow, been there every time I've been there. We do their yard first thing in the morning. This guy shows up about nine. Stays until just before noon."

"And?"

"He drives a green Taurus. Florida license plates."

Connolly's eyes grew wider with interest.

"A green Taurus?"

"Yeah. Mean something to you?"

"I'm not sure," Connolly said. "There was a green Taurus behind me the other night when I stopped to see Toby. He thought it might have been following me."

"Toby LeMoyne?"

"Yeah. What was the second thing?"

"That's it."

"You said you had two things. You only told me one."

"No. I told you both," Hollis insisted. "The guy was there, and he drove a green Taurus."

Connolly smiled and shook his head.

"What?" Hollis asked.

"Nothing," Connolly replied, amused. "Got anything else?"

"Nope. Place is quiet. Whole neighborhood is quiet. Don't even see any of the neighbors."

"Think Leigh Ann and this fellow in the Taurus are having an affair?"

Hollis cocked his head to one side and gave Connolly a knowing look.

"Alright. Alright," Connolly said. "I guess it's obvious."

"I guess so."

"Ever see them together?"

"I don't run around looking in the windows, if that's what you mean."

"No. I mean, does she come out to greet him? What happens when he arrives?"

"He pulls in the driveway, drives right up to the garage. Goes around to the side and goes in through the kitchen. Let's himself in. Doesn't knock."

"Huh." Connolly rocked the chair back and propped his head against the wall. "Does he have a key?"

"I don't know. Looked to me like the door was unlocked already."

"She didn't come to the door?"

"Not that I saw."

"Interesting."

"Yeah," Hollis said.

Connolly sat forward in the chair.

"Alright," he said. "I need you to keep going over there. Ronnie Goleman satisfied with your work?"

"Satisfied?" Hollis snorted. "Don't insult me like that."

"I just meant are you having any problems?"

"No," Hollis replied. "I ain't having any problems. Ronnie Goleman ain't never had an employee like me. I do more than any three of those other loafers he has."

Connolly nodded.

"Any way to get some kind of listening device over there?"

"No way," Hollis said, waving his hands in protest. "I ain't about to bug a federal judge's house."

Connolly smiled.

"I guess you have a point," he said.

"I told you before. I don't mind helping you out. But I'm not doing anything illegal."

"It was just an idea," Connolly said.

"And a bad one at that," Hollis replied.

He stood and started toward the door. Connolly came from behind the desk and followed him up the hall.

"They paying you alright?"

"Yeah," Hollis said. "They're paying me."

They passed Mrs. Gordon's desk. Connolly opened the door to the corridor and held it for Hollis.

"If you need anything, let me know."

"Yeah," Hollis replied. "I'll do that."

Connolly watched from the door as Hollis walked down the corridor and turned the corner toward the elevator. When Hollis was out of sight, he stepped into the office and closed the door.

"You two are going to wind up in jail one of these days," Mrs. Gordon said.

Connolly frowned at her.

"For what?"

"I don't know what it'll be," she said. "But there isn't an ounce of sense between you."

Connolly smiled.

"You may be right," he said. "You may be right."

He turned away from the door and walked down the hall toward his office.

Thirty-One

A few days later Judge Cahill called Connolly and Henry McNamara and asked them to meet with him that afternoon. The courtroom was deserted when Connolly arrived. As he made his way to the front, Walter emerged from the door behind the judge's bench. He sipped from a cup of coffee as he walked to his desk.

"Henry here yet?"

"Not my day to watch him," Walter grumbled.

"Where'd you get that coffee?"

"In the back."

Connolly walked through the door to the office area behind the judge's bench. The coffee machine sat on a shelf under a window across from the door. He found a Styrofoam cup and poured it full. As he sipped the coffee and waited, Henry McNamara entered.

"Mike, you have any idea what the judge wants with us?"

"Probably just going over the ground rules," Connolly replied. "You do many preliminary hearings for capital cases?"

"Not many. We have a team that handles major felony cases. Most of the time one of them comes in for the hearing."

"You got this one alone?"

"Looks like it."

The door to Judge Cahill's office opened. He stepped out dressed in a black robe.

"You two ready?"

"Yes, Your Honor," they replied.

They followed him through the door and into the courtroom. Judge Cahill took a seat at the bench. Connolly and McNamara stood at the counsel tables in front.

"Have a seat, gentlemen," Cahill said.

Connolly sat at the table to the right. McNamara sat at the table to the left.

"I called you two down here today so we could go over a few things while we still have time to handle any problems before we get to the preliminary hearing. You realize this case is scheduled in less than two weeks?"

"Yes, Your Honor," McNamara replied.

Connolly nodded.

"Mike, I understand your client is now at Harwell Psychiatric Facility," Cahill said. "Did you know that?"

"Yes, Your Honor."

Cahill sounded irritated. "Some reason why you didn't tell me about it?"

Connolly stood."Yes, Your Honor. There is."

He took some papers from his satchel and stepped toward the bench.

"Judge, this is a copy of the file they have on my client at Aikers Hospital in Jackson. This is where he was sent first on the order you signed." He handed the documents to Cahill.

"As you will recall, your order said Mr. Thompson was to be evaluated to see whether he was competent to stand trial."

Cahill nodded as he scanned the documents.

"The last page of the file I just handed you is an order that purports to be signed by you," Connolly continued. "As you can see, this is a different order from the one in the court file. The order in the hospital file indicates Thompson was sent to Aikers because of the severity of his mental condition and the jail's inability to handle him. Do you see that document?"

Cahill looked at the document.

"That's not my signature," he said. "Look at this, Walter." He turned the file to one side and held it for Walter to see. "That's not my signature."

Walter shook his head.

"No, Judge. That's not your signature. That's not even one of our orders."

Cahill turned back to Connolly.

"He's right. This isn't one of the orders we use. This is ridiculous. Any idea who did this?"

"No, Your Honor."

"Walter, get Sheriff McNeil on the phone and tell him to come see me. We need to get to the bottom of this. When I find out who did this, they're going to jail." He continued to look at the documents a moment, then glanced at Connolly. "Go ahead. I didn't mean to interrupt you."

"When Thompson got to Aikers, someone administered a large quantity of drugs. Doctors at Harwell have examined him and determined that substance was phencyclidine."

"Pheny what?" Cahill frowned.

"PCP, Your Honor. Angel dust."

Cahill grimaced and shook his head. Connolly continued.

"The doctors tell me Mr. Thompson was given enough of this stuff to kill him. He survived because the PCP they used was diluted with water and not ether or cleaning fluid. And, it was injected."

Cahill looked more puzzled than before.

"Ether? You mean that stuff they put you to sleep with?"

"Yes, Your Honor. As a powder," Connolly explained, "PCP is hard to dissolve unless you use a solvent. That's what they do with it on the street, which is why so many people have a bad experience with it."

Cahill shook his head again.

"If you try to dissolve it in water, it gets gooey, like a paste. That's what happened here, and when they injected this stuff into Mr. Thompson, it formed a clot in an artery in the left side of his brain stem. He lost some of the use of his right side, but the clot prevented the dose from being fully absorbed by his body. That and the fact that someone discovered him shortly after it was given to him, saw what shape he was in, and alerted the director at Aikers. Thompson was sent off to Harwell immediately. They identified the problem rather quickly and started treating him."

"You got somebody who can testify to all this?"

"Yes, Your Honor," Connolly said. "But I don't think that will be necessary."

"Sounds like it will to me," Cahill chortled, "and my opinion's the one that counts in here."

Connolly glanced around the courtroom to make certain no one else was present.

"I went to see Mr. Thompson not long after he got to Harwell," he said. "I've been back up there since and talked to the doctors who are treating him. Mr. Thompson has improved remarkably, and they are willing to issue a report stating that he is competent to stand trial, but they don't want to do that until closer to the preliminary hearing. They're a little concerned about Mr. Thompson's safety. Frankly, I am too. If they give their report now, they'll have to send him back to the county jail. They feel like he would be better off up there than down here."

Cahill thought for a moment, then turned to McNamara.

"Henry, what do you know about all this?"

"This is the first I've heard of it, Your Honor."

"You still want to handle this case, or you want to get somebody else from your office to do it?"

"I'm ready to go forward, Your Honor."

"I'll put it off a while and give you some time to get someone else up to speed."

McNamara shook his head.

"That won't be necessary," he said. "I'm ready. I can handle it."

Cahill turned again to Connolly.

"I'm going to wait until I receive the report from Harwell before deciding what to do," he said. "If they say he's competent, and you don't challenge it, I reckon we'll go forward. But I'll decide that once we have a report."

"Very well," Connolly replied.

Cahill turned to McNamara.

"Henry, you got all your people ready?"

"Far as I know, Judge."

"No important witnesses who've said they're going to have difficulty getting here?"

"No, Your Honor."

"You going to have the coroner here? Live?"

"No, Your Honor," McNamara replied. "We plan to get his report in through the detective for the preliminary hearing."

Cahill frowned.

"I don't know what they told you in the office, but I prefer to have the main witnesses testify live. This is a capital case. It's not like your garden-variety robbery. Supreme Court's liable to get this case automatically after the trial. You don't want to be back in here in two or three years retrying this thing. Witnesses forget. Die. Get lost in the shuffle."

McNamara smiled.

"I think we have everything covered," he replied.

Cahill frowned and shook his head.

"You got any more experts you plan to bootstrap into evidence?"

"Forensics on the bullets."

"The bullets?"

"Ballistics tests, Your Honor."

Cahill groaned.

"Just going to get the report in through your detective?"

"Yes, Your Honor."

Cahill stared at him.

"Let me say this, if I may," McNamara said.

Cahill nodded for him to continue.

"I don't care to discuss a lot of this in Mr. Connolly's presence, Your Honor. Witnesses, experts, how we plan to prove our case. This goes to our trial strategy, and I'd rather not divulge it."

Cahill's face was flush. His eyes were narrow and bore down on McNamara. He gripped the edges of the desktop in front of him. Then, like a volcano, he erupted.

"Listen to me," he roared. "I'm the judge in this courtroom. If I want your witnesses here, then that's the way it will be." McNamara dropped his head. Cahill continued to unload. "And if I want to ask you questions about it, you very well better answer me. Is that clear?"

McNamara lifted his head.

"Yes, Your Honor."

Cahill wasn't finished.

"You try a couple of these cases, and you'll see," he continued. "There isn't much strategy for the district attorney." He pointed his finger toward Connolly, but his eyes remained fixed on McNamara. "He knows who every one of your witnesses are. He knows what you're going to ask them. If he's worth anything, he already knows how the witnesses will answer."

McNamara mustered a strained smile.

"Yes, Your Honor."

"All that zealous advocacy stuff they told you about in law school is fine. But in practice, trying a case is not about springing a trap on someone. It's about controlling the evidence that gets admitted. Understand?"

"Yes, Your Honor."

"Your goal here is to establish probable cause without committing reversible error. And the only way you can commit reversible error in a preliminary hearing is to play hide and seek with the evidence."

Judge Cahill took a deep breath and tried to relax. He turned to Connolly.

"Mike, you going to put on any witnesses?"

"That depends, Your Honor."

"On what?"

His voice was gruff.

"On who the State calls," Connolly replied.

"Who you want to hear from?"

"They've identified one eyewitness, Bill Sisson. If they don't put him on, I am."

"Anyone else."

"I may put on a lay witness to identify another vehicle that was present at the scene."

Cahill frowned.

"You think that goes to probable cause?"

"It may, Your Honor. We're still developing it."

Cahill sighed and leaned back in his chair. He draped both arms across the top of his head.

"I thought we could meet and iron out any problems y'all might have while we didn't have a crowd in here. But you two seem determined not to be candid about this."

Connolly spoke up, anxious to end the hearing on an amicable note.

"Judge," he began, "I appreciate the help. I don't have any witnesses yet who have indicated a problem in getting to court. If I do, I'll advise the court as soon as I'm aware of it."

Cahill dropped his arms and leaned forward.

"Alright." He turned to McNamara. "Henry, same goes for you too. If I don't hear about any witness problems from you, I'll assume you have what you need for the hearing."

"Yes, Your Honor."

"Now, one more thing." Cahill paused to make sure he had their attention. "As you know, Keyton Attaway was a well-known lawyer. Assuming I'm satisfied with the report from Harwell, and we go forward with the hearing, there's likely to be a courtroom full of people here when we get started. I'll do my best to keep things under control. If you have any trouble getting in and out of the courtroom, let Walter know. You can use the elevator there." He pointed to a door at the side of the courtroom near Walter's desk. "Takes you to the holding area on the first floor, but you can get out from there pretty easily."

Connolly nodded.

"Anything else?"

"Nothing from me," McNamara replied.

Connolly shook his head.

"Very well," Cahill said. "You may go."

Cahill bounded from the bench and disappeared through the door to the right. When he was gone, Connolly turned to Walter.

"What was that all about?"

An embarrassed grin broke across Walter's face.

"Judge is real worried about this case."

"What about?"

"Thinks he might have made a mistake appointing you."

Connolly frowned.

"Really?"

Walter nodded.

"Why?"

"Afraid you'll do something silly," Walter said. "Make him look foolish."

"Is he afraid I'm going to show up drunk?"

Walter nodded again.

"I'd say that's it in a nutshell," he said.

Connolly shook his head.

"Things may get out of hand," Connolly replied. "But it won't be because I'm drunk."

Thirty-Two

At noon a few days later, Father Scott phoned the office. Connolly was fast asleep when the telephone rang. His first inclination was to ignore it, but after four or five rings he slipped his feet from the desktop and grabbed the receiver.

"I just got off the phone with Karen Attaway," Father Scott said. "You got time to meet me at her house?"

"You mean now?" Connolly replied.

"Yes. If you still want to talk to her, she'll see you."

Connolly hung up the phone and hurried out of the office. The Chrysler was parked around the corner on Conception Street. He was behind the wheel in less than five minutes.

The drive down to Dog River took almost an hour. Connolly turned in under the moss-draped oaks and jumped from the car almost before it stopped. He crossed the yard and bounded up the steps to the porch.

Karen met him at the door. She was dressed in a cotton shirt and long baggy shorts that came almost to her knees. She led him through the house to a room along the back. Large windows gave a commanding view of the savannah marsh between the house and the river. Father Scott stood at one of the windows waiting for them. He turned to greet Connolly as he entered the room.

"Sorry it took me so long," Connolly apologized.

"That's alright," Father Scott replied. "I've just been enjoying the view."

Karen picked up a glass of iced tea from a nearby table and moved toward the sofa.

"You want something to drink? Tea? A glass of water?"

"No thanks," Connolly replied. "I had some bottled water on the way."

She sat on the sofa and curled her feet underneath her thighs.

"Have a seat," she said, pointing to a wicker rocking chair in front of her.

Connolly took a seat. She turned to Father Scott.

"Father Scott, you want to pull a chair over here by us?"

"No. I think I'll sit over here." He moved across the room to a well-worn recliner farther away. "Y'all take as much time as you need."

Connolly turned to Karen.

"Let me first say that I'm sorry for upsetting you the other day. I didn't mean to do that."

She smiled and nodded.

"Don't worry about it. I shouldn't have been so touchy. I tried to reach you last week."

"I've been ... out of the office," Connolly said.

"Look," she said, "why don't I get right to the point. You asked a lot of questions the other day. Questions I didn't want to answer and some for which I really have no answers. But one thing you asked me about was Keyton and Truman Albritton."

Connolly nodded.

"Keyton saw Truman a lot. And he saw John Agostino too. The three of them had something going on. I don't know what it was, but I've heard that name you mentioned, Al ..."

"Alpaca."

"Yes. I ... heard them talking about that once or twice."

"You mean you actually overheard them talking about it?"

"Yes. But I don't really know what it was all about. I do know this. Whatever it was, Keyton wanted out, and that infuriated Truman."

"He told you that?"

"No. But during the last month or so something was really bothering him. He would sit out here by himself at night after everyone had gone to bed. Just sit here. Right there in that rocking chair, as a matter of fact. And stare out the window."

"You think this Alpaca thing had something to do with it?"

"I think so. In the last week or so, Truman called every evening. Sometimes two or three times. Came by too. The last few weeks they had some terrible arguments. I stood over there in the kitchen one day and watched them out in the yard. I thought they were going to get in a fight."

"Do you think Keyton might have kept some kind of notes ... maybe a diary ... that might give some details about what he was involved in?"

Karen shook her head.

"He didn't keep a diary. At least, not one I knew about. I've gone through all of his stuff here at the house, and I haven't found anything like that around here. Might have something in his office, but I doubt it. They wouldn't let me in there. I tried to—"

Connolly interrupted her.

"You mean you couldn't get in there after he died?"

Karen shook her head.

"The night he died, they changed all the locks in the entire building. We went by there on the way home from the hospital and couldn't get in."

Connolly frowned in disbelief.

"I sent my brother down there to see about his personal things a day or two later," she continued. "They wouldn't let him in. Said they'd box everything up and send it to us."

"Did they?"

"Yeah. Wasn't anything much there."

"Do you still have it?"

"The box?"

"Yes."

"It's in the bedroom."

"Mind if I take a look?"

"No. I'll get it for you," she said. "There might be something down at the beach house. Keyton had a closet down there he kept some things in."

She slipped off the couch and crossed the room to the hall. Connolly turned to say something to Father Scott, but he was sound asleep in the recliner.

In a few minutes Karen returned with a cardboard box. She set it on a table in front of the sofa.

"This is the stuff the office sent us. I still think we're entitled to other things, Day-Timer, that sort of thing. But they insist they have to keep it."

Connolly reached into the box, then hesitated. He looked at Karen, suddenly conscious of how personal the items must be.

"Go ahead," she said. "I brought it out here so you could go through it."

Connolly picked through the box, removing each of the items and setting them on the table. The box contained mostly trivial items. A brass pencil holder, a letter opener with Keyton's name engraved on it, two or three collectible golf balls, and an assortment of odds and ends. In the bottom, however, he found the photograph of Keyton, Truman, John Agostino, and Hogan Smith from the credenza in Keyton's office. He lifted it from the box.

"You have any idea where this photograph was taken?"

She slid forward on the sofa and looked at it.

"That was taken in the Bahamas. Last summer I think. I'm not sure where, exactly. The four of them had been going down there for the last three or four years. Usually went at least once a year. They stayed at a place called Greycliff Manor. Might have been taken there."

Karen slid back on the couch. Connolly continued to study the picture.

"Looks like they had a good time."

She smiled.

"They did when that was taken." The smile vanished from Karen's face. "That's one of the things Keyton and Truman fought about."

"Really?"

"They were supposed to go down there last month. But at the last minute Keyton changed his mind."

Connolly laid the photograph in the box.

"Did he say why?"

"No. Not really. All he said was, 'I can't do this anymore.' I didn't push him on it. He changed a lot over the last year. Became a completely different man. I figured whatever it was, it came from who he had been, not who he was now, and I wasn't going to nag him."

Connolly leaned back in his seat.

She slipped her hand into the pocket of her shorts and pulled out a key ring with two keys.

"If you want to look at the beach house, you're more than welcome." She leaned forward and handed the keys to him.

"It's down there at the end of Gorgas Street on the east side of ... you know where it is. The closet is in the back bedroom, on the beach side. One of those keys fits the front door. One goes to the closet. He was pretty weird about keeping it locked. I have no idea what's in there."

Connolly held the keys in his hands.

"You don't want to be there when I look at it?"

"No," she answered, dismissing him with the wave of a hand. "There's nothing in there you can hurt. But there is one condition." Her eyes were fixed on him, intent, unflinching. "Whatever's in there, whatever you find, I don't want to know about it. Like I said, Keyton was a totally different person this past year. It was a marvelous transformation, and whatever he did before that doesn't matter. I don't want to know about it now."

Connolly nodded.

"I appreciate this," he said.

"You're welcome. If what you're looking for isn't in the closet, the only other place to look is the hunting lodge. But you'd probably need a court order and an army to get in there."

"Keyton had a hunting lodge?"

"He and some of the guys in the firm had a cabin on the river up above McIntosh. I think Albritton was in on that too. They used to meet up there a lot."

"Any idea where it's located?"

"No," she said, shaking her head. "I've never been there."

Connolly nodded.

"I really appreciate this, Karen," he repeated.

"After you left the other day, I thought about what you said. Maybe you're right. Maybe there's more to this than anyone has said."

Tears welled in her eyes. She managed a smile and wiped her cheeks. Connolly stood.

"I've taken enough of your time," he said. "Thank you for seeing me."

Across the room, Father Scott roused from his nap and stood. Karen slid to the edge of the couch to stand as well.

"No," Connolly said. "Don't get up. I can let myself out."

She stood anyway and followed him toward the hall.

"You mentioned Leigh Ann Agostino the other day too," she added. "I think you were wondering if Keyton was having an affair with her."

Connolly paused in the doorway and turned to face her.

"It was a bad question," he said. "I'm sorry I brought it up."

"No need to be sorry," she replied. "Leigh Ann Agostino is Keyton's half sister."

Connolly's chin dropped. Karen smiled.

Thirty-Three

The Attaways's beach house was located on Dauphin Island, a narrow barrier island that lay five miles off the Alabama coast south of Mobile near the mouth of Mobile Bay. A concrete bridge connected it to the mainland. Connolly crossed the bridge and drove the Chrysler to the center of the island. There, he turned left. Three-quarters of a mile down the road he passed a park known as Cadillac Square. There, he turned right on Fort Charlotte Avenue, a narrow lane that wound around behind the park to Gorgas Street. At Gorgas Street he turned left. The beach house sat beneath a grove of pine trees at the end of the street, facing the water.

The house rested atop thick wooden pilings that held it ten feet off the ground to protect it from flooding during the all-too-frequent hurricanes. Connolly moved up the steps that led from the ground to the front door. He unlocked the door and pushed it open.

Inside, he went straight to the bedroom on the surf side of the unit. The closet was situated along the wall opposite the door. He crossed the room, took out the key, and unlocked the door. Inside, two cardboard file boxes were stacked on the floor against the back wall. They were covered with a blanket. A loaded revolver lay on top. In the corner to the right, an automatic shotgun leaned against the closet wall. A single bar stretched from side to side across the width of the closet. It was empty, as was the shelf above it.

Connolly moved the revolver to the floor, pulled aside the blanket, and opened the top box. It was stuffed with papers and documents. He carried the box out of the closet and set it on the bed.

With the box on the bed, he lifted out a handful of papers and flipped through them. The documents were statements for a bank account from ThomasBanc, located in Nassau, Bahamas. The statements bore only an account number and a Nassau post office address. Stuck in with the first handful of statements were receipts for wire transfers from ThomasBanc to an account at Tidewater Bank in Mobile.

For the next hour and a half Connolly worked methodically through the box, sorting the documents into separate stacks on the bed, one pile for the account statements and one for the wire transfer receipts. As he did, he found an assortment of other scraps of paper with notes and numbers scribbled on them.

When he emptied the first box, he took the second from the closet and sorted through its contents. Like the first, it held account statements, transfer receipts, and odd scraps of paper with notes and numbers. Statements in the second box were from an earlier period than those in the first. He added them to the stacks already on the bed. Then, at the bottom of the box, he found a manila file folder.

He opened the folder and slowly leafed through the documents inside. As he did, a grin spread across his face.

"Alpaca," he whispered.

The file contained incorporation documents establishing Alpaca as a Bahamian corporation. John Agostino was listed as president. Leon Barclay, an attorney in Nassau, was the company's sole shareholder. Connolly wasn't well versed in the use of foreign corporations, but it appeared this one was created to allow money to flow to Agostino while still qualifying as a domestic Bahamian corporation. With Agostino holding no ownership interest, it would avoid detection by U.S. Treasury officials. The only thing that puzzled Connolly was the wire transfers back to Tidewater Bank in Mobile. Those transfers would have been easily noticed by U.S. authorities.

He spent the remainder of the day putting the account statements and wire transfer receipts in chronological order. As he did, it became obvious that a large sum of money had passed through the account. Several million dollars had found their way through the Bahamian account and into the account at Tidewater.

But what was the connection to Attaway?

Nothing in either box offered any hint of the type business Alpaca was engaged in or where the money came from that was in the Bahamian account. He was certain the bank account was owned by the corporation, but without a paper trail linking the two it was all useless information. He needed a document or a witness who could explain what it all meant.

As darkness approached, he replaced the documents in the boxes in an orderly fashion, locked the closet door, and carried the boxes to his car.

From Dauphin Island, Connolly drove north along the shore of Mobile Bay to Mon Louis Island and East Fowl River. The sun was only a glow on the horizon when he turned onto the muddy trail that led to Hollis Toombs's shack. The car bounced and swayed as he negotiated the deep ruts and mud holes. At the shack, he brought the car to a stop near the front door and got out. Hollis appeared from around the corner.

"If you're looking for anything new on Agostino, you're all out of luck," Hollis said.

"Don't believe in luck," Connolly replied. "That's why I came to you."

Hollis disappeared around the corner. Connolly followed.

Behind the shack a large black pot boiled on a cooker fired by butane gas from a small tank. A pot of fresh shrimp sat on the hood of Hollis's pickup truck, which was parked a few feet away. Three ears of corn lay beside the pot of shrimp. Beyond the truck, a brown burlap sack hung from a nail in the trunk of a scrubby oak tree. Hollis took a seat on a five-gallon bucket near the cooker. He pointed to the burlap sack.

"Better get a couple ears of corn out of that sack if you want anything with your shrimp."

Connolly stepped behind the truck and took two ears from the sack. He dropped the green shucks on the ground near his feet. When he finished cleaning both ears, he brought them to the hood of the truck and laid them beside the pot of shrimp.

In a few minutes, Hollis rose from his seat on the bucket and took the corn from the hood of the truck. He placed it in the boiling water, then returned to his seat. Connolly leaned against the truck and watched.

"There's a log over there by that pine tree you can sit on," Hollis said. His voice was low, and the words oozed from his mouth like syrup.

"I'll stand a while," Connolly replied.

"Suit yourself."

When the corn was almost done, Hollis retrieved the shrimp from the hood of the pickup and dumped them into the pot with the corn.

"Be better if we had some new potatoes to go with it, but I didn't feel like going anywhere to get some today."

Connolly smiled as he watched the shrimp and corn boiling together in the pot.

They ate supper in the dark, boiled shrimp and corn on the cob. Both men sat in silence. When the last of the shrimp was gone, Hollis walked to the pickup truck. An ice chest sat in the back behind the cab. He lifted the lid and took out two cans of Coca-Cola. He tossed one to Connolly.

"Hope you don't mind Coke," he said. "Fresh out of beer. Didn't go nowhere today. Ain't got no gin neither." He paused. "Got a bottle of scotch inside if you need it."

"No, thanks," Connolly replied.

Hollis sat on the ground and leaned against an oak tree. Connolly sat a few feet away on a wooden step at the end of the pier.

"I hope you're feeling better," Hollis drawled. "You didn't look too good when you arrived."

"Rough week."

Hollis took a sip of Coca-Cola.

"I quit that grass-cutting job," Hollis said.

"Yeah?"

"Yeah. Too hot."

"See anything else at the Agostinos's?"

"No. Not really."

"The man in the green Taurus still coming around?"

"He was there the last time I was over there. Truman Albritton was there too."

"Albritton?"

"Yeah. Standing in the garage talking to the judge when the green Taurus arrived."

"Hear what they were talking about?"

"Nah. Lawnmower makes too much racket. Pretty serious looking conversation between the judge and Albritton. They seemed to know the other guy too. Though I think they were a little surprised to see him."

"What about Leigh Ann, did she come out?"

"Leigh Ann?"

"Mrs. Agostino."

"No," Hollis chuckled. "She didn't come out. Probably hiding under the bed."

They sat in silence a while longer. Connolly heard a mullet splash in the bayou a few feet away. In the east, a large, full moon rose through the pines.

"Got something else I need you to do," Connolly said finally.

"I ain't interested in no more of your jobs," Hollis replied.

Connolly was unfazed by the response.

"Keyton Attaway and some other lawyers had a hunting lodge on the Mobile River below McIntosh."

Hollis slipped one foot toward his body, raising his knee. He propped his arm on his knee and took another sip of Coca-Cola while he waited for Connolly to finish.

"Think you could find it?"

Hollis sighed.

"That's all you know? Mobile River, below McIntosh?"

"Yeah," Connolly replied. "That's it."

"Why you need to find this place?"

"I got a feeling there's something important up there."

"You don't know nobody that knows where it is?"

"Yeah." Connolly answered. "Several people know exactly where it is. But if I tell them I'm looking for it, it'll give the whole deal away."

Hollis did not reply. Crickets and cicadas chirped in the trees above. The moon rose above the treetops. Another mullet splashed in the water near the dock. Hollis slid away from the tree and stretched out on the ground.

"I'll see what I can do," he sighed. "You staying the night?"

"Nah," Connolly said. "I've got a trunk full of documents to decipher. I better go back tonight."

Connolly stretched out on the dock and stared into the night. Above him the sky was filled with stars. A light breeze blew through the tops of the pine trees. He closed his eyes.

Sometime before midnight he forced himself up and headed for Mobile. Hollis was sound asleep when he left.

Thirty-Four

*T*he next morning Connolly was at the office before dawn. When Mrs. Gordon arrived, she found him on the floor behind the desk, digging through a drawer.

"What are you doing?"

"Looking for something," he replied.

"Well, if you're looking for a bottle, you won't find one."

"What are you talking about?"

He raised his head above the desktop and glared at her.

"Last week while you were out, I turned this place upside down," she said. "Went through everything. You won't find a bottle of gin anywhere. So you might as well get up off the floor."

Connolly smiled.

"I'm not looking for a bottle of gin," he said.

"Oh," she said, glancing away.

"I'm looking for a legal pad with some notes I made when Henry McNamara and I went to the property room."

He moved from behind the desk and crossed the room to the filing cabinets.

"Not likely in there," she said. "Most of the Thompson file is on your desk."

He opened a drawer and looked inside.

"I know," he said, continuing to plunder through the drawer. "But I stuck some notepads in here the other day."

In the back of the drawer, Connolly found a cell phone. He took it out and turned to Mrs. Gordon.

"This thing still work?"

"It would if you charged the battery."

"You know where the charger is?"

"Yes."

He handed it to her.

"We've been paying the bill for it?"

"Every month."

"Get it charged and see if it works."

She gave him a skeptical look.

"Are you actually going to use it?"

"Might as well. I forgot it was in there."

Connolly turned back to the filing cabinet and continued his search. Mrs. Gordon laid the cell phone on the desk and began straightening up.

"Maybe you didn't have a legal pad with you," she suggested.

"Yes!" he shouted.

Mrs. Gordon jumped.

Connolly shoved the drawer closed with a bang and darted across the room. He snatched his jacket from the coat rack and thrashed through the pockets.

"What now?" Mrs. Gordon scowled.

"You're right," he said, almost giddy. "I didn't have a pad with me." He jerked his hand from a coat pocket triumphantly holding a business card. "I wrote it on this."

"Wrote what?"

"Henry let me see the evidence they collected from Attaway. One thing they had was his wallet. When I went through it, I found a small scrap of paper with a name written on it and some numbers. I scribbled the numbers on this business card."

The boxes of documents from the closet in the Attaways's

beach house sat on the floor beside the desk. He lifted one of the boxes to the desktop and set it on the pile of papers Mrs. Gordon was trying to straighten. She moved out of the way and scowled at him from near the door.

Connolly flipped the top off the box and pulled out a stack of bank account records. Holding the business card in his hand, he checked the number on the card against the account number on the bank statements.

"That's it," he said, triumphantly.

The numbers matched. He now had a paper trail linking Alpaca to Attaway, Agostino, and the documents in the boxes from Attaway's beach house.

"So," Mrs. Gordon said, "what good does all that do Avery Thompson?"

Connolly sank into a chair behind the desk.

"I don't know," he said. "At least, not yet."

He stared into space, thinking.

"Gives you something to talk about at the preliminary hearing," she said.

"Yeah."

He jumped up and slipped on his jacket.

"Where are you going now? You need to clean up this mess."

"If Leigh Ann Agostino was in the car with Attaway, that means she knew something about this. I think it's time I had a talk with her."

"Leigh Ann Agostino?"

"I'll explain later," he said.

He started for the door.

"What about this mess?" she repeated.

"Leave it," he called. "Leave it all right where it is."

From the office, Connolly drove west to Spring Hill. It took all of ten minutes to get there. He parked the Chrysler on the street in front of the Agostinos's home and walked to the front door. The door opened before he could ring the doorbell. Leigh Ann Agostino appeared, holding the door open with one hand, the other lying deliberately on her hip. She smiled a fake beauty pageant smile, her lips stretched tight pushing her cheeks up slightly, her head tilted to one side.

"Mike Connolly," she said, stepping back and taking the door with both hands. "I haven't seen you in ages."

Connolly stepped inside. She closed the door behind him.

"How have you been?" she continued. "I saw Barbara at the flower shop a few days ago."

She was still smiling, but the tone of her voice was unmistakably cruel and condescending.

"Hello, Leigh Ann," he replied.

"Come on back to the kitchen," she said. She led him down the hall. "Believe it or not, I'm trying to cook."

He followed her through the house. In the kitchen, several pots and pans sat around the counter top. Another boiled on the stove.

"I'm trying to get ready for my bridge club. They're coming for lunch. Have a seat." She pointed toward a bar stool on the opposite side of the counter. Connolly sat. "You know most of them. Trudy, Kathy, Mitzi Kaylor. Want something to drink?"

"No. Thanks."

She looked at a page in a cookbook, then turned to a mixing bowl and began stirring.

"So, what's on your mind?"

"You want to tell me what you and Keyton were talking about?"

"Keyton?" She did her best to look puzzled. "When?"

"Right before he was shot?"

A frown appeared on her forehead, but she did not lift her eyes from the mixing bowl.

"How would I know? I wasn't there."

She lifted a carton of milk and began pouring it into the bowl. Connolly pressed the conversation further.

"I didn't know until yesterday that he was your brother."

The carton slipped from Leigh Ann's hand, spilling milk across the counter. She grabbed a towel to clean it up.

"I don't think I have anything to say to you," she said.

Her voice was ice cold. She picked up a second towel to wipe the milk.

"Ever hear of a Bahamian corporation called Alpaca?"

Leigh Ann continued to clean the spilled milk.

"Has a large bank account in Nassau," Connolly said. "There were wire transfers from that account to an account at Tidewater Bank here in Mobile."

She avoided looking at him and continued to sop the milk with a towel as he spoke.

"What does that have to do with me?"

"Your husband is president of the corporation."

She stopped wiping the counter. Milk dripped from the towel in her hand as she stared at him.

"You have no idea what you're talking about," she said. She tossed the towel in the sink. "You need to leave."

No longer the genteel, Southern housewife, her countenance turned nasty, cold, heartless. Her eyes were narrow and dark. Her lips thin and taut. Connolly was amused at her reaction.

"Tell me why your husband, a sitting federal judge, has an offshore corporation and an offshore bank account."

She walked around the counter to the back door and snatched it open.

"Leave," she ordered.

"Tell me why someone would murder Keyton in your presence and not kill you too."

"Leave," she shouted. "Now!"

Her face was contorted in a grotesque display of raw anger and rage. Connolly slid off the bar stool and walked to the door.

"What did John say when your boyfriend showed up the other day?"

"My boyfriend?"

"Yeah. That guy in the green Taurus."

Leigh Ann's face was suddenly red.

"Get out of my house," she hollered.

Connolly stepped outside. Leigh Ann slammed the door closed. A smile spread across his face.

Connolly returned to the office at noon. Mrs. Gordon was out. His desk was still strewn with papers from the Thompson file. On top of it all sat the box of account records where he left it. He slid the box to one side and sat in the chair behind the desk. As he relaxed he leaned farther back in the chair, propped his feet on the desk, and closed his eyes. He was soon fast asleep.

An hour later he awoke to the sound of Mrs. Gordon's voice.

"Did the infamous Mrs. Agostino solve all your problems?" She was standing in the doorway.

"No," he said. "She threw me out, actually."

"Imagine that."

She stepped toward the desk. He took his feet off the desktop and stood.

"What are you doing?"

"I'm going to clean up this mess," she replied.

"Not yet."

She paused between the door and the desk.

"Copy this box of documents first," he said, pointing to the box on the desk. "Make a copy of all the account statements and transfer receipts. Do the same for the box in the floor."

"Why don't you send them out to a copying service?"

"If I send them out, they may never come back."

"What do I do with them when I finish?"

"Put the originals in a box and take them to your house."

"My house?"

"Yes," he replied. "Your house."

"Why my house?"

"Because no one will think to look there."

A look of concern spread across Mrs. Gordon's face.

"You think someone might try to take this stuff?"

"I don't know," Connolly said. "But I'm not taking any chances. Truman Albritton is a dangerous man."

"Truman Albritton? What's he got to do with anything?"

"I'm not exactly sure yet."

Mrs. Gordon rolled her eyes as she picked up the documents and started toward the copier.

Thirty-Five

The following morning Connolly parked the Chrysler on the street in front of the office building. Instead of going directly upstairs, he walked up the street to the Port City Diner for coffee and doughnuts. As he sat there sipping coffee, Hollis Toombs walked in.

"You out early or late?"

"Early," Hollis replied. "Been up at your office waiting for you."

"Not usually anyone there before eight. Want a doughnut?"

"Sure."

Connolly waved at the waiter behind the counter.

"Two doughnuts and a cup of coffee for him," he said, pointing to Hollis.

"So, why are you looking for me?"

The waiter set a plate of doughnuts and a cup of coffee in front of Hollis. Hollis took a sip of coffee before replying.

"Found that place you asked about."

Connolly was puzzled.

"That place?"

"Below McIntosh."

Connolly's eyes lit up.

"That was fast."

"Got a friend lives up that way," Hollis said. "Knows all those places. Told me how to get to it."

"Sure it's the right place?"

"I'm sure."

Hollis stuffed half a doughnut in his mouth.

"Who's your friend?"

"Game warden," Hollis replied. His voice was muffled by a mouthful of doughnut.

"Got time to ride up there with me?"

Hollis choked down the mouthful of doughnut.

"Yeah," he said. "Let me finish my doughnuts first."

"Good idea," Connolly chuckled. "I think I'll have another myself."

He raised his hand to get the waiter's attention.

Connolly and Hollis reached the town of Calvert, ten miles south of McIntosh, in about an hour.

"Keep on going," Hollis said. "We get on the north side of town, start looking for a place called Hattie's One Stop."

"Hattie's One Stop," Connolly repeated.

Hollis nodded.

"It'll be on the right."

A mile or two farther, they approached a rambling shack of a building a few feet off the highway. Two faded red gasoline pumps sat between the building and the edge of the pavement. Three or four pickup trucks were parked out front.

"Slow down," Hollis said. "This may be it."

The building once had been a single-story wooden frame house. Over time, rooms had been added on either side. A service bay stood at one end with a lean-to in the back. Gray and weathered, most of it had never seen a coat of paint. A rusted Royal Crown Cola sign hung above what appeared to be the front door. As they drew closer, Hollis saw the words "Hattie's One Stop" faded and barely legible in the middle of the sign.

"Yeah," Hollis said. "This is it. Turn right."

Connolly turned right onto a dirt road. He pressed the accelerator. The Chrysler picked up speed. Soon they descended into the delta swamp that surrounded the upper reaches of the Mobile River. Huge oak trees with thick trunks and sprawling branches interspersed with towering pines and scrubby bushes created a thick wall along both sides of the road. The road was dry and dusty, and a red cloud rolled behind them, but a few feet to either side dark brown water oozed from the swamp into ditches that ran along the shoulders.

"We're going to come to a fork in the road down here a little ways," Hollis said. "Take the road to the left."

The road was wide, but rough as a washboard, and it bounced the car around. Connolly eased off the accelerator and moved farther to the right where the road was smooth and sandy.

"Don't get too far over here," Hollis warned.

"Just looking for a smooth place," Connolly replied.

"Well, there's a ditch over here about four feet deep."

"I see it."

Before long they reached the fork in the road. Connolly steered the car to the left. The rear end of the Chrysler slid around. Hollis grabbed the dashboard. Connolly laughed.

"Now what?"

"Looking for a blue board nailed to a tree," Hollis replied. "Better slow this thing down or you'll never find it."

"A blue board?"

"Yeah. Two by four. Not very long."

"Which side?"

"I don't know."

Connolly frowned. Reluctantly he lifted his foot. The Chrysler slowed.

"You watch that side," Connolly said. "I'll watch over here."

Both men peered out the window as they rolled along. In a few minutes Hollis stuck his head out the window. He craned his neck to see behind them.

"Back up," he shouted.

Connolly shoved the brake pedal toward the floor and brought the car to a sliding stop.

"Back up?"

Hollis slipped his head inside.

"Yeah," he said. "I think that's it back there."

Connolly put the car in reverse and backed up. The cloud of dust that had rolled behind them now enveloped them. Fine grains of red dirt covered the car.

"How far?"

"Not far," Hollis said. "Keep going."

"Hope nobody runs up behind us."

Connolly drove the car backward several hundred yards.

"You sure we don't need to just turn around?"

"There it is," Hollis said, pointing to a blue board nailed to a pine tree.

"Okay," Connolly said, looking around. "What next?"

"A mile from here we should come on a road to the left. Might be a little rough."

"Why didn't you tell me that before? We didn't have to back all the way up here."

"Hey," Hollis countered, throwing his arms in the air. "You want to find this place or not?"

"Yeah, I want to find it," Connolly sighed.

Hollis pointed toward the road.

"Then drive," he said.

In about a mile and a half they came to a rough, two-rut road to the left.

"That's it," Hollis said, pointing.

By the time Connolly stopped the car, they were a hundred feet past it. He put the car in reverse and backed up.

"You sure about this?"

"It's the first road I've seen, and look yonder," he said, pointing again. "See the sign on that tree." A sign nailed to a nearby tree read, "Hunting Club. No Trespassing."

"Looks like the place to me," Hollis said.

Connolly turned the car left and started down the road. Thick woods on either side encroached the road. Pine trees towered high above them, and large oaks spread their branches in an unbroken canopy, blocking out the morning sun.

"This is like driving in a cave," Connolly said.

The car bounced along between the ruts, twice bottoming out. Tree branches raked the sides of the car, and weeds made a slapping noise underneath the floor. Mud splattered against the fenders and up the sides. Connolly grimaced at the thought of making a mess of the car, but kept going.

In a few minutes, the woods fell away, and a clearing opened in front of them. To the left stood a two-story cabin. Built of cypress, it was gray from the weather, but appeared sturdy and solid. A porch ran across the front and around the corner to a chimney.

To the right, across the clearing, stood a large barn. It too was constructed of cypress and, like every other structure in that part of the world, was gray from years in the sun and rain.

Connolly stopped the car and got out.

"This look like what your friend described?"

"Yeah," Hollis replied. "This is it."

Connolly stepped onto the cabin porch and looked inside. The entire first floor was a single, open room. To the left of the door was a fireplace, to the right the kitchen. In between was a long table with benches on each side and a chair at either end. He jiggled the doorknob. It was locked. He stepped away from the door.

"Come on," he said. "Let's try the barn."

Hollis followed Connolly across the clearing.

Large double doors stood in the center of the front wall of the barn. They were locked together with a chain and a padlock as big as Connolly's fist. Lean-tos on either side of the main structure were crammed with equipment and junk.

"Looks like a hunting club to me," Hollis said.

Ignoring him, Connolly walked around the corner to the rear of the barn.

In back was another set of large double doors. Unlike the front, however, these doors were not chained together but held together from inside by a single timber lodged in u-shaped brackets on either side.

"Come here," Connolly called.

Hollis appeared from around the corner.

"Find something?"

"See if you can find something to slide between these doors."

"You going to break in?"

"I imagine there's a board across here inside holding these doors together. If we can lift it up, we can get inside."

"We? I didn't agree to break into nobody's barn."

"Just find something," Connolly insisted. "Something thin and strong."

Hollis glared at him.

"Hurry up," Connolly said.

Hollis disappeared around the corner.

In a few minutes, he returned with a kaiser blade, a curved

blade about a foot long with a solid wooden handle about three feet in length.

"Will this do?"

"Perfect," Connolly said.

He slid the blade into the crack between the doors and moved it up until it contacted the board holding the doors together.

"Alright," he said. "Give me a hand."

Together, they pushed the handle up, lifting the board out of the slots on either side of the door. It fell to the floor inside with a thud. The doors came open. Connolly grasped one and pulled it wide.

Morning light streamed into the darkness of the barn. He squinted against the glare, trying to see inside. Finally, he stepped through the doorway.

A few feet beyond the door sat a car. It was covered with a cloth for protection. Connolly lifted the corner of the cloth and peeled it back, exposing the right rear fender of a white Cadillac. He looked at Hollis and smiled.

"That what you were looking for?"

"Yeah," Connolly replied. "That's what I was looking for."

He threw the cover back further and walked up the side of the car to the front passenger door. With a hard tug he removed the cover from over the door. The glass in the door was shattered. Connolly pulled his shirt out of his trousers and used the tail as a glove to open the car door. He bent low over the front seat as he looked around.

"I wonder if Toby is at work today."

"LeMoyne?"

"Yeah."

"I have no idea," Hollis said. "Why?"

"We need him up here."

Connolly walked out of the barn and went around front to his car. He picked up a cellular telephone from the front seat and dialed Toby's number.

Thirty-Six

*C*onnolly and Hollis spent the remainder of the day at the hunting lodge with Toby LeMoyne and a crime scene investigation unit from the sheriff's office. They returned to Mobile late that evening. Connolly made it to the office shortly before noon the following day.

Mrs. Gordon glared at him as he passed her desk.

"What?" he asked.

The corners of her mouth turned up in a knowing, but disappointed, look.

"You laid out all night, didn't you?"

"No."

"Right," she said, her voice laden with skepticism. "I called your apartment. You weren't there. Where were you?"

"Hollis Toombs and I were looking for Attaway's hunting lodge."

"Now that's a creative story," she replied.

He pulled a chair close to her desk and sat down.

"We found it," he said, his voice low. "And we found a white Cadillac. Toby checked the tag. The car belongs to Leigh Ann Agostino."

"And this proves ... ?"

"I'm not sure what it proves, but it certainly raises some doubt."

Mrs. Gordon was unconvinced.

"Like I said, what does it prove?"

"I don't know," he said, jumping to his feet. "I don't have it all worked out yet."

He started down the hall.

"I almost forgot," she called after him.

Connolly stopped near the door to his office.

"Robert Knodel called this morning. Said you'd been trying to reach him."

"I saw him on the street a few minutes ago," Connolly replied. "I'm going by to see him in a little while."

"Talk about crooks. What are you going to see him for?"

"He's not a crook, he's a stockbroker."

"Like I said ..."

Connolly stepped into the office and closed the door. He crossed the room and flopped into the chair behind the desk. Even though he was getting a late start on the day, it was already noon. Time for his nap. He propped his feet on the desktop, leaned the chair against the wall, and closed his eyes.

When the telephone rang, he was sound asleep. He moved his feet to the floor and struggled to open his eyes. Groggy and only half awake, he shoved papers and files around in an attempt to uncover the telephone. Finally, he found it on the floor at the end of his desk.

"Meet me at Municipal Park, near the pond," the caller said. It was a male voice, brusque but not rude. "Second entrance. We need to talk about Keyton Attaway."

"Who is this?"

"Half an hour, and don't be late."

Connolly hung up the phone and leaned back in the chair. He stared at the ceiling and did his best to figure out whose voice it was. He checked his watch and sighed.

"What do I have to lose?" he thought.

Thompson's preliminary hearing was fast approaching, and he was still no closer to understanding why Attaway was killed. If someone could tell him something that would help him, he owed it to Thompson to listen.

Reluctantly, he pushed himself up from the chair and took his jacket from the coat rack.

With afternoon traffic, the drive from the office to Municipal Park took twenty minutes. Connolly made his way to the Spring Hill Avenue side and turned in at the second entrance. Ahead, a picnic pavilion sat at the end of the drive near the pond. He eased the Chrysler along, watching for anything that looked suspicious.

The parking area around the pavilion was empty. The pavilion itself was deserted. A swing set stood across the drive, the swings drifting gently to and fro in a light breeze. Connolly brought the car to a stop near a water fountain alongside the pavilion. He turned off the engine and got out.

He looked nervously about as he closed the car door and moved to the front fender. He stopped near the front bumper and stood beside the car. In the next pavilion, a hundred yards away, two children played on a picnic table. Their mother sat nearby reading a book. At the far end of the pond, a small child fed the ducks.

The day had been hot and muggy downtown, but there in the park the air felt cool and refreshing. The breeze that moved the swings blew through Connolly's hair. He ran his fingers across the top of his head to smooth it in place. The sound of the breeze in the treetops and the hum of traffic going by in the distance gave the park an eerie stillness.

In a few minutes, a dark green Taurus turned off Spring

Hill Avenue. The car rolled quietly toward him. Two men sat in the front seat.

He glanced behind him toward the pond. The child who had been feeding the ducks was gone. In his place was a man in a dark suit. The man wore dark sunglasses that hid his eyes, but Connolly was certain he was staring in his direction.

Connolly turned quickly away and focused on the oncoming Taurus. The two men in the front seat stared ahead at him, their faces resolute and emotionless. The car was close enough now that Connolly heard the gravel crunch beneath its tires.

Suddenly, the laughter of children drew near. He glanced to the right and saw the children from the next pavilion running toward the swing set across the drive in front of him. Their mother followed behind them.

Connolly's heart began to pound. He stole a quick glance over his shoulder. The man at the pond moved forward.

The children stopped at the swings. Their mother continued toward Connolly. She crossed the drive and walked in front of him, passing between the Chrysler and the oncoming Taurus. At the edge of the pavilion she bent over the fountain and took a drink. When she lifted her head she glanced at Connolly and smiled, distracting him for a moment.

The Taurus came to a stop a few feet away. Connolly turned away from the woman to face the car. The man on the passenger side said something to the driver. The car backed slowly away and turned around. Connolly watched as it drove toward the entrance. At Spring Hill Avenue, the car made a right turn and disappeared in traffic.

With the car gone, Connolly suddenly remembered the man behind him. He spun quickly around expecting to see him still standing there. But he saw nothing. Only the blue-green water of the pond and a group of ducks floating quietly by.

He turned again toward the fountain. The woman who had been there only a moment before was gone too. The swings at the end of the pavilion were empty, floating on the breeze just as before. The children he had seen only minutes before were not there.

Thirty-Seven

wo days later, Connolly was busy at his desk preparing for Thompson's preliminary hearing which was only four days away. Mrs. Gordon appeared at the door to Connolly's office. In her hand was a small piece of paper. She had a puzzled look on her face.

"A little boy brought you this note," she said. "I'm not sure what it's about."

She walked to his desk and handed him the slip of paper.

"Is he still out there?" Connolly said, glancing at the note.

"No," she replied. "He left this and scooted out the door. Said a woman out front told him to bring it to you."

"Courtyard. St. Alban Cathedral." The message read. "Ten minutes."

Connolly stared at the note. The handwriting was neat and legible, but not one he recognized.

"Any idea who wrote it?" Mrs. Gordon asked.

He tossed the note on the desk and stood.

"Not really," he replied.

He walked to the coat rack by the door and slipped on his jacket. Mrs. Gordon still stood in the doorway.

"Where are you going?"

"St. Alban," Connolly replied.

"What for?"

"Going to find out who wrote the note."

Connolly started up the hall toward the door.

Instead of leaving through the lobby downstairs, Connolly took the service elevator and exited the rear of the building to Ferguson's Alley. He walked down the alley to Conti Street and turned right.

St. Alban Cathedral was located on Claiborne Street and occupied the entire block between Dauphin and St. Francis Streets. Only five blocks north of Connolly's office, he could have walked up Dauphin Street but after the incident in the park a few days earlier he was a little leery of anonymous calls and notes. He walked up Conti to Claiborne and turned right. Taking the more circuitous route allowed him to approach the cathedral from the side.

A delivery truck was parked near the corner at Claiborne and Dauphin. Connolly moved from the sidewalk to the street and stepped behind the truck. He stood at the bumper on the left corner and peered slowly around. From there, he had a clear view of the front of the cathedral.

On the corner to the left was Embry's Drugstore. Directly across the street was the cathedral. He scanned the area carefully but saw no one suspicious. He ducked behind the truck again and moved to the right side.

Across Claiborne Street, in front of the cathedral, was a square that covered most of the block. A fountain sat in the middle with sidewalks extending from it. Benches were scattered about and there were small patches of grass, but there were no trees or other obstructions. From his place beside the truck, Connolly could see all the way across the park to Eddie's Pawn and Gun on St. Francis Street. Several people sat on the benches. He studied each one, but found nothing unusual. A woman sat on a bench in one of the patches of green between the sidewalks. She read a book while two small children played in front of her. Connolly was about to turn away when he noticed a man standing outside the pawnshop on St. Francis Street.

Dressed in a dark suit, he seemed to be just another downtown businessman. But as Connolly watched, he noticed the man did not move and he appeared to be searching intently for something or someone. In his left hand he held a newspaper rolled into a tight cylinder.

Connolly moved to the left side of the truck for another look in that direction. As he peered around the truck, he caught a glimpse of a man in front of Embry's Drugstore. He appeared to be moving nervously, turning from left to right affording Connolly a brief view of his shoulder with each move. He wore a dark gray business suit. Connolly slipped back behind the truck and waited. A moment later, he peeked around the truck again for another look.

The man in front of Embry's had moved further out from the corner of the building. He stood near the edge of the sidewalk. Like the man on St. Francis Street, he was dressed in a dark gray suit and seemed to be just another downtown businessman. As Connolly watched, the man turned to the right. Connolly caught a glimpse of his face. Unlike the other man, this one wore sunglasses. Connolly's heart began to pound.

He slipped behind the truck and sat on the bumper. The man at the corner was the same man he had seen standing behind him in the park.

While Connolly tried to focus his mind on what to do, a deliveryman wheeled a hand truck from the sidewalk to the back of the truck. His sudden appearance startled Connolly.

"Sorry to bother you," the man said. "But I've got to go."

Connolly stood. The deliveryman shoved the hand truck into the back of the truck and pulled the door down. Connolly waited while the man moved around the truck and climbed in behind the steering wheel. As the truck eased forward, Connolly followed it toward the corner. At the last minute, he darted from the street to the sidewalk beside Embry's Drug Store and slipped in the side door.

He slipped behind a display rack and watched. Through the large windows in front of the store he could see the man standing at the corner. Across the park the other man was still outside the pawnshop. A few minutes later, a dark green Taurus rolled slowly up Claiborne Street and came to a stop in front of the cathedral. Leigh Ann Agostino emerged from the cathedral. She stalked across the street to the Taurus and flung open the door. She leaned inside and spoke to the driver in what appeared to be an excited conversation. Connolly could see her arms flaying the air as she spoke. Finally, exasperated, she got inside and slammed the door closed. The car drove away.

Connolly turned on the stool and looked toward the corner. No one was there. He glanced across the park. The man outside the pawnshop was gone too.

He slipped from the stool and laid a five-dollar bill on the counter.

Thirty-Eight

Mrs. Gordon was waiting at her desk when Connolly returned to the office.

"Judge Cahill called for you," she said.

"What did he want?"

"Said he needed to see you."

Connolly started past her desk toward the hall.

"He meant this afternoon," she said.

Connolly stopped and turned toward her.

"Anything else happen?"

"No," she said. "How was it at the church?"

"Interesting," he said. "I'll tell you later."

He stepped toward the door.

"Who was it?"

"Leigh Ann Agostino."

Mrs. Gordon looked puzzled.

"What's she got to do with this case?"

He opened the door.

"I'll tell you about it later," he said.

He stepped through the door to the corridor and walked to the elevator.

Cahill's courtroom was empty when Connolly arrived. Walter's desk was clean, and his coffee cup was missing.

Connolly smiled to himself. It was a sure sign Walter was gone for the day.

He walked past Walter's desk and stepped through the door behind the judge's bench. Judge Cahill was standing outside his office near the coffee machine.

"I see you got my message," Cahill said.

He stepped inside his office. Connolly followed him. Cahill crossed the room to his desk and took a seat. Connolly lingered near the door.

"Close the door," he said. "Have a seat."

Connolly closed the door and sat in a chair in front of the desk.

"Got a report from Dr. Fitzhugh Brundige at Harwell Psychiatric Facility," Cahill said. He tossed the report across the desk. "Says your man has some permanent damage from what happened to him, but he's fit to stand trial."

Connolly picked up the report and scanned the first page.

"You still agree he's competent?"

"Yes, sir. We're ready to go forward." Connolly tossed the report on the desk.

"We'll need to get that on the record before we do the preliminary hearing."

Connolly nodded.

"Any more word on who filed the motion and did that order?"

Cahill sighed. He toyed with a pencil a moment before replying. "I talked to Sheriff McNeil about it," he said. "He wasn't too interested in pursuing it."

"Must be an election soon."

Cahill laughed.

"As a matter of fact, it won't be long." Cahill leaned back in his chair and draped his arms over his head. "I think I'm satisfied nobody from the sheriff's office or the jail was involved. If what happened to him occurred at Aikers, it would be out of my jurisdiction anyway. DA's office couldn't do anything about it. Have to go up there to pursue it."

Connolly crossed his legs.

"You know, Thompson has a claim against somebody for the way he's been treated."

Cahill stopped toying with the pencil.

"You mean me?"

Connolly shrugged.

"I don't know about you. You might have immunity. But this man was in custody. He was in a vulnerable position. Somebody at the jail, or Aikers, or Harwell deliberately did this, or let it happen."

Cahill let the pencil slip from his fingers. He leaned over the desk.

"If Thompson wants to file a lawsuit, I'd let somebody else handle it if I were you," he said.

Connolly stared at him a moment.

"What are you saying?"

"I'm saying, after years of handling cases you learn which ones to hold onto and which ones to let go. My sense is, this is one you want to let go." He leaned back in his chair. "You got anything else we need to talk about?"

"No," Connolly replied. "I don't think so."

Cahill stood. "Okay," he said. "I have to run."

He started around the desk toward the door. Connolly rose to follow. Cahill picked up the report from the desk and handed it to him.

"This is your copy."

Connolly took the report and stepped to the door.

Thirty-Nine

 onday afternoon, Judge Cahill rapped his gavel promptly at two o'clock.

"Order," he said. "Order in the court."

The courtroom was packed. Keyton Attaway's wife and children sat on the front row of the audience behind the counsel tables, along with his mother, an uncle, and Jake and Connie Patronas. On the second row, Avery Thompson's mother sat with his cousins. Behind them the remaining seats were filled with attorneys from Attaway's law firm and curious spectators.

Reporters from three television stations and four newspapers stood against the wall along both sides of the courtroom. They scribbled notes on their notepads and waited. Walter had already banished the cameramen to the hallway. Judge Cahill would not allow them to videotape the proceedings.

At the counsel table to the judge's right, Henry McNamara sat alone. A box of documents sat beside him on the floor. A file folder lay open in front of him on the table.

The table to the judge's left was occupied by Connolly and Avery Thompson. Connolly's worn and battered leather satchel sat on the floor beside his chair. The tabletop was clean and uncluttered.

As Judge Cahill rapped his gavel, spectators and family

members wedged themselves into the last remaining seats, and the courtroom grew quiet. Laughter and noise from the crowd in the hallway drifted into the courtroom.

"Walter," Judge Cahill said, "go see if you can get them quiet in the hall."

Walter stepped from behind his desk beside the judge's bench and strode across the courtroom to the door. Judge Cahill tossed his gavel on the bench and leaned back in his chair, crossing his arms behind his head.

"Tell them I'll give them lunch and a place to eat it if they can't be quiet," he called.

Walter shoved the door open and stepped into the hall.

"Hey," he barked.

His voice cut through the noise like a knife. Startled, the crowd in the hall fell silent.

"You folks want to continue this conversation in a jail cell?"

They all shook their heads.

"Alright then, keep it down."

Walter returned to the courtroom and closed the door. He glanced at Judge Cahill as he walked toward his desk. Both men struggled to suppress a grin.

Judge Cahill leaned forward and smiled at the court reporter.

"Are you ready?"

"Yes," she replied.

He settled into his chair.

"Alright," he began, his face suddenly serious, "we're here today for a preliminary hearing in case number 99489. State of Alabama versus Avery Lee Thompson." He looked to Henry McNamara. "Mr. McNamara, is the State ready?"

McNamara stood.

"Yes, Your Honor," he said. "We're ready."

Cahill turned to Connolly.

"Mike, are y'all ready?"

Connolly stood.

"Yes, Your Honor. We're ready."

"Very well. State, call your first witness."

Connolly took a seat and removed a yellow legal pad from the leather satchel. He turned to a clean sheet and prepared to take notes.

"The State calls Mrs. Karen Attaway."

"Mrs. Attaway," Cahill said, "come on up if you would, please ma'am."

Karen Attaway slipped past those seated next to her and made her way to the witness stand on the opposite side of the judge from Walter's desk. Judge Cahill placed her under oath.

"Have a seat, please ma'am," he said. "I know this is difficult for you, but if you would, please speak up so everyone can hear you."

She nodded in response. McNamara approached the witness stand. Cahill nodded toward him.

"Alright, Henry."

"State your name for the record, please," McNamara began.

"Karen Attaway."

"Are you married?"

"I was."

"What was your husband's name?"

"Keyton Andrew Attaway."

"Mrs. Attaway, do you recall seeing your husband on or about June 15 of this year?"

"Yes. I saw him when he left the house that morning. Said he was going to the office. I was having breakfast with our children."

"At your home?"

"Yes."

"Is your home in Mobile County?"

"Yes, it is."

"When did you next see your husband?"

"The evening of that same day."

"And, where was he when you saw him that evening?"

She put her hand to her top lip. Her eyes squinted closed. Her chin quivered.

"At the ... hospital," she sobbed.

"Was he alive?"

She shook her head.

"Please ma'am. I know it's hard, but I need a verbal response so the court reporter can have a clear record of your answer."

"He was dead," she blurted.

"No further questions," Henry said.

Cahill looked to Connolly.

"Mike, you have any questions for Mrs. Attaway?"

The tone of his voice and the look on his face indicated Connolly should avoid questioning the witness.

"Just a few, Your Honor."

Cahill frowned.

"Make it quick."

"Yes, Your Honor."

Connolly rose and moved across the room in front of the witness stand.

"Karen," Connolly began, his voice soft and concerned, "did you actually identify your husband's body at the hospital?"

"No," she said, shaking her head. "They called me and said he was there. I went to the emergency room. They wanted me to see him. I got as far as the hallway. He was lying on a cart in the morgue."

"You saw a body there?"

"Yes."

"You knew that was the body they wanted you to view?"

"Yes."

"But you didn't actually walk up to it and say, 'Yes, that's my husband.'"

"No."

"Who did? Who made the official identification?"

"Truman Albritton."

Cahill interrupted.

"Is identification really an issue?"

McNamara stood.

"Judge, everyone knew it was Mr. Attaway's body. The coroner knew who he was. They just had to have someone to officially identify the body. When Mrs. Attaway wasn't able to walk back there, Mr. Albritton went. There's no doubt it was his body."

"That right, Mike?"

"I suppose we could put Henry on the stand, and he could get that on the record," Connolly replied. "But Judge, this is a capital murder case. I'm not conceding the point until we have some testimony to that effect."

Cahill was exasperated. He turned to Karen.

"Is that essentially what happened?"

"Yes," she said, nodding her head.

"Alright," Cahill snapped. "I find that the corpus has been sufficiently established. Mike, you got any other questions for Mrs. Attaway?"

"Yes, Your Honor. One or two."

Cahill sighed and leaned back in his chair. He draped both arms over his head again, and rolled his eyes.

Connolly turned to the witness stand.

"Karen, do you recall discussing with me earlier an entity known as Alpaca?"

"Yes."

A rustling sound arose in the back of the courtroom. Cahill sat up and scanned the audience. Charlie Miffin entered the courtroom and crammed himself into a tiny space on the last row of the audience.

"And, do you recall telling me there were records on that entity which were stored at a beach house on Dauphin Island owned by you and your husband?"

"Yes."

McNamara jumped to his feet.

"Your Honor, I object. This is a preliminary hearing on a murder. I have no idea what he's talking about."

Again, there was a noise in the back of the courtroom. Connolly turned toward the audience and scanned the crowd. Truman Albritton slipped from his seat and stepped to the door.

"Mike?" Cahill scowled.

Connolly turned to face the judge's bench.

"You going some place with this?"

"Judge, I can tie this up later with other witnesses, or I can wait and recall her later, but I intend to offer evidence in opposition to the State at this hearing, and I'm entitled to put on enough to establish my theory of what happened."

"Get whatever you want out of her now, she's not coming back," Cahill sighed. "Objection overruled, for now."

Connolly turned again to Karen Attaway.

"Where were those records kept?"

"In a closet in the beach house."

"Was that closet locked?"

"Yes."

"And did you give me a key to that closet?"

"Yes."

"And told me I could go down there and get those records?"

"Yes."

"Did you ever hear your husband mention this entity called Alpaca?"

"Yes."

"Do you recall when you heard him mention it?"

"No, not specifically. He and Truman Albritton used to have these hushed conversations in Keyton's study sometimes. I overheard them talking about it."

"Did you ever overhear them arguing?"

"Yes."

"Heated arguments?"

"Yes."

"Thought they were going to get in a fight?"

"Yes."

"Did they argue any in the week or two prior to your husband's death?"

"Yes."

"You saw them?"

"Yes. Truman was at the house. They were standing in the back yard."

Connolly stepped to the table and took a photograph from the leather satchel. With it in hand, he returned to his place in front of the witness stand.

"Have you ever seen this photograph?"

He handed the picture to Karen.

"Yes."

"Where was this photograph regularly kept?"

"In my husband's office."

"Can you identify the people in that photograph?"

"Yes."

McNamara rose from his seat and moved behind the witness. He looked at the picture over her shoulder.

"Who are they?"

"Hogan Smith, John Agostino, Truman Albritton, and Keyton."

"Do you know where this photograph was taken?"

"Yes."

"Where was it taken?"

"In the Bahamas, summer before last."

She laid the picture on the edge of the witness stand. Connolly retrieved it. McNamara returned to his seat.

"The men in this photo were down there in the Bahamas together?"

"Yes."

"Did they regularly go there together?"

"At least once a year during the past three or four years."

"Were they scheduled to travel there together this year?"

"Yes. They had a trip planned in May."

"Did they take that trip?"

"I don't know about the others. Keyton didn't."

"He refused to go with them?"

"Yes."

"Did that cause a problem?"

"He and Truman Albritton argued about it several times. That's what I was talking about earlier."

"Mr. Albritton wanted Keyton to go. Keyton didn't want to go."

"Yes."

"Was this a pleasure trip?"

"No," she replied. "It was business."

"What kind of business?"

"I don't know, but it was very serious. Keyton sat up at night worrying about it, but he wouldn't tell me any details."

Connolly turned away from the witness stand.

"No further questions, Your Honor."

Cahill leaned forward.

"Henry, any follow up?"

"No, Your Honor."

Cahill relaxed and gestured for Karen to step from the witness stand. When she was seated in the audience, he turned to McNamara.

"Call your next witness."

McNamara stood.

"We call Bill Sisson."

Sisson took the stand. Judge Cahill administered the oath, and McNamara began.

"Do you recall the events of June 15?"

"Yes."

"What do you recall about that day?"

"I was driving home from work at Ingram Shipbuilding—"

McNamara interrupted him.

"Which location? You work at Ingram's yard on Pinto Island?"

"Yes." Sisson replied. "I was coming down Short Haul Road. When I rounded a curve in the road, a man darted out in the highway in front of me."

"Do you see that man here today?"

"Yes. He's seated over there with Mr. Connolly."

"Now Short Haul Road ... is that in Mobile County?"

"Yes. I think so," Sisson said. "It's over there just off the causeway."

"When the defendant darted in front of you, where did he go?"

"He ran across the road and into the swamp."

"Did he look scared?"

Connolly rose part of way out of his chair.

"Objection."

"Sustained," Cahill droned.

"Mr. Sisson, you said you saw Mr. Thompson dart in front of you. Did you see anything else?"

"There was a white Cadillac parked on the left side of the road. He was running from there."

"Was anyone in that Cadillac?"

"I'm not sure. When he ran in front of me, I was trying to avoid hitting him. I wasn't really looking that close at the car."

"What did you do after that?"

"I drove a little farther down the road, then thought I better go back and see if somebody needed some help. I turned around, and when I got back, the car was gone. That's when I noticed the body lying by the road."

"Keyton Attaway's body?"

"They told me it was him. I didn't know him."

"You saw the body. Then you called the police?"

"Yeah. I waited to see if someone would come by to help. I didn't really want to leave the body there alone. But when no one came after a few minutes, I drove down to the causeway and called from a pay phone."

"No further questions."

McNamara returned to his seat at the counsel table. Connolly rose and moved in front of the witness.

"Mr. Sisson, was there a second vehicle there at the point where you saw Mr. Thompson?"

"Yes. A blue Ford pickup was parked behind the Cadillac."

"Was anyone in it?"

"I don't know. Like I said, I was trying to keep from hitting your client."

Connolly stepped to the counsel table and retrieved a photograph from his file.

"Let me show you this picture," he said.

He stepped toward Sisson to hand him the photo. McNamara stood.

"Can I see that?"

"Sure," Connolly replied.

McNamara scanned the photo, then handed it back to Connolly. Connolly handed it to Sisson.

"Mr. Sisson, take a look at this photograph," he said. "Is that the truck you saw parked behind the Cadillac?"

"Yes."

"And how do you know that?"

"Well, it's the right color and make. It has this scratch down the side, along the bed and the rear fender. And it has this green sticker on the windshield."

"Let me see that," Cahill said.

"Judge," McNamara interrupted, "I object. This is a photograph of a truck in a junkyard. Half of it's covered in rust. I don't see how he can identify it."

"Mike?"

"Your Honor, he's already said why he can identify it. I can tie this up later. I'm just getting what I need out of the witness now so we don't have to recall him later."

"Overruled."

"We would ask the photograph be admitted as Defendant's Exhibit Two. And the other photograph that Mrs. Attaway identified, as Defendant's Exhibit One."

"Admitted."

Connolly returned to his seat.

"Nothing further from the witness, Your Honor."

Cahill turned his chair to the side and stood.

"Let's take a break, gentlemen."

Before anyone could answer, Cahill bounded off the bench and disappeared through the door to his office.

Forty

*F*ifteen minutes later, Judge Cahill returned. Spectators climbed over each other to reclaim their seats and wedged themselves in place, hip to hip and shoulder to shoulder. Cahill waited a moment for everyone to find a place. When the courtroom grew still and quiet, he turned to McNamara.

"Go ahead, Henry. Call your next witness."

McNamara stood.

"The State calls Detective Anthony Hammond."

Hammond was seated on a bench directly behind the prosecutor's table, inside the railing that separated the audience from the business area of the courtroom. Beside him sat a large cardboard box. He picked up the box and carried it to a table in front of the judge's bench, then made his way around to the witness stand. Judge Cahill administered the oath, and McNamara began his examination.

"Detective Hammond, did you investigate the death of Keyton Attaway?"

"Yes, I did."

"And in the course of that investigation, did you collect various pieces of physical evidence?"

"Yes."

"Is that what's in the box you brought with you here today?"

"Yes."

"As a result of your investigation, were you able to determine how Mr. Attaway died?"

Suddenly, Judge Cahill lurched forward.

"Just a minute, Detective."

He waved his hand for McNamara and Connolly to approach the bench. When they were in front of him, he looked to Karen Attaway.

"Mrs. Attaway, could you come up here, please?"

She slipped out of her seat and walked to the judge's bench. Judge Cahill covered the microphone in front of him with his hand.

"Henry, are you going to get into the wounds and that sort of thing?"

"We'll have to some, Judge."

Cahill turned to Karen.

"Mrs. Attaway, this might be a little graphic. I notice you have your children with you. You might want to take them out of the courtroom for this part."

Karen shook her head.

"No, Your Honor," she said. "I appreciate the thought, but they know what happened to their father. I told them how he died."

"You sure they'll be able to handle it? I don't want any outbursts."

She nodded.

"Yes, Your Honor. They'll be alright."

"Very well."

Judge Cahill sat up straight in his chair. Connolly, McNamara and Karen Attaway returned to their places.

"Go ahead, Henry," Judge Cahill said.

"Detective, were you able to determine how Mr. Attaway died?"

"Yes. According to the coroner, he died of a gunshot wound to the head. A shot near his temple."

"Did the coroner retrieve any bullets from Mr. Attaway's body?"

"Yes."

"Were those bullets submitted for testing?"

"Yes. The forensic report indicated they came from a thirty-eight caliber pistol."

"In the course of your investigation into this matter, did you find a pistol?"

"Yes. The defendant, Mr. Thompson, had a thirty-eight in his pocket when we picked him up."

McNamara's questions sounded like a well-rehearsed litany. Hammond's answers came almost before the questions were finished.

"Was the pistol tested against the bullets?"

"Yes. The bullets from Mr. Attaway's body matched the pistol we took from the defendant."

"Did you conduct a criminal history background check on the defendant?"

"Yes."

"What did you find?"

"The defendant has three prior felony convictions," Hammond replied. "One for murder. A burglary. And robbery."

"Do you have a certified copy of the judgment of conviction for the murder case?"

Hammond removed a copy of the document from his file and handed it to McNamara.

"Your Honor, we offer this as State's Exhibit Number One," McNamara said, handing the copy to Judge Cahill. "And, we offer the ballistic report on the gun and the spent bullets as State's Exhibits Two and Three."

"Admitted."

McNamara returned to Hammond.

"Where did you find Mr. Attaway's body?"

"He was found lying on the shoulder of the road," Hammond said. "Short Haul Road, out on Pinto Island."

"Was that the same location identified by the prior witness, Mr. Sisson?"

"Yes. Mr. Sisson is the one who called us. He was at the scene when patrol officers first arrived. They took a statement from him."

Cahill interrupted the examination.

"Henry, did you furnish Mike with a copy of that statement?"

"Yes, Your Honor."

"And any other statements you have?"

"Yes, Your Honor."

Cahill turned to Connolly.

"Mike, you agree you received copies of those statements?"

"I received one for Mr. Sisson, Your Honor."

Cahill again leaned back in his chair.

"Very well. Go ahead, Henry."

McNamara moved closer to the witness stand.

"Did you find a white Cadillac automobile at the scene?"

"No," Hammond said.

He could not suppress a smile.

"Did the patrol officers find a white Cadillac at the scene?"

"No."

Connolly jumped to his feet.

"Judge, he's impeaching his own witness. He can't do that. And he's using collateral evidence to do it."

McNamara turned to Cahill.

"I didn't elicit testimony from Mr. Sisson about the car, Your Honor. He did."

Cahill raised his hand.

"Calm down, both of you. This is a preliminary hearing. Mike, your objection is overruled. Go ahead, Henry."

McNamara resumed his questioning.

"No blue Ford pickup there either?"

"No."

"The only mention of either vehicle comes from Mr. Sisson, is that correct?"

"That is correct."

"And there isn't any mention of that automobile in his written statement, is there?"

Hammond shook his head.

"No, there isn't."

"And, that statement was signed by Mr. Sisson, wasn't it?"

"Yes."

"I don't have anything further from this witness."

McNamara returned to the counsel's table. Cahill turned to Connolly.

"Mike."

Connolly rose from his chair.

"How many bullets were removed from Mr. Attaway?" He spoke as he moved across the room to stand near Hammond.

Hammond looked through the papers in his file.

"Three were intact," he said. "There were additional bullet fragments."

"So, he received more than the one wound you told us about?"

"Yes."

"Where were the other wounds?"

McNamara leaped to his feet.

"Objection," he snapped. "This witness is not here to testify as a medical expert."

"Judge," Connolly said, smiling, "he's already testified from the coroner's report about the cause of death. Henry can't object to a little cross-examination."

"Overruled."

Connolly turned again to Hammond.

"Where were the other wounds?"

Hammond glanced at the coroner's report.

"There was the one wound to the temple. Above his right ear. And then there were multiple wounds that were made through his mouth."

"But the coroner has concluded the wounds to the mouth were wounds made subsequent to death, hasn't he?"

"Yes," Hammond said. "The gunshot to the temple would have been fatal."

Connolly moved to the cardboard box on the table in front of the judge's bench.

"You brought this box in with you. Does it contain evidence from this case?"

"Yes."

"I'd like for you to open it and take out Mr. Attaway's wallet, please."

Hammond stepped from the witness stand and moved around to the table. With a small pocketknife, he cut open the top of the box. Carefully, he sorted through the contents laying each item on the table. When he came to the wallet, he took it out and handed it to Connolly.

"This is the wallet from Keyton Attaway's body?"

"Yes," Hammond said.

"It's been in your possession since it was recovered?"

"Yes. Sealed in this box and locked in the evidence room."

Hammond stepped away to return to his seat on the witness stand. Connolly grabbed his arm.

"Wait right here," he directed. "Open this wallet and remove the papers from it, please."

Hammond took the wallet, opened it, and pulled out the papers from the money fold portion.

"You want me to remove the rest of the stuff in here?"

"No," Connolly replied. "This is enough."

Hammond laid the scraps of paper on the table. Connolly picked up one and handed it to him.

"Detective Hammond, what is written on this paper?"

"The word 'Alpaca,' and the numbers '41556943.'"

Connolly let go of Hammond's arm.

"Thank you," he said. "You may return to the stand."

Connolly waited while Hammond returned to his seat.

"Now, Detective, about Mr. Sisson. You have a typewritten copy of that statement Mr. McNamara has referred to, do you not?"

"Yes."

"Do you have the notes from the original interview with Mr. Sisson?"

Hammond leafed through the pages of the file. Connolly did not know whether any notes existed, but he had a hunch. Hammond pulled a handwritten document from the file. He handed it to Connolly.

"I believe that's it."

Connolly smiled as he scanned the paper, then handed it back to Hammond.

"Take a look at that," he said, "and tell us if those handwritten notes indicate whether the witness mentioned a white Cadillac."

Hammond quickly studied the page.

"Ahh ... down here near the bottom," he said, pointing. He had a blank look on his face. "There's a note that the witness told the patrol officer there was a white Cadillac parked on the shoulder of the road."

Connolly turned to Judge Cahill.

"No further questions, Your Honor."

Hammond gathered the contents of the box and resealed the top. As he did, Judge Cahill turned to McNamara.

"Henry, do you have anything else for this witness?"

"No, Your Honor."

Cahill nodded.

"Call your next witness," he said.

McNamara stood.

"The State rests, Your Honor."

"That's all you have?"

"That's all we need, Your Honor," McNamara replied. "We've established Mr. Attaway is dead. His body was found at the scene. The defendant was at the scene. Mr. Attaway was murdered by a gunshot to the head. The defendant was found in possession of the murder weapon. He has a prior murder conviction, which was rendered within the last twenty years. That establishes probable cause for capital murder."

Cahill turned to Connolly.

"Mike, you still want to put on some evidence?"

Connolly stood.

"Yes, Your Honor," he said. "We have several witnesses we'd like to call."

Cahill looked at his watch.

"Why don't we start on that first thing in the morning. It's almost five now. We'll be in recess until tomorrow morning. Nine o'clock."

He slipped from the bench and disappeared through the door behind Walter's desk.

Forty-One

*C*onnolly walked from the courtroom to the office. Mrs. Gordon was waiting for him.

"How'd it go?"

"Well as could be expected," he replied. "Did you check to see if our subpoenas have been served?"

"Took care of that late last week," she said. "All your witnesses are waiting on a call."

"Good. Call them. Tell them to be at Judge Cahill's courtroom tomorrow morning. Eight o'clock."

He passed Mrs. Gordon's desk and moved down the hall.

"Robert Knodel came by," she continued, following him down the hall. "Said to tell you it was all taken care of. Said you'd know what that meant. He left an envelope for you. I put it on your desk."

"Great."

"I still think you need to use a different broker," she called. "I use Oscar Howell myself. Knodel is a relic."

"Oscar's too aggressive for me," Connolly replied over his shoulder. "Besides, relic or not, I like Robert. Never have to worry about losing my money."

Connolly stepped inside his office and turned to face Mrs. Gordon.

"Are you working tonight?" she asked.

"Not long," he said. "Why?"

"Just wondering what to expect," she replied. "Sometimes you work late when you're in a trial."

"Not tonight," he said. "Just make those calls, and then you can go."

He closed the door. She returned to her desk.

He hung his jacket on the coat rack and sank into the chair behind the desk. He picked up the envelope from the desktop and opened it. Inside was a two-page document. He glanced at it briefly and propped his feet on the desktop. He laid the document in his lap and fell asleep.

When Connolly awoke, the office was dark. He walked to the window and opened the blinds. Light from the streetlights below sent an eerie glow through the room. He checked his watch. It was eight-thirty. He hesitated—it was later than he had intended—then grabbed his jacket from the coat rack and hurried downstairs.

The drive to Ann Street normally took ten minutes, but without the daytime traffic he made it in five. From there, it was only two blocks to Barbara's house.

He pulled to a stop at the curb out front and scanned the windows. Lights were on inside near the back. He got out and walked to the front door. On the steps, he hesitated again. Twice he turned to leave. Then, with determination, he jabbed the doorbell button with his finger. The porch light came on, and Barbara peered through the window. His heart leaped at the sight of her.

She moved away from the window and opened the door.

"You know, it would be easier if you'd call first," she said.

"I'm sorry," he replied. "I've been in court most of the day."

"Come on in," she sighed.

She held the door for him and stepped aside to allow him into the hallway. He brushed past her and into the living room.

"Let's go back here," she said, pointing down the hall. "I have something in the oven."

She led him into the den at the back of the house. The television was on when they entered the room. She switched it off and took a seat on the sofa. He sat in a nearby chair. A wonderful aroma drifted out of the kitchen.

She wore a blue and white cotton dress that hung loosely from her shoulders. Her hair was undone, and she had on no makeup. Even so, he found her mesmerizing. He watched as she settled on the sofa and crossed her long, slender legs.

"Did you come here for something in particular?" she said.

The look in her eye said she'd noticed he was staring at her.

"Sorry," he said.

He glanced away, suddenly nervous and self-conscious.

"I've been ... ahh ..." He turned to her with an embarrassed smile. "This is hard for me to talk about."

She sighed impatiently and waited for him to continue.

"When we divorced, I told what's-his-name ... your lawyer ..."

"Bill Mills."

"Yeah. I told Mills we didn't own much more than what we owed. But," he took a deep breath, "I lied."

Her face grew cold. Her eyes narrowed, and her jaw slid forward.

"Wait," he said, gesturing with his hand. "Let me finish ..." He looked her in the eye now. "I was wrong to do that. I'm sorry for it. I know you've had to work in that flower shop, and it's been tough on you, especially having your friends see you like that. I want to make it as right as I can."

He paused and took an envelope from the inside pocket of his jacket. Stretching forward, he handed it to her.

"I had some money in an investment account with Robert Knodel. It came from that oil rig case I had a few years before we divorced."

She was livid.

"Don't think I'm going to let you get away with this," she hissed through clenched teeth.

"Calm down for a minute," he said. "I'm not finished yet."

She re-crossed her legs and folded her arms tightly across her chest.

"As far as I can remember, I haven't taken any money out of that account. You can check with Robert to verify it."

"You can bet I will." Her words were like bullets. "And don't think we're splitting this evenly either."

"That's what I'm coming to." He paused and gathered himself, then plunged ahead. "I don't want to split it evenly. I don't want to split it at all. I've already signed the papers with Robert transferring the entire account to you. There's a copy in that envelope. The account is worth a little over three hundred thousand dollars."

Her chin dropped. Her mouth gaped open. Connolly stood.

"I'm sorry," he said. "I shouldn't have hid this from you."

He walked out of the room and up the hallway. Barbara stepped into the hall behind him, a puzzled look on her face.

"Mike, why are you doing this?"

He stopped near the front door and turned to her.

"I ... ahh ..."

The words stuck in his throat. He swallowed hard. He

wanted to tell her all that had happened to him, the encounter at St. Pachomius, the days he spent ridding his body of alcohol, the struggle each day to stay sober, but he couldn't.

"The ..." He tried again, and again the words would not come. He cleared his throat and looked away. "The other day ... when I saw you at the flower shop, I ... ahh ... I heard the way Tootsie talked to you, and I saw the way those other women looked at you, and I remembered what I had done. It never seemed too big a deal until I saw ..." He turned to look at her. "Things are different now. I don't want to be like I was. I just wanted to make it right."

Tears came to her eyes.

"I'm not asking for anything," he continued. "I don't expect anything from you. I just wanted to let you know I was wrong, and I'm sorry."

They looked at each other a moment.

"I've got to go," he said. "Got a big day in court tomorrow."

He opened the door and was gone.

Connolly returned to the office a little after nine o'clock that night. A few details required his attention prior to returning to court the following day. The streets were deserted when he arrived downtown. He parked in front of the lobby entrance and took the elevator to the office. When he grasped the doorknob to insert the key, the knob came loose in his hand. He kicked the door open with his foot and ducked, but nothing happened.

Inside, the office was dark. In the light from the corridor he could see the top drawer of Mrs. Gordon's desk was open. Papers and books lay in the floor. He reached inside the doorway and turned on the light. As he did, two men, their faces covered with ski masks, charged toward him.

Without stopping, the first lowered his shoulder and crashed into Connolly sending him sprawling on his back. The second jumped over him. Both men were down the corridor and into the stairwell before he could recover.

He heard them clattering down the steps as he rolled to a sitting position. He picked himself up from the floor and stumbled to the chair behind Mrs. Gordon's desk. From there he phoned the police, then called Mrs. Gordon.

The police spent several hours examining the scene, taking photographs, lifting fingerprints. Connolly was forced aside while technicians sorted through the files and documents the intruders left scattered about the room. Correspondence from clients, notes from conversations with witnesses in countless cases, most of them criminal cases, all exposed now to the eyes of investigators. He cringed at the sight.

"So much for attorney-client privilege," he mumbled.

Painful as it was, Connolly stayed near his office. If they were going to sort through his clients' lives, he felt obligated to watch. Mrs. Gordon retreated to the front.

It was after midnight when the police left.

"You go on home," she called from her desk. "I'll straighten this place up."

Connolly gathered the pens from the top of his desk and replaced them in the holder. As he set the cup near the telephone, he paused. The office seemed unusually quiet. His heart pounded in his chest. He listened, straining to hear beyond the silence for the slightest sound of the danger he felt inside.

He placed the holder full of pens on the desk and walked up the hall to Mrs. Gordon's desk. Without stopping, he took her by the elbow and pulled her toward the door.

"Leave it," he said. "Let's go."

She drew away from him.

"Somebody has to get this place in order," she protested. "You have to be in court. I don't mind staying."

He took her elbow again.

"It'll be here in the morning," he said. His voice was calm but firm.

They moved toward the door.

"We can't just leave it like this," she protested.

Connolly opened the door.

"Let's go," he said.

They stepped into the hall. Connolly switched off the light and closed the door. What was left of the doorknob fell to the floor.

"What about the lock? We can't just go off and leave the door unlocked."

"It didn't stop them the first time," he said.

Connolly felt overwhelmed by the need to leave the building. He ushered Mrs. Gordon down the corridor to the elevator and pressed the button. The elevator doors opened. They stepped inside. Connolly pressed the button for the lobby. As the elevator doors shut, he heard the stairwell door bang closed.

"Do you still have those two boxes of documents I told you to take home?"

"Yes," she said. "Why?"

"Bring them to the office in the morning," he said. "I have a feeling we'll need them."

Forty-Two

The following morning Connolly was at the office before sunup. From the corridor near the elevator he could see the door was open. His heart sank as he walked cautiously to the door and stepped inside.

Mrs. Gordon's desk looked the same as when they left the night before. Papers and books were stacked on it where Mrs. Gordon had started to pick things up. Client chairs sat along the wall across from the door in front of her desk.

From her desk he could see the hallway was clear. He made his way as far as the copier room and peeked inside. The copier sat in its usual place. The sink was still attached to the wall, and the refrigerator was closed. Nothing looked out of place there.

At the end of the hall the door to his office was open, but he could tell by the way the morning light shone in the room that things were out of place. He moved from the doorway at the copier room and walked toward his office. His heart began to pound as he drew closer. Veins in his neck throbbed as he anticipated the condition of his office. By the time he reached the doorway, his muscles were tense and ready to pounce. He stepped inside.

The desk lay upside down in the center of the room. The filing cabinets along the wall to the right lay face down on top of a pile of papers and files that had been inside. Drawers from the desk were tossed about the room.

Connolly picked up the coat rack and set it by the door. With his foot, he kicked the papers aside and cleared a path from the door to the desk. Grasping the edge of the desktop, he lifted it from the floor. He rested it against his thighs and positioned his hands underneath it. Then, with a burst of energy, he flipped it over. It landed right side up and banged against the wall.

He slid it away from the wall and put it in its place. His desk chair lay in the far corner. He climbed over the filing cabinets to retrieve it and placed it between the desk and the wall.

With the desk and chair in place, he righted the filing cabinets and pushed them back in place along the wall. In a few minutes, he had the drawers back in the desk. He followed the telephone cord and dug the phone from under the pile of papers in the floor. When he found it, he placed it on the desk.

Beneath the pile of files and papers he located the leather satchel. He opened it and looked inside. It was empty. He found a couple of clean legal pads and shoved them inside. He located two or three pens and tossed them in as well.

He laid the satchel on the desk and picked up the telephone. As he dialed the number, Mrs. Gordon appeared in the doorway.

"I see they came back," she said.

He hung up the phone.

"I was just trying to call you. I need that box of documents you took home," he said.

She nodded to one side and pointed over her shoulder with her thumb.

"They're in the copier room. I brought them with me this morning."

He grabbed the satchel and started toward the door. Mrs. Gordon stepped inside the office and looked around as he passed by.

"Anything in here you need?"

"Nothing worth taking the time to find," he replied.

She followed him to the copier room.

"Think we ought to call the police again?"

"I don't want them plundering through my files anymore," he said. "They saw too much last night. Besides, they'll never catch the people who did this. Let's concentrate on Avery Thompson."

They spent the next two hours sorting through the two boxes of documents.

Connolly arrived at Judge Cahill's courtroom shortly after eight o'clock. Larry Yates was waiting for him. In a few minutes Toby LeMoyne arrived with Vernon Eubanks. Connolly met with each of them privately.

While Connolly met with the witnesses, Walter brought Avery Thompson from the jail. When Connolly finished preparing Yates, LeMoyne, and Eubanks, he entered the courtroom and took his seat at the counsel table next to Thompson.

As nine o'clock approached, spectators drifted in and took their places in the rows of seats. The room was full, but it was a much calmer and somewhat smaller gathering than the day before. Reporters returned in mass but, unlike the day before, they found seats near the back.

Karen Attaway arrived in the company of Jake and Connie Patronas at ten minutes before nine. They sat together on the front row. Her children did not attend. Thompson's mother and cousins returned to their seats on the second row.

Henry McNamara was already in the courtroom when

Connolly took a seat next to Thompson. He sat quietly at his table sorting through a large cardboard box of files from other cases. His work on this one complete, he was confident he had nothing to do but await what was sure to be an order sending this case to the grand jury for an indictment and then on to circuit court for trial.

Promptly at nine o'clock, Judge Cahill strode through the door from his office and bounded to his seat behind the bench. Walter stood as he announced the judge. His voice interrupted Connolly's thoughts.

"All rise."

A rumble swept through the courtroom as audience and lawyers rose from their seats.

"The District Court of Mobile County is now in session. The Honorable Robert Cahill presiding. Be seated."

The rumble rolled back across the courtroom as everyone took their seats. When the room was quiet, Cahill began.

"We're here today for the continuation of the preliminary hearing in the case of State of Alabama versus Avery Thompson. This is a charge of capital murder. Mr. Connolly, I believe you had some witnesses you wanted to call."

Connolly rose to address the court.

"Yes, Your Honor."

"Very well. Call your first witness."

"The defense calls Larry Yates."

Yates entered the courtroom and walked to the witness stand. He identified the blue Ford pickup from the photograph and told how it had been brought to his junkyard for storage by the sheriff's department. He brought with him a record from his own file that contained information about the truck.

"The front of the truck appears rusted," Connolly said.

"Yes," Yates responded. "They found this truck down on

Mon Louis Island. The engine compartment and some of the cab had been burned."

"But the tag and vehicle identification number were still on it."

"Yes."

"Do you have those numbers recorded somewhere in your file?"

"Yes."

Yates flipped through the file and located a page with the information. He handed it to Connolly.

"And those numbers are accurately recorded on this document you brought with you today?"

"That's correct."

"Judge, we'd offer this document from Mr. Yates's file as an exhibit. I think this will be Defendant's Exhibit Three."

Connolly stepped to the judge's bench and handed the document to Cahill. Cahill glanced at McNamara as he scanned the document. McNamara was engrossed in one of the files from the cardboard box and paid no attention.

"Admitted."

Connolly stepped away from the bench.

"I have no further questions."

"Henry," Cahill barked.

McNamara scrambled to his feet.

"You have any questions for this witness?"

"No, Your Honor. How much longer is this going to take? I have some other cases we need to address this morning."

Cahill ignored the question and turned to Connolly.

"Call your next witness, Mr. Connolly."

McNamara took a seat.

"Judge, I issued a subpoena for a witness who is not

present," Connolly said. "I need her testimony. The court file shows she was served."

"What's the name?"

"Leigh Ann Agostino."

Cahill leaned back in his chair. A frown wrinkled his forehead.

"Leigh Ann Agostino?"

Connolly nodded his head in response.

"Yes, Your Honor."

"You issued a subpoena for Judge Agostino's wife?"

"Yes, Your Honor."

"What for?"

"I'd rather not say just yet."

Cahill looked at the file for a moment, then turned to Walter.

"Call over to the sheriff's office and see if they can go pick her up."

Walter picked up the telephone. Cahill turned back to Connolly.

"This better be good," he said, "or you'll be having lunch with Mr. Thompson over in the jail."

"Yes, Your Honor."

"You got any more witnesses besides her?"

"Yes, Your Honor."

"Good. Call your next witness."

"The defense calls Vernon Eubanks."

Eubanks took his time coming from the back of the courtroom. Connolly waited patiently for him to take a seat on the witness stand. When Eubanks was finally seated, Connolly began his examination.

"Mr. Eubanks, were you once the owner of a blue Ford pickup truck?"

"Yes. I owned it once."

Connolly retrieved the photograph of the truck taken at Yates's junkyard and handed it to Eubanks.

"Does that look like the truck you owned?"

"Looks like it."

"The tag number on this truck is 2-ARX401."

Eubanks nodded his head.

"That's the right number," he said. He was still holding the picture. He pointed to it as he spoke. "And I remember that big scratch down the bed," he said.

"What did you do with this pickup?"

"I took it in on trade from a fella what owed me some money. I kept it a few months and sold it."

"Do you know who you sold it to?"

"Said his name was Sanders … Sanderson, something like that. I pointed him out in them pictures for you."

The audience snickered at the remark.

"Think you'd recognize him if you saw a picture of him this morning?"

"Sure," he said.

"You looked at some pictures at the jail, didn't you?"

"Yes," Eubanks said. "You was there. You know I did."

Connolly stepped to the counsel table and lifted his leather satchel from the floor. He set it on the table and took out another picture. McNamara laid aside the file he had been reviewing and watched with growing curiosity. Connolly returned to stand in front of Eubanks.

"Take a look at this and see if you recognize this man?"

McNamara stood. "Could I see that, please?"

"Sure," Connolly replied.

He handed the picture to McNamara. McNamara looked at it, jotted a note on a legal pad, and handed it back. Connolly handed the picture to Eubanks.

"That's him," Eubanks said. "That's the man what bought my truck."

"The same truck that's in this picture."

Connolly held up the picture of the blue Ford pickup.

"Yes, sir."

Connolly turned to Judge Cahill.

"No further questions, Your Honor."

Cahill looked to McNamara.

"Henry?"

McNamara stood and walked to the table in front of the judge's bench.

"Mr. Eubanks, you said you looked at some photographs at the jail."

Eubanks nodded his head.

"You mean the county jail here in Mobile?"

"Yes, sir."

"Who was with you?"

"That lawyer there," he said, pointing to Connolly, "and that policeman."

Eubanks pointed to Toby LeMoyne who sat on a bench between the counsel table and the railing behind Connolly and Thompson.

"You're pointing to a deputy seated behind Mr. Connolly?"

"Yes."

McNamara turned to the deputy.

"Sir, could you identify yourself, please?"

Connolly jumped to his feet.

"Judge, we'll get to him in a few minutes."

Cahill turned to McNamara.

"Stick to this witness, Henry."

"So, a deputy had you look at photographs at the jail?"

Eubanks nodded his head.

"How many did you look at?"

"Hundreds."

McNamara smiled.

"Hundreds?"

"Yeah. Thousands maybe. We was there most of the night seemed like."

"You did this at night?"

"Yes, sir."

Frustrated, McNamara returned to his seat.

"No further questions, Your Honor."

Cahill turned to Connolly.

"Mr. Connolly, any other questions for this man?"

"No, Your Honor."

Eubanks stepped from the witness stand and left the courtroom. When he was gone, Cahill turned once again to Connolly.

"You got any more witnesses?"

"The defense calls Toby LeMoyne."

Toby made his way to the witness stand. He carried with him a small file folder. McNamara rose from his chair once again.

"Judge, I object to this deputy testifying in this case." His voice was thin, and he was starting to whine. "He's from the sheriff's department. This case was investigated by Mobile city police. The crime occurred within their jurisdiction. They had a right to investigate and they did, and this man did not participate in that investigation."

"Now, Henry," Cahill smiled, "none of that disqualifies him from testifying. Let's hear what he has to say." Cahill turned to Connolly and nodded for him to proceed.

Connolly moved from the counsel table to the table in front of the judge's bench. There, he picked up a photograph, then moved closer to the witness stand.

"Officer LeMoyne, take a look at this photograph, please." He handed a picture to Toby. "Mr. Eubanks previously testified this was the man to whom he sold a blue Ford pickup. The same blue Ford pickup Mr. Sisson said he saw out at the scene where Keyton Attaway's body was found."

Toby nodded.

"Can you tell us this man's name?"

Toby looked at the picture.

"This is a copy of a booking photo," he explained. "When this man was processed through the jail, he was processed under the name Ralph Martin."

"Did you attempt to locate any information on this man?"

"Yes. I did."

"What did you find?"

"I ran a check on him." Toby opened the file in his lap and took out a sheet of paper. He glanced at it as he spoke. "His real name is Frank Torelli. Born in New York. Raised in New Orleans. Arrested in New York City for murder a few years ago, apparently acquitted. Did time in Illinois for racketeering. FBI says he's suspected of murdering at least three other people, but they can't really pin anything on him."

"These other three murders, what were the circumstances of those?"

McNamara jumped to his feet.

"Judge, I object. What happened in some other case is irrelevant to these proceedings and a waste of time."

Connolly turned to Judge Cahill.

"Your Honor, I'm not going to get into all the details of each case. But I want him to tell us whether there was something in common about these three murders."

Cahill frowned.

"I'll allow it."

Connolly turned to Toby LeMoyne.

"Was there anything peculiar about these other three murders you referred to?"

"They were all what people sometimes call 'mob style hits.'"

"What's a 'mob style hit'?"

"It's an execution," Toby began. "Basically, the victim is shot once or twice with a fairly clean, fatal shot. And then the victim's body is either sprayed with bullets in a disfiguring manner or shot in some particular part of the body. The eyes, the mouth, the nose. Something like that. They're murders designed to send a message."

"Rather like the shooting of Keyton Attaway?"

McNamara rose from his seat.

"Yes," Toby said, answering before McNamara could voice an objection.

McNamara sat down without a word. Connolly continued with his next question.

"Now, a witness has previously testified that a white Cadillac was parked on the side of the road at the same location where Keyton Attaway's body was found." Connolly paused for effect, then asked the question. "Did you find the Cadillac?"

"Yes."

The audience gasped. Cahill rapped his gavel.

"Alright," he droned. "Keep it quiet."

Connolly continued.

"Where did you find the Cadillac?"

"It was stored in a barn at a hunting camp up around Calvert, south of McIntosh."

"Who owns that hunting camp?"

"As best I could determine, Keyton Attaway, John Agostino, and Charlie Miffin."

The audience murmured. Cahill rapped his gavel.

"Keep it quiet," he said. "One more outburst, and I'll send you out of here."

Connolly ignored the interruption.

"Did you process the Cadillac for evidence?"

"Yes, we did. We got a crime scene unit out there and went through the barn and the car."

"What did you find?"

"The front passenger window of the Cadillac, that's the right side door window, had two bullet holes through it. A large portion of the window was blown out. There was blood residue in the upholstery of the seat and the carpet of the front floor on the passenger side. A large amount of residue."

"Were you able to collect a sample of that blood?"

"Yes," Toby replied. "Someone had attempted to clean the seat and carpet, but like I say, there was a lot of blood. It had soaked through the carpet. We got enough for the lab."

"You sent a sample to the lab?"

"Yes." He glanced again at the file in his lap. "They found it to be human blood, type B positive. I have a report here in my file."

Toby took a copy of the report from his file. Connolly handed the report to Judge Cahill.

"Judge, for the record, I'd like to point out that the coroner's report indicates Keyton Attaway's blood type was B positive."

Cahill nodded as he read the lab report.

"We offer that report as one of our exhibits," Connolly said.

Cahill laid the report in front of him and leaned back in his chair.

"It's admitted," he replied.

Connolly returned to Toby.

"This Cadillac, who was it registered to?"

"It was registered to John and Leigh Ann Agostino."

The audience gasped and murmured. Cahill rapped his gavel.

"Order," he barked. "Order."

The audience grew quiet. Toby took another piece of paper from his file.

"This is a copy of the registration for the Cadillac."

Connolly handed it to Judge Cahill.

"We offer this as well, Your Honor."

Cahill nodded. Connolly returned to the counsel table, reviewed notes on a yellow legal pad, then took a seat.

"No further questions, Your Honor."

Cahill turned to McNamara. Henry was already up and moving toward the witness.

"You found this Cadillac?"

"No," Toby replied. "Mr. Connolly and another gentleman actually located it."

"Mr. Connolly found it and called you?"

"Yes."

"What condition was it in?"

"Good condition. It had been covered with a car cover. Stored in a barn there at the hunting lodge."

"How long had it been there?"

"No way to know for sure," Toby said. "It hadn't been operated in a while."

"A while. Days? Weeks?"

"I'd say a couple of weeks, maybe a little longer."

"Where is this car now?"

"We have it secured."

"Where?"

"If you want to see it, I can make it available to you at a secure location. I'd rather not say in open court where it is."

"You said the blood type is B positive?"

"Yes."

"Other people besides Keyton Attaway have that same type blood, don't they?"

Connolly was on his feet.

"He's not here as an expert on blood types, Judge. He's just testifying to what he found and what the reports say."

"They opened the door to this," McNamara retorted.

"We opened the door to the report to which the witness referred, Judge," Connolly countered. "Mr. McNamara can ask about the content of the report, not this witness' opinion. He's not qualified to give an opinion on blood types in general."

Cahill turned to McNamara.

"He's right, Henry. Confine your questions to the content of the report. Objection sustained."

McNamara was angry and frustrated.

"Does that lab report indicate how many people in the state of Alabama have type B positive blood?"

"No."

"Does that report indicate whether the blood you found was, in fact, that of Keyton Attaway?"

"No."

McNamara picked up his file from the counsel table and turned through its pages. Still angry, he tossed it on the table and took a seat.

"I don't have any further questions," he snapped.

Toby stepped from the witness stand and took a seat on the bench behind Connolly. Cahill turned to Connolly.

"Call your next witness."

Connolly stood.

"Judge, our next witness would be Leigh Ann Agostino, but she isn't here yet."

"You going to call anyone else?"

"No, Your Honor."

Cahill turned to Walter.

"Did you call the sheriff's office?"

"Yes, Your Honor."

"What did they say? Can they go pick her up?"

"Said they'd send somebody after her," Walter replied. "Ought to be here before long, if she was at home."

Cahill checked his watch.

"Okay," he said. "Let's adjourn for lunch. We'll start again at one-thirty." He rapped his gavel on the bench. "We'll be in recess until one-thirty."

Cahill disappeared through the door to his office. Walter stepped from behind his desk and approached Avery Thompson. In his hands he held a pair of handcuffs.

"Come on, Mr. Thompson. We got to get you downstairs for lunch." Walter turned to Connolly. "You need him back here early?"

Connolly shook his head.

"No," he said. "Just bring him back in time for the hearing."

Walter led Thompson out of the courtroom through a separate doorway.

Forty-Three

*C*onnolly took the elevator to the lobby and walked outside. At the corner, he bought a hot dog from a pushcart vendor. He sat alone on a nearby bench and ate. Restless and unable to relax, he returned to the courtroom. When he arrived, two sheriff's deputies were seated inside the railing behind the counsel tables. Between them sat Leigh Ann Agostino.

Connolly walked up the aisle to the defense table and took a seat. Leigh Ann turned away, avoiding him. He looked through some papers in the leather satchel, then turned toward her.

"I don't have anything to say to you," she hissed, still looking in the opposite direction.

Amused, Connolly turned away, folded his hands in his lap, and closed his eyes. It was noon. Time for his usual nap. In spite of the surroundings, he was soon fast asleep.

Sometime later, the sound of shuffling feet and the rattle of metal handcuffs awakened him. Walter and Avery Thompson stood at the end of the counsel table. Walter removed the handcuffs and pointed to the chair beside Connolly.

"Take a seat," he ordered. "Don't get up without asking me."

Thompson did as directed and took a seat at the table. Connolly, now awake, organized his notes for the afternoon session. Behind them, the audience filled the courtroom. Word that Judge Agostino's wife would testify had spread quickly through the courthouse. Lawyers and court officials crowded the room to see what would happen. Journalists filled the back rows. Television cameras clogged the hallway outside the door.

At a quarter past one, two tall, well-built men entered. Dressed in identical charcoal gray suits, white shirts, and red ties, they looked like clones of each other. Six feet two inches tall, with broad shoulders, square chins, and close short haircuts, they moved like robots through the door and up the aisle. They pushed aside the gate at the rail and stopped in front of Leigh Ann Agostino. The deputies seated at her side looked puzzled and amused.

One of the two took a document from the inside pocket of his suit coat and thrust it toward the deputies.

"I'm Tom Allen, United States Marshals Service," he said. "We have an order to produce Mrs. Agostino in Federal District Court."

The deputy seated to her right scanned the order.

"We have her here on an order from Judge Cahill," the deputy said.

The man accompanying Allen stepped forward and reached for Leigh Ann's arm. The other deputy blocked him with his own arm and pushed him away.

"What do you think you're doing?" the deputy demanded.

"Our order is from a federal judge," Allen argued. "We're taking her into custody."

The deputies jumped to their feet. Suddenly, all four men were nose to nose. Before they could say more, the door opened, and Judge Cahill appeared.

"All rise," Walter droned. "The District Court of Mobile County is now in session. The Honorable Judge Robert Cahill presiding."

Cahill took his seat at the bench and looked down at the cluster of officers squared off beneath him.

"Be seated," Walter droned.

Judge Cahill glared from the bench.

"You men got a problem?"

Allen turned to face Cahill.

"Your Honor, my name is Tom Allen. This is Bill Henck with me. We are from the United States Marshals Service. We have an order to bring Mrs. Agostino to Federal Court."

Allen stepped to the bench and handed Cahill the order. Cahill read it and laid it aside.

"We have her here in court on a subpoena. She's about to testify in a preliminary hearing. You can take her after that."

"No, Your Honor," Allen countered. "We have a federal order. That order supersedes any state subpoena."

Cahill thought for a moment, then turned to Walter.

"Walter, are you thinking what I'm thinking?"

Walter grinned, and stepped from behind his desk, a pair of handcuffs in his hand.

"Mrs. Agostino," Judge Cahill began, "you were served with a subpoena to appear in this courtroom this morning at nine o'clock. You ignored that subpoena. As a result, I find you in criminal contempt of court and sentence you to five days in the county jail. You're in custody. Walter, put the cuffs on her."

Walter slipped the handcuffs gently over Leigh Ann's wrists. Cahill glared at Allen.

"Mr. Allen, she's my prisoner now."

Allen slipped his arm through Leigh Ann's elbow as if to

take her anyway. Judge Cahill exploded. His voice rushed from his body in a blast.

"You think you can come in here and disrupt my courtroom, just because you work for the federal government?" His face was red. The veins in his forehead throbbed. "You can turn her loose right now, or I'll put you in my jail. I don't care who you work for."

Allen hesitated.

"Walter," Judge Cahill barked.

Walter took Allen by the arm. The deputy to Leigh Ann's left removed a pair of handcuffs from his pistol belt.

"Now," Cahill said, forcing himself to sound calm. "You two can leave, or spend the night in jail."

Allen hesitated, uncertain what to do next. Then, without a word, he released his grip on Leigh Ann's arm and moved toward the center aisle. Henck followed, and together they walked to the door and into the hall. Leigh Ann Agostino, bewildered, stood before the judge's bench with Walter and the two deputies still by her side.

When the marshals were gone, a wide grin broke across Cahill's face.

"I love backing those guys down. They think they rule the world." The audience chuckled. "Walter, take those cuffs off her. Mrs. Agostino, come around here to the witness stand."

Judge Cahill administered the oath to Leigh Ann, then turned to Connolly.

"Mr. Connolly, you may proceed."

Connolly stepped from the defense table and stood in front of Leigh Ann.

"Mrs. Agostino, are you acquainted with Keyton Attaway?"

"Yes."

"How are you acquainted with him?"

She hesitated, her eyes darted around the room.

"He's my brother ... half brother actually."

"You own a white Cadillac automobile, do you not?"

"Yes. I did."

"You did?"

"It was stolen."

"When was it stolen?"

"I ... uhh ... don't recall."

"We have a witness who says there was a white Cadillac at the spot where Keyton Attaway's body was found. Was that your automobile?"

Again, Leigh Ann hesitated.

"Ahh ... no."

"Were you with your brother that day?"

"N-n-no."

"Are you aware your Cadillac has been recovered by the sheriff's office?"

Her eyes opened wide.

"No."

"Were you aware your Cadillac was found, neatly covered with a car cover, in a barn at a hunting club owned by your brother, Keyton Attaway and your husband, John Agostino?"

Her face appeared calm, but her eyes belied the panic she felt inside. She did not answer.

"Well, Mrs. Agostino," Connolly lowered his voice, "were you aware that when the sheriff's office recovered your Cadillac, they found the window on the passenger side in the front had been shot out?"

Leigh Ann slumped backward in her seat. Her face turned pale.

"When evidence technicians went through the car, they

found a large amount of human blood in the carpet and upholstery on the passenger side of the front seat."

She propped her arm on the edge of the witness stand, rested her head in her hand, and closed her eyes.

"Any idea whose blood that might have been?"

Again, she did not respond.

"The lab tested that blood residue and found it to be of the same blood type as that of your brother, Keyton Attaway."

Leigh Ann's body shook. She turned her body sideways in the chair in an attempt to hide her face.

"Would you like to tell us what happened to your brother?"

The sound of sobbing drifted across the courtroom. Judge Cahill took a box of tissues from his bench and dropped it on the witness stand in front of her. She snatched a tissue from the box and wiped her face.

"I ... didn't know ... they were going to kill him," she blurted between sobbing sounds.

She folded her arms along the ledge of the witness stand and rested her forehead on them. The muffled sound of sobbing drifted across the quiet courtroom.

Cahill looked to Connolly. Connolly shrugged his shoulders. He was sure it was all an act.

"Mrs. Agostino," Cahill said. "You need to sit up."

Leigh Ann lifted her head, took another tissue from the box, and wiped her eyes and nose. Walter brought a glass of water. She took a sip. Her eyes were red but dry, and her makeup was not smudged.

"Tell the court what happened that afternoon, the afternoon of June fifteenth," Connolly said.

She took a deep breath.

"Keyton called me," she began. "He wanted to go for a ride so we could talk. I picked him up in front of his office, and we rode around. We kept talking and riding. We went through the tunnel to the causeway, and I turned on a side road, and we rode some more. Finally, I just pulled off the road and stopped. While we were sitting there, a truck pulled in behind us. Then, about the same time, that man there tapped on my window."

She pointed to Avery Thompson.

"You're pointing to the defendant?"

"Yes. He tapped on my window and said something about his car had broken down. As I was rolling up the window, I heard a gunshot."

She made a snorting sound as if choking back tears.

"Did Avery Thompson shoot Keyton Attaway?"

She shook her head.

"No," she blurted as if between tears. "He didn't have anything to do with it."

"What happened after Keyton was shot?"

She wiped her eyes.

"He opened the door ..."

"Who opened the door?"

"The man with the gun," she said. "The man from the pickup truck."

"Did you get a look at him?"

"Not really. I was too scared. I thought he was coming for me, but Keyton's body rolled out on his legs and knocked him backward. The car was running because we had the air conditioner on, so I put the car in gear and drove away as fast as I could."

"You didn't call the police?"

"No. I drove home. I was scared. I didn't know who the man was, or why he was there."

"How did the car wind up in a barn at your husband's hunting camp?"

"I told John what happened. He said he would take care of it. The next day, the car was gone, and I had a new one."

Connolly turned aside, trying to collect his thoughts. Leigh Ann was not exactly telling the truth, but she had given him room to defend his client without having to go into all the details. But was it enough?

Just then, Avery Thompson waved him over. Connolly turned to Judge Cahill.

"May I have a moment with my client, Your Honor?"

"Certainly," Cahill nodded. "Why don't we take five minutes and let Mrs. Agostino relax."

Judge Cahill stepped from the bench. Connolly crossed the courtroom to Thompson at the counsel table.

"She's lying," Thompson whispered. "Her husband picked her up right there on the spot. Those other men took the car."

"I know she's lying, but we don't have to prove all of that," Connolly whispered. "We only have to show enough to show they don't have probable cause to proceed against you. She's already said you didn't do it. I think Judge Cahill will dismiss the case."

"But she's lying," Thompson repeated.

"This isn't a trial," Connolly replied. "We don't need to get into all of that."

As they talked, Judge Cahill returned. He took a seat at the bench and looked to Connolly.

"You ready, Mike?"

Connolly stood.

"Your Honor, this witness, who was the only eyewitness to the shooting, has testified my client did not shoot Mr. Attaway. She has identified the man from the blue Ford pickup truck as the shooter. I don't think I have any further questions for her."

Cahill nodded and turned to McNamara.

"Henry?"

McNamara walked to the table in front of the judge's bench and picked up a photograph.

"Mrs. Agostino, is this the man who shot your brother?"

She looked at the picture.

"It looks like him," she said, suddenly composed and in control.

"You said you were talking to Mr. Attaway that afternoon. What were you talking about?"

Cahill slid forward and opened the court file.

"Henry," he said, interrupting, "I don't think we need to get into that. This isn't a trial."

Connolly felt his body relax. Even if he didn't know all the details, Cahill knew when he had heard enough. And he knew with this case he didn't want to hear any more.

McNamara turned to Judge Cahill.

"Your Honor, she's already testified she was talking to him. I just want to—"

"And she's identified someone else as the person who did the shooting. You have any questions for her about that?"

"No, Your Honor."

"Is there anyone else you know of who was there at the scene when the shooting took place besides this woman and the defendant?"

"No, Your Honor."

"Very well." Judge Cahill turned to Leigh Ann. "Mrs. Agostino, thank you for coming today. You are free to go."

Leigh Ann slipped from the witness stand and hurried toward the door. Cahill turned to Connolly.

"Mr. Connolly, you have anything else?"

Connolly stood.

"No, Your Honor. The defense rests."

Cahill bent over the court file and began to write.

"Judge," Connolly continued, "I believe we've put on enough evidence to show that the State has no probable cause to proceed further against Mr. Thompson. We move to dismiss."

"I agree," Cahill said.

He continued to write in the file. McNamara was on his feet.

"Judge, we put on evidence of a ballistic report that matched the bullets from the victim with a gun in the defendant's possession. That ties him to the crime and establishes probable cause. It doesn't matter what they put on about anything else. They haven't rebutted our evidence."

Cahill stopped writing and looked to McNamara.

"Henry, you might be able to show he was at the scene, but you can't show he did it. We heard the only eyewitness to the shooting say he wasn't the one who shot Keyton Attaway. You've got this man in here on a capital murder charge. I can't hold him on this evidence. If you don't like it, you can always present the case to the grand jury on your own."

McNamara slumped in his chair. Cahill scribbled something else in the file, then looked to Thompson.

"This case is dismissed. Mr. Thompson, you are free to go. Walter will take you downstairs. A deputy will take you back to the jail, and they'll process you out over there."

Thompson shook Connolly's hand. Walter stepped from his desk and escorted him from the courtroom. Connolly gathered his things from the counsel table and stuffed them in his satchel. The audience stood to leave. Karen Attaway stepped to the rail behind the counsel tables.

"That's it?" she shouted. "Leigh Ann gets to go?" She pointed to Thompson. "He gets to go? End of story?"

Her voice was loud, her face red, her clenched fist struck

the rail as she spoke. Judge Cahill was taken aback by the sudden disruption.

"Mrs. Attaway, I'm very sorry you've lost your husband," Cahill said, trying to calm her. "But you've heard what was said. You can see the State has no basis to proceed against Mr. Thompson. If they did, if I let them proceed, the case would be dismissed in circuit court. They don't have a single witness who can testify against this man."

"But what about her story?"

"Whose story?"

"Leigh Ann Agostino's. She's only told half the truth." She turned to Connolly and continued to shout. "What about the bank records? What about that Alpaca thing you were talking about? What about all that?"

Connolly did not reply.

"Mrs. Attaway," Cahill soothed, "I'm sure the district attorney's office will be glad to listen to anything you have to say. But this case today was about Avery Thompson."

"But what about—"

Jake Patronas took her by the arm.

"Come on, Karen," he said softly. "Let's go."

"But I want to know—"

He pulled her toward the aisle.

"Let's go," he repeated.

Connolly closed his leather satchel and waited. Reluctantly, Karen followed Jake to the door. After she was gone, Connolly stood to leave.

Forty-Four

*L*eather satchel in hand, Connolly stepped from the counsel table. At the rail he was beset by a horde of reporters, all clamoring for a statement.

"What was Judge Agostino's involvement in this case?" someone shouted.

"No comment," Connolly replied.

He pushed forward, trying to reach the door.

"Was anyone else involved?"

"No comment," Connolly replied again.

"What about Truman Albritton?" someone asked. "Was he present when the shooting took place?"

"No comment."

He pushed past the reporters and started down the aisle. Several continued to shout questions to him as he reached the door. He ignored them and pushed open the door.

In the hallway he was met by a second cluster of reporters, all shouting questions at once. Toby LeMoyne emerged from the courtroom and held them at bay while Connolly headed for the stairway.

Two floors below the courtroom Connolly abandoned the stairway and took the elevator. Minutes later, the doors opened at the lobby. Connolly poked his head out and looked around.

Surprisingly, the lobby was empty. He walked quickly to the front and out to the sidewalk.

The evening was balmy but not unbearable. He walked alone the few blocks to the office building. The Chrysler was parked in front. He tossed the leather satchel onto the back seat and slipped in behind the steering wheel.

It was late when he reached his apartment on Carondolet Street. Tired and emotionally drained, he trudged up the steps, opened the door, and switched on the light.

In an instant, the entire apartment was consumed by a fiery explosion. Glass and debris blew out the front windows and scattered in the street below. Flames engulfed the apartment and swept through the door singeing Connolly's hair and scorching his clothes. As flames swirled around him, the force of the blast rushed through the doorway. He sailed backward through the air, arms and legs thrashing helplessly about as he flew across the landing at the top of the steps. With a sickening thud, he crashed hard against the wall of the apartment on the opposite side of the stairs and tumbled to the floor.

When he regained consciousness, he was lying on a stretcher in the street behind a fire truck. Paramedics and ambulance attendants huddled over him. Blazes from the apartment cast an orange glow across the faces closest to him. Others farther away were lost in a blur. Connolly struggled to focus his eyes.

His head was strapped to a backboard, and a collar fit tightly around his neck. Unable to turn his head, he rolled his eyes as far to the right as possible and strained to see the apartment.

"How is it?" he mumbled.

"What's that?" someone shouted.

"What'd he say?"

A paramedic leaned over his face.

"You're going to be alright," he said. "We're just fixing it so you can't move until we get you to the hospital and get you checked out."

"How's my apartment?"

"I wouldn't worry about that now, sir. The important thing is to get you to the hospital."

"How's my apartment?" he insisted.

Connolly's eyes demanded an answer.

"It's pretty much disintegrated, sir," the paramedic replied.

"Anyone else hurt?"

"We're still trying to get the fire out."

Connolly closed his eyes and drifted into unconsciousness.

When he awoke again, he was lying on a treatment table at Mobile General Hospital. Electrodes attached to each side of his chest sent impulses through a tangle of wires to a monitor beside his shoulder. It beeped at regular intervals. Barbara stood to one side at the foot of his bed. Mrs. Gordon stood beside her. Toby LeMoyne leaned against the wall on the opposite side of the bed.

A curtain separated the treatment room from the remainder of the emergency room. As Connolly looked around, the curtain parted, and Ted Morgan, the county coroner, appeared. He stepped to Connolly's side.

"You come for me?" Connolly mumbled.

"Yeah," Morgan chuckled. "Business was kind of slow tonight. You seemed like the most likely prospect."

A young doctor appeared behind Morgan and stepped forward. Morgan moved aside.

"Mr. Connolly, my name is Mark Perry. I'm the chief resident around here."

Connolly managed a faint smile.

"How am I?"

Perry lifted Connolly's eyelid and flicked a small flashlight at his pupil.

"You're bruised and banged up," he said. He continued to flick the flashlight at the pupil in Connolly's right eye. "You have a broken rib or two, but you look to be in pretty good shape considering you took a blast to the face and flew fifteen feet through the air."

"When can I go?"

"In a few minutes," Perry replied. He moved the light to the left eye. "We're waiting on some x-rays of your back and neck." He turned off the flashlight and shoved it in his pocket. "Can you move your feet for me, please sir?"

Connolly moved his feet back and forth.

"Good," Perry replied. "How about your fingers? Remember where they are?"

Connolly moved the fingers on each hand.

"Okay. Just lay here and try to relax. We'll have those x-rays ready in a few minutes."

Perry stepped away without waiting for Connolly to reply. He slipped past the curtain to the hall. Connolly closed his eyes.

Sometime early the following morning, Dr. Perry released Connolly. The x-rays showed he had two broken ribs and a large bruise to his back, nothing further. Barbara was by his side as he limped out of the emergency room.

"Come on," she said. "My car is over here."

Connolly took her arm to steady himself as they walked across the parking lot.

"If you don't mind," he said, "take me to the Admiral Semmes. I'll get a room there until I can settle with the insurance."

"There's plenty of room at the house," she suggested.

He squeezed her arm.

"Barbara, I love you. I have always loved you. Nothing that's happened between us has ever stopped me from loving you. But I can't go back to that house. That house is full of traps for me. I don't want to go back to who I used to be."

Tears filled Barbara's eyes. She blinked them away and helped him into the car.

Forty-Five

The Admiral Semmes Hotel was located on Government Street, one block from the courthouse. Connolly rented a room there and went to bed. Two days later, he felt well enough to go to the office. Sore and stiff, it took a while for him to walk the short distance to the building. He arrived there around ten o'clock.

"Your insurance agent has been looking for you," Mrs. Gordon said as he walked through the door. Her head was bent low over the work on her desk. "He needs a list of what you lost in the explosion."

"Good morning, Mrs. Gordon."

Connolly eased into a chair near her desk.

"Barbara take you home with her?"

"No," he replied. "I'm over at the Admiral Semmes. Where's my car?"

Mrs. Gordon brightened some and lifted her head to look at him.

"On the street in front of Port City Diner," she replied. "Toby LeMoyne brought it down here this morning. Keys are in the top drawer of your desk."

Connolly nodded.

"Anthony Hammond has been calling here for you," Mrs. Gordon continued. She handed him a slip of paper from the desk. "Said he needs to talk to you about your apartment."

"Why's he working on that?"

"Didn't say. Henry McNamara called twice yesterday."

"What's he want?"

"I don't know. But it might have something to do with this."

She tossed a newspaper toward him. It landed in his lap. He winced with pain. In bold type across the top of the front page the headline read, "Federal Judge Found Dead." Connolly's eyes grew wide.

"John Agostino," he whispered.

"Found him over in Florida yesterday, near Grayton Beach," Mrs. Gordon said, her head once again bent over her work. "Highway Patrol noticed his car on the side of the road. Stopped to investigate. Found Agostino slumped over the wheel, a bullet in his head."

Connolly struggled to his feet and walked down the hall-way toward his office. He read the newspaper as he went. He finished the article while reclining in the chair behind his desk.

When he was through, he called Henry McNamara.

"My secretary said you called."

"Yeah," McNamara replied. "I wondered if you knew how to get in touch with Avery Thompson."

"Why?"

"FBI called. They wanted to know where he was. I told them I'd check into it."

"I have no idea," Connolly said. "What do they want with him?"

He knew how to find Thompson, but after what happened to him in jail, he wasn't eager to help.

"They're interested in talking to him about Judge Agostino."

"They think he had something to do with that?"

"No," McNamara replied. "They're just tracking down as much information as they can."

"I'll see if I can find him," Connolly replied. "Did you want me to help you follow up with Leigh Ann Agostino?"

"Mr. Connolly, I have to be in Judge Cahill's court in fifteen minutes." McNamara's voice was suddenly curt. "I have more on the docket than I can possibly get done today. I don't have time for Mrs. Agostino."

Connolly was beside himself.

"Is someone in your office following up with her?"

"I don't know. I haven't talked to anyone about it."

Connolly was incredulous.

"You haven't talked to anyone?"

"No," McNamara laughed. "Why?"

"Henry," Connolly railed, his voice rising, "Keyton Attaway is dead. Judge Agostino is dead. Somebody tried to kill me. Don't you think you ought to be a little curious about whether all three of those are related?"

"I've got more than enough to do without being curious. The FBI is investigating Judge Agostino's death. If they want to follow up and see if Attaway's murder is somehow related, I'll be happy to tell them what I know. But right now, I've got to get up to Judge Cahill's courtroom."

Connolly hung up the phone and eased back in his chair. He stared in disbelief at the ceiling. Judge Cahill's suggestion a few days earlier drifted through his mind.

"This is one of those cases you have to let go."

And then he thought about Avery Thompson; he hadn't done anything except be in the wrong place at the wrong time.

He felt angry. Angry at McNamara for caring so little. Angry at Leigh Ann for lying to protect herself, even implicating her husband to deflect attention from her own conduct. But most of all, he was angry at himself for not doing more to help Thompson.

Connolly snatched his jacket from the coat rack by the door. Pain shot through his side. He leaned against the wall to catch his breath, then walked up the hallway.

Downstairs, he ducked out the back entrance to Ferguson's Alley and walked to the courthouse. Once there, he passed through the lobby and out the back near St. Pachomius Church. He crossed in front of the church to the rear entrance at the sheriff's office.

Inside the sheriff's office he asked for Toby LeMoyne. A deputy directed him to a conference room down the hall. Toby emerged from the room as Connolly approached.

"No, no, no," he said. He was polite but firm. "I can't even be seen talking with you today."

Toby continued down the hall, away from Connolly.

"What are you talking about?"

"The district attorney's mad at the sheriff. The sheriff's mad at me. The city police department wants to know why we went behind their backs, and the FBI wants to know what I know about Judge Agostino."

Connolly ignored Toby's protests.

"Listen," he said, "Henry will never do anything about this case. If you don't pick it up, the whole thing will be dropped."

"I can't do anything about it," Toby said, as he continued down the hall.

Connolly followed close by his side.

"I'll tell you what I know."

Toby shook his head.

"Between my notes and Karen Attaway's records, you could indict Leigh Ann and Truman Albritton."

Toby stopped and faced Connolly.

"Look, I'd love to help, but I've done all I can do. If the sheriff finds out I did something like what you're suggesting, after all that's happened, he'd fire me on the spot. I'm sorry." His voice was less cordial, and there was an irritated scowl on his face. "You're on your own."

Toby strode down the hall. Connolly watched as he disappeared around the corner.

Disgruntled, Connolly walked out of the sheriff's office through the rear door. He crossed the street and started up the steps at St. Pachomius. At the top, he took off his jacket and sat. He felt alone.

The day was miserably hot, but as he sat there a cool, refreshing breeze blew across the portico. As the breeze washed over him, he remembered praying with Father Scott that day when he found himself lying on the floor in front of the altar. He glanced around at the building and smiled.

Forty-Six

*L*ater that afternoon, Connolly returned to the office. As he stepped toward the entrance to the lobby, a horn blared on the street behind him. He turned to see what the noise was about.

At the curb was a dark blue BMW. A woman sat behind the steering wheel. Dressed in a baggy shirt, she wore dark sunglasses and a baseball cap that sat low on her brow. He did not recognize her, but she seemed to be waving at him, motioning for him to come to the car.

Connolly crossed the sidewalk to the car. As he reached for the door handle, he realized the woman in the car was Leigh Ann Agostino. He opened the door.

"Get in," she said. "We need to talk."

"What about?"

"About John," she said.

He hesitated.

"Get in," she said. "Before someone recognizes us."

Connolly slid into the front seat. Leigh Ann steered the car away from the curb as he pulled the door closed. Immediately he sensed he had made a bad decision.

From the office building at Bienville Square, they drove toward the docks along Mobile Bay. When they reached Water Street, Leigh Ann turned right and drove past the rows of warehouses. A few blocks further she steered the BMW toward the ramp onto the interstate highway. The car picked up speed.

"I thought you wanted to talk," he said.

Leigh Ann did not reply.

She glanced in the rearview mirror, then turned her head to look out the side window. Connolly's mind raced trying to figure out what was happening.

"What do you want from me?"

Leigh Ann did not reply. Connolly glanced at her. Her face looked as hard and cold as stone.

This, he thought to himself, *is not going to turn out well.*

Leigh Ann glanced in the rearview mirror again. They were traveling in the far-left lane. Suddenly, without warning, she jerked the car to the right across three lanes of traffic and shot up the Broad Street exit ramp. At the end of the ramp she turned left, drove over the bridge crossing the interstate, and into Brookley Industrial Park.

A former Air Force base, the industrial park sprawled over hundreds of acres. In the center were two all-weather runways capable of handling anything that could fly. Huge hangar buildings stood at the Broad Street end of the runways surrounded by acres of low, single-story industrial buildings.

At the end of Broad Street they turned left and drove around the perimeter, past the busiest areas. When they reached the far side of the park, they turned right.

Ahead, three abandoned hangars stood near a taxiway at the far end of the runways. They drove past the first hangar and turned right. The car came to a stop in front of the hangar's main doors. Directly opposite it, to their left, stood a second hangar. A third was located farther down the tarmac. It sat at a right angle to the other two. Together, the three hangars were arranged in such a way that no one passing by had a clear view of the tarmac area in the middle.

Leigh Ann switched off the engine. Surrounded by the empty and abandoned hangars, it was very quiet. As the sun sank lower in the afternoon sky, shadows from the buildings stretched across the pavement. It was a lonely place. Connolly felt along the armrest for the door handle. His fingers slid along the leather upholstery and slipped around the chrome handle.

"I wouldn't do that," Leigh Ann said.

Connolly turned to face her and found himself staring down the barrel of a revolver.

"I'd hate to make a mess of a second car."

Her voice was as cold as the look on her face. Even with the sunglasses on he could tell her eyes showed no sympathy.

To his right, the main doors of the hangar slid open. In the shadows beyond the door he could see a white twin-engine airplane. Truman Albritton stepped from the hangar.

Albritton walked to the car and opened Connolly's door.

"I see you two are getting better acquainted," he said, smiling.

A third man appeared near the nose of the aircraft. Dressed in blue jeans, a white shirt, and sunglasses, he seemed aloof, discreet, professional. An automatic pistol protruded from the waistband of his trousers.

Leigh Ann opened the door and stepped out of the car. Albritton backed away from the door on Connolly's side of the car and motioned for him to get out.

"Step this way, Mike."

Connolly twisted his torso and put both feet on the ground outside the car. Pain from the broken ribs forced him to move carefully. Using the door for leverage, he slid out of the BMW.

"Taking a trip?" Connolly said, nodding toward the plane.

"Thought we might run down to the Bahamas," Truman replied.

"Need to pick up some extra cash?"

"Something like that." Albritton said. He stepped behind Connolly. "Let's go," he ordered, pushing Connolly toward the hangar.

Connolly walked slowly forward.

"You should have stuck to the gin bottle," Albritton said. "I went to a lot of trouble to see that you were appointed to represent Thompson. You should have let him go."

"Well, you know how it is," Connolly replied. "Curiosity gets the better of me sometimes."

"It's gotten you in a mess now. You pieced things together really well. Frankly, I was surprised at how hard you worked. A little too hard, as it turns out. I tried to tell you to leave this case alone."

"You weren't the only one," Connolly said.

Albritton snickered in response.

They continued walking toward the plane. When they were between the wing and the tail section, they stopped.

"Mike," Albritton began, "in spite of the way you treated me the last time we spoke, I've always liked your sense of humor. So, I tell you what I'll do. I'll give you a choice." A smile broke across his face. "You can die right here. Quick, painless gunshot to the head. Or, I can throw you out of this plane when we're over the Gulf." He paused to give Connolly a moment to consider the options. "What'll it be?"

As Albritton waited for an answer, Leigh Ann stepped to his side. She slipped her arm through his and nuzzled against his shoulder.

"Tell me something, Truman," Connolly said. "Whose idea

was all this? Getting Agostino appointed judge, the bank account in the Bahamas, the decisions in all those cases. Whose idea was all that? Yours or Attaway's?"

"Oh, Attaway's," Albritton acknowledged. "Brilliant idea, too. We all get rich, and no one can touch us. Then he had to go and get religion on me. It was his idea, but he had to have some help. This thing goes a long way. Much further than you can imagine. Involves a lot of people. Big people. That's why we can't leave any loose ends. And, it's also why we have some assistance here today." He nodded toward the man beside the plane. "What'll it be? Here, or in the air?"

Connolly glanced at Leigh Ann.

"What's your choice?" Albritton insisted.

"Here's fine," Connolly replied. He looked slowly around the hangar as he spoke. "I've never cared much for flying."

"Sorry it has to come to this," Albritton said.

He nodded to the man beside the airplane, and stepped away. Leigh Ann clung to his arm as they moved across the hangar. The man who had been standing near the nose of the plane walked forward in a business-like manner.

Slender, muscular, tanned, he had the appearance of someone who worked outside. Construction perhaps. But the blue jeans he wore were neatly pressed with a razor-sharp crease down each pants leg. The white shirt he wore was starched stiff enough to stand by itself and made a rustling sound as he moved. His hair was neatly trimmed above his ears. His low-quarter shoes were buffed to a high-gloss shine. There was no emotion about his face. Only the confident manner of a man who knew his business. Connolly stared at him as he approached, trying to see behind the dark tint of the Rayban glasses that hid the man's eyes. He took Connolly by the arm and led him past the airplane toward the back of the hangar.

An arc of sunlight streamed through the open door and formed a circle around the airplane, but beyond the tail section the building was dark. As they passed beyond the sunlight, the building became strangely quiet. Sounds from outside faded away. Albritton's voice grew more faint. Soon, the only sound was that of their own shoes against the concrete floor.

Connolly took slow, careful steps. He had trouble picking his way through the building, and he listened intently for the slightest hint the man was about to stop. In spite of the pain in his side and back, he was ready to spring at the first indication the man was about to shoot. He might die, but not without a fight, sore ribs or not. With each step, his muscles grew tighter.

From somewhere behind him, a cool, refreshing breeze swept through the hangar. At first blowing lightly, then stronger and stronger, it picked up dust and trash from the floor in a swirl around him. Every cell in his body seemed energized by the touch of the cool, moist air on his skin.

In a moment the breeze subsided around him, but he could hear the rustling of the trash as it swept through the building. Still, he could not stop walking. As long as he put one foot in front of the other, he was alive. Finally, he stumbled across a pile of twisted steel and rubble too large to negotiate. He stopped.

"There's some stuff in front of us," he said. "I can't go any further."

There was no reply.

He stood, waiting. Waiting to feel the cold steel muzzle of the pistol as it pressed against his head. Instead, all he felt was the stillness of absolute silence.

He moved his head ever so slightly to the left and cut his

eyes as far that way as possible. The man was not beside him. Slowly, he moved his head to the opposite side. He wasn't there either. Connolly's heart pounded against his chest as he imagined the man standing behind him, the pistol raised, inches from his scalp, ready to fire.

In an instant, he wheeled around ignoring the stabbing pain in his ribs, his left arm extended in a sweep, his right fist cocked and ready. His left foot landed squarely on the concrete floor, but his left arm met only air, and he stumbled forward, off balance. There was no one behind him. He blinked his eyes and did his best to focus.

Facing the light from the front doors, he could see the airplane and Leigh Ann's car outside, but no one was in the hangar.

He hurried toward the front, coming out of the dark behind the tail of the airplane. There, he stopped and listened. Trash from the swirling breeze lay piled against the back of the doors, but the breeze was gone. The sun was fading fast too. The arc of light that had encircled the plane had now retreated toward the door. Outside, shadows from the hangar buildings covered the tarmac.

Satisfied no one was in the hangar, he moved past the plane and stepped cautiously to the tarmac. He glanced to the left and right, then scanned the area around the other buildings. No one was in sight.

Leigh Ann's blue BMW was parked where she left it in front of the main doors. He looked inside through the front passenger window. Her purse was missing. The car keys were gone from the ignition.

By then, the sun had begun to dip below the horizon. Darkness closed in. With no other option but to walk, Connolly started on foot. He walked down the street alongside the hangar to the perimeter road and followed it toward the front of the complex several miles away. The evening was warm and humid. Before he was out of sight of the hangars, his clothes were damp with sweat.

Halfway to Broad Street he came to the clubhouse at Bayshore Golf Course. The course previously had been part of the officer's club when the complex was an Air Force base. It was now owned by the city and maintained as a public facility. A pay phone hung on the wall near the cart shack. Sweaty and drained, he telephoned Mrs. Gordon. She did not answer. He thought about calling Barbara, but then he would have to explain what happened, and he wasn't ready for that. Instead, he telephoned the Mobile Taxi Company.

Forty minutes later a yellow cab pulled to a stop at the clubhouse. The window on the driver's side lowered an inch or so.

"You call for a cab?"

Connolly was already moving toward the car.

"Yeah," he said.

He opened the door and sank into the rear seat.

"Admiral Semmes Hotel," he said.

Forty-Seven

Connolly fell fully clothed across the bed in his hotel room. He awakened the next morning with a start. Confused and disoriented, he stumbled to the window and drew back the curtain. Outside, dawn was breaking. The streets below were gray in the early morning light. Across Government Street he saw the Presbyterian church. Down the street a ways the sign at the *Mobile Register* gave the time and temperature. It was five o'clock.

He stepped away from the window and crawled back into bed, but by then he was wide awake. In his mind he replayed the events at the hangar. He struggled to make sense of it. It all seemed like a dream. Perhaps it was a dream. Finding himself unable to return to sleep, he showered, dressed, and went downstairs to the hotel restaurant for breakfast.

At eight o'clock he left the hotel and took the long way to his office, walking up Government Street and then right on Conception. At Dauphin Street he turned right again and walked toward Bienville Square and his office. By then, he had almost convinced himself the whole thing really had been a dream.

Just then, a sheriff's patrol car approached from behind and drew abreast of him. The front window lowered, and the horn sounded. Connolly glanced at the car. Toby LeMoyne leaned through the open window and waved him toward the car. Connolly stepped from the sidewalk to the street. The car stopped. Connolly leaned against the front door.

"You're out rather early," Connolly said.

"We need to talk," Toby said.

His face was grim, his voice serious. Connolly knew at once the previous day had not been a dream.

"You still mad?"

"No," Toby replied. "Get in."

Connolly opened the door and slipped into the front seat.

"Where were you yesterday afternoon?" Toby scowled.

"Around ..." Connolly said, suddenly cautious. If he wasn't sure what happened, he was certain Toby would never believe it either. "Why?"

"Leigh Ann Agostino collapsed yesterday ... at lunch. She's out at St. Joseph's Hospital. Last I heard they weren't sure what happened to her. You know anything about that?"

Connolly struggled to make sense of what he heard.

"No," he said.

Toby looked aggravated.

"Truman Albritton had a massive heart attack yesterday morning," he said. "He's dead. You know anything about that?"

"Yesterday morning?"

"Yeah. Wife said he went into the bathroom to shave. When she went to see about him, he was lying on the floor. He was dead by the time they got him to Mobile General. You know anything about that?"

Connolly's mind was reeling.

"You sure it was yesterday morning?"

"Yeah," Toby replied. "I'm sure. What happened to them? Sheriff's asking all kind of questions. FBI called my house this morning." He paused. When Connolly didn't respond, he continued. "I like my job. My wife likes me to bring home a paycheck. My kids like new shoes. So, I want to know what you know about John Agostino, Leigh Ann, Truman Albritton, and all the others. And I want to know before you tell anybody else. You owe me that much."

Connolly slumped against the car window.

"Talk to me," Toby insisted. "Tell me what this is all about. You tell me, I can help us both."

By then, they were near the foot of Dauphin Street, well past Connolly's office. Ahead lay Water Street with the docks a little way beyond that.

Connolly groped for a response.

"Ahhh, I don't feel so good. Pull over and let me out," he said, pointing to the curb.

"Not until you tell me what's going on," Toby replied.

They continued on, turning left at Water Street. The car rolled slowly past rows of warehouses that lined the docks along Mobile River. Connolly, his head still resting against the car window, was unable to respond.

"Am I under arrest?" he croaked. His mouth was as dry as cotton.

"Tell me what happened," Toby demanded.

"Am I under arrest?" Connolly repeated.

"No," Toby said. "You're not under arrest. But I want to know what's going on."

"Let me out," Connolly said.

"Talk to me," Toby replied.

"Let me out," Connolly insisted. "We can talk later. I'm about to be sick."

Toby turned the car into the parking lot at Raphael's Cafe, a greasy diner between Water Street and the banana wharf. He brought the car to a stop. Connolly flung open the door.

"We can talk later," Connolly said.

He rolled from the car seat and shoved the door closed. The patrol car roared away.

Connolly stepped inside the cafe and sat at the first empty table. A waitress appeared, her blonde hair teased out from her head in all directions.

"What'll you have?" she asked.

Her jaws worked a wad of chewing gum as she spoke.

"Coffee," he said.

"Anything to eat?"

Connolly glanced across the room. A sign on the wall behind the counter advertised the morning specials.

"The two-egg special," he said, reading from the top of the sign.

She walked to the counter and returned with a cup and a pot of coffee. She set the cup in front of him, filled it with coffee, and walked to the kitchen window. Connolly saw her. He heard her voice. He even heard himself order the two-egg special, though he had already eaten breakfast. But his mind was far away, replaying for the hundredth time the events of the previous afternoon. The hangar. Albritton. Leigh Ann. The man approached him. A breeze blew from the far end of the hangar. Then there was silence.

One question rocked his mind. If Truman died yesterday morning, and Leigh Ann collapsed at lunch, how could they have been at the hangar yesterday afternoon?

The waitress returned.

"Two-egg special," she said.

She set the plate in front of him and moved away. He stared toward the front door, the images and questions turning over and over in his mind. Without noticing what he was doing, he picked up a fork and began to eat. Three bites later, he laid a ten-dollar bill on the table and walked out.

On the street out front he hailed a taxi and rode to St. Pachomius Church. He climbed the steps from the street and pushed open the door. Inside, a janitor was busy vacuuming the sanctuary. Connolly took a seat on a pew near the front.

In a few minutes the janitor switched off the vacuum cleaner. He was startled when he turned to find Connolly.

"Excuse me," he said. "I didn't notice you come in."

He rolled up the cord and carried the machine from the room. Connolly sat alone. In the peace and quiet his stomach began to settle. Before long, Father Scott appeared. He entered through the door to the right.

"Mike," he said, "you look a little tired this morning. Rough night?"

"Rough yesterday. Rough morning. Rough everything," Connolly replied.

Father Scott took a seat on the pew beside him.

"What's up?" he asked.

"Well ... I don't know ..." Connolly searched for a place to begin. "Yesterday, I was ..." He took a deep breath and tried again.

For the next thirty minutes, he told Father Scott about Attaway and Albritton and their scheme to pay off Judge Agostino. About finding the car, the preliminary hearing, and the explosion at his apartment. And then he told about going with Leigh Ann the day before and about Albritton at the hangar that afternoon. When he came to the part about his conversation with Toby LeMoyne that morning, and his failing grip on reality, his voice broke.

"Am I crazy?"

Father Scott smiled and shook his head.

"No. You're not crazy. And, what that deputy told you is true. Truman Albritton is dead. Leigh Ann Agostino is in the hospital."

Connolly shook his head in disbelief and confusion.

"So, what happened to them? Were they really there yesterday?"

"Oh, I'm sure they were there," Father Scott replied.

"But how can it be? They were there, and then at the same time they were somewhere else?"

Connolly propped his elbows on his knees and buried his face in his hands.

"Look," Father Scott said. "Like I told you before. I don't have all the answers. I can't tell you why. I can only tell you Who. You have encountered the One who made something from absolutely nothing. He's not like us. Day is the same as night to Him. Time doesn't set boundaries for Him. He exists beyond time." Father Scott paused, to let the thought sink in, then continued. "You'll never understand what's happened to you unless you allow yourself to consider something other than the existence you have previously known."

Connolly sighed. He sat up for a moment then slid low in the pew.

"We're not just talking about a concept or a theory," Father Scott said. "The One who created time has stepped into your life in a dramatic way. You need to find out why."

Connolly ran his fingers through his hair and tugged on it as if to pull it out.

"I could handle it if they were there and then suddenly not there. That would be tough, but I could manage it. But to have them there, then not there, and then to find out the next day that what happened in the afternoon the day before was impossible the day I actually experienced it ..." He threw his hands in the air. "See, I can't even articulate the thing."

Father Scott put his arm around Connolly's shoulder. His voice fell to a whisper.

"You are encountering One for whom then and now are always the same. He lives in an eternal present. For Him, it is always now. He simply is not limited by our limitations, and he has chosen to relate to you in a real and unique way. Yield to it, don't fight it."

Connolly looked Father Scott in the eye, desperate to understand.

"But they vanished from the hangar," he pleaded. "I mean, they were there. I saw them. We talked. And then they were gone. Disappeared. And now I find out today that things happened to them yesterday that would have prevented them from even being there. Were they really there? Was I really there?"

"You were there," Father Scott replied.

He leaned away and withdrew his arm from Connolly's shoulder.

"Think of it this way," he offered. The tone of his voice changed from serious to light. There was a sparkle in his eye. "You now have the upper hand."

"The upper hand?"

"Sure," Father Scott replied. "You know what Leigh Ann was going to do if she had finished lunch yesterday. No one else but the two of you knows that." A mischievous smile spread across his face. "And she doesn't know you know."

Connolly smiled too. He hadn't thought of that.

Forty-Eight

Connolly left the church and walked to the Port City Diner. The Chrysler was parked out front. He got in and drove south past Bienville Square and the office building to Water Street. From there, he made his way up the ramp to the interstate. At the edge of town he took the Broad Street exit and entered the Brookley complex. About a mile from the front entrance, he passed the golf course where he had called the taxi the evening before. A little further, he turned right onto the street that led toward the abandoned hangars.

His pulse quickened as he neared the first hangar. He lifted his foot from the accelerator. The engine slowed to an idle. Momentum carried the car silently up the street. By the time he reached the back of the hangar building, he was breathing hard, and his palms were sweaty. He glanced in the rearview mirror to make sure no one was following, then turned the corner.

The blue BMW sat where Leigh Ann parked it the day before, in front of the main doors of the first hangar to the right. The hangar doors were still open. The white, twin-engine aircraft sat inside. Connolly brought the car to a stop and got out.

A breeze blew off Mobile Bay and swept across the tarmac. It tousled Connolly's hair and sent trash swirling along the ground. In an instant, the scene from the day before inside the hangar flashed before his eyes. The darkness. The man with the gun. The sound of his footsteps on the concrete floor.

Connolly closed the door of the Chrysler and stepped slowly toward the hangar. He paused at the hangar door.

In front of him, the airplane sat in the midst of a semi-circle of sunlight. Beyond the plane, there was nothing but darkness. He looked around to make sure no one was present, then stepped inside to the airplane.

The windows of the plane were tinted. Even standing with his face against the glass, his hands cupped around his eyes to block out the glare, he could not see inside.

Near the tail section he found the door to the baggage compartment. He lifted the latch and pulled. The door was locked. He stepped onto the left wing and tried the cabin door. It was unlocked. He opened the door and looked inside.

On the pilot's seat lay a chart book. Connolly picked it up. The book was open to a chart showing Mobile and the surrounding area. A second chart for southern Florida and the Keys was marked with a paper clip. Still another chart was marked with a Post-it note. He opened the book to that page. It was a chart for the Bahama Islands.

Connolly turned to the instrument panel. He flipped the main battery switch to the "On" position and checked the gauges. The fuel tanks were full. He switched off the battery.

He folded the pilot's seat forward and crawled into the first row of passenger seats. They were empty. He swiveled one of the seats to the side and moved to the rear of the plane. Beyond the last row of seats was the baggage compartment. By looking over the top of the seats on the last row he hoped he could see inside the compartment. Connolly crawled into the last row and looked over the top, but it was too dark to see. He scrambled back to the pilot's seat and turned on the main battery. He found a switch for the cabin lights and turned them on, then returned to the back of the plane.

Peering over the last row, he saw two pieces of luggage in the compartment behind the seat. One bore a luggage tag with Leigh Ann's name. The other was without a tag. Connolly slid down in the seat and thought.

With millions of dollars in the bank in Nassau, and John Agostino dead, Truman Albritton wouldn't have trusted anyone else to obtain the money. But why only luggage for two? He was certain neither Albritton nor Leigh Ann could fly the plane. The man who was going to shoot him must have been the pilot. Yet, there were only two bags in the compartment.

Connolly crawled to the front of the plane, switched off the battery, and climbed out of the plane. Alone in the hangar, he leaned against the fuselage and thought about what to do next. If Toby wouldn't help, there was no one else to whom he could turn. He wasn't going to the FBI. They would want to know how he knew about the plane and the car, and they would never believe his answer.

He glanced toward the front. Through the open hangar doors he saw Leigh Ann's BMW sitting on the tarmac. He walked from the plane to the car. A quick glance at the back seat revealed nothing. He moved to the front passenger door and peered inside. A pistol lay on the floor on the driver's side. He grasped the door handle and pulled. To his surprise the door opened.

Connolly leaned inside and reached for the pistol. He paused as his fingertips brushed the pistol grip. If he picked it up, his prints would be on the only weapon at the scene. Instead, he took a seat and slipped his foot to that side of the floor. Using the toe of his shoe, he nudged the pistol out of sight under the seat.

He glanced around the interior of the car but found nothing unusual. He opened the glove compartment, expecting to find it cluttered. It was empty. No receipts. No owner's manual. Nothing. He ran his finger across the bottom of the compartment. It was clean.

"Not even any dust," he mumbled.

He checked the tray above the radio, but found nothing there either. As an afterthought, he opened the ashtray on the console near the gearshift. A small piece of white paper was stuffed inside. He took it out and unfolded it. The paper was a cash register receipt.

Across the top of the receipt was the name Zirlot's Grocery. The name sounded familiar, but he couldn't remember why. He scanned down the receipt. It was a list of grocery items. Bread, milk, the usual things. Then, at the bottom, he saw an item that seemed out of place. Gillette shaving cream. He wondered out loud.

"Why would Leigh Ann Agostino buy Gillette shaving cream?"

At the bottom, the receipt indicated the purchase had been made with cash the morning of the previous day.

Two bags in the airplane, he thought. And Leigh Ann bought groceries yesterday morning. She wouldn't buy groceries if she was going away. Yet, her suitcase was there.

"Where is Zirlot's?"

There was Buddy Zirlot, at Bayou La Batre. Nathaniel Zirlot ran a boatyard at Coden. Zirlot Road ... Zirlot's. A smile broke across his face. There was a store on Dauphin Island named Zirlot's Grocery Store. Not much of a store, it was used mostly by weekend vacationers. He stopped there once. It wasn't far from Keyton Attaway's beach house.

"That's it," he whispered. "Keyton's beach house."

He jumped from the BMW, slammed the door closed, and started toward the Chrysler.

Connolly drove back to the interstate and headed west. A few miles beyond Broad Street he turned onto Dauphin Island Parkway and drove south. Fifteen minutes later he crossed Dog River. From there, it was a thirty-minute ride to Cedar Point at the mouth of Mobile Bay and the end of the mainland.

South and west of the point lay a body of water known as the Mississippi Sound. Shallow and murky, it was a narrow band of shoals marking the area where the Gulf of Mexico mingled with brackish water draining from the thousands of acres of swamp along the coast below Mobile. Dauphin Island sat five miles due south from Cedar Point.

Connolly drove the Chrysler onto the Dauphin Island Bridge, a concrete span across the Mississippi Sound that linked the island to the mainland. Traffic was light on the bridge. He pushed the accelerator toward the floor. The car picked up speed.

Forty-Nine

From Cedar Point, Connolly reached the end of the bridge at the center of the island in a matter of minutes. There, the road ended at the intersection with Bienville Boulevard. A wide thoroughfare, the boulevard traversed the length of the island from east to west. Connolly turned left and headed east.

Three-quarters of a mile down the road, he passed Cadillac Square. He turned right on Fort Charlotte Avenue, then left on Gorgas Street. Keyton Attaway's beach house sat at the end of the street. Connolly lifted his foot from the accelerator and let the Chrysler slow to an idle. The car rolled silently down the street and coasted to a stop. He switched off the engine, slid out of the front seat, and gently closed the car door.

He moved lightly up the long flight of steps to the porch, ten feet above the ground. Surf crashing on the beach behind the house muffled any noise he made. He reached the front door undetected and turned the knob. It was unlocked. He eased the door open and stepped inside.

The house was quiet and still. To the right of the door sat a sofa. A newspaper lay on the far end. A coffee cup sat on a low table next to the sofa. Further to the right, a doorway led into the kitchen in the rear of the house. Connolly stepped to the right and peered through the doorway.

From the living room, he could see through the kitchen to

the deck that extended across the back of the house. A man sat in a chair on the deck, reading a magazine. He was dressed in shorts and a T-shirt and wore a baseball cap that was pulled low over his forehead. Sunglasses hid his eyes, and he was unshaven. Had Connolly not known him most of his life, he would not have recognized the man. He was John Agostino.

Connolly walked quickly through the house and onto the deck. His sudden appearance caught Agostino by complete surprise, so much so he did not bother to lay the magazine aside.

"Mike," Agostino greeted him. "Didn't expect to see you here."

He continued to read the magazine as he spoke.

"Didn't expect to see you here either," Connolly replied. "Whose house you going to break into next?"

Agostino hooked his foot around the leg of a nearby chair and pulled it closer.

"Relax," he said. "Have a seat. Keyton gave me a key to this place a long time ago."

Connolly sat in the chair and looked across the beach to the surf. He watched in silence as the waves crashed to shore, unsure what to say.

"I suppose you have a few questions," Agostino said, his face still buried behind the magazine.

"Yeah," Connolly replied, still staring at the beach. "A few."

Agostino waited, then prodded him on.

"Well ... ?"

"To tell the truth," Connolly replied, "I don't know where to begin."

Agostino laid aside the magazine. Connolly turned to face him.

"You didn't leave me much choice, you know," Agostino said.

Connolly was taken aback.

"I didn't leave you much choice?" he repeated. "What did I have to do with any of this?"

"After what you did in that hearing on Keyton's case, I had no choice. I could either find a way to disappear, or go to prison. That or wait for someone to kill me."

"Kill you?" Connolly made no effort to hide his disbelief. "I think it was the other way around."

Agostino cocked his head in an arrogant, knowing look Connolly found all too familiar. His voice took on a condescending tone.

"You don't know half of what you think you know," he said.

"Well, if you didn't set Keyton up, how did you know to pick up Leigh Ann after he was shot? Why did you hide the car?"

Agostino looked away, but the glint in his eye indicated he was caught by surprise that Connolly knew he was actually at the scene of the murder.

"Who told you I picked her up?"

Connolly ignored Agostino's question.

"Why did you hide the car? At your own hunting lodge?"

The insolent confidence vanished from Agostino's face. In its place was a blank gaze.

"That ... ahh ... that wasn't my idea," he said.

His words trailed off, and he had a look of sudden realization about him, as if aware for the first time the car was at the camp.

"I had no choice but to go along," he mumbled.

"No choice?"

Just as quickly, the blank expression vanished from Agostino's face. An arrogant look returned.

"Albritton was the one who was worried about Keyton," he replied. "Not me. Taking care of him was Albritton's idea."

"You just happened to be in the neighborhood."

Agostino did not reply. Connolly continued to press for details.

"So, whose idea was it to leave a dead man in your car so everyone would think it was you?"

"That was my idea," Agostino said, raising his hand in mock frankness. "I'll take credit for that."

"You're admitting to murder," Connolly quipped. "That's good. Now we're getting somewhere."

"No," Agostino replied. "I didn't say I murdered anyone. Like I told you. You don't know all you think you know."

Connolly threw his hands in the air.

"So, enlighten me, John," he said.

Agostino let out a long, deep sigh.

"That man they found in my car was sent to kill me," he explained. "We fought. I managed to get the gun pointed toward him and pulled the trigger, but it was self-defense."

Connolly shook his head.

"I find that hard to believe. You couldn't win a wrestling match with your mother. Much less a professional hit man."

Agostino smiled.

"That may be true, but I managed to get it pointed at him."

"Then what?"

"He was dead. We were about the same size. I shoved him in the car, drove to Grayton Beach, and propped him behind the wheel. Put my wallet in his coat pocket. Made sure all his other pockets were empty, and left."

"Good plan," Connolly smirked. "Except you're a federal judge. FBI must be all over this by now."

Agostino smiled.

"The FBI isn't a problem," he said.

"What do you mean?"

Agostino crossed his legs and folded his arms in his lap.

"Mike, that's one part of this I'm not going to talk about. Just believe me. The local FBI office is not a problem."

"And what about the part where Leigh Ann and Albritton were going to kill me? You going to explain that part, too?"

Agostino looked puzzled.

"What are you talking about?"

"You know," Connolly explained. "She gets me in the car and drives me to an abandoned hangar at Brookley Field. When we get there, Albritton's waiting for us with an airplane. Has a man with him to kill me. Take me in the back of the hangar, shoot me, take the plane to the Bahamas for the money, end of story."

"I have no idea what you're talking about. Leigh Ann was here yesterday morning. She stayed in Mobile last night. She should be back here this afternoon."

Connolly leaned forward in his chair. His face was flush with anger.

"John, don't tell me you don't know, because I know you do. Let me hear your explanation for it. Tell me how it was all Albritton's idea. You were just going along with it because you didn't want to go to jail. You've already explained away two murders that way, why not one more?"

Agostino leaned forward in his chair. The two men were only inches apart.

"Mike, I have no idea what you're talking about."

"You expect me to believe that? How do you think I knew you were down here?"

Agostino shrugged his shoulders and leaned away.

"A hunch," he said, "A guess. I don't know."

Connolly pulled the receipt from Zirlot's out of his pocket.

"I found this in Leigh Ann's BMW."

He held it for Agostino to see.

"What were you doing in her car?"

"I just told you," Connolly said. "She stopped me on the street yesterday and said she wanted to talk. About you, by the way. Sounded desperate. She picked me up in front of my office and drove me to a hangar at Brookley Field. She and Albritton were going to kill me. By the looks of things, I'd say they were going to fly off to the Bahamas together and clean out your bank account. The way she was cuddled on his shoulder, I'd say they were going to leave you high and dry."

"Impossible."

"Don't you think it's just a little odd that between all of you … you, Keyton, and Truman, your name is the only one on the documents. You're the president of the corporation. You're the owner of the account at Tidewater. You're the—"

Agostino interrupted him.

"Tidewater? What account at Tidewater?"

"The account," Connolly replied. "Your account."

Agostino looked puzzled.

"What account?"

"There were wire transfers. Thousands of dollars from the bank in the Bahamas to an account at Tidewater National Bank in your name."

Agostino shook his head.

"I don't have an account at Tidewater."

"See," Connolly cried. "That's what I mean. All the evidence points to you. Leigh Ann says you took care of hiding the Cadillac. You insisted on the transfers to the Tidewater account."

Agostino sat in dazed silence.

"I'm telling you, John," Connolly continued. "All the evidence points straight to you. They have you in a box. You can live on the run, with nothing, or you can talk and go to prison. Either way, Leigh Ann and Truman, or Leigh Ann and somebody, were going to take the money and run."

"You're crazy," Agostino growled.

"You think so?" Connolly stood. "Come on," he said. "Let's take a ride."

"A ride?" Agostino snorted. "I'm not going anywhere with you."

Connolly took him by the arm.

"Come on," he insisted. "I want you to see for yourself. Leigh Ann's probably up there right now getting ready to leave."

Connolly tugged on Agostino's arm. Agostino stood, finally. Connolly guided him across the deck and into the house. When they reached the kitchen, Connolly froze.

"Hold it," he whispered.

He halted Agostino with a quick jerk of his arm. Ahead, he saw a man peering through the living room window.

"You know that man?"

Agostino shook his head.

"No," he replied.

Connolly, still holding Agostino by the arm, pulled him toward the back door.

"That's the man who was at the hangar with Albritton," Connolly said. "He's the one who was going to kill me."

The man on the front porch drew a pistol from the waistband of his trousers. An automatic pistol, it was equipped with a silencer. He raised the pistol and fired a shot through the front window. The bullet whizzed through the room and struck the refrigerator.

Connolly let go of Agostino's arm and darted out the back door. He crouched out of sight near the steps that led from the deck to the beach behind the house. Agostino stood in the kitchen and watched, bewildered.

The gunman raised the pistol again. Instinctively, Agostino turned his head and torso to one side. The shot grazed his left arm. He dove out the back door and landed on the deck near Connolly.

"I don't think he came here looking for me," Connolly said. "I think he's after you."

Agostino clutched his arm.

"Albritton," he muttered.

"Albritton's dead," Connolly replied. "We gotta get out of here. That man will kill us if we wait around."

Connolly started down the rear steps. Agostino grabbed his arm.

"Truman is dead?"

"Yeah. Had a heart attack yesterday morning."

"I talked to him yesterday morning," Agostino replied.

His face looked perplexed, but his eyes were wide with fear.

"I'm sure you did," Connolly replied. "I saw him yesterday afternoon too. But he had a stroke yesterday morning. He was dead before lunch."

"I don't understand," Agostino protested.

"It's a long story," Connolly replied. "Let's talk about it later. Come on."

Connolly started down the back steps. A third shot struck the railing near Agostino's head.

"Come on," Connolly repeated.

Agostino followed him. Together, they scrambled down the steps.

The man with the gun hurried through the house and onto the deck. Connolly and Agostino ducked underneath the house and ran. As they reached the front, the gunman reached the rear steps.

Connolly hurried toward the Chrysler. Agostino followed close behind.

"Get in," Connolly shouted.

He rounded the corner of the car and reached for the door handle. On the other side of the car, Agostino opened the front door and dove into the floor. He pulled the door closed and curled himself under the dashboard on the passenger side. Connolly slid behind the steering wheel and shoved the key in the ignition switch.

By then the gunman was at the bottom of the steps. When he saw them in the car, he slowed to a walk and swaggered confidently toward them. He lowered his arm and let the pistol dangle at his side. A knowing smile stretched across his face. The smile grew to a broad grin as he approached.

Connolly turned the key in the switch. The engine in the Chrysler came to life. He jerked the gear lever into reverse and backed the car away from the house. The man with the pistol stopped and stared. His mouth dropped open in amazement. As the car reached the street, he recovered and raised the pistol to fire.

At the last moment, Connolly whipped the steering wheel to the right. The front of the car slid to the left, spinning around in a half-circle to face away from the house. A shot rang out. A bullet bounced off the front door post on the passenger side.

"Whoa," Agostino cried from the floor. "He's shooting at us."

Connolly snatched the gear lever into drive and stomped the accelerator to the floor. The rear wheels spun on the dirt driveway sending a cloud of dust and gravel in the air behind them. A second shot blew out the rear window and shattered the rearview mirror above Connolly's head. He ducked low in the seat and pressed the accelerator hard with his foot.

When the spinning rear tires reached the pavement, the Chrysler shot forward. The car raced to the opposite end of the street. At the corner, Connolly whipped the steering wheel to the right. The back of the car came around to the left as they made the turn, but Connolly kept the accelerator pressed against the floor. Inches from sliding into the ditch on the far side of the road, the tires caught traction with the pavement, and the car lunged forward.

Connolly and Agostino reached Bienville Boulevard in less than a minute. Connolly turned to look behind.

"I don't see anyone behind us," he called.

Agostino raised his head from the floor.

"You sure?"

Connolly glanced over his shoulder once again.

"I don't see anyone."

They raced up Bienville Boulevard. Ahead was the entrance onto the bridge back to Cedar Point and the mainland. A few hundred feet from the turn, Connolly lifted his foot from the accelerator and rested it on the brake pedal. He slowed the car enough to make the turn, then pressed the accelerator to the floor once again.

Fifty

From Dauphin Island, Connolly and Agostino retraced the drive back to the interstate. There they traveled east to Broad Street and entered the Brookley Industrial Complex. At the end of Broad Street, they turned left and drove along the eastern perimeter. A mile past the golf course, they turned right toward the hangar.

Connolly lifted his foot from the accelerator as they approached the building. The Chrysler's engine slowed to an idle. The car rolled quietly toward the corner.

Agostino glanced in Connolly's direction.

"You really expect me to believe Leigh Ann came to a place like this on her own?"

Connolly's heart rate increased as the car rolled forward.

"Just wait," he replied. "You'll see."

"Probably got the police or somebody waiting around the corner," Agostino grumbled. "I can't believe I let you bring me up here."

"You didn't have much choice, remember," Connolly replied. "That guy was shooting at you when we left."

"He was shooting at you," Agostino retorted.

"Yeah?" Connolly replied. "Then why were you running so fast?"

They reached the corner of the hangar before Agostino could

reply. Connolly turned the wheel, and the car rounded the building.

The BMW was still there, parked in front of the hangar where Leigh Ann had left it. The hangar doors were open. The airplane was parked inside. Connolly brought the Chrysler to a stop behind the BMW. Agostino looked puzzled.

"How'd her car get out here?"

"Like I told you twice already," Connolly replied. "She drove it out here. Brought me out here in it so Albritton could have me killed."

"You brought it out here," Agostino said.

Connolly opened the door and got out.

"Don't be ridiculous," he replied.

Agostino stepped from the car and walked to the BMW. He cupped his hands around his eyes and looked inside. As he looked inside, Connolly remembered Leigh Ann's pistol was lying in the floor of the car.

"The plane's more interesting," he called, hoping Agostino would move away from the car before he noticed the gun.

Agostino stared through the car window a moment longer, then turned away and stepped toward the hangar.

"Come on," Connolly called. He waved his arm in a gesture for Agostino to follow. "Take a look over here."

Agostino followed him into the hangar. Connolly walked to the plane and stepped onto the wing. He grabbed the door latch and opened the door, then moved aside.

"Come on," he said, waving his arm again and gesturing to Agostino. "Get up here and take a look."

Agostino stepped onto the wing and climbed through the door.

"Crawl into the back seat," Connolly said.

Agostino backed out of the plane.

"I'm not getting back there," he protested. "No telling what you'll do to me."

"Crawl back there and look over the back seat," Connolly insisted. "If I'd wanted to do something to you I wouldn't have waited 'til now."

Agostino frowned, then reluctantly climbed inside the cabin of the plane. He moved to the rear seat and looked into the luggage compartment. In a few moments, he retreated to the door and back onto the wing.

"Okay," he said. "So her bag is in the plane. Big deal."

Connolly smiled.

"You didn't know it was back there, did you?"

"It doesn't mean anything," Agostino replied.

"Sure it does, John. If she and Albritton were just setting me up so they could kill me, they wouldn't have gone to the trouble of loading luggage in the plane. I never got in the plane. I wasn't going to see it."

Agostino stepped from the wing to the hangar floor.

"I'm sure there's an explanation for it," he said.

"Yeah," Connolly replied. "They were going to the Bahamas and leave you in that beach house to fend for yourself."

"I don't think so."

"Listen, John. That man with the gun. The one who was shooting at us. He didn't know I was coming down there to Attaway's beach house. No one followed me."

"So?"

"He wasn't down there for me. He was there for you."

Agostino thought for a moment.

"Where's Leigh Ann?"

"Story I heard was she's in the hospital. Supposedly, no one knows what's wrong with her."

"The hospital?"

"That's what they say."

For the first time, Agostino displayed genuine anger.

"You dragged me all the way up here, knowing my wife was in the hospital?"

"If I'm right," Connolly replied, "she'll be feeling fine by this afternoon."

Agostino glared at him.

"What difference does it make?" Connolly chuckled. "You can't go over there anyway."

Agostino thought for a moment.

"That man," he said, finally. "The one at the house. He was the man you were looking for before the hearing. The one from the blue Ford pickup."

Connolly nodded his head slowly. Hearing that made him uneasy. A sense of foreboding swept over him.

"We better go," he said.

"Let me ask you something," Agostino said. "You claim they brought you out here to kill you. How did you get away?"

"We don't have time for me to explain all that," Connolly replied. He glanced around, checking the other hangar buildings, unable to shake the feeling someone was watching. "I don't like this place," Connolly replied.

"Answer my question," Agostino demanded. "How did you get away?"

Connolly walked to the Chrysler. Agostino followed him and slid in on the passenger side.

"It didn't happen, did it?" Agostino said. "You made this whole thing up just to get me to talk."

Connolly sat behind the wheel. He placed the key in the ignition switch and turned it. Nothing happened. He tried again. Again, nothing happened.

Agostino looked perplexed.

"What's wrong?"

Connolly shook his head.

"I don't know," he replied.

He opened the door, stepped to the front of the car, and raised the hood. He leaned against the radiator and stared into the engine compartment. Agostino climbed out and walked to the front.

"What is it?"

Connolly pointed to engine. A black wire dangled from the center of the distributor cap.

"When did that happen?" Agostino's voice betrayed a hint of panic.

Connolly propped his head against the hood.

"Your friend with the gun must have removed it before he came in the house."

Agostino scanned the surrounding hangars.

"Then how did it start and run all the way up here?"

Connolly looked at him and smiled.

"I don't know," he said. "It's the coil wire. I guess it was close enough to arc."

"Tell me how a car runs without a coil wire," Agostino insisted. "And while you're at it, tell me how you got away from Albritton and the man with the gun."

"Not now," Connolly said. "You wouldn't believe me if I told you, and we don't have time. We need to get out of here."

As they argued, Connolly heard a noise. He raised his head to look around. Agostino grew frantic.

"What's that?" he asked.

"It's a car," Connolly replied. "Come on."

Connolly ran from the Chrysler toward the far side of the hangar, Agostino followed. They reached the corner as a green Ford Taurus rounded the building and stopped on the tarmac near the Chrysler. Connolly and Agostino crouched behind a scrubby bush and watched.

Leigh Ann Agostino was driving. The gunman from the beach house was riding with her. He jumped from the car as soon as it stopped and ran to the Chrysler.

"See," he shouted, pointing to the engine compartment. "I told you. I took the coil wire loose from the distributor. There's no way it could run."

"Come on," Leigh Ann called. "We don't have time for that. You sure you know how to fly this thing?"

"Yeah," the man replied. "I can fly it."

"Well, let's get moving," Leigh Ann said. "I have to get to Nassau before John figures out what's happening."

The man walked quickly to her side.

"You sure they'll give you the money?"

"Yes," she said. I'm sure."

"And we split it."

"Yes," she said, exasperated. "We split it. Now let's get moving."

Still crouched at the corner of the hangar, Agostino was enraged by what he had seen and heard. He stepped around the corner of the building and started toward the hangar doors. Connolly grabbed him by the shoulder and pulled him back.

"They'll shoot you," he said, his voice a coarse whisper. "Just wait a minute."

Connolly pulled Agostino away from the corner a few feet down the side of the building. Holding him with one hand, he slid a cell phone from his pocket with the other. Using his thumb, he punched in a number. Agostino started for the corner of the building again. Connolly held tightly to his arm and hauled him back. Seconds later, the dispatcher at the sheriff's department answered his phone call.

"Toby LeMoyne," he whispered.

"Excuse me?"

"Toby LeMoyne," he repeated.

In a moment, Toby came on the line.

"Toby, this is Mike Connolly."

"I told you I can't talk to you," Toby snapped.

Connolly ignored him.

"Get over here to Brookley Field," he said. "I'm at an abandoned hangar down past the golf course. You can't miss it. On the right. I'm here with John Agostino. Get here quick."

"What are you talking about?"

"Get here quick. And bring some help. I'll explain it when you get here. We can bust this case wide open."

"Who are you with?"

"John Agostino."

"His body?"

"No. Him. He's alive. Get here fast."

Connolly switched off the phone and shoved it into his pocket. He dropped to the ground and pulled Agostino down beside him.

"What now?"

"I don't know," Connolly replied. "Wait for help, I guess."

Agostino sat for a moment, then jumped to his feet.

"Forget about the money," he said. "You were right. She sold me out. Let's get out of here."

He climbed over Connolly and started toward the far end of the hangar.

"It's a long way," Connolly protested.

"I don't care," Agostino replied. "I'm not waiting around here to die."

Connolly pulled himself up and followed. Halfway down the building a shot rang out.

"Stop!" someone shouted.

Agostino dove to the ground. Connolly froze, then slowly turned around.

Behind them stood the gunman from the beach house. In his hand he held the automatic pistol. This time, the silencer was missing. Holding the pistol in front, he walked toward them.

"Get up," he ordered, gesturing toward Agostino with the gun.

Agostino stood.

"You two somehow managed to get that heap of junk Chrysler up here. You can move it. It's blocking the door."

Connolly and Agostino stared at him.

"Don't just stand there," the man ordered. "Come on. Get moving."

They stepped toward him. As they did, he backed toward the corner. At the corner of the building he stepped onto the tarmac and held the pistol on them as they passed.

"Push it out of the way," he ordered.

They started across the tarmac.

"Think you two old men can handle that?"

Connolly walked to the Chrysler and closed the hood. Out of the corner of his eye he saw Leigh Ann standing by the plane.

"How about if we just crank it and back it out?" he said.

The man laughed.

"You tried that once today already," he chided. "Don't push your luck."

"It's not luck," Connolly replied. He looked to Agostino. "Get in," he said.

The gunman stepped forward.

"Not so fast," he barked. "Just push it out of the way."

Connolly ignored him and got in on the driver's side. Agostino hesitated, then slid in on the passenger side.

The man with the gun raised the hood and looked inside. The black wire dangled from the distributor. He slammed the hood closed.

"Get out of the car," he demanded. A sly grin spread across his face. "I don't know what you think you're doing, but I want this car out of the way." His face was suddenly cold and emotionless. "Now," he shouted.

Connolly slipped the key into the ignition switch and turned it. The engine started. With one quick move, he snatched the gear lever into drive and pressed the accelerator to the floor. The Chrysler shot forward. The gunman dove to the side to avoid being hit as the car sped past him.

At the corner of the building Connolly whipped the steering wheel to the right and drove into the grass and down the far side of the building. At the end, he steered the car to the right again and pointed it toward the street.

The gunman gathered himself from the pavement and ran to the opposite side of the building. When the car emerged from the far end of the building, he fired four quick shots. Agostino slid into the floor. Connolly ducked low in the seat and drove the car while looking through the spokes of the steering wheel.

The first shot struck the right rear fender of the car and passed through the trunk. The second shot struck the ground near the front passenger's door. The other two shots sailed over the top of the car.

As the gunman fired at Connolly and Agostino, three sheriff's patrol cars turned from the perimeter road and sped up the street toward the hangar. The last shot from the gunman's pistol sailed over the top of the Chrysler and struck the lights atop the first patrol car. They exploded in a shower of plastic and glass.

Fifty-One

Connolly ducked low in the seat as the shots whizzed past. He struggled to control the Chrysler, glancing over the dash as he dodged the bullets.

The Chrysler careened across the street in front of the approaching patrol cars. Connolly jerked the wheel to the right and pushed on the brake pedal with both feet. The car spun around in a circle and came to a stop alongside the first patrol car. Toby LeMoyne was driving. Toby leaned out the window and shouted.

"What's going on? Who's doing the shooting?"

"Leigh Ann Agostino's up there," Connolly shouted in reply. He nodded over his shoulder toward the hangar. "There's a man with her. He's shooting at us. You better hurry. They have a plane in that first hangar. They're trying to take off."

Toby barked orders on the radio to the patrolmen in the other cars. The two cars behind him sped around his car and drove toward the hangar. As the first car rounded the corner at the front of the hangar, shots rang out again.

Toby turned to Connolly. He stuck his arm out the window of the patrol car and pointed to Judge Agostino.

"Bring him and follow me," he ordered.

Toby raced ahead to catch up with the other patrolmen. Connolly pressed the accelerator to the floor, turned the steering wheel hard to the left, and sent the rear of the Chrysler sliding around. When the front of the car faced the hangar, he lifted his foot from the pedal long enough to let the rear wheels gain traction, then pressed it to the floor again.

The sound of gunfire rang from the hangar once again.

"Maybe we shouldn't be in such a hurry," Agostino suggested.

Connolly kept the accelerator pressed to the floor. The car sped forward. Agostino turned to him.

"Mike." Agostino grabbed Connolly's arm. "Do we have to go up there?"

"Yeah," Connolly replied. "It'll all be over in a few minutes."

"Couldn't we just sort of drift off?" Agostino said.

Connolly turned to Agostino.

"What do you mean?"

He lifted his foot from the accelerator as he waited for Agostino to answer. The Chrysler slowed.

"You know," Agostino said. "Maybe it would be easier if I just ... disappeared."

Agostino slipped his right hand around the door handle. His fingers gripped the latch lever.

"Don't even think about running," Connolly warned.

He shoved the accelerator to the floor. The sudden surge of power from the Chrysler's engine threw Agostino back against the seat. His hand slipped from the door handle.

They reached the hangar as Toby leaped from his patrol car. Connolly brought the Chrysler to a stop behind Toby's car but left the engine running. He watched as the patrolmen secured the area. To the right, through the open hangar doors, Leigh Ann stood beside the airplane. Her hands against the fuselage, she faced away from them. A patrolman stood nearby, holding her at bay with a pistol.

The gunman lay face down on the floor a few feet away. Blood ran from underneath his body. A rattling, gravelly moan emitted from his mouth between gasps.

Toby walked to the passenger side of the Chrysler and opened the door.

"Alright, Agostino," he ordered. "Out of the car, slowly."

Agostino glared at him.

"That's Judge Agostino to you, son," he replied.

"Out of the car," Toby repeated.

Agostino climbed slowly from the car. As he emerged, Toby took him by the shoulder and lifted him to his feet, then turned him around to face the car.

"Hands on top of the car," he said. His voice was stern but not angry. Agostino reluctantly obeyed. Toby ran his hand down Agostino's side, searching for a weapon, then cuffed his hands behind his back.

"John Agostino," Toby began, "you are under arrest. You have a right to remain silent. If you give up that right—"

Agostino interrupted him.

"Don't you think I know my rights?"

His tone was sharp and sarcastic. Undaunted, Toby continued.

"... anything you say can and will be used against you in a court of law."

"I don't need the Miranda routine," Agostino snarled. "I'm not some kind of common criminal."

"You have a right to an attorney and to consult with an attorney prior to any questioning. If you cannot afford an attorney, one will be appointed for you by the court. Do you understand these rights?"

Agostino chuckled. Toby grabbed his hands and jerked backward against the handcuffs, forcing him to stand erect.

"I said, 'Do you understand these rights?'"

Agostino was livid.

"I'm still a federal judge," he hissed.

"Then act like one," Toby replied. "Do you understand these rights as I've explained them to you?"

Agostino sighed.

"Yes," he seethed, "I understand them."

Toby led Agostino to his patrol car.

Connolly stepped from the driver's seat of the Chrysler and walked to the front of the car. He raised the hood, reached across the engine, and shoved the coil wire back in place. As he closed the hood, Toby returned.

"I suppose you have an interesting explanation for all this," he said.

"Yeah," Connolly replied. "I have an explanation."

He moved around the car to the door on the driver's side. Toby followed.

"Am I going to believe it?"

Connolly smiled.

"Probably not," he said.

Toby sighed and rubbed his forehead.

"Give us a couple of hours to process them in at the jail," he said, "then come down to the office. We'll need a statement from you."

Connolly nodded.

"Think they'll still be mad at you?"

Toby looked puzzled.

"Who?"

"You know, the sheriff, district attorney, FBI. All those people you were so worried about before."

"No," Toby growled. "They'll think I'm a hero now."

"Then why aren't you smiling?"

"Because now I've got to attend who knows how many hearings and meetings, file a bunch of reports, and," he swept his arm around in a broad gesture, "explain all this to everyone over and over again. And, worst of all, I have to listen to you tell me 'I told you so.'"

Connolly grinned.

"See," Toby exclaimed, pointing to Connolly. "That's what I'm talking about. That little smirk of a smile."

Connolly started the car and began to back away.

"Could be worse," he said.

"Two hours," Toby reminded him.

Connolly backed the Chrysler beyond the corner of the hangar and turned it around. As he did, an ambulance passed in front of him and came to a stop near the hangar doors. The ambulance doors burst open. Paramedics rushed to the gunman. Two more lowered a stretcher to the ground from the rear of the ambulance. Down the street more patrol cars approached. Soon, the place would be crawling with detectives and investigators.

Connolly put the car in gear and started forward. A few feet past the hangar, he eased the car into the grass and drove alongside the pavement as the line of patrol cars raced past him toward the hangar.

Fifty-Two

*I*t was late when Connolly finally arrived at Toby's office. He parked the Chrysler in front of St. Pachomius Church and stepped from the car. The church was dark, but much more inviting than what lay across the street. He paused a moment, then reluctantly crossed the street and entered the sheriff's office through the rear door. Toby LeMoyne was waiting for him.

Connolly followed him down a long corridor to an interview room. Furnished with only a table and three chairs, the room was cold and intimidating. Toby took a seat, placed a small tape recorder in the middle of the table, and glared at Connolly.

"Alright," he growled. "Begin at the beginning and tell me what happened. Exactly. And don't leave anything out."

Connolly smiled.

"You think you're ready for this?"

Toby sighed.

"I doubt it," he said. "But tell me anyway."

It took Connolly almost an hour to tell what happened. When he finished, Toby called two detectives to the room and made him tell it all again. Then, Toby and the two detectives questioned him about each detail. Unable to shake him, they finally gave up at midnight and agreed to let him leave.

Toby walked him to the door.

"I'm more confused than ever," he said, as they walked down the corridor.

"Got to think beyond yourself, Toby," Connolly replied, repeating what he'd heard from Father Scott.

Toby chuckled.

"You gone from law to philosophy?"

"No philosophy could explain this," Connolly said.

They reached the exit. Toby unlocked the door and held it open for Connolly to leave.

"Well, whatever," Toby said. "But the FBI will probably contact you tomorrow. For your sake, I hope you don't give them the same story."

Connolly laughed as he stepped outside.

The next morning, Connolly walked from the Admiral Semmes Hotel to his office. Mrs. Gordon was waiting at her desk for him, as usual.

"You made the papers," she said, as he entered the office.

She tossed the newspaper onto the desktop. It landed with a thud.

"Good morning, Mrs. Gordon," Connolly replied.

He picked up the newspaper from her desk and scanned the front page. There was a large article about Judge Agostino's return, along with a photograph of Connolly.

"How about that," Connolly replied. "Made the front page, above the fold. Might be good for business."

Mrs. Gordon rolled her eyes.

"Since when have you been interested in business?"

"Now, now, Mrs. Gordon," Connolly teased, "it's too early in the morning for sarcasm."

She handed him a stack of phone messages.

"These are your calls so far this morning." She glanced at her watch. "I've been here forty-five minutes. The phone hasn't stopped ringing."

The phone rang as she spoke. She gestured in frustration as she reached to answer it.

"See what I mean?"

Connolly grinned and laid the newspaper on her desk. Mrs. Gordon answered the phone. Connolly walked down the hall to his office.

He spent the morning returning phone calls and catching up on what little pending business he had. Compared to events of the past several weeks, he found sitting behind the desk boring. By eleven o'clock, he'd had enough. If the FBI wanted to talk, they would have to wait. He retrieved his jacket from the coat rack and walked to the door.

"I have another stack of messages for you," Mrs. Gordon said.

She held up a handful of yellow message notes.

"Keep them," he replied, dismissing her with a wave of the hand. "I'll be back this afternoon."

"What do I say ... "

Connolly ignored her and stepped into the corridor outside the office. The door banged shut behind him.

Downstairs, he made his way to the sidewalk and walked to the Chrysler. It was parked in its usual place near the Port City Diner. He slid in behind the steering wheel, placed the key in the ignition switch, and turned it. The engine came to life at once. At the sound of it starting he remembered that moment on the tarmac in front of the hangar when he first realized the car had been running without the coil wire attached. A broad grin spread across his face.

He looked up to check the traffic in the rearview mirror. But the mirror was gone, shot away by the gunman as he and Agostino sped away from Attaway's beach house. He chuckled at the thought of it, then looked over his shoulder to check the traffic, and steered the car away from the curb.

From the diner, he drove down Dauphin Street to Water Street. As he waited for the traffic light, he glanced to his left toward the banana wharf. Between the rows of warehouses he saw the sign outside Raphael's Cafe, where Toby LeMoyne let him out of the patrol car the morning before. He smiled. The traffic light turned green, and he steered the Chrysler around the corner.

At Government Street, he turned right again and meandered west past the downtown office buildings. When he reached Ann Street, he turned left and made his way to Barbara's house. He parked out front, walked to the door, and rang the bell. In a few minutes, Barbara opened the door, dressed in housecoat and slippers, her hair tied in a kerchief, a dust cloth in one hand.

"You really ought to call first, you know."

Her voice was stern, but there was a sparkle in her eye.

"You know me," Connolly replied. "Mr. Spontaneity."

Barbara laughed. Connolly smiled.

"You want to come in?"

She stepped back from the door and held it open for him.

"No," he replied. "I want to take you to lunch."

"Lunch? I hardly look like lunch," she replied.

"Well, get ready," he suggested. "I'll come back in thirty minutes."

She hesitated. The smile disappeared from her face.

"I don't know if ..."

"It's lunch, Barbara," he countered. "That's all. Just lunch."

"I ... ahhh ..."

"You'll like it," he said. He turned away and moved down the steps. "Thirty minutes," he called as he walked toward the car.

Half an hour later, Connolly returned to Barbara's house. He parked on the street out front and walked up the sidewalk. The door was open. He stepped inside.

"Have a seat," Barbara called from upstairs. "I'll be down in a minute."

He stepped inside to the living room and took a seat on the sofa.

Before long, Barbara entered the room. She wore a sleeveless yellow linen dress. Knee-length, it followed the curves of her body in a way that made Connolly take notice without giving him reason to think he could do more than look.

He stood when she entered the room.

"You look lovely," he stammered.

Suddenly, he felt scared, like a schoolboy on his first date.

"Thank you," she replied.

He gazed at her. There was a moment of awkward silence.

"Ahh ... shall we go?"

"Certainly," she said.

He stepped past her into the hallway and opened the front door. At the top of the steps he felt her jump when he took her hand. When she reached the sidewalk, he folded her hand under his right arm and escorted her toward the Chrysler.

At the car, he opened the front door and held it as she sat down. When she was seated, he closed the door and hurried around to the other side.

He slipped deftly behind the wheel.

"Sorry about the car," he said, suddenly self-conscious.

The rear glass was shattered and held together by tape.

"Had a little trouble the other day," he explained.

"So I heard," she replied.

"Sorry."

"I love this old car," she said. "I remember the day you brought it home. You got it from that lady on Japonica Street for helping with her husband's estate."

He placed the key in the ignition switch and turned it. The car started immediately.

Connolly drove away from the house.

"Where are we going?" she asked.

"I thought we'd ride over to Camellia's in Daphne," he said, glancing at her as he spoke. "Is that alright with you?"

She smiled.

"I thought places like that were too prissy for you."

"Oh, I'm sure I'll scare most of their customers away," he said, only half in jest. "Especially when they see this car." Connolly glanced at her. His eyes were misty. "But I thought you might enjoy it."

She looked at him and smiled.

/

READERS' GUIDE

**For Personal Reflection
or Group Discussion**

Readers' Guide

Mike Connolly wasn't looking for God when he walked into St. Pachomius Church that rainy afternoon. He was just a lawyer, trying to solve a case. But much to his surprise, he learned God was looking for him. Connolly didn't find religion. He didn't find philosophical principles to apply to his life. Instead, he found the Ancient of Days, the Lord of All Time. As events unfolded, he learned by experience that God wasn't just in the church building, but in the daily events of his life. Ready, willing, and able to intervene for the purpose of giving Connolly the desires of his heart. Not the ones Connolly could articulate but the ones God knew. The desires deep inside where Connolly couldn't consciously reach.

He came looking for Connolly, and He's looking for you with an invitation to an adventure. An invitation to a journey. Your journey begins now. No altar calls. No music. Just you and the Spirit who brooded upon the face of the deep at the beginning of time. Come on. Why would you ever refuse?

The questions that follow may help you move ahead. I guarantee you, He will show up.

1. Mike Connolly encounters God at a time in his life when he really isn't looking for Him. Can you think of examples in your own life when God found you at a time when you weren't looking for or interested in Him?

2. Father Scott presents Connolly with a challenge. What is that challenge and what is Connolly's response?

3. Do you think of your own relationship to God as a journey? Where did your journey with Him begin? What are some of the important events along the way?

4. Connolly's life is radically changed by his encounter with God at St. Pachomius Church. How important was the role of Father Scott to that transformation? Do you have a mentor? What is the difference between a convert and a disciple?

5. What changes are evident in Connolly's life as he progresses through the story?

6. The changes Connolly experiences are a gift to him. Yet they also cost him something. List some of the things he loses as he changes.

7. Have you ever lost a relationship with someone because of your commitment to Christ? How did you feel? What else has following Him cost you?

8. Near the end of the book, Connolly finds himself in a life or death situation and yet the Lord comes through, changing time and space to accomplish his purposes.

What are some Biblical examples of how He has done this in the past? Can you think of similar examples from your own life? The life of others you know?

9. What was the effect of this incident on Connolly? What do you think the Holy Spirit was saying to him through this experience? What are some examples of how Jesus used miracles to reveal Himself to His followers?

10. Is it really possible for God to reorder events that have already occurred? Are time and space absolute?

11. In discussing his experience in the hangar, Father Scott refers to an event in the book of Acts in which Philip was translated by the Holy Spirit from one location to another. Is this possible? Can you think of other similar incidents recorded in the New Testament? Is this kind of thing possible today?

12. Connolly seems to experience God as One who is actually alive and active in the daily conduct of his life. How do you perceive God?

13. What is the difference between understanding the Christian life as the application of a set of principles deduced from Scripture and understanding that life as a dynamic relationship with the God who is really there and actively involving you in His redemptive work?

14. What is the role of the Holy Spirit? How does He fulfill that role? How is He fulfilling that role in your life?

15. How does the transformation of Connolly's character affect those around him?

16. Connolly is an alcoholic. Does alcoholism arise from a genetic predisposition or from a choice? Does it matter?

17. The book alludes to an incident in Connolly's life in which he opened himself to the possibility of addiction to alcohol. What areas of sensual pleasure have you exposed yourself to? What were the consequences?

18. What emotional scars do you see in Connolly that came as a result of the choices he made in his life?

19. Connolly made choices for himself that led him to the condition he was in at the beginning of the book. How did those choices affect his family?

20. What challenge does Connolly's transformation pose for Barbara and Rachel? If you were counseling them, what would you say? What would your response be if you were the former spouse or the child in a similar situation?

21. Connolly finds himself drawn to St. Pachomius Church, and particularly to the building. Is place important to the work of the Holy Spirit? What are some Biblical examples of places that were significant to God? What are some Biblical examples of places that were significant to mankind? Is there a particular place that is significant to you and your relationship with God?

22. In the book, Connolly avoids partaking of Communion until after he repents. Was this necessary? Is Communion a means of grace, or a result of grace?

23. The Sacraments are sometimes overlooked as an effective tool for evangelism. What does the term *sacrament* mean? What are the sacraments of the church?

24. Every church has a liturgy it follows in conducting its worship service. Yet, the traditional liturgy is often scorned as an obstacle to effective worship. What is the traditional liturgy of the church worship service? Why has it come to be viewed as an obstacle to worship? What is the value of a liturgical approach to worship? What is the value of an informal approach?

25. God engages Connolly at several different levels in an attempt to woo him into a redemptive relationship. What are some of those approaches? What is the approach that finally moves Connolly to act on what he has heard? How did God first approach you? What moved you to finally respond?

26. *Sober Justice* is a fictional story. What is the value of fiction to the growth of your relationship to God? How does God use fiction to reveal Himself to you and to expand your understanding of Him?

27. A number of symbols appear in the book. Some are obvious, like the stained glass windows in the church and the design of the sanctuary. Others are somewhat less noticeable. For instance, where direction is important to the story, the good characters are almost always

on the right side, the bad are almost always on the left. With the exception of Connolly, favorable characters are referred to by their first name, unfavorable by their last. What symbols are important in your life? Are they important to your relationship with God? How has God used symbols to reveal Himself to you?

28. Connolly drives a 1959 Chrysler Imperial. The car develops a personality and becomes a character in the story. What role does it play? What is its effect on the lives of the other characters? What does the car symbolize?

29. As the story unfolds, the car becomes a tool God uses to bring about change in Connolly's life. What are those changes? Describe a time in your life when God used an unexpected object to move you on in the next step of your journey with Him.

30. The story takes you to two churches, St. Pachomius Church and St. Alban Cathedral. Revelation occurs at both places. Compare and contrast the revelation Connolly receives at each place. What is the role of each church in the story? How does God use the church to reveal Himself to the world? How does God use the church to reveal Himself to you?

The Word at Work . . .

What would you do if you wanted to share God's love with children on the streets of your city? That's the dilemma David C. Cook faced in 1870s Chicago. His answer was to create literature that would capture children's hearts.

Out of those humble beginnings grew a worldwide ministry that has used literature to proclaim God's love and disciple generation after generation. Cook Communications Ministries is committed to personal discipleship—to helping people of all ages learn God's Word, embrace his salvation, walk in his ways, and minister in his name.

Opportunities—and Crisis

We live in a land of plenty—including plenty of Christian literature! But what about the rest of the world? Jesus commanded, "Go and make disciples of all nations" (Matt. 28:19) and we want to obey this commandment. But how does a publishing organization "go" into all the world?

There are five times as many Christians around the world as there are in North America. Christian workers in many of these countries have no more than a New Testament, or perhaps a single shared copy of the Bible, from which to learn and teach.

We are committed to sharing what God has given us with such Christians.

A vital part of Cook Communications Ministries is our international outreach, Cook Communications Ministries International (CCMI). Your purchase of this book, and of other books and Christian-growth products from Cook, enables CCMI to provide Bibles and Christian literature to people in more than 150 languages in 65 countries.

Cook Communications Ministries is a not-for-profit, self-supporting organization. Revenues from sales of our books, Bible curricula, and other church and home products not only fund our U.S. ministry, but also fund our CCMI ministry around the world. One hundred percent of donations to CCMI go to our international literature programs.

. . . Around the World

CCMI reaches out internationally in three ways:

· Our premier International Christian Publishing Institute (ICPI) trains leaders from nationally led publishing houses around the world to develop evangelism and discipleship materials to transform lives in their countries.

· We provide literature for pastors, evangelists, and Christian workers in their national language. We provide study helps for pastors and lay leaders in many parts of the world, such as China, India, Cuba, Iran, and Vietnam.

· We reach people at risk—refugees, AIDS victims, street children, and famine victims—with God's Word. CCMI puts literature that shares the Good News into the hands of people at spiritual risk—people who might die before they hear the name of Jesus and are transformed by his love.

Word Power, God's Power

Faith Kidz, RiverOak, Honor, Life Journey, Victor, NexGen — every time you purchase a book produced by Cook Communications Ministries, you not only meet a vital personal need in your life or in the life of someone you love, but you're also a part of ministering to José in Colombia, Humberto in Chile, Gousa in India, or Lidiane in Brazil. You help make it possible for a pastor in China, a child in Peru, or a mother in West Africa to enjoy a life-changing book. And because you helped, children and adults around the world are learning God's Word and walking in his ways.

Thank you for your partnership in helping to disciple the world. May God bless you with the power of his Word in your life.

For more information about our international ministries, visit www.ccmi.org.

Additional copies of *Sober Justice* are available
from your local Christian bookseller.

If you have enjoyed this book,
or if it has had an impact on your life,
we would like to hear from you.

❖❖❖

Please contact us at:

RIVEROAK BOOKS
Cook Communications Ministries, Dept. 201
4050 Lee Vance View
Colorado Springs, CO 80918
Or visit our website: www.cookministries.com

RIVEROAK®
Good News in Fiction